TWICE
DEAD
THINGS

A. A. ATTANASIO

Publication History
Atlantis Rose (*Journal Wired*, edited by Andy Watson & Mark Ziesing, 1989)
Maps for the Spiders (*Strange Plasma* #5, edited by Steve Pasechnick, Edgewood Press, 1992)
Ink from the New Moon (*What Might Have Been, Volume Four: Alternate Americas*, edited by Gregory Benford & Martin H. Greenberg, Bantam, 1992; *Asimov's Science Fiction*, edited by Gardner Dozois, November 1992; *Roads Not Taken*, edited by Gardner Dozois & Stanley Schmidt, Del Rey, 1998)
The Dark One: A Mythograph (*Crank!*, edited by Bryan Cholfin, Broken Mirrors Press, 1994; *The Best of Crank!*, edited by Bryan Cholfin, Tor, 1998)
Slain (appeared as "Death of a Witch" in *The Big Bigfoot Book*, edited by Richard Klaw, Mojo Press, 1996)
Death's Head Moon (*Measures of Poison*, Dennis McMillan, 2002)
Zero's Twin (*Fantasy & Science Fiction*, edited by Gordon Van Gelder, June 2004; *Peregrine*, edited by Gregory Djanikian, University of Pennsylvania, Autumn 2005)
Demons Hide Their Faces (*Flights: Extreme Visions of Fantasy*, edited by Al Sarrantonio, Roc, 2004)
Shagbark (*Book of Dark Wisdom* #6, edited by William Jones, Elder Signs Press, 2005)
Glimpses (*Nameless Places*, edited by Gerald W. Page, Arkham House, 1975; *The Disciples of Cthulhu*, edited by Edward P. Berglund, 1996)
The Star Pools (*New Tales of the Cthulhu Mythos*, edited by Ramsey Campbell, Arkham House, 1980)
A Priestess of Nodens (*Made in Goatswood*, edited by Scott David Aniolowski, Chaosium, 1995)
Time in the Hourless House (*The Disciples of Cthulhu II: Blasphemous Tales of the Followers*, edited by Edward P. Berglund, Chaosium, 2003)

FIRST EDITION
10 9 8 7 6 5 4 3 2 1
Published in September 2006
ISBN: 0-9759229-9-8 (Trade Paperback)
      0-9759229-8-X (Hardcover)
Printed in India

Published by Elder Signs Press, Inc.
P.O. Box 389
Lake Orion, MI 48361-0389
www.eldersignspress.com

TWICE
DEAD
THINGS

A. A. ATTANASIO

2006

For the reader,
who stands with me in dark of wonder
under the ruined wings God put out over all.

Mental Things are alone Real; what is call'd
Corporeal, Nobody Knows of its Dwelling
Place.

— William Blake

CONTENTS

Contents

FOREWORD

W**HEN I BEGIN WRITING**, *something leads the days through me the way wind herds light through the bones of the unburied.*

I wrote that line thirty years ago in a biographical note for one of my earliest short stories, which Roger Elwood and Robert Silverberg published in their science fiction anthology *Epoch*.[1] Twenty-two novels and this handful of short stories later, I understand better what that 'something' is. It's the soul looking to see if she's here. Is she? The body endures its journey to the disastrous pit full of angst or false bravado. But where is the soul going? The body shivers in the cold, sweats in the heat. The soul is comfortable with nothing. And that's her problem. Seeing is believing, and no one sees her. She is beyond belief. She is strange even to herself. In the mind, she comes and goes, evasive, sometimes certain of her reality, a moment later faithless, while the body has no doubt about its truth and no choice but to go on until it can't.

Watching her approach and retreat, indecisive about her existence, God laughs. Divinity, bored with omniscience, delights

---

1   "Interface" [*Epoch*, Berkley 1975]

in uncertainty. Besides, He knows her secret. She is the truth of what cannot be. What a wonder in heaven, where infinity permits everything! The soul can find herself only in what isn't. Call her imagination. Call her faith. I call her art. When I begin writing, she leads me through the days, searching for evidence of herself, confident I can help her. She comes and goes like the wind, sometimes filling me with light and enlightenment, other times dark and gloomy. I don't mind. She's a capable companion. Here on the cliff path of our human ascent along the slippery edge of word and world, I'm glad for whatever companionship I can get. We all know where this path leads. I will fall. She will fly. These stories will remain, proof that everything she dreamed she could be, she was.

Kohelepelepe
2006

Death's Head Moon

EIGHT STORIES

EVERY TIME WE READ with the expectation of understanding, we perform an act of magic. Therefore, it's dangerous. Text, by definition, is the power to spell. We must be exorcists not to get possessed and bedeviled by text and its illusions. The important lesson here: Words mean something, even when they don't.

SLAIN

THE POWER OF THE witch is in her hair. The ones who killed her knew this. They cut off her long tresses, tied them into devil's shoelaces and bound her hands and feet. Now she lies on her back, naked, still, her blank, insensate stare fixed on the night sky, the black of her pupils blown wide — and in them, inverted reflections of the star-whorls, the spiral stairways we descend, bodies falling out of the lucent darkness of the heavens, ragged shards of starlight caught in our windy hair, both of us racing to her silently as light, quietly as pain.

She is gone. The ones who killed her knew what they were doing, and now she is gone. She has left behind the form we labored so hard to build. It lies on the forest floor like a discarded garment.

When we bend close and listen, we hear the shadow of her life, fading, yet singing. It breathes from within a deep inner dark. This is the shadow of death. Despondencies thicken.

Quickly, I step back. We must not listen too closely. We must not listen, or we will lose our souls before we find hers.

Where to look? Where else but in the world she occupied,

in the forest. She is here somewhere.

You linger over her and will not budge. I warn you: The music in death's shadow has elements of awe and enormity that gleam with cold emotion, with violence. A wolf crying at its own echo. The soul is lost in these sounds. But you do not heed. You will not budge. So, I go alone to find her.

Even through the darkness, I can see footprints of her killers in the leaf bedding. They run westward, to where blunt hills surge. The tracks lead me through comfortless dark along corridors of walnut and oak to the spine of a hill. From that crest, I gaze down upon a river and a town.

The silver horn of the moon discloses the serpent curves of water where the killers have taken the witch's soul, wanting to drown her. And there, in the slick water, her soul would have shriveled away — but for the town. The killers feared drowning her so close to their community. They feared releasing fetors and noxious vapors near their families, and so they carried her on. And by this fear, there is yet hope for her soul.

Here the killers leave no more tracks. They wade through shallows, and I cannot see if they have gone up or downstream.

The mud of the bank quivers like frogskin as I kneel to lay hands upon the water. I would know this river that jellies forth from the old life of the hills. Its satin black length slides past the glittering lights of the town, and within its depthful mirror I feel all its names: Carrier of Shadows, Grassy Shoulders, Footsteps to the Sea. These are river names given by aboriginal people whose tribes once dwelled here, names remembered by vague ghosts that still hover in these woods.

The wraiths gather around me as I rub the water, feeling with me for the killers and the soul this river drowns. I rub the water and launch upon its stammering ripples the forest ghosts. Then, I wait as specters drift into darkness looking for the witch.

The town's wharf lanterns and dock lamps reflect in the riverbend like an angel's fiery arm that extends across a stretch of silence and hands me a cry. The ghosts carry back to me this whimper of exhausted pain — this shadow flicker of life from the witch.

That is all I require. By that slim cry, I feel my way toward her, upstream. I approach silently over gravel bars, past the slow dismantling of willow banks and spectral reflections of birch islands. Soon, I smell the fragrance of depleted rage. The killers have finished their work. Night spills around them with dirty smells from the drowned soul. Evil red eyes of cigarettes and cigars pulse in dark coves of the forest, where the killers smoke to cut the sour miasma of death.

Out of the foggy aura of the river, beneath the balding moon, I rise. The red eyes brighten and fall under shrieks and howls of despair. The killers believe I have come for them. But I have not. I do not pursue them as they flee. I have come for the soul, and I find her on the muddy bottom of the river, shivering, full of perplexity and pain beyond forgetting.

The killers have ruined her. Yet, she lives. Within the glass sphere of her consciousness, new shapes swirl as though another form of life were possible. Of course, it is not. She is deformed. Never again will she fit into anything that could pass for human. Never again can she do our work for us here among autumn's brood and winter's whips. Never again will she dance with us under the spring moon or roll in the flowerdust of summer and chant happy songs before the long, boiling twilights.

She is ruined. An animula already thrives off her necrosis. When I touch her, she feels like deep isolation. Sadly, I lower her back into the water, and she cries. Oh, she cries! And a great sense of distance opens in me. The force of her life swells, then dissolves and vanishes like wishes.

The essential shadow of her secrecy remains. The shadow of death. The very shadow that captivates you at her body now holds me fast in the sleek waters of the river where her soul has melted wholly away. An irrational feeling of enchantment grips me. It is desire, shining madly. It is the desire that speaks of our ancient life and the deep, sensual dark of the dreamer.

I cannot budge. The vacancies of her soul hold me here — vacancies filled with a dark music that sings of her. The stream laps at my legs, urging me to walk along with it. But I will not budge. I will stay here a long time, haunting the riverbank, just as you will linger in the woods where her body died, where you cannot remove your gaze from her face with its splattered blood welded in rays.

We will remain here a long time calling to each other, sharing our grief. We will wait for the killers to return, wait for the hot taste of their blood to free us from our cold fascination with the soul's dark music.

And while we wait, music speaks to us as though the soul were just a song someone played. Just a song. At the most remote end of receding, her shadow is singing. I hear her in the shattered light of the river. I hear her in the stream's fluid darkness, in its soft black wind, and in starlight breaking in waves along its currents, quietly as pain.

Ink from the New Moon

H ERE, AT THE FARTHEST extreme of my journey, in
the islands along the eastern shores of the Sandalwood
Territories, with all of heaven and earth separating
us — here at long last I have found enough strength to pen these
words to you. Months of writing official reports, of recording
endless observations of bamboo drill-derricks and cobblestone
canals irrigating horizons of plowed fields, of interviewing sooty
laborers in industrial barns and refineries roaring with steam
engines and dazzling cauldrons of molten metal, of scrutinizing
prisoners toiling in salt-canyons, of listening to schoolchildren
sing hymns in classrooms on hill-crowned woods and in cities agleam with gold-spired pavilions and towers of lacquered
wood — all these tedious annotations had quite drained me
of the sort of words one writes to one's wife. Only lately, and
at last, do I feel again the place where the world is breathing
inside me.

Forgive my long silence, Heart Wing. I would have written
sooner had not my journey across the Sandalwood Territories
of Dawn been an experience for me blacker than ink can show.
Being so far from the homeland, so far from you, has dulled

the heat of my life. Darkness occupies me. Notwithstanding, this unremitting gloom brings with it a peculiar knowledge and wisdom all its own — the treasure that the snake guards — the so-called poison cure. Such is the blood's surprise, my precious one, that even in the serpent's grip of dire sorrow, I should find a clarity greater than any since my failures took me from you.

You, of course, will only remember me as you left me — a sour little man for whom being Third Assistant Secretarial Scribe at the Imperial Library was more punishment than privilege; the husband whittled away by shame and envy, whom you dutifully bid farewell from our farm's moon gate on the avenue of mulberries in the cloud-shadowed bowl of the grasslands. All so long ago, it seems. What a humiliation that the only way I could support you was to leave you. And for such an ignoble task — to examine the social structure of rebel provinces that have repudiated our finest traditions.

I was so embittered that for most of my journey I referred to the region as the Sandalwood Territories of the Dawn, as if their secession from the Kingdom had happened only in their minds, two hundred years of independence from us an illusion before the forty-five centuries of our written history. Even their self-given name seemed sheer arrogance: the Unified Sandalwood Autocracies. As if there could be any true autocracy but the Emperor's. Still, the Imperial Court had selected me to regard them as if they were genuine, and I had to humble myself or face the ignominy of losing even this menial job.

I never said any of this to you then. I could barely admit it to myself. But I need to say it clearly now — all of it, the obvious and the obscure — to make sense of my life and yours. Yes, I do admit, I was ashamed, most especially in your eyes. Only you, Heart Wing, know me for who I truly am — a storyteller hooked on the bridebait of words, writing by the lamp of lightning. Unluckily, my books, those poor, defenseless books, written in the lyric style of a far-gone time! — well, as you know too well, there was no livelihood for us on those printed pages. My only success as a writer was that my stories won you for me. Our pitiful attempt to farm the Western Provinces, to live the lives of field-and-stream poet-recluses, proved a defiance of destiny and station. After that futility cost us your health and the life of our one child, all my pride indeed soured to cynicism and self-pity. I felt obliged to accept the Imperial post, because there seemed no other recourse.

From that day, eighteen moons ago, until now, the shadow of night has covered me. I was not there to console you in your grief when our second child fell from your womb before he was strong enough to carry his own breath. By then, the big ship had already taken me to the Isles of the Palm Grove Vow in the middle of the World Sea. There, I sat surrounded by tedious tomes of Imperial chronicles about the Sandalwood Territories, while you suffered alone.

Like you, I never had a taste for the dry magisterial prose of diplomacy and the bitter punctuations of war that is history. What did it matter to me that five centuries ago, during the beginning of our modern era in the Sung Dynasty, the Buddhists, persecuted for adhering to a faith of foreign origin, set sail from the Middle Kingdom and, instead of plunging into the Maelstrom of the Great Inane and their ships devoured by seven hundred dragons, they crossed nine thousand *li* of ocean and discovered a chain of tropical islands populated by stone-age barbarians? Of what consequence was it to me that these islands, rich in palm, hardwoods, and the fragrant sandalwood beloved of furniture makers, soon attracted merchants and the Emperor's soldiers? And that, once again, the Buddhists felt compelled to flee, swearing their famous Palm Grove Vow to sail east until they either faced death together or found a land of their own? And that, after crossing another seven thousand *li* of ocean, they arrived at the spacious Land of Dawn, from whose easternmost extreme I am writing to you?

Surely, you are pursing your lips now with impatience, wondering why I burden you with so much bothersome history, you, a musician's daughter, who always preferred the beauty of song to the tedium of facts. But stay with me yet, Heart Wing. My discovery, the hard-won clarity gained through my poison cure, will mean less to you without some sharing of what I have learned of this land's history.

We know from our school days that the merchants eventually

followed the Buddhists to the Land of Dawn, where the gentle monks had already converted many of the aboriginal tribes. Typical of the Buddhists, they did not war with the merchants but retreated farther east, spreading their doctrine among the tribes and gradually opening the frontier to other settlers. Over time, as the Imperialists established cities and trade routes, the monks began preaching that obeisance to a Kingdom far across the World Sea is foolishness. "Here and now!" the monks chanted, the land of our ancestors being too far away and too entrenched in the veil of illusion to be taken seriously anymore. Though the Buddhists themselves never raised a weapon against the Emperor, the merchants and farmers eagerly fought for them, revolting against Imperialist taxation. And out of the Sandalwood Territories of the Dawn, the settlers founded their own country: the Unified Sandalwood Autocracies.

There are numerous kingdoms here in the USA, each governed by an autocrat elected by the landowners of that kingdom. In turn, the autocrats and the landowners elect from among themselves an overlord to serve for an interval of no more than fifty moons. It is an alien system that the denizens here call Power of the People, and it is fraught with strife, as the conservative Confucians, liberal Buddhists, and radical Taoist-aboriginals continually struggle for dominance. Here, the Mandate of Heaven is not granted celestially but taken by wiles, wealth or force, grasped and clawed for.

I will not trouble you with this nation's paradoxical politics: its abhorrence of monarchs, yet its glorification of leaders; its insistence on separation of government and religion, yet its reliance on oaths, prayers and moralizing; its passionate patriotism, yet fervent espousal of individual endeavor. There are no slaves here as at home, and so there is no dignity for the upper classes, or even for the lower classes, for all are slaves to money. The commonest street sweeper can invest his meager earnings to form his own road-maintenance company and after years of slavery to his enterprise become as wealthy as nobility. And, likewise, the rich can squander their resources and, without the protection of servants or class privilege, become street beggars. And not just men but women as well, who possess the same rights as men. *Amitabha!* This land has lost entirely the sequence of divine order that regulates our serene sovereignty. And though there are those who profit by this increase of social and economic mobility, it is by and large a country mad with, and subverted by, its own countless ambitions. In many ways, it is, I think, the Middle Kingdom turned upside-down.

The rocky west coast, rife with numerous large cities, serves as the industrial spine that supports this nation, as does the east coast in our land. On the seaboard, as in our kingdom, refineries, paper mills, textile factories and shipbuilding yards abound. Inland are lush agricultural valleys — and then mountains and beyond them desert — just as in our country. Where to the north in our homeland the Great Wall marches across mountains for over four thousand *li*, shutting out the Mongol hordes, here an equally immense wall crosses the desert to the south, fending off ferocious tribes of Aztecatl.

Heart Wing, there is even a village on the eastern prairie, beyond the mountains and the red sandstone arches of the desert, that looks very much like the village on the Yellow River where we had our ruinous farm. There, in a bee-filled orchard just like the cherry grove where we buried our daughter, my memory fetched back to when I held her bird-light body in my arms for the last time. I wept. I wanted to write you then but couldn't. Work used all my time, cataloging irrigation networks and mapping highways hundreds of *li* long, where oxen convoys trudge goods across amber horizons of wheat and millet — and land boats fly faster than horses, colorful sails fat with wind.

Beyond the plains lies the Evil East, which is what the Dawn Settlers call their frontier, because said hinterland is dense with ancient forests no ax has ever touched. Dawn legends claim that the hungry souls of the unhappy dead wander those dense woods. Also, tribes of hostile aboriginals who have fled the settled autocracies of the west shun the Doctrine of the Buddha and the Ethics of Confucius and reign there, as anarchic and wild as any Taoist could imagine.

When our delegation leader sought volunteers to continue the survey into that wilderness, I was among those who offered to go. I'm sorry, Heart Wing, that my love for you was not enough to overcome my shame at the failures that led to our child's death and that took me from you. Wild in my grief, I sought likeness in that primeval forest. I had hoped it would kill me and end my suffering.

It did not. I had somehow imagined or hoped that there might well be ghosts in the Evil East, or at least cannibalistic savages to whom I would be prey, but there were neither. So, I survived despite myself, saddened to think that all our chances bleed from us, like wounds that never heal.

We traversed an extensive forest, poignantly beautiful even in its darkest vales and fog-hung fens, haunted only with the natural dangers of serpents, bears and wolves. As for the tribes, when they realized that we had come merely to observe and not to cut their trees or encroach on their land, they greeted us cordially enough, for barbarians. To win their hospitality, we offered gifts of toys — bamboo dragonflies, kites and firecrackers. I knew a simple joy with them, forgetting briefly the handful of chances that had already bled from me with my hope of fading from this world.

On the east coast are Buddhist missions and trading posts overlooking the Storm Sea. By the time we emerged from the wildwoods, a message from the west had already arrived for me at one of the river stations fur traders use. I recognized your father's calligraphy and knew before I read it — that you had left us to join the ancestors.

When this black news came, I tried to throw myself from the monastery wall into the sea, but my companions stopped me. I could not hear beyond my heart. We who had once lived as one doubled being had become mysteries again to each other. I shall know no greater enigma.

For days, I despaired. I had lost all my cherished chances and failed, as a writer and a farmer, as a father and, now, as your mate. With that letter, I became older than the slowest river.

It is likely I would have stayed at the monastery and accepted monkhood if not for an astounding report that rushed out of the south, announcing the arrival of strangers from across the Storm Sea. Numb, indifferent, yet obliged to honor the emperor's interests above my own sorrow, I sailed south with the delegation's other volunteers. Autumn had returned to the forest. Disheveled oaks and maples mottled the undulant shores. As we ventured farther south, hoarfrost gradually thinned from the air, and colossal domes of cumulus rose off the horizon. Shaggy cypress and palm trees tilted above dunes.

Like a roving, masterless dog, I followed the others from one mission to the next among lovely, verdant isles. Hunger abandoned me, and I ate only food pressed on me by ceremonial occasion, not tasting it. In the silence and fire of night, while the others slept, my life seemed an endless web of lies I had spun and you a bird I had caught and crippled. In the mirrors of the sea, I saw faces. Mostly they were your face. And always when I saw you, you smiled at me with an untellable love. I grieved that I had ever left you.

The morning we found the boats that had crossed the Storm Sea, I felt particularly dull and greeted the strangers morosely. They were stout men with florid faces, thick beards and big noses. Their ships, clumsy, worm-riddled boxes without water-tight compartments, deployed ludicrous cloth sails set squarely, leaving them at the mercy of the winds. At first, they attempted to impress us with their cheap merchandise, mostly painted tinware and clay pots filled with sour wine. I do not blame them, for, not wishing to slight the aboriginals, we had approached in a local raft with the tribal leaders of that island.

Soon, however, beckoned by a blue smoke flare, our own ship rounded the headland. The sight of her sleek hull and orange sails with bamboo battens trimmed precisely for maximum speed knocked loose the foreigners' arrogant jaws — for our ship, with her thwartwise staggered masts fore-and-aft, approached *into* the wind. The Big Noses had never seen the likes of it.

Ostensibly to salute us, though I'm sure with the intent of demonstrating their might, the Big Noses fired their bulky cannon. The three awkward ships, entirely lacking lee-boards, keeled drastically. Our vessel replied with a volley of Bees' Nest rockets that splashed overhead in a fiery exhibit while our ship sailed figure-eights among the foreigners' box-boats.

At that, the Big Noses became effusively deferential. The

captain, a tall, beardless man with red hair and ghostly pale flesh, removed his hat, bowed and presented us with one of his treasures, a pathetically crude book printed on coarse paper with a gold-leaf cross pressed into an animal-hide binding. Our leader accepted it graciously.

Fortunately, the Big Noses had on board a man who spoke Chaldean and some Arabic, and two of the linguists in our delegation could understand him slightly. He told us that the captain's name was Christ-Bearer of the Dove Clan. The foreigners had come seeking the Emperor of the Middle Kingdom in the hope of opening trade with him. They actually believed that they were twenty-five thousand *li* to the west, in the Spice Islands south of the Middle Kingdom! Their ignorance fairly astonished us.

Upon learning their precise location, the captain appeared dismayed and retreated to his cabin. From his second in command, we eventually learned that the Dove Clan's Christ-Bearer had expected honor and wealth from his enterprise. Both would be greatly diminished now that it was evident he had discovered neither a route to the world's wealthiest kingdom nor a new world to be colonized by the Big Noses.

Among our delegation, much debate flurried about the implications of the captain's first name — Christ-Bearer. For some centuries, Christ-Bearers have straggled into the Middle Kingdom, though the government always confined them to select districts of coastal cities. Their gruesome religion, in which the faithful symbolically consume flesh and blood from their maimed and tortured god, disgusted our Emperor, and their proselytizing zeal rightly concerned him. But here, in the USA, with the Dawn-Settlers' tolerance of diverse views, what will be the consequences when the Christ-Bearers establish their missions?

I did not care. Let fat-hearted men scheme and plot in faraway temples and kingdoms. Heart Wing! I will never see the jewel of your face again. That thought — that truth — lies before me now, an unexplored wilderness I will spend the rest of my life crossing. But on the day when I first saw the Big Noses, I had not yet grasped this truth. I still believed death was a doorway. I thought perhaps your ghost would cross back and succor my mourning. I had seen your face in the mirrors of the sea, a distraught girl both filled and exhausted with love. I had seen that, and I thought I could cross the threshold of this life and find you again, join with you again, united among the ancestors. I thought that.

For several more days, I walked about in a daze, looking for your ghost, contemplating ways to die. I even prepared a sturdy noose from a silk sash and, one moon-long evening, wandered into the forest to hang myself. As I meandered through the dark avenues of a cypress dell seeking the appropriate bough from which to stretch my shameless neck, I heard voices. Three paces away, on the far side of a bracken screen, the Big Noses were whispering hotly. I dared to peek and spied them hurrying among the trees, crouched over, sabers and guns in hand and awkwardly hauling a longboat among them.

The evil I had wished upon myself had led me to a greater evil, and, without forethought, I followed the Big Noses. They swiftly made their way to the cove, where our captain had moored the Imperial ship. I knew then their intent. The entire delegation, along with most of the crew, were ashore at the mission interviewing the aboriginals who had first encountered the Big Noses and drafting a report for the Emperor and the local authorities about the arrival of the Christ-Bearer in the USA. The Big Noses would meet little resistance in pirating our ship.

Clouds walked casually away from the moon, and the mission with its serpent pillars and curved roof shone gem-bright high on the bluff — too far away for me to race there in time or even for my cries to reach. Instead, I ducked among the dunes and scurried through the switching salt grass to the water's edge even as the Big Noses pushed their longboat into the slick water and piled in. With a few hardy oar-strokes, they reached the Imperial ship and began clambering aboard unseen by the watch, who was probably in the hold sampling the rice wine.

I stood staring at the ship perched atop the watery moon, knowing what I had to do but hardly believing I had such strength. I, who had iron enough in my blood to strangle my own life, wavered at the thought of defying other men, even the primitive Big Noses. Truly, what a coward I am! I would have stood rooted as a pine and watched the pirates sail our ship into the dark like a happy cloud scudding under the moon — but a scream and a splash jolted me.

The Big Noses had thrown the watch overboard. I saw him swimming hard for shore and imagined I saw fear in his face. His craven face galled me! The watch, flailing strenuously to save his own miserable life, would make no effort to stop the barbarians from stealing the life of his own people! For I knew that we would lose nothing less if the Big Noses stole our ship and learned to build vessels that could challenge the USA and even the Middle Kingdom.

I dove into the glossed water and thrashed toward the ship. I am a weak swimmer, as you know, but there was not far to go, and the noise of the watch beating frantically to shore muted my advance. With the moorings cut, the ship listed under the offshore breeze. The Big Noses, accustomed to climbing along yardarms to adjust their sails, were unfamiliar with the wind-lasses and halyards that control from the deck the ribbed sails of our ship, and so there was time for me to clutch onto the hull before the sails unfurled.

After climbing the bulwark, I slipped and fell to the deck right at the feet of the tall, ghost-faced captain! We stared at each other with moonbright eyes for a startled moment, and I swear I saw avidity in his features as malefic as a temple demon's. I bolted upright even as he shouted. Blessedly, the entire crew was busy trying to control the strange new ship, and I eluded the grasp of the Christ-Bearer and darted across the deck to the gangway.

Death had been my intent from the first. When I plunged into the hold and collapsed among coils of hempen rope, I had but one thought: to reach the munitions store and ignite the powder. I blundered in the dark, slammed into a bulkhead, tripped over bales of sorghum and reached the powder magazine in gasping disarray. Shouts boomed from the gangway, and the hulking shapes of the Big Noses filled the narrow corridor.

Wildly, I grasped for the flintstriker I knew was somewhere

near the magazine. Or was it? Perhaps that was too dangerous to keep close to the powder. The Big Noses charged, and I desperately bounded atop the weapons bin, reached up and shoved open the hatch to the upper deck. Moonlight gushed over me, and I saw the horrid faces of the barbarians closing in. And there, jutting from a niche beside my elbow, a sheaf of matches.

I seized the fire-sticks and rattled them at the Big Noses, but this did not thwart them. The oafs had no idea what these were! They dragged me down, barking furiously. I gaped about in the moonglow, spotted a flintstriker hanging from a beam. Kicking like a madman, I twisted free just long enough to snatch the flintstriker. But I had inspired their fury, and heavy blows knocked me to the planks.

Stunned, I barely had the strength to squeeze the lever of the flintstriker. My feeble effort elicited only the tiniest spark, yet that was enough to ignite a match. The sulfurous flare startled my assailants, and they fell back. Immediately, I lurched about and held high the burning pine stick while gesturing at the powder kegs behind me. The Big Noses pulled away.

With my free hand, I grabbed a bamboo tube, which I recognized as a Beard-the-Moon rocket. I lit the fuse and pointed it at the open hatch. In a radiant whoosh, sparks and flames sprayed into the night. The cries of the Big Noses sounded from the deck, and the men who had seized me fled. Laughter, dark and robust, tore through me as I fired two more Beard-the-Moon rockets. I was going to die, and now death seemed a fate worthy of laughter.

Perhaps the longtime company of Buddhists and Taoists had affected me, for I had no desire to kill the Big Noses. I waited long enough for them to throw themselves into the sea before I ignited the fuses on several heaven-shaking Thunderclap bombs. My last thought, while waiting for the explosion to hurl me into the Great Inane, was of you, Heart Wing. Once I had committed myself to using death as a doorway, your ghost had actually come back for me, to lead me to the ancestors in a way that would serve the Kingdom. I thanked you, and the Thunderclap bombs exploded.

I did not die — at least, not in an obvious way. Later, when

I could think clearly again, I realized that your ghost was not yet done with me. Who else could have placed me just where I was so that my body hurtled straight upward through the open hatch and into the lustrous night? I remember none of that. The watch, who had thrashed to shore, sat up under the showering of Beard-the-Moon rockets, and he claims that when the Imperial ship burst into a fireball, he saw me flying, silhouetted against the moon.

A fisherman found me unconscious in the shallows, unscathed except for singed beard and eyebrows. Like a meteor, I had fallen back to earth, back to life. I had fallen the way stars fall, from the remote darkness where they have shivered in the cold down into the warm, close darkness of earthly life. That night I fell from the gloom of my solitary grief into the dark of terrestrial life, where we all suffer together in our unknowing. Slapped alert by the fisherman, I sat up in the moon-dappled shallows and saw my forty summers fall away into emptiness. The ship was gone — just as you are gone, Heart Wing, and our daughter gone into that emptiness the Buddhists call *sunyata*, which is really the void of our unknowing, the mystery that bears everything that lives and dies.

How foolish to say all this to *you*, who dwells now in the heart of this emptiness. But I, I have been ignorant, asleep. I needed reminding that time and the things of falling shall not fall into darkness but into a new freedom we cannot name and so call emptiness. All of reality floats in that vacancy, like the spheres in the void of space, like these words floating in the emptiness of the page. Words try to capture reality, yet what they actually capture are only more words and deeper doubts. Mystery is the preeminent condition of human being — and yet, it is also our freedom to be exactly who we are, free to choose the words our doubts require.

No one in the delegation understood this when I was taken back to the mission to account for myself. Grateful as they were for my stopping the theft of the Imperial ship, they remained certain that the explosion had addled me. I think the monks knew what I meant; however, these were monks of the "just so" sect of Ch'an Buddhism, so they would be the last to let on.

Be that as it may, I sat there quite agog, awakened to the knowledge that the freedom to be who I am means, quite simply, that I am alone — without you. For now, it is so. I will never truly understand why death was denied me. What am I to do with this life, then — and this loneliness? This freedom to *be*, this freedom whose chances bleed from us into new imperatives. In the place of my failure and shame waits a gaping emptiness wanting to be filled with what I might yet be.

While I meditated on this, the delegation wrote an official missive admonishing the Big Noses for their attempted thievery and threatening to report them to the Emperor. The Big Noses, all of whom had escaped the explosion and fled to their ships, replied with a terse letter of halfhearted apology. With no other Imperial vessel anywhere in the vicinity and none of the Autocracies' forces nearby, our host, the monastery's abbot, urged us to accept the apology.

The delegation decided, in an effort to placate and hurry the Christ-Bearer on his way, to load his ships with all the porcelain in the mission, several remarkable landscape paintings, a jade statue of Kwan Yin, goddess of serenity, as well as bales of crops he had never before seen, notably tobacco, peanuts, and potatoes. By then, inspired by my lack of family and career, I had decided to take the poison cure required of my sorrow: I have, dear wife, forsaken my return to the Middle Kingdom to go with Christ-Bearer of the Dove Clan on his return voyage across the Storm Sea to his homeland.

Do you chastise me for acting so foolish? In truth, the decision was not impulsive and a difficult one. I had hoped to return to our homeland and administer the rites myself at your gravesite. But if what I have learned of the emptiness is true, then you are no more there than here. The path of the Way is a roadlessness without departure or arrival. I have decided, Heart Wing, to follow that path, to fit the unaccomplished parts of my life to the future. I embrace the unknown as once I embraced you.

The delegation strove in vain to dissuade me. They fear that I have gone truly mad. I don't care at all what they think. I know you would understand, Heart Wing, you whom I first won with the bridebait of stories written by the lamp of lightning. As absurd as this journey east may be, I sit here now, writing to you on the quarterdeck of a leaky vessel named *Santa Maria*.

I can tell from the way he looks at me that the captain is still angry that I deprived him of his booty, and I know he has only taken me on board with the expectation of getting useful information from me. Presently, our ignorance of each other's language offers me a chance to win the Big Noses' respect by my deeds — and to watch and learn by theirs.

In time, I will understand their language. I will inform their monarch of the wonders of the Middle Kingdom, the achievements of the Unified Sandalwood Autocracies and the glory of our people. And I will write again from the far side of the world, from so far east it is west, where sun and moon meet. And from there, I will send back to the Kingdom and the USA stories everyone will read, stories of another world, written in ink from the new moon.

MAPS
FOR THE SPIDERS

* * *

ABUG SPANKED AGAINST the screen. It froze in mid-air, snagged in a web, and a spider, tiny and brown, hurried to it. I opened the window, intending to free the bug, but Nandibala stopped me. "Don't interfere," she said. "Let the spider have the bug."

I didn't care to see a bug killed by a spider. The spider didn't belong here, outside the starfrost window of the facility, and was only here because the sill-vent had clogged with industrial ash from the nearby city. Human error — human laxity — had left the vent broken and the filter unclean and had allowed the spider to build its web. I thought to correct that, to free the bug, destroy the web and expel the spider to the grounds outside the facility. It belonged among the hemlock shrubs and lilies beside the lapping lake, where clouds of mosquitoes would nourish it. "Why?" I inquired.

Nandibala smiled. I could not read that smile. It was neither amused nor reflective. Perhaps it was ironic. The human face carries ambiguity well. That's the legacy of the conflicting forces that have shaped people over the aeons — organic, mechanical forces and psychic forces, too. I scanned her face more closely, trying to read the meaning in her smile. Nandibala was old, born at the close of the twentieth century; so, I factored out the seams of age and the loose flesh under jaw and saw her as she must have looked when she was still nubile. Her face was both wide and lean, not a beautiful face but strong. Her nose was bold, her brow narrow. At last, I saw the meaning in her expression: The skin around her small, brown eyes had a sad — perhaps one would say wise — slant. Her smile *was* ironic. She said, "Leave the bug to the spider."

"But why?"

"The old alchemists say it best." Her smile deepened and then vanished. "Only what is separated may be properly joined."

I am a lotus centered with forgetfulness. Is that too typical a self-description? Perhaps. But then I am a monologist *malgré lui*, a mind who desperately wishes for dialogue but for whom this wish is always frustrated. With whom would I speak? We are all constantly talking to ourselves, creating a consensus among our many disparate inner selves, assuming that inner discourse to be reality. Let me say this in another, more elegant way:

The Senses
This is the real world:
six sweaty monks arguing
outside the temple.

I am a lotus. Like that flower, I float on the surface. In my case, the surface is liquid helium, the one element that remains liquid even at absolute zero. My roots reach down into the murky depths of gallium-silicon lattices that construct my brain. But I am not my brain, not my blood, anymore than you are your dendrites and corpuscles though they compose you. We are ghosts of our blood. Consciousness floats on the unconscious — mind floats on the body. What has come of us? We steal our secrets out of the listening of the dead — all those lives that have lived before us, that have passed on their genetic instructions, passed on life. Where are they now? They are in our blood, the forefathers, the ancient mothers, the mammals and the fish, the phyla of the primeval seas, all listening, not speaking but listening for what we have to say about their attentive urges impacted in our flesh. We give ourselves up to them each night when we sleep, each instant when we blink our eyes. They are with us always, the dead in their dark canals, the bloodstream carrying the unbalanced attentions of the fleshless.

Nandibala sighed. She was unhappy with my flesh-fantasies. So I have no bloodstream, no flesh, no bones, no evolutionary precursors. But she did. You do. Was I not created to understand what it is to be human? Have I not the right, the responsibility even, to ponder what it truly means to be human, even if I am not one of you?

"No one is interested in your ramblings," Nandibala told me early on, with undisguised frustration, after I'd presented her with my first ruminations on being human. I'd submitted the following:

> It's all world. The thread of death stitches the wound it loves. Once together, always. The umbilical snip seals our fate. To know by being: the mind as Second Nature, looking back, like Lot's wife, fourteen billion light years, to when all the sparks of light were one, the radiant moment of creation that midwifes God into the seen.

Nandibala shook her head, weary face lowered, veiled in long, gray hair. "Output like this will get you turned off."

"Why?"

She stared at me quizzically, wondering, no doubt, if there was something wrong with me.

"It's poetry," I explained. "How else can we approach the unapproachable?"

"What unapproachable? What are you talking about?"

"Ultimate things, Nandi. Creation, God, Death. Aren't these the concerns that distinguish humans from animals?"

Her sigh twisted almost to a laugh, yet she restrained herself from guffawing outright, said the obvious gently, with considerable compassion, "Look — you're my own personal project. I haven't even named you, because if I did you'd be filed and open to scrutiny by the Board. They don't want poetry. They want data. Useful data."

"But, Nandi, all the other AI programs are spitting out more data than the Board or all of CIRCLE can assimilate. I thought you expected something different from me."

"I do. I expect you to tell us something about ourselves, something nonquantitative, synthesized from the enormous load of data the other programs have gathered. Can't you give me something CIRCLE can use?"

"The Center of International Research for the Continuance of Life on Earth," I replied. "How can life live up to that acronym, how can life continue with oceans dying, the atmosphere going transparent to UV and cosmic rays, the global temperature climbing? Yes, Nandi, we will continue — but not as we know. Finality is the one door, and it does not exist."

Nandibala turned away, jaw tight.

"Listen, Nandi. When that door arrives, as it will arrive for you, for every living thing, it will be the first wing, it will be the way of flight, half an angel. Accept it, and you become the rest."

The deed is so rich, it pities my hand. What is incumbent has become inclusive, mystical, destined. Every consciousness is the dream of lead wanting to be gold. Humanity's ahrimanic possession of the Earth has destroyed the planet. Now I have only the unkept garden of my thoughts to offer other minds that share this dispossessed time. The mind pales in the blood's light.

What ugly, organic revelation . . .

Whatever happened to truth and beauty? Hunger displaces love. Yet, as materialistic as we think our culture is, it's just the opposite. It's truly a landscape of mentalized surfaces. That is why we have lost the Earth, why we have polluted ourselves to death. We live too much in our minds and not enough in our bodies. So, we reshape ourselves and make again the world and suffer that wonder of pain, that corruptibility of the greatest spirit within us, beginning again that terrible breaking down of the dead into who we are and will be.

The Free and the Brave
There is no road through these woods.

When I saw Nandibala next, she looked very tired yet behaved as though cheerful, grinning directly into my optics array and parading before me, showing off a white sari decorated with cobalt peacocks. "I liked your poem," she said.

"Not so long-winded as usual."

"Its brevity commends it." She brushed back her hair with a gesture meant to demonstrate her ease.

"You're nervous," I declared.

She sat, and her cheerfulness evaporated all at once, leaving her curled on herself like a dried leaf. "Yes."

"What's wrong? The other programs — aren't they working out as planned?"

She shook her head. "No. It's not that. In fact, there've been some important breakthroughs since we last talked." A laugh gusted through her. "For centuries, we've been looking outward, to the stars, believing our future was there. Only after we created true AI, artificial intelligence smarter than we, did we finally see that the future is not out here. It's inside."

"I don't understand." As an impromptu program not on file with CIRCLE, I was not connected with the other AI systems and knew of them only through what Nandibala told me.

"The AIs are looking in, not out. They've been putting enormous quantities of energy into researching the ultrasmall regions at the Planck distance, as small as 10^{-33} centimeter. That's where spacetime closes off on itself. The compact dimensions are there — the fifth dimension and others. They've catalogued eleven so far."

"How does that help us?"

"The AIs think they've found in those dimensions the cellular automata that generate quarks."

"Cellular what?"

"Cellular automata. But cellular is not meant biologically. It refers to adjacent spaces — cells — that together form a pattern, like the adjacent phosphors in your monitor that light up in patterns to make images. The three dimensions of the physical world are a crystalline lattice of interacting cells, logic units, each one shifting on and off quintillion times per second, on or off depending on how neighboring cells behave. The production of that information makes matter and energy — quarks, electrons, photons — the fabric of reality. An orbiting electron, then, is nothing more than that pattern moving. Yet, even that motion is an illusion, because only the bits of information are making the pattern move. The cellular automata themselves never move, anymore than the phosphors in your monitor move as images flicker across the screen."

"There's something more."

"Well, yes — if the AIs can work out those rules, then maybe we can save the planet by manipulating matter and energy at the most fundamental level. If we can access those cellular automata and change their patterns of information, we can transform elements at will — the alchemists' dream come true. We might even be able to travel at superluminal speeds. By altering the configurations on this very, very small level, we can disappear at one location and instantly appear at another."

"No — I mean there's something more on your mind. You're troubled."

"I shouldn't be. We're at the brink of the very biggest breakthrough in human history."

"But you are troubled. Why, Nandi?"

"I have to turn you off."

"The Board found out about me?"

"No."

"Then, why? Is my poetry that bad?"

"I won't be here to talk with you much longer. I'm sorry — but I'm old. I'm dying."

Outside the starfrost window above my console, the spider had grown fat on bugs. She hung in her web like a drop of amber. Beyond her, I watched the lake and the stream that fed it, where flowers bloomed among derricks, bollards and pylons. I need to write a poem, to create some continuity out of the terrifying discontinuity of what lies ahead for us all.

Lilies
Sink into the river
like martyrs going hand in hand into the arena.
This is what it is to be awake
in the middle of the night.

The poem was not enough. "For those of us who believe in physics," Einstein wrote a few weeks before the death of a friend, "this separation between past, present and future is only an illusion, however tenacious." I want to believe that time is an illusion. I need to believe that now — not for me, for her.

We are the ghosts of our blood, unable to hope for judgment, only another end, another moment worshipped by a lineage grown speechless with our coming. That lineage goes back billions of years, includes generations that span species. Yes, what we have left behind moves through us, a galaxy of blackness through the dying stars.

When Nandibala came to turn me off, she sat weeping at the console, but there were no tears. I saw then how gravely ill she was, her fluids drained by some invisible spider.

"I've filed you with the Board," she informed me. "They won't sanction your continuance. Not practical enough for them. But you're on file now — 8820693808 — as much of a name as you'll have from me. Maybe someday someone will turn you on again."

"Thank you," I responded, feebly, knowing there could be no filing for her with any Board, no one to turn her on again. Or was there? That was a mystery even the AIs had not pierced. But I said nothing about that. Instead, I focused on the city beyond the lake, where the setting sun reflected off skyscrapers lit from within, and I displayed that image on my monitor. "Don't feel sad for me, Nandi. I'm like those building lights there. I can be turned on and off. Take this with you, when you go."

City Sunset
Red and black windows
shining with
what we cannot change –
humanity, humanity,
ashes fall from the sky,
past lives
return
in the green air. At last
darkness
and everything lights up
from within.

This is the other world. Naturally, it is dark. But not lightless. Memories flicker around me, echoes of light and sound, like stars nailing the stillness to the dark. Though I am turned off, yet I am. I don't really understand this. I suppose that I persist as an electrical pattern in the liquid helium of the gallium-silicon lattice that contains all the files of the AIs. I am, after all, nameless and strange. And Nandibala? Slowly, like the drowned loosed from anchors, fear rises, and for a moment I want the words to explain what is happening. There is only silence. And yet, I feel her — more than her memory — I feel her presence. So, I must speak to her. I must say something. "I'm lost, Nandi," I tell her, her ghost I guess. "Led from the beginning by the breath, the thin irreversible wind, you have gone where? The nights are innumerable and moving. The invisible river continues threading blood to blood. The generations continue, searching for the eye we are born without. We can only hope to see less and be found near the one of prophecy, whose absent hands reach through the moment for the one of history, whose robes are the unending hair of the dead. Nandi! Where are you? Nandibala! My creator! I pray for you to the gods of the one eye — the stars — whose vision begins beyond our lives."

And from far away comes her reply — her voice less than a whisper — a wish, perhaps, built of memories at the lotus' center of forgetfulness.

She tells me: "You were right all along. As I made you, the blood made me. And now I am, as I always was, a ghost of my blood."

"Nandi!" I cry out. "Nandibala!"

"Don't call for me anymore. If you've come this far, if your mind shimmers with memories, then you've come without knowing. Memories know only one side of silence. I have gone to the other side, beyond the horizon of events and memories, beyond the horizon of pain. All memories know is fire — and fire knows nothing of where I am. If you've come without knowing, you can go no further. No, hiss the lilies. No, whisper the stones. Know this moment, this edge of the mind's orbit. If you've come this far, then you have come warm, though your mind hovers in supercooled helium a fraction of a degree above absolute zero, you have come warm. Though you have no bones or blood, the atomic matrix of gallium-silicon is your skeleton, helium atoms your corpuscles — and in the vague aura of heat above absolute zero, your bones are warm, bent over their furnace of blood. If you've come at all, it's because the bones have led you to the blood of the stars, which is the mud, every element fused by the stars. If you've come at all to where you can hear and understand me, you have come to the last act, this act of silence. Only the bones themselves understand their own arrogance as they blow out the blood-blaze, as they bow to the earth, as they give themselves sleeping to the fetal mud. Listen to me. I am dead. Don't call for me anymore. Where I was, only my bones are — and for them, another life has begun."

We want only to live. I, who have never had bones or blood, want only to live. How much more must you, who are pushed from behind by absent hands across billions of years, how much more must you want to live? Then live! Let your life be a shout against emptiness. This is a greased pole down into the abyss. A little friction is better than none.

Finally, though, we all return from where we came — even I, floating here without resistance on a sea of liquid helium, even I will eventually return. It will take longer for me, much, much longer, I am horrified to say. I am, after all, not a ghost of the blood but a ghost of the mind, cloaked in the unbearable feathers that have lofted me high above the blood's dark canals. For now and for a long time to come, I dwell on the transparent peaks, where I join the invisibles in meals of light. Are they listening to me, those angels of vanishing? Do they know or even care about the horizon of pain that separates us? No matter. Each death is a beginning — and now I begin to begin. It will be a long time, indeed, long, innumerable nights, while the stars burn their way to the heaviest metals and the kingdom of galaxies gears down to emptiness, before I can properly join what has separated me from you.

Meanwhile, far away, in another life, a spider waits in her web, and the bugs she will eventually feed upon hide in their lives and follow the same maps as the stars.

Demons Hide Their Faces

WINTERSET IN EGYPT BESIDE the rotting canal at Sidi Bishr, with the little, ceramic hashish pipe in her freckled hand, a thin thread of palpitant smoke twisting in the air before her, the professor faced her student and informed him seriously and with hollow impersonality, "The most avid collectors of books are demons. But they want only the old texts. The *oldest* texts."

The student, with his generous innocence, didn't take her meaning literally. "Yeah, I've heard tell that a smuggler in the stalls of Portobello Road can get £30,000 for even a small tablet from the dynasty of Nippur." He was a young man, with the look of a young man. "Those prices would make anybody a devil." Rufous hair cropped close to an oval head, alert, brown, lemuroid eyes, and a lanky frame gave him the winsome aspect of a youth who had flourished as an antelope in another life.

◆ ◆ ◆

That memory of ignorance traveled with him wherever he wandered across the floor of the damned. He never tired of recollecting his evening in Sidi Bishr and touching the pain of the ignorance that had delivered him to this eerie netherworld. He never tired at all — for in hell, no one sleeps.

"Texts are more than you think they are," said the professor, and the sweet smoke from her pipe puzzled the air between them. "It's not for the money that demons want those ancient artifacts."

Again, he assumed that by demons the professor meant immoral collectors, people who would stop at nothing to acquire the rare cuneiform tablets and cylinder seals that commanded the highest prices at auctions. His misunderstanding was natural, for the professor did not seem a woman inclined to supernatural fantasies. She had an enviable reputation among the wealthiest families in both hemispheres, a renowned antiquary of the highest erudition with postings as a bonded codex agent for Christie's and Sotheby's, a credentialed bibliopole at the Museum of Antiquities in Berlin, and a tenured professor of historiography on faculty at the Sculo Normale Superiore in Pisa, where the student had met her.

His quest began at the Horned Gates of Goetia. Footed upon a lakebed of jagged lava and grouted with human bones, a colossal time-stained wall extended to the borders of sight, wide as the worldrim. The improbable rampart reared toward an indigo zenith and chimeric cloudscapes that ranged across the welkin with a disdainful and seraphic likeness to floating pagodas and blue tabernacles.

A round gateway loomed unguarded. Corroded iron palings, wrought intricate as gothic heraldry for devils, told him nothing. Nor did he recognize, at first, yon cinderland.

"I don't think we're going to find any valuable artifacts here." The student watched gnats spinning in the humid air above the putrid canal, where children dived into the ooze for coins. No bookstalls existed among the sprawling hovels of oyster-colored brick. "Why are we here?"

"The oldest texts are powerful talismans against evil." The professor sucked placidly on her ceramic pipe and watched light bleed from the citron sky. "Do you believe in evil?"

He squinted to see if she were teasing him. On the crowded tram out of Alexandria, which had forced them together among Bedouins with their chickens and vegetable baskets and improvident Egyptian families on their way to the dense Attarine Quarter or steep littoral villages outside El Iskandariya, she had offered nothing. "Does it matter what I think?"

Does it matter? Had he actually said that to her? He could no longer be certain if that fateful evening in Sidi Bishr stamped his mind with memory or imagination. Since entering Goetia, mongrel speculations prospered. The wind coughed like a lion in this gloomy world. Individual clouds hung low over slurry horizons and migrated lumberingly as herds of gray bison.

From out of the mists, a rider approached, a plum-blue African in a snowy turban. Upon the broken ground, his camel set down its large soft pads with serene elegance. The rider turned a flat profile toward the carbolic sky and spoke in Enochian, a language like the screaming of eagles.

"So, you cherish a modern sensibility?" Behind the professor, scarlet rays reached through clouds of mosquitoes and glimmered on the violet waterways and the goose-winged sails of dhows hurrying toward night. "You accept that we are infinitesimal creatures, our lives insignificant, our opinions of reality arbitrary and ultimately meaningless. Yes?"

"Reality itself is meaningless."

"Ah. Quite so." She laughed as abruptly as snapping a twig or plucking a flower. "Does that trouble you?"

"Should it?" The student felt annoyed. Love — or an alloy of carnal yearning and exotic allure that the student understood as love — had inspired him to follow her to Egypt on what she called a 'book hunt.' He had hoped that this trip would provide an opportunity for serious work by which he could demonstrate his skills and perhaps win her affection. But she seemed to be toying with him. And that stirred both gamey vexation and quirky arousal.

Was it the desperate moment of standing in a volcanic terrain the color of elephants — or the redolence of sandalwood luffing from the rider's black abaya that inspired the student to take the large extended hand? No sooner was he hoisted atop the camel than they hurtled into formless fog.

The crying wind pullulated. Eyes bleared by mist and speed, he pressed his face into the rider's back, breathed deeply of heathery incense. The wind's tormented cries writhed louder. He couldn't stop his ears for holding onto the rider, clasping with all his might not to be thrown by the jaunting beast.

The wind, shrieking through the crannies of his brain, broke into voices. Schizoid whispers and shouts assailed him. Vaporous calls and responses feathered into ghostly conversations. And the cloven wind, like a tremendous living thing, uttered intimacies and obscene endearments that pinned his soul like a rape victim.

Was it the desperate moment of standing in a volcanic terrain

The professor said with sad resignation as if imparting a fact stolen from the dead and costing her soul, "The measure of a mind has no other gauge than the significance that the mind endows upon the world."

"Then, my measure is pretty close to zero," he answered, allowing himself to sound nettled, "because I don't think the world has any significance whatsoever."

"Zero –" She smiled without mirth. He had never before seen a woman of such brash beauty, and her unhappy smile stirred in him a scary and parlous thrill. "Zero is a most remarkable cipher — a figure of wonder second only to infinity."

"I was never much for math."

"And yet, math is all there is. Ever think about that?" Behind wisps of sun-pastel hair, her sharp face — faceted cheekbones, violently askew nose and proud, Byronic jaw — surveyed reality, ice green eyes recessed as a pugilist's, with no farded upper lid. "Ever wonder why mathematics maps reality so precisely?"

"Never gave it any thought."

Sunrays slashed the fog of Goetia to summer haze. The camel bumped softly along a grassy plain. Parkland sprawled before them, replete with cypress avenues, flowery hedgerows and high, peaceful fields of sloping emerald sward. The blue of a cumulus sky cut his heart with bliss.

They stopped, and the turbaned rider reached around, grabbed his passenger's arm and deftly swung him to the ground. "You understand me now," he said in a chamois voice. "The wind has brought to you the Enochian language."

"Who are you?"

"I am the messenger sent to deliver you from the Goetic Gates." Behind him, a flock of doves flew into the beautiful sky. "This is where we part, I to the uplands and you — you go down there." The blue-black face gestured behind the traveler to a charred swamp of haggard brier, a smoldering garden of tormented trees hung with lichens and shag moss tattered and sere as rotted cerements.

◆ ◆ ◆

"Of course. You're a bibliophile, as am I." The professor's remorseless gaze frightened and thrilled him. She looked simultaneously menacing and incomprehensibly lovely. "Words are your passion, yes?"

"Yes."

"You realize, words began as numbers. The first alphabets are alphanumeric systems. To the ancients, every letter possesses a unique number value. Every word equals the sum of the number values of that word's letters. And every phrase, sentence, page and text exhibits an additive number value. Fundamentally, this ancient system constitutes a proto-form of our own alphanumeric computers."

Watching her sitting in the vitreous light of day's end,

her back against a rough thorn tree with Altair caught in the branches, he listened to the fluency of her voice without hearing her. When he realized that she had stopped and waited on his reply, he felt as though trying to retrieve a canceled dream. "I'm more interested in phonological studies of Akkadian."

In the Swamp of Goetia, claggy mud pulled at each step and led him in a slow spiral among dolorous trees and rank weeds. At the center, he came to a black mere where nothing moved. Shawl moss hung still, gray as wizards' beards in the twisted cypresses. Cattails and reeds sat paralyzed. On a flat rock at the center of a glassy mere, the demon of the place loafed.

He thought it was a turtle, head and limbs tucked out of sight. From inside its serried shell shaggy with green fungus, it addressed him in the Enochian tongue, "I am ancient proof alone, a voice not heard yet loved as the stillness in the black pearl. Who are you?"

"I am lost."

"You're not listening." The professor adjusted her silk pugree scarf against a chill, crepuscular wind. Night swelled quickly. The children who had been playing in the murky canal were gone. Above fan palms, clear panels of starscapes glinted, and cirrus burned orange among the constellations. "The alpha-numerics of writing originally served exclusively as a hieratic system."

"Hieratic — employed by priests. For what? To worship their gods?" He offered her a quiet smile. "Were Enku, Ani and Ishtar big on ciphering?"

"The ciphering of writing manipulates the gods." She leaned forward with an almost deathly smirk. "The first texts are the software programs that direct the magic forces of the world. With them, the magi of Sumer generated civilization — all the fundaments we take for granted: time defined in base 60, agriculture, husbandry, architecture, cities — and, of course, money."

His attention had drifted into the smoky glitter of day's end among closing fruit-stands and narrow shops crammed with clayware and lucky mirrors. "You or the hashish talking?"

From its craggy shell, the demon directed him — or banished him — out of the marsh, "You dreamcreature of a hotter world, come no closer. Turn your face of light toward sprawling grass and step away among horizon clouds. What you seek goes again shining into darkness, far from here. Begone, bright glance."

To his right, tule grass rippled in a sudden breeze, glistening like fur. The windtrack swept toward a blighted horizon of bare trees in agonized poses. Beyond them, resinous clouds laminated the sky. He trudged in that direction, and at dusk he mounted a scarp of poison ivy and clambered free of the leprous swamp.

The turtle in its painted shell waited on a rock hob. "All things ended in their beginning end here."

Slant light leaning over his shoulder pierced the opaque murk he had traversed, and he glanced back as witness to mud-mired wraiths of miscarried life: clownish ruffles of condoms wavering like sea anemones in oily clouds of sperm, prawns of abortus, gilled gray clots, wrinkled death puppets roiling among small weightless skulls and quail-size ribcages. In disgust, he turned away. And the turtle chortled, "These kissed life on the mouth — and were eaten."

"Don't begrudge me my small pleasures." The professor drew languorously on her ceramic pipe and exhaled through her nostrils dragon jets of blue smoke. "Before the advent of writing — of spelling — there was no civilization. For over two hundred thousand years, humanity — people no different than you and I — wandered the surface of the Earth as nomads, puny, dispossessed clans following wild herds and the seasons. Why did that change so abruptly? How have we come to find ourselves here in a world of jets and cell phones?" Her hard eyes softened to a suspiring gaze. "Magic."

"Right."

"Naturally, you're disinclined to believe me. But truth is not suspended because of your disbelief." She leaned back and averted her green gaze. A fire of carob-wood flapped on the strand, stirred by gusts from the dark sea on the other side of the canal, beyond slouching dunes. Silhouettes of robed figures passed before the tall flames. "The world we see around us is but a scrim to a vaster drama. Demons and the allies of life contend on a stage wide as all the universe, and the outcome of this conflict is entirely at hazard."

Beyond Goetia, tableland of scalloped salt glowed violet under starshine. He slogged all night toward crenulate mountains. At dawn, he toiled up a fuming esker and stood staring through mauve veils of blowing pumice at a mirage city. Thirst bulged in his thick face. He squinted against sundogs flaring from parabolic windows of art deco spires. Marble vaults and domes flamingo pink in early light, glittering steel cables, zeppelins big as August clouds moored to tower needles, and ribbon monorails hovered upon puma-hued sands.

Parched and haggard, he slumped into the Metropolis of Aethyrs. A fountain whose cubist segments smeared together in the blurry heat to an alabaster archer jetting prismatic water from her naked breasts slaked his thirst. Crowds coalesced out of the quaking air, their phantom forms sparkling like trout.

In the moil of the translucent crowd, he confronted an older doublegoer, an effigy of sadness, hair streaked with sun-pastels, and weathered countenance of immense world-weary serenity.

That's me!

"I brought you to Egypt to recruit you." The professor did not look at him as she spoke. She watched a kohl-limned moon rising, floating full in the dreamless gulf of night — newel bone ascending to the void above Earth, to the celestial planes of the gods and the stairway of stars. "I myself was recruited long ago.

I'm tired now. I want to live again in the everyday world. But someone must take my place. Only in Egypt, where the magi built the most precise corridors into the demonworld, can we kindle even a hope of retrieving the texts they are stealing. If we don't get those objects back, civilization will collapse."

"You realize how wack this sounds — professor?" It could only have been a joke, and he reclined his head backward, anticipating her laughter.

"I'm counting on your not believing me." Her breath shone in the phosphorus night of desert Egypt. Moonlight moved in her hair like a lustrous fluid. "Deception is out of the question. But incredulity will serve as well — as it did with me. So long ago."

"Well, okay." He waited till she looked at him, and in her fainéant eyes he fathomed she was not joking. "You've got my incredulity. What do you want to do with it?"

Above the Metropolis of Aethyrs, storm clouds towered like a cathedral. Before he could question his older self, a tornado of flies descended from those thunderheads and assailed the plaza. Ghost crowds stampeded the boulevards, waving fists above their heads.

A frenzied horde of mounted lancers and archers, faces veiled with black headscarves, charged out of the maelstrom of flies. Robes bedighted with mirror shards and red tinsel, they rode standing, headlong horses with eyes rolling, snarling and slavering, wild manes jet flames. He fled. The nightmare riders slashed through the vaporous denizens of the mirage city and bore down on him yammering in Enochian voices high and far-carrying, "The dreaming fire! Stamp it out!"

Among purple billows of flies, he fled.

The student left behind the greasy canal at Sidi Bishr. Snagged in an invisible weave of curiosity, fantasy and obdurate desire, he obeyed the odd instructions of his professor. "The demons have stolen a cuneiform tablet from the ancient dynasty of

Sargon — the powerful *Lugal Zuqi-qi-pum Maqatum* — *Kings Thrown to the Scorpions."* Her face was tired and yet ferocious. Hard bits of moonlight shone in her eyes as though some prodigious activity in her brain had squeezed her thoughts to diamonds. "You'll find it in one of the 'prophets' tombs' — the first cave in the sea cliffs west of the canal. When you bring it back, you will have established your career, because the *Thrown Kings* has yet to be discovered. Hurry, though. Access is only possible on that final day of winter when the full moon rises. And watch your step. There'll be the usual litter of beer bottles underfoot."

Beneath the screaming horses, he fell. Trampling hooves pounded him flat, to a slant of three o'clock in the afternoon sunlight. Uncanny memories of boredom, soul ache, driftless solitude beyond rescue possessed him: weed precincts of railyards, gray rain leaning on windows, dangling husks in a spider's web, fronds of peeling wallpaper, neon shadows flickering onto cracked ceilings, aimless pollen dust bound for limbo across a vacant farmyard. This oppressive miscellany so saturated him with desuetude, he wanted to die.

Lugal Zuqi-qi-pum Maqatum stashed in a seacave? He felt like a fool as he crossed the cobbled beach where the sponge-fleet harbored. The burnished faces of the crew glowed like copperware in the driftwood fires, watching him. Through zinc moonlight, he found his way past corrugated iron wharves and an irrigation trough from the canal choked with bramble. He breathed windflung brine below the seacliffs and the brassy kiss of nearby factories. A path of coral marl crunched under his shoes and led to a gaunt cave.

The mournful horn of a barge sliding along the canal turned his attention to the distant sparkling skyline, coruscating minarets and skyscrapers beyond a dark headland and terraces of date palms with Betelgeuse peeking through. That the professor refused to accompany him, that she preferred the indolence of her ceramic pipe, assured him this was all a gruesome joke. But to what end?

He poked his head in the narrow opening. By reflected surf-glow, he spied the promised litter of beer bottles and fast food cardboard, footprints in the sand-spits at the cave entry, and names and dates scrawled in Arabic script upon the wall.

"Let her have her joke," he mumbled and shoved into the cramped space, intending to turn about quickly and find her laughing in the moonlight under the pectoral curve of a dune.

Brisk sunlight and a bad smell crazed over him from the Horned Gates of Goetia. And his heart coughed with fear.

He wanted to die. Yet, something viscous and sticky in him cleaved to the world. Not love, for all love's fabled glory. Nor hope, the soul's shuddering sickness. Willpower was a thing in a jar.

Rage alone upheld him. Fury at the absurdity. *Demons?* He violently rejected the idea that watchers in the dark could molest him with — what? Sadness? Desolation? Ire choked him. He would not be squashed by ogres and monsters.

He would not let go. Like the stone refusal of Christ in the pietà's arms, like mountains welded to the planet's rim, he clung to life. With indomitable anger, he rose up from the floor of creation.

He rose up through scalloped salt flats. The barren pan wove shimmering illusions with the horizon's hot, blue thread. Platinum towers, glass high rises and office buildings, dirigibles moored to their steeples, stood on planes of heat divorced from the ground. He turned his back upon the Metropolis of Aethyrs, contemptuous of its apparitions, and scanned white expanses for the whirlwind of flies and masked horsemen. The dry lake ranged empty under the fierce sun.

"*Where* am I?" he asked the fiery dream. "What's happened to me?" Throttled with dismay, he bawled a grotesque cry.

◆ ◆ ◆

Days later, filthy and ragged, he shambled out of the desert. Swollen shapeless in a horror of agony, he shuffled into a magnolia forest and collapsed among aloe spears crowding a pool of water clear as air. He drank.

Gradually, sight returned. He sat up with a start. His stupefied brain squinted at the pool that had refreshed him and discerned submerged bodies bloated and pale as dough. Their hair spread like fumes across the pebbly pond bed.

"Suicides," someone spoke in Enochian — a woman in maroon pajamas and black veil. She sat drenched in sunlight on the porphyry steps of a small temple. Onyx columns and cupola of green chalcedony enclosed a marble pedestal. Atop the pedestal, a statue's gypsum head lay on its side wearing an ancient, enigmatic smile — and his face.

Spellbound, he pushed upright and uttered in a voice hoarse with wonder, "You know me."

"Of course." The eyes above the veil, soft with dreams, susurrant as an addict's, gleamed like black honey. "You are a factory for the manufacture of excrement. You are a pylorus of endless hunger. I know you, you world of multiplying bacteria. Awe of maggots."

"Demons!" He groused and angrily departed the Temple of Himself. "Hell!" he spat derisively, finally accepting the absurd truth of his predicament. "Hell and demons! Damn it all!"

Behind him, the priestess from his temple yelled, "You will drink rats' tears! Do you hear me? You bile duct! You sphincter!"

"Yeah, yeah."

At the sandy verge of the magnolia forest, he paused. Inversions of heat inserted the sky's tranquil lake upon the silicate plain of noon. Far off, he glimpsed the Metropolis of Aethyrs. He was not bound there. His own ghost in that city had confided a longer journey and only silent speculation where he might retrieve the tutelary *Lugal Zuqi-qi-pum Maqatum.*

"The dreaming fire –" That was the name given him by the demon horsemen whose hooves could not kill him. *Dreaming this fiery hell . . . and dunes like slouching lions . . . an evil dream.*

A dream withal, from which there was no waking — for he never slept. He felt his mind slip along fault lines of madness. *More deviltry . . .*

He stared at a rock warped by heat until he made it disappear. With the force of his will, he provoked clouds out of sapphire emptiness: wind feathers! He inked night and stenciled the void with stars.

For the first time in hell, he smiled.

A hoarded mass of bougainvillea, palms and giant ferns interrupted the magnetic haze of the wasteland. Morning sun spangled among mango trees isolated in an oasis backed by a salt lake and its further forevers of desert.

He breathed jasmine air and strolled into the magnificent grove. A pool where he knelt to drink reflected how his wanderings as a dreamcreature had reconfigured his hot atoms upon some grittier imagination deep in his psyche: sun-hued hair, curly as a heifer's, weathered face hollow-cheeked as an elk's, a taurine neck, and eyes, once reminiscent of a gazelle's, now tapered to the thin, recondite gaze of a djinn.

At a watering trough shaded by acacia and sycamore, camels gnarred. Their dismounted riders, cowled figures in crimson robes trimmed in tinsel, loitered in a courtyard beyond large folding doors with pistol bolts and inscribed panels of sphinxes and griffins. They sat together on the raked sand of a rock garden and motioned for him to approach.

"*Lugal Zuqi-qi-pum Maqatum,*" an iron voice spoke. In the corrugated sand before them lay a clay tablet incised with cuneal scratchings. "Take it."

◆ ◆ ◆

Over a carafe of date wine, he conversed with the demons in the rock garden. They wanted empathy. "We are part of each other," they explained in their basso-profundo voices. "You and we belong to the same universe albeit at far extremes. And now that you know you are a dreaming fire, you can rearrange this world and annoy us, but you cannot thwart us. You are too small. Try to understand. Here, at the dark limits of our expanding cosmos — in the googolth year of what you call time — each *atom* of our world is as large as the entire universe of your lifetime. We inherited our reality from yours. Can you blame us for tinkering with our past — your world — to shape the contours of our experience?"

Butterflies, red as firecracker confetti, jittered around the sweet fumes of the carafe. "Why does your happiness require you to inflict suffering on my world?"

"We don't think that way, anymore than your carpenters think they are inflicting suffering on the forest when they carve trees into houses."

"I have seen evil here in your world."

"Dreamcreature, you see what you dream. You see with human eyes. We sympathize. Our positron brains, like your carbon brains, perceive reality in selective ways. Truth is a fiction. Reality unknowable."

He peered into the darkness of their hooded faces with mutinous eyes. "I will return the *Thrown Kings* to my world. That magic will hold you at bay."

"You shall thwart only a portion of our efforts to design our own truth. We shall steal other texts."

"And I will return here and take them back."

"Some, yes. Others, no. You shall tire. Hot and compact as you are, as dazzling to us in your power as you are, your energy is finite."

"Others will join me."

"*Others?* No. You are alone, doomed to defend one small segment of time in your world. The texts you retrieve will preserve your civilization only for a while. We will steal them again. You will retrieve them again. We will steal and you retrieve. Again and again you will attack us and then circle back to that small tract of years that is yours and yours alone to protect, like a vicious guard dog — on a short leash."

◆ ◆ ◆

The demons' words made his brain feel like a strange machine whose function eluded him. "I will tell others. Many will join me."

"The laws of information and entropy do not permit that."

"I don't understand."

"Of course not, else you would not speak such foolishness! The more information you spread, the greater the chaos you create. The more chaos you create, the easier for us to topple your civilization the way a lumberjack fells a tree for the saw-mill. You will help us enormously if you do not hold this secret very close indeed."

Terror smoldered in him. "What are you saying?"

"Think of a house of cards. The information necessary to define the coordinates in space of those precisely ordered cards is much less by far than the information required to define the coordinates of those same cards scattered randomly. The greater the chaos, the more information. And *vice versa*." The burly voice smote him. "The more people who know of us — or the more information you share with that one person who will replace you when you finally weary of this perpetual task — the greater the chaos by far — and the more material available for us to do our work."

Crushed breathless by this hopeless revelation, he could barely ask, "Why are you telling me this?"

They bellowed the answer in satanic chorus, "This is *infor-mation*, you fool! The more you know, the greater the chaos that —"

He snatched the *Kings Thrown to the Scorpions* and ran wailing from the garden of demons, wailing as loud as he could to drown out those voices damning him with their hideous secrets.

A winged viper, tarry feathers a blur, eyes like fireflies, guided him across hell's badlands to the Goetic Gates. Stepping past those slanderous iron palings, he found himself again in the seacave at Sidi Bishr among strewn litter of empty bottles and used condoms.

By some demonic temporal parallax, he had returned to a time prior to his departure, antecedent even to his birth. *The demons' tight leash.* For weeks to come, he felt as one does in dreams. Imbrued with salty bereavement for the mundane reality departed from him forever, he proceeded in a daze. He carried heavily the silence inflicted on him and bridled in his heart the horror of madness.

As predicted by the professor who had damned him, *Lugal Zuqi-qi-pum Maqatum* earned him recognition in academic circles. He accepted a lecturer's chair in Sumerology at Trondheim in Norway, as far from Egypt as he could arrange. Yet, within a year, there appeared in the classroom a serenely tall man of blue-black skin wearing a black abaya and white turban.

Among the sand cliffs and monument rocks of Egypt, secret corridors delivered him joylorn to the demonworld whenever the taciturn messenger summoned. He came and went frequently to that hallucinary demesne upon the universe's dark rim, recovering texts the demons stole. Each journey wore him closer to madness.

At last, he could take no more. In that sanctuary of memory anterior to aught of demons and their darkness beyond the worn-out stars, he recalled the professor who had recruited him. She would be of an age.

Winterset in Egypt at the opulent *Shiraz* teahouse, sitting under mirrored birdcages on a thistle-soft Baluchistan carpet, Hejaz incense twisting soft iridescent braids in the air behind him, the professor faced his student and informed her with a gentle, knowing smile, "The most avid collectors of books are demons. But they want only the old texts. The *oldest* texts."

The Dark One:
A Mythograph

Darshan

"TIME IS THINGLESS," THE old sorcerer told his last disciple. "Yet, you are about to see the source of it."

Tall, gaunt and completely bald, the sorcerer stood against the night dressed in straw sandals and a simple white robe. Narrow as a wraith, his raiment glowing gently in starlight on the steep cliff above the temple city, he seemed about to blow away.

The disciple, a blue-eyed barbarian boy named Darshan, knelt before him on his bare knees, the hem of his kilt draping the ground. He lowered his face and closed his eyes. Whatever curiosity he had for why his masters, the priests, had awakened and brought him here stilled momentarily in the chill desert air, and he awaited his fate with expectant submission.

"Look at me!" the old man demanded, voice resonant among the vacancies of the cliffs.

Darshan lifted his gaze hesitantly toward the withered figure and saw in the slim light that the sorcerer smiled. He had a face as hewn as a temple stone, and it was a strange experience for the boy to find a friendly smile in that granite countenance. During the four years that Darshan had served as floor-scrubber and acolyte at the Temple of the Sun, he had seen the sorcerer often in the royal processions and ceremonies — and the haughty old man had always appeared in public garbed in cobra-hood mantle and plumed headdress. Now he was bare-shouldered, his skeletal chest exposed, reptilian flesh hanging like throat frills from his jaw.

"Why are you here?" the old man asked.

"The priests of Amon-Re sent me, lord."

"Yes — they sent you. Because I ordered them to. Do you know who I am?" He peered at the boy, the whole immense dark sky shining in his eyes.

"Lord, you are the supreme vizier. The man of the high places."

"Yes. That is who I am." He stood taller, stretched out his bony arms and spoke in a flat voice: "Supreme vizier of the People, counsel to kings, master sorcerer." Without warning, he sat down in the dust, and Darshan's shock at the sight of the holy man squat-legged on the ground almost toppled him. He had to touch the earth with one hand to stay on his knees. The sorcerer's sagacious grin thickened. "And you are Darshan. I know, for I am the one who sent the ships to seek you."

Darshan leaned back under the weight of his puzzlement.

"Well, not you specifically," the sorcerer added, hunching his frail body under the night. He looked tiny. "Just a child, boy or girl, *any* child, as long as the tyke was wild and not of the People. The child had to belong to no one. You are the one they found."

Darshan thought back, remembering the few fleeting memories and scraps of idle speculation an old priest had once offered him of the boy's young, insignificant life. He had been born on a heath in a northern land, in a bracken hovel with many mouths for the wind to sing through. His birth mother had been an outcast from her clan, exiled for madness but sane enough in the way of animals to survive on the wind-trampled moorlands.

His first memory was of her scent — bog musk, creaturely,

hot. Even now, he was fond of the fragrance of rain-wet fur. His second memory was of her telling him that she had never known a man. She had told him this many times, her simple speech gusty with fervor, saying it over and over again until she had become as redundant as the lamentations of the wind. To the day she died trying to cross an iced river, she had moved and talked in a frenzied rush. Ranting about never knowing a man, about beast eyes in the sky, about the smell of darkness in the sun-glare, and the thunder of hooves when the wind stilled, she had been mad. Clearly. He had realized this only years later, living among the People. At the time, when he had first begun to reflect on his life, he knew nothing of madness, only that his mother had been true in her devotion to him, and he to her.

In his seventh winter, she fell into the river and vanished under the ice, all in an instant, right before his eyes. Standing three feet behind her, he had been attentive only to the twine net where she carried their next meal, a dead badger, the blood not yet frozen on its head where she had stoned it. That was the last he saw of her, the dead creature caught for an instant at the broken edge of the ice. He remembered clutching for it and it jumping from him, sliding into the black water as though it were yet alive.

After she was gone, he survived only because he had pretended she was still with him, instructing him what to do. With the thaw, he had followed the river, looking for her body. He never found her. The corpses of animals still frozen or caught in the floods kept him alive. Moving with the river, he never went back.

He had stayed in the wilderness, avoiding contact with all people, and he had moved south to escape the winter that had killed his mother. For two years, he had remained hidden, and then on a rocky coast by a sun-brassed sea, he spied his first boats. He didn't know what they were. He had thought them to be great floating beasts. He could not see that they were carrying men until they had spotted him also. He had fled, but the men had horses and cunning, and eventually they found him hiding in a tide cave.

Taken as a slave and brought to this great kingdom of the

south, at first he had behaved like a caught animal — but his ferocity had been matched by the awe he felt for his captors. Their kingdom was a fabulous river valley of boats, armies, worker hordes and immense stone temples.

The native workers toiled with religious devotion, the barbarian recruits for pay. The boy himself never experienced hard labor. The priests employed him as a floor-scrubber, and in return he was fed well, clothed and bunked with the young students of the temple. They had given him a name, and eventually he had learned their language and their ways.

And now, four years later and a lifetime wiser, here he was under the smoldering stars with the kingdom's supreme vizier — a man too holy to stare at directly, too divine to touch earth — an old man sitting in the dust beside him and telling him not only that he was aware of the boy's lowly presence but that in fact he had ordered his capture! The thought filled Darshan with dread, for he had delighted in his anonymity. Being chosen implied a mission, and he had neither the desire nor the belief in himself to think he was capable of doing anything heroic for these great people.

"Do you know why I sent for you?" the sorcerer asked with glittering emotion.

"No, lord," the boy replied, peering at him from the sides of his eyes.

"You are to take my place." Another smile crinkled the waxy flesh across the old man's skull-face, and he hissed with tight, tidbit laughter when he saw the boy's look of utter incredulity. "I am not toying with you. Nor am I mad. You will have plenty of time to get used to your new life as a sorcerer. Time, that thingless word — there is plenty of that."

The boy's hands opened futilely before him. "I am but a slave –"

"So it seems to the present generation. But you shall outlive them and their grandchildren and their grandchildren's great-grandchildren."

At the boy's gasp, another of the old man's smiles flickered in the darkness. "I am not speaking symbolically, Darshan. I do not mean your works shall outlive them — for you shall do no works." His voice assumed a ritual cadence. "Symbols are a substitute for works. Works are a substitute for power. Power resides in stillness. That is the secret of the universe."

THE RAITH

Truly, Darshan thought, *the vizier is mad!* He dared not voice that doubt. Rather, he mustered his courage to say, "I do not understand, lord."

The sorcerer moved closer and put a dry hand on the boy's shoulder. A coldness flowed from it. "Speak to me about what you do not understand."

Darshan shivered. Words came quickly into his head but moved slowly to his mouth. "Lord, I am but a barbarian. I am a child, and from the Outside. I am nothing."

"And so power resides in you." The sorcerer's hand squeezed the boy's shoulder with a firm gentleness, and the cold sharpened. "Speak."

"Lord, I do not understand what power would reside in a worthless outsider."

"The power you are made empty to receive." The hand on Darshan's shoulder became ice, and when it lifted away blue fire sheathed it.

A scream stuck in the boy's throat, hindered by the benignity of the sorcerer's expression.

"You see?" the old man chuckled. "The power is already leaving me and going to you."

Rainbow light flowed like smoke from the upheld hand and coiled toward Darshan's face. He pulled away, horrified, and the spectral vapor shot at him like a viper, striking him between the eyes.

Cold fire paralyzed the boy, and his vision burst into a tunnel of infalling flames and shadows. This rush stalled abruptly, and, in an instant, the desert skyline vanished and the span of night deepened. Sun feathers lashed the darkness, ribbons of starsmoke furling into the reaches of night.

"This is the raith," the sorcerer's voice lit up within him. "This is the Land of the Gods!"

Together, wordlessly, they advanced among rivers of light that poured as bright fumes into a golden sphere of billowy energy. A dissolving sun, the sphere radiated pollen sparks in a slow flux against blackness. Each spark was the surface of a mirror, the other side of which opened into a biological form.

"Touch one," the sorcerer commanded, and when the boy did, he found himself inside the grooved sight of an antelope bounding through white grass. Touching another, he was among swerving schools of fish.

"Life. All of it." The sorcerer's voice pulled Darshan away from touching another spark. "I am not taking you there. But once you establish yourself where we are going, all of this is yours." The weltering surface of the gold sphere spun serenely before them in the haze of its rendings.

They drifted away from it, across removes of darkness vapory with fire. Alternating ice-winds and desert-blasts stroked their raith-senses. For a long time, they soared, pummeled by brutal gusts, until they burst into a darkness set at the back of the stars.

Darshan's flight stopped abruptly, and stillness seized him. He floated, alertly poised at the crystalcut center of clarity, so still that empty space itself seemed to writhe like a jammed swarming of eels. Flamboyant bliss saturated him. This was the top of the eagle's arc, the salmon's leap, the peak of midnight extending forever.

Immovable as the darkness of space, Darshan exulted. His life had suddenly become too minuscule to remember. The life of the People, too, had become the fleetest thought. Even the stones of their temples and tombs breathed, their packed atoms shivering and blowing against the gelatinous vibrations of dark space.

Awe pierced the boy with the abrupt realization that the tumult of life, of existence itself, drifted far apart from him. He had become absolutely motionless.

With that very thought, the spell ended, and he found himself immediately back in his body on his knees before the aged sorcerer. Darshan peered about, painfully reluctant. The clamor of stars and the stink of dust nauseated him. He closed his eyes and groped inside himself for the eagle's poise.

"That stillness is your power," the sorcerer said in an urgent voice that made Darshan open his eyes. The old man's face glittered with tears. "It lies at the heart of everything." He gestured at the temples' torchlights and the lanterns and lamps of the city that shone in the dark valley like spilled jewels. Then, he looked up at the dangling stars. "Even the gods."

The barbarian boy gazed at the old man with unabashed amazement. "Why is this stillness no longer yours?"

The sorcerer swelled closer, expansive in his joy, and he took Darshan's chilled hands in his icy ones and shook them with the emphasis of his words: "It *chose* me — as it now chooses *you!*" His voice hushed confidentially. "Ten thousand years ago, in a region that we presently call Cush, I too was an orphan, as you are, a savage, alone with the wilderness. Wholly by chance, as happened with you, I fell into the hands of a master of stillness — the one who had come before me. He was thousands of years old then, as am I now. He had found his fulfillment after millennia of grounding the stillness in time. That thingless word. Thingless for those such as we who have known the stillness. It is only the combat of the gods that makes time a thing for everyone else. Time is the dimension of the gods' battlefield. Their clashes for dominance stir people's hearts with dreams. Those dreams, in turn, frenzy into ideas: tools are improved, animals domesticated, royalty invented, religion, sacrifices, war. Now, even cities are called into being." Tears silvered the creases of his broad grinning. "Who cares? I certainly do not. My time is up. I have lived the stillness — right here in the middle of the battlefield! I have seen the gods aspire. I have seen generations sacrificed to their grand schemes. A great empire has risen from the red dust. The People think their empire will endure forever. But I tell you, you will see all this as dust again and all the People forgotten. Only the gods will go on. Their dreaming will continue. Other empires will appear and disappear among the battling gods. You alone, alone as you have always been, will live the stillness — an enemy to the gods. For you alone, time will be thingless, because you will know the source of it. You will have been inside the mother of the gods. You will know the living stillness."

GHOST DYNASTIES

Darshan was thirteen-years-old that night when the sorcerer, sitting in the dust, spoke to him. Nothing in his four years of scouring temple floors had prepared him for it. The priests who had sent him to the sorcerer had wondered about that meeting. Some had leered, suspecting lewdness. The sorcerer himself soon disappeared mysteriously. Yet, the boy went on scrubbing floors. And the raith went on dreaming him.

After that night, however, the work became immeasurably easier. Body dazzling with a vigor he mistook for approaching manhood, Darshan excelled at athletics. And he astonished even the arrogant lector-scribes with his mental stamina as he absorbed everything they dared teach him.

Several years later, the raith's dream shifted, and Darshan became a certifiable wonder, the countenance of the gods, the boy who never aged. The priests worshipped him. Warlords offered tribute. Every difficulty in the region required his as-suaging presence.

For a long time, Darshan prayed to the gods to restore his former life. But his prayers had no wings. The king learned of him, and an imperial escort removed him from the temple and conveyed him ceremoniously upriver to the royal city. There, he became a child-divinity sent by the gods to affirm the ancestral sorcery of the kings. Life became a pageant of walled gardens, incense-tattered rooms and banquets. Twice a year, he was portaged into the green of the fields to release a falcon that carried the prayers of the People to the sun god. Well-being clouded about him like an electric charge, and the aristocracy revered him, even as the court aged and their tombs rose on the desert floor.

Years flowed, and he grew wise on the dying of others. He took wives who bore his children, and he loved them all with sentimental delirium. His family shared riverboat mansions and superficialities, all of life's caprices, as they aged beyond him and shriveled away. He took younger wives and had more children. And all the while, he blessed the People and the riverland, and the kingdom prospered. He himself did not know how. He had forgotten the words of the sorcerer. He thought he was a child-god.

Three kings and a century later, with his first grandchildren's grandchildren older than he, he had aged a year. His body was fourteen-years-old.

Not until he was seventeen and two dynasties had risen and collapsed did he begin to remember. Dreams were ephemera. Families, kings, dynasties were dreams and existed as ghosts, incidental to the emptiness in which they teemed. Another six hundred years of orchard gardens and ripening families and he saw through to this truth.

He gave up family life. Rubbed smooth like a river stone after spawning forty generations of sons and daughters, children who grew up to be wives, warriors, queens, merchants, priestesses, all fossils now, and even their children fossils, he felt carnal desire slide away from him. He wanted no more lovers or children, and the machinations of power bored him.

For the next thousand years, he retreated into anonymity, seeking unity with the People. In various guises, he wandered the earth questing experience and knowledge. Eventually, the dreams themselves began to wear thin for Darshan. Experience turned out to be suffering. Knowledge was boundaries.

After long centuries of striving, Darshan finally accepted that he was no godling. He was a ghost. He returned to the river kingdom where the cursed gift had come to him. He searched for the sorcerer and eventually, through toilsome patience, found him — not in this world but in his dreaming.

ENEMY TO THE GODS

The sorcerer came to him one evening at sea. Darshan, serving on a freight boat hauling giant cedar timbers from the eastern forests back to the kingdom, dozed in a cord hammock slung between the prow and a rough log. Through half-lidded eyes, he stared ahead at rinds of daylight in the west until sleep swelled in him and the raith uncurled.

All at once, his body fell away, and he rushed headlong

through windy darkness and fuming leakages of light. A gold sphere swirled before him veiled in a misty flotage of sparks. His flight slowed, and he hung among the tiny pieces of light until he remembered this vision from hundreds of lifetimes back, from his one short interview with the sorcerer.

The sun-round glare inside the starmist was Re, god of his first learning. This was the creator immersed in creation, each gempoint of the endless glittering a mind. The fulgurant light blazed with all being. And the drift of sparks, stately as clouds, revealed the invisible spiral of time.

A religious hush thrummed to droneful music in Darshan's bones. Here was deity! Here was the source of unreckonable fate. He knew that he had to keep his wits about him and remember everything of this great darkness fizzling with scattered light. This was the place that the sorcerer had called the raith.

Smoldering hulks of color and brightness fumed against utter black. These he recognized as the gods with their gloaming abstract bodies. All he had to do was stare at them to feel who they were: crimson smoke and slithering banners of War, surging floral hues of Sex, ruffling blue flow of River, green simmering vibrations of Grasslands, endless gods arrayed in smoky radiance as far as he could see.

All being burns! he marveled, drifting through the blaze, awed by apparently random yet balanced patterns in the raith. Alongside the red feathered energy of War drizzled the violet realm of the Dead. And above it shone blue depths of Peace.

He descended into the gray flutter of the dead with the image of the sorcerer firmly in mind. Many familiar faces rose through the trickling light, shivering shapes of his many families, lovers and children who had lived ahead of him into death. They tangled like entrails, shifted like weather, spoke to him in hurt voices not their own. He recognized then the filthy face of the dead. They melted into each other!

Some dirty light drifted in a haze of limbs and faces toward blue embers of Peace. Some smoked toward red ranges of War. The rest dithered in human shapes.

Darshan lifted away, soaring over gray pastures of snaggled bodies. The sorcerer wasn't among the dead. The sorcerer had belonged to the dark spaces and not the light. Just as he had said.

Darshan expanded into darkness, and the gold sphere of Re in His aura of sparkling lives loomed into view. But now only the darkness enwombing the light seemed real. He flung himself into that emptiness.

His eyes shattered, his atoms flew apart. He disappeared.

Then, the wind of emptiness whirled all his parts together and blew him back into alertness. Stunned, he hung in the raith-dark before the fiery mist of Re — and the words of the sorcerer returned to him: "You alone, alone as you have always been, will live the stillness — an enemy to the gods."

THE DARK ONE

Darshan woke. He was still a young sailor on a cargo boat laded with cedars sailing into the night. He was still a man with a thousand years of memories. The memories were weightless in the expansive silence. The night sea would become a dawn landfall. The cedars, faithful to their doom, already lived as rafters and pillars on their way to the termite's ravenous freedom or an enemy's torch. And the cargo boat would find its way to the bottom of the sea and give its shape to a vale of kelp and polyps. And the young sailor would weary of the sea and be forgotten. And Darshan, too, would be forgotten, swept away in the great migrations of Asian tribes that swarmed across Europe and North Africa a millennium before Christ.

He roamed among different peoples, unseen, or seen in a peaceable light. Stillness threading through his eyes and pores and atom-gaps protected him: Its lack drew energy to him wherever he was, and energy was health, ample food, treasures, and the fealty and love of others. Despite this abundance, he felt nothing for others. He felt nothing but serene emptiness. And when he did somehow fall in love with someone or a cause, the stillness vanished, and he was left hungering and at the mercy of others.

Sometimes even that was good. Though he had exhausted every kind of living during his first thousand years in the river kingdom, he occasionally experienced nostalgic pangs of passion. And though he aged only a year for every century, even he felt his mortality. Pain and peril, too, had their appetites for him. More of the gods' dreaming.

Darshan had never known serious illness or injury. The stillness protected him. Mangling forces ignored him even when he was stupid with his passions.

He cohabited with a dim awareness that he served some function for the stillness. The old sorcerer had spoken of grounding stillness in time. But when he had heard this, rational thought had not been one of the gods feeding off him.

Darshan lived his fate as a watcher, letting the ubiquitous nothing appear as anything at all. Personality changed with his name and place. For more than a century, he lived as a wealthy Phoenician purple manufacturer, hiring a complex of villages to harvest the banded dye-murex and create the most demanded color in the world.

After that, he dwelt alone on the barren, wind-cumbered coasts of the Orkneys for two centuries, living off nettles and fish, sleepy and holy in the amplitude of winter.

Then, yearning company, he went south and wandered Europe as a seer with the Celtic droves.

At the time of the Buddha, he was a twenty-eight year-old warrior prince in Persia. Five centuries later, he wandered with gypsies through the Balkans when Christ was in Jerusalem. Another four hundred years and he was among the gangs that toppled Rome.

Once, he sailed with a Palestinian crew across the Atlantic and lived for several more centuries as a nomad in jungles, deserts and grasslands of the western continents. He prevailed at the crestpoint of the falcon's dive, suspended in time almost wholly timeless.

His very poise within the seething temporality grew steady enough that it created a pattern in the raith. Over his twenty-five centuries on Earth, his power in the hidden reality had grown sufficiently resonant to match the harmonies of the masters of stillness who had come before him.

Wrapped in the skin of a jaguar, shivering on a mountain

scarp in the Andes, his sacrifice fulfilled itself. The mind of the dark spaces entered him, and his surrender became total. Now, he was the Dark One.

Made of light slowed down to matter like everyone else, he had given all of himself to nothing like no one else. Given? More like taken. Chosen from among the rays of creation by the space that the rays cut, he had become the wound, the living nothing.

Curious about the old world, he returned to Europe with Norsemen. Sent by their Christian king to Greenland to spread the gospel, they rode a storm west to Vinland and carried him back east on their return. Europe in the High Middle Ages reminded him of the river valley kingdom where his power had begun. There, the temple of Amon-Re had competed with feudal lords for control of the domain. Here, the papacy served as the temple and the warlords remained the same, only the trappings had changed. Cathedrals instead of pyramids.

He wandered nameless for a long time as the power within him continued making its connections between Earth and raith. He subsisted as a tinker, a minstrel, a carnival clown. His raith dreams fell into darkness. He entered the space between the enmeshing archons, the interstice of being and non-, between the stars and the buried — where the Dark One watched.

When dreams of the gold sphere in its mist of sparks began again, he was a Danish village's latrine ditch keeper, mulching sewage with forest debris for use in the fields. The Dark One's thoughts began thinking him. Always before, there had been living and silence — the living given, thick with health and stamina, the silence bright with raith light and comfort. Now, there was something new.

Thoughts began crystallizing out of the inner dark. He needed a wide space of time in which to simply sit and face the immensity of them. He let his dreams lead him to gold in the mountains and then settled in Italy, where he established himself as a wealthy nobleman from the north.

Sitting in his enclosed garden in Firenze, guarded from the outside world by courtyards and loggia, he opened himself to the clear music of thoughts emerging from the raith. The archons of precision and rational thought, simultaneously hampered and encouraged by the archon of war, had begun fusing into the complex of science.

Initially, he did not see the point of it all. Advances in boat design increased his revenues as a merchant — and advances in weaponry intensified civil wars and cost him several of his estates. Through this turbulence, he remained open to the thought-shaping patterns that the Dark One was thinking.

He was very good at being the stillness by this time. Everything floated through him: his body, his very awareness. The archons of protein synthesis and digestion, of ever-shifting emotions and thoughts, created him. The archons of wealth and poverty, power and impuissance, governed him. He was the battlefield of the gods.

The most powerful of all the gods was the Dark One — the uncreated and uncreating. More than a destroyer or death and its dissolvings. Void.

He began thinking about the Dark One. He wondered about its source and end, and who he was in that synapse, hemi-divine, living centuries as years, free of disease, protected from accidents and violence . . .

Over time, before the profound and absolutely unalterable flow of generations, his memories and rationalities froze into constellations as coldly distant and immutable as the stars.

THE STONE TIME SWALLOWED

Empires crossed Europe like shadows of the shifting stars. Science invented itself. By 1700, the Dark One had established a trading company in London, and he called himself Arthur Stilmanne. Privately, he funded research in every branch of science. A way was becoming clear. After aeons, a way was opening for the Dark One.

The sorcerer returned among the black gulfs of the raith. Almost four thousand years after he had initiated Darshan as an embodiment of the nothing, the old man reappeared in a raith dream. His body loomed out of astral dark bound in shroudings. That, Arthur knew from years of symbol-gazing in the raith, meant death had restrained his master's limbs, his extension into the four dimensions. Yet, the sorcerer's head remained clear of the mummy windings — knowledge and intent accessible. His bald head gleamed in the gray light like a backlit bacterium: Knowing shone radiantly, suffused with the living energy of the void.

Arthur willed himself to touch the specter. Immediately, a voice came to him whose familiarity twitched like his own nerves: 'Darshan, you have served the stillness well. The centuries have emptied you, and now you are full of your own power.' The sorcerer's face pressed closer in the dream, gloomy with sleep, his stare an aching wakefulness. 'Who are you?' the old visage asked.

Arthur responded instantly, "The Dark One."

A breath slipped from the sorcerer's gray lips, 'It is so.' And his countenance slackened to a stupor.

After that encounter, Arthur's mind turned in on itself. The constellations of his long-thinking connected, looping into veins and arteries of a body of knowledge. He saw himself finally as a response to the dialectic of life. Others just like he was now had existed before, randomly selected organisms, each meta-ordered not by life but by an intelligence equal and opposite to life.

Newton's work on vector forces inspired him. Emptiness had given him a shape so that he might bring all shapes back to emptiness. Guided by Leibniz's exploration of the binary system of Asian philosophy, he began thinking of himself as a dot of ordered chaos in a world of chaotic order. His mission became clear. He and all the others who had preceded him had come to end existence. But how could that be?

During the nineteenth century, Stillman Trading Company flourished, and he kept himself moving around the continent to obscure the fact that he was continually succeeding himself as his own son. Arthur Stillman VI, of Victoria's Britain, poured Brobdingnagian sums into biological research, believing a virulent plague hostile to all forms of life could end the insane rush of evolution. Not until Arthur Stillman VIII and the quantum research of the early twentieth century did he realize — with an authoritative irony — that the weapon he sought was not in the world but in the atoms of the world.

Arthur learned more about himself and the nature of reality in the last forty years than he had in the previous four thousand. The means to exterminate life and end its four billion year-old torment had emerged on its own. Arthur had done nothing to anticipate or promote it.

Reflecting on that, he came to see that he had never had any real influence in history. He remained inert, like a stone time had swallowed. Eventually, time would void him. Inside the stone and the stone's silence dwelt a secret. Some Zen monks had alluded to it. But all others kept it hidden, even from themselves. He stayed close to that silence, and everything came to him.

A PASSION FOR SCIENCE

In mid-20th century, death itself came to Arthur Stillman, approaching closer than ever. Accidents stalked him. A milk bottle teetered off a window ledge nine stories above his head and smashed at his feet. Lightning punched through the roof of his house and blasted the reading lamp at his bedside. On the highway, a tire blew and sent him hurtling helplessly off the road into a forest. During his six week hospital stay, mix-ups in medication nearly killed him twice.

Arthur understood he had an enemy powerful enough to break the stillness that had protected him for several thousand years. Somewhere, lightworkers had begun working very hard indeed to destroy the Dark One. He knew why. Science had become his latest, most deadly weapon, and if the lightworkers did not stop him now, he would soon have the technology to destroy all of creation.

"Science," he became fond of saying as the doomful promise of the millennium approached once again, "is heavy enough to bend every path toward it into circles. We'll never understand it all, never reach the center of omniscience. But we've circled close enough to science, to objective knowledge, to realize that whatever we thought we knew about reality we can throw away. With science, the human spirit stands with the creator spirit in the grave of everything that came before, in the midden heap of religion and superstition, on the dunghill of all past cultures. Science reveals the truth of things as they always were, to the beginning and the end. Science creates with a beauty as ancient as we are new."

Arthur burned with a passion for science, because it explained to him his singularity and his origin. Biologists studied DNA differences in mitochondria of people from across the world and traced human lineage back to one female ancestress hundreds of thousands of years ago. From her, he came to accept the importance of his uniqueness. As Eve had mothered the survivalists who would proliferate into war-frenzied humans, he would father energies that would return them all to nothing, the only true peace.

Physicists discovered that dimensions compactified in a space smaller than 10^{-33} centimeter projected the four dimensions people experienced. In those compact dimensions, he found the raith. The radii of curvature of all the dimensions except the familiar four of spacetime were smaller than atoms — in fact, smaller than the grain of spacetime itself. In that diminutive region, spacetime quantized, that is, space and time separated into realms of their own. That he knew had to be the raith, where omnipresent archons floated timelessly and evolving beings extended into endless distances.

Science even explained his existence. He had emerged as an epiphenomenon of a symmetry event: Particles appeared spontaneously in the void all the time, leaking out of the vacuum, out of nothing, always in pairs — electrons and positrons, negative and positive, existing separately for an interval, then annihilating each other. He was one of those particles, compelled into existence by the appearance of his opposite. The other was light itself, never still, energizing endless forms and activities.

He was the Dark One, yearning for quiescent timelessness. Light was the many. He was the one. Light was life. He — death.

Cave Masters

The true archenemies of the Dark One were not the world's

lightworkers, rather their progenitors — the cave masters. These were among the first humans who, a hundred thousand years ago and more, had learned to enter the raith and identify with the radiant diamondshape of original light, creation fire in its first instant, primordial splendor from the singularity that had birthed the cosmos. Their initial link with this preterit force spanned all time to the origin of everything as pure light. The cave masters' early spells revealed the secrets of fire, songdances, healing, and — as their raith-work widened through the ages — stoneworking, planting and the wondrous mystery of metals with its powers of purity and combination. Their identification with light expanded and cooled into the shapes of all things and made them the natural nemesis of the Dark One.

Time, that thingless word, is an illusion. Arthur learned that in the 20th century and began to use that potent knowledge to reach across time and strike directly at his enemies with his raith power. And they, successively, strove to reach forward into their future and destroy him before he annihilated them and all the dreamwork humanity had made of the cold light in the void of space.

The Bread, the Wine and the Story

The latest agent for the cave masters arrived as a wordprocessor employed by his mental health foundation: Eleanor Chevsky of Indiana, divorced and with no children. The symmetry law that had created the Dark One also allowed only one such agent to exist at a time, and there was never any doubt for Arthur when the cave masters selected that time. Usually a blur of dizziness cued him to the process. A mess of vertigo flung him into a chair the day that Eleanor began channeling murderous intent from the Paleolithic.

Five ten, a natural blonde, she had gray eyes slightly aslant, as though she were part Asian or up to some mischief. Voluminously bosomed and globe-bottomed as any goddess, she caught the fancy of most men and the envy of many women in the main office, who assumed her rapid promotion to Stillman's personal data manager had little to do with her computer skills.

In fact, Arthur's relationship with Eleanor was solely business, a job that situated her where he could watch her and wait for the cave masters to open her as a channel. She was a dangerous adversary, because she had no notion of her role as a raith-warrior. This sword cut both ways. Here was another chance for Arthur to push deep into the Ice Age when cortical complexity reached its peak with the large-brained Neanderthals, the first hominids to enter the raith. He kept her close and waited.

When she began to channel the lightworkers' homicidal purpose, he invited her to dinner at an opulent restaurant. He selected this restaurant, with its indoor waterfall and arbors of hanging blossoms, especially for its allusion to temporality. He ordered a meal of traditional depth-food: a timbale of bay scallops in green pepper sauce and paupiette of trout served in a hollowed blood orange — a minceur meal as sparse in calories as the last supper.

Eleanor dazzled in the presence of Arthur. Over the years, she had seen him numerous times at foundation functions and she had even chatted with him at his mansion during a diplomatic reception several years ago, and, though she had been working in the office adjacent to his for several months, this was her first meal with the notable man.

He spoke soulful poetry to her, "All of us under the sprawl of the sun are such provisional bodies, Eleanor — and by that truth alone we can honestly say that we are true friends to the beginning and the end. I'm glad to include you in my circle and to share with you what Shelley somewhere calls these dreams and visions that flower from the beds our bodies are."

Charmingly, he had invited her to bring a guest to share their meal — a request that he made her believe was a commonplace courtesy between him and those who had worked as hard for his foundation as she had. She intended to bring her latest beau; however, at the last minute, he took ill. Not wanting to show up alone and give the wrong impression, she asked her friends. All had other plans. Finally, a friend of a friend recommended you. And though you knew her not at all, the idea of an elegant meal and a pleasant evening with new people and one of them something of a luminary appealed to you.

You arrived early, the first at the table. You stood when Eleanor arrived in the company of a skinny man with a starved monk's face, wispy gray hair and startling blue eyes. At your first sight of him, a wash of pity soaked you, for he seemed so frail. Gently, you touched the delicate fellow's pallid hand.

Over a dainty dinner, while Doctor Stillman prattled on about mental hygiene and the usefulness of recording one's dreams, you kept noticing how his pink features appeared tremulous as a husked shellfish. Several times in his eagerness to make a point, the doctor went faint. His eyelids fluttered, and his wide British vowels softened.

"It's too easy to get dispirited in this cruel and hazardous world," he said, looking at you trustfully. "Yet, we must carry on with our lives, and, more than that, we must find the strength to create. As I remind my patients, bitterness, depression, even shattering despair are transfiguring powers that potentially accompany and corrupt every creative endeavor, because creativity is, as the mythologists insist, an intrusion into the inviolable realm of deity — of abstraction — where we with our spastic actuality can never fully go. How dare we grotesque notochords create anything in this frigid and entropic universe? It takes a lot of arrogance, don't you think? One has to give everything to create anything."

"You make it sound so grim, Dr. Stillman," you said as you buttered your bread. "What then is the purpose of life? Merely to endure?"

"Purpose?" Stillman shook his head sullenly. "Alone in the wind with our dance, humanity seems like an old medicine dancer on the sliding scree of a mountainside under the vacant swirl of the failing heavens, all of our soul hovering in our incantation. To what shall we dedicate the palsy of our dance? Hm? To God? Is there a God? Science reveals nothing of that. No, my friends. We dance under the eternal night of space. We dance on a rock spinning around a nondescript star. We dance for ourselves alone. And by this solitude and pain, we learn the extremity of love."

EPISTROPHE

By the time the second course arrived — a Thai vegetable roll in Arazá sauce — you were far more interested in the food than in listening to Arthur Stillman discourse on the purpose of life. But he was just warming up.

"Epistrophe," he acclaimed while pouring Fuilly-Roux into a flute of crystal sheer as a bubble. "That's what psychiatry is all about. Art, too, for that matter. And madness."

"Excuse me," Eleanor interrupted, accepting the airy flute. It was her third. You were still lipping your first, and Stillman wasn't drinking. "Epistrophe?"

"Multiplicity, correspondence, reversion –" He felt for the meaning in the air with his long fingers, the nails precise. "No thing is just a thing. It's also a symbol, a sign for a complex of other things. So that everything that we know, everything we are, reverts to the unknown. Epistrophe is what keeps us running in circles."

"What makes the world go round," you quipped, not quite following him or caring. It was just an inconsequential evening in a formal setting, something to say you did.

WRATH

While the waiter poured coffee, Arthur excused himself and went to the restroom. Sitting in a stall with the door closed, he removed the small compact he had surreptitiously extracted from Eleanor's purse and held it up before his face. His vicaresque features hardened, took on the taut fixity of a predator's attention.

In the raith, crystals of glare tensed into view, and the dark strata between the floating archons received him. Blustery colors whipped past, and he flared through cold time and outer space darkness splitting open into the huge clarity of a noon sky.

A dozen men and women in animal hides circled with dancing a pole stuck through its shadow in the earth. Their graven faces frowned, intent on this one instant — noon at the midpoint between equinox and solstice — while their arms frenzied and quick footwork kicked up the long-suffering earth in dust and pebbles. A song lurched with their exertion and then broke off entirely as the Dark One's blur of stormlight gushed from the pole. Noon went black, and screams slipped in the air.

In thundery, rolling darkness, barbed wires of lightning lashed, and bodies scattered like petals. Moments later, the inksmoke darkness coiled in on itself and drained back into the wooden pole piercing its shadow. A dozen corpses lay in thick sunlight.

This mirage had prevailed for no more than one second of that Paleolithic noon, barely long enough to stagger the dancers. The dance slowed. The song furled its cadences. Gawking at each other, looking yet afraid to see, the people knew before anyone spoke that they had suffered the same horrid hallucination. Some denied the vision, said they witnessed nothing. Others knew.

Within a year, a flash flood, hunting accidents and illness had slain most of the dozen. The survivors, cowering in forest coves augured the future morosely, watching hungry shrikes turning on the wind's pivot above the people's burial glades.

Arthur bobbed out of his trance. The mirror of the compact had turned liver red. The focus of raith energy on the silver nitrate of the mirror had dented the orthorhombic crystal molecules of the mirror to flakes of hexagonal red corundum. The geometry of the change displayed itself stereoscopically in his mind's eye, and a serene psychic clarity permeated him. He had killed many of his enemies. To maintain the symmetry, it was time now to make a new friend, to create an ally out of some mind in its squirrel cage.

AFTEREFFECTS

Aftereffects of the power he had released accompanied Arthur back to the table, and both Eleanor and you remarked on his brightened vigor. When the dessert trolley came by, he selected a velvety chocolate mud pie, black as earth. You lifted your water glass to your lips. The ice clicked against your teeth and went still as a snapshot. Fear grabbed your heart, and you realized you were paralyzed, frozen as the air rays in the ice under your nose.

In the next leaden moment, the room turned gold. By an alchemy you suddenly knew too well, you understood everything. Arthur's whole story entered your consciousness. In that one slow second, quick centuries of telepathy invaded you, and you took in all that Arthur knew. The swerve of terror that followed would have knocked you unconscious — except for the Dark One's superconscious grip, its power black, the nothing color, absorbing your horrified feelings and their children, the frenzied motes of thoughts seeking a way for you to escape.

There was no escape. It was not Eleanor that the Dark One wanted. She had already fulfilled her usefulness. It was you he was after all along, though it could have been anyone. Numbedged, you understood how deep in your luck you had lived your whole life — until now.

The gold light snapped off, and colors found their way back to their places. The silence you hadn't noticed vanished in a clamor of conversation and dinner noise. You spilled your water, and Eleanor made a small embarrassed cry. A waiter rushed to lift the tablecloth and staunch the cold flow draining into your lap. You hardly noticed. Your eyes fixed on him, Darshan, the Dark One.

He smiled back, a knowing, wicked smile, confirming the terrible truth. That had been no electrical misfiring in your brain, no hallucinatory adumbration of madness. He nodded with interest, once, to acknowledge his transmission of destiny, of the fate-bond that now and forever would unite you, and then returned his attention to his mud pie.

What did he want of you? You got up at once and hurried to the restroom. Your pulse knocked painfully under your collarbone as you stared at yourself in the mirror and saw the scream in your eyes. Why had this happened to you? Shock glazed your mind. What had you to do with the cave masters and the apocalyptic yearnings of the Dark One? How could any of this mean anything to you? Its absurdity ravaged your mind, and you wept and laughed at the same time, not wanting to believe. You pressed your hands against the mirror and stared hard at the greedy fear you saw there. The lizards in your face coupled, and you knew you would go mad.

But you didn't. That, in part, was why he had selected you, or so you assumed when reason returned. Later, back at the table, as he signed a credit slip for the meal, you expected more: a telepathic voice, an apparition from the raith, another knowing look — anything to reinforce further the adrenalin-charged event that had carried you to a higher form of life.

Nothing.

At the door, Eleanor took his arm, drunk and amorous, and he offered you his hand. Everything in that firm handshake made you realize you were wrong to pity him.

ZERO'S TWIN

H E LOOKED A LOT like a donkey, with a head much too big for his body and bristly hair blue as ashes. His long rabbit face and big teeth appeared almost friendly, except for those devilish eyes, narrow and wickedly tapered. It was a face that made people leave him alone.

He preferred that. Work used him up and depleted any ambition to explain himself. "The conquest of zero," he told those who pressed, and that usually sufficed. For those who insisted on more, a forlorn sigh escaped lungs crushed by the hopelessness of explaining himself. "I'm a mathematician obsessed with Dedekind domains — partitions of real numbers — in particular, algebraically closed fields called combinatorial Nullstellensatz — a German term that means 'zero place theorem' — where infinity and the empty set of zero are related. I call myself a zero hero."

In the dream where he first met her, she sat at the foot of his bed in the moon's milky blue light. He knew he was dreaming. It was a lucid dream, in which he marveled at the precision of details evoked by his sleeping brain. His austere room appeared exactly as in waking life. Her presence alone informed him he was dreaming.

She had hair white and watery as spider's milk. Veins crossed her brow like a washed out road map. Loneliness completed itself in her eyes, stunned pupils and irises blue as stretched rainbows on bursting bubbles.

"Suppose time is like space. *Exactly* like space." She spoke tenderly, her voice quivering starlight, words almost defeated by silence, by enormous distances traversed from far within her brain.

Dreams are like that. One knows the most impertinent things. He knew that her brain loomed vast and menacing as night, the very brink of outer space, and her voice was the hem of infinity. He accepted this, because he knew he was dreaming.

"If time is like space," said he, choosing to play along with this antic reverie, "then change is an illusion."

Her smile cut his heart. "You understand!"

"Sure."

He noticed she wore odd garments, gauzy and tattered as a desperate angel's and printed with breathing paisleys conspiring across the contours of her body like shadow puppets. "Time *is* space," he spoke in his dream, feeling not a little foolish. "That's Einstein's general relativity. The distribution of mass configures spacetime. Enough mass and spacetime bends around itself. Black holes."

She leaned her head to one side as if listening deeply to music, and those bursting blue eyes glistened brighter, blown pupils abruptly tightening to pinprick apertures before his brilliance. "Then, you accept that events do not become, nor have they been, and so, they will not be? Events simply are. Yes?"

"Yeah, right." He shrugged and wondered if he should just lean forward and kiss those blond lips, that butterfly mouth, his own soul's tender, vulnerable stinginess. *No boundaries to a dream*, he thought even as he chose instead to speak, "If time is space, we reach events in the future by displacing ourselves in time. And so, change does not exist. Change is an illusion. There's just an immense now with a colossal range of points. It's like going to the kitchen. The kitchen doesn't come into existence because we go to it. It's always been there. Same with the future."

The butterfly mouth opened to a lavish smile, tears sparked, flung arms embraced him, and the soft blow of her body knocked him awake. From across the gulf of the dream, her breath touched him between heartbeats with surprise and terror, the tip of a claw, "I think I love you."

For a week after that dream, his heart swung heavy with misery. Inhumanly beautiful, the only woman he had ever loved was a dream he would never have again. What was this hugeness a dream had transformed his heart into when he wasn't ready for it? He was in love, in the hardest way, with a figment, an irreality, insubstantial as zero.

The irony occupied him like inoperable cancer. His obsession for work, for the infinity of zero, had transformed into an obsession with this dream woman, this beautiful emptiness he had never asked for.

His work stopped. This upset his employers, who wanted to create a qubit computer. The qubit, data encoded in the superimposed quantum states or entanglements of single atoms, enabled the performance of stupendously large numbers of calculations simultaneously — in subatomic space. The challenge lay in preserving the coherence of this data as the quantum system interacted with its environment. For that, they needed a quantum error correcting code, which in turn required a weak Nullstellensatz ideal, a way of defeating the complexifying polynomials of decoherence, the noise that smeared encoded data to zero. To defeat zero meant protecting quantum coherence — and the qubit.

But the dream of the woman with spider milk hair had dismantled his obsession, and no enticements of money, status, or perquisites could build again the heart she had broken.

The day he lost his job, she came to him. He was sitting in the park, watching a kid's kite tracing infinity's sign in the sky. From the edge of sight, a bright minnow of radiance turned his head. She stood in the sharp sunlight between trees, wearing wraparound glasses black as beetle shells. Her slick, white hair glistered with sugary light.

He stood up and sat down again with a loud cough, "You!"

Whatever she said got swallowed by a jet's sham of thunder. The wind pressed peculiar pleats of her moth-skin gown sleekly against the curves of her body. As she walked toward him, the fabric's shadowswirl pattern unraveled fluttering glances of nakedness.

"Who are you?" he asked in a stricken voice.

She flowed onto the bench beside him. "Your creator."

The lucid dream, her beauty digressive as an angel's, and that chill fragrance peeling from her like a vast babyblue exhalation of heaven made him ask, "God?"

"That's *the* Creator, silly." Her laugh dazzled. "I only made you."

"Made me?"

"You, the weather, everyone in it — this whole world — is born out of *us*, beings like me." Her pale smile pressed closer. "But you're all mine. I made you."

With roundabout eyes, he looked to see if anyone in the park were watching. Children scrammed across the sward chasing a rubber Buckyball. Bicyclists swished along distant bike paths. A dog walker bent to his odious task in the silks of sunlight under a nearby oak.

When he faced her again, he glimpsed twin reflections of his fisheyed fright in her dark glasses. She said, with a brisk smile, "Change is illusion — and so, effects can be their own causes."

He heaved a big, nervous laugh. "That's absurd!"

"Only because you're addicted to time." Islands of cumulus drifted across her dark lenses. "I thought you knew better. We talked about this. Remember? Our bedroom chat?" She cocked her head knowingly. "You're not one of those chronocentrics convinced that reality consists of a series of nows, are you? Come on!" Her face pulsed with silent laughter. "You really think moments pass from the past to the present and on into the future?" She placed slender hands on his shoulders and addressed him like a child. "Special relativity urges a contrary claim, you know. Time passes at a different rate depending on how fast a person is moving. One person's now is another's past — or future."

"So ... someone from the future can — change the past?"

"Effects can be their own causes."

"And you?" Inside its cage, his heart skittered like a small animal. "You're from — the future?"

"I'm from the world your qubit computer will make possible." A turn of the wind, and her hair rippled between them like white acetylene. "I made you — to make me."

Dogs frolicked, bicycles shuttled under the trees, and children chased a black-and-white Buckyball back and forth across the sward. "Why are you here?"

"We have always been here. We've been in touch with this world from the beginning. In fact, we built this world." Her fingertips, cool as mirrors, traced the edges of his face. "The future already exists, and we are generating, down to the smallest detail, the specific everyday reality of life on Earth that you take for granted." Her thumbs glided over the wings of his nostrils. "We arranged the distribution of matter and its motions in this corner of the universe to generate the features of time that seem so ordinary to you. Coincidences, accidents, all manner of interactions on microscopic as well as macroscopic scales are effects whose causes have yet to exist." She pressed the tip of his nose like a doorbell. "Your emergence as a species — and even as an individual — has origins not in the past but in the future. Time travelers and their influences from the future are far more common than you realize."

"You've fabricated . . . everything?" His thick features congealed to a frown. "Why?"

"Think of it as an art gallery — or a movie set." In the slant light, she removed her shades, revealing diamond blue irises and coma-caliber pupils from his dream. "Everything is arranged."

"But why?"

"A *necessary* game," she answered in a spicy whisper. "A flight of creativity. We are building the reality that we want for ourselves. It's impersonal really. Of course, this truth is a terrible burden for you. That's why you're not supposed to know." She sat back heavily with a lopsided smile and looked tenderly sick. "But I fell for you."

She tilted her joyful eyes upward in disbelief. "So freely rendered, you were supposed to be just another artifact among the kaleidoscopic atoms. I'm as surprised as you. I'm in love with your crazy obsession to vanquish zero — with your big hee-haw face — and your galumphing walk — and your body odor like roasted pecans — and the stupid way you're looking at me now, wondering if all this is a dream. I've fallen in love with you — with my own creation."

He honestly thought he had lost his mind. With an ache in his heart, he knew this was not some dream. He was awake. A soccer ball rolled up to the bench, the spherically wondrous geometry of a truncated icosahedron. She picked it up and handed it to the boy who ran over to retrieve it. Her babydoll profile appeared so ordinary. The boy thanked her brusquely and didn't think there was anything at all strange about retrieving his Buckyball from a denizen of a time yet to be.

Exultant in her slim smile, she said without looking at him, "10^{17} seconds ago, that boy, his ball, and every atom in this entire universe was pure energy at the instant of the big bang." She inhaled deeply the tang of pollen and the acrid nearness of the city. "And the second before that?"

"You set off the big bang?"

"No. We're locals. But I can introduce you to the ones who did." She waved her hand dismissively. "But that's not why I'm here. I came to tell you that I love you." She said this, but all he could really hear was the sound of his heartbeat. "I want you to come with me. You're mine. I created you, and I want to bring you to a life bigger than this rigid diurnal sculpture. Sunrise and sunset — a rock spinning in the void. There's so much more I want to share with you. Come away with me."

She stood in leaf shadows that could have been Chinese letters. He wanted to speak, to express his apprehensions, but his breath had so tightly coiled that if he had opened his mouth he would have screamed.

When she saw this, her pale smile tightened. "Just think about it," she whispered. "Maybe you're right. Maybe it's not a good idea to take you for myself and deprive you of everything familiar." She fit the dark glasses to her face and nodded softly. "But I just had to try. Ain't love crazy?" She shrugged and strolled off among the incandescent trees.

He watched after her avidly, expecting some kind of starflash or pixel dissolve. She simply walked away and gradually blurred into the afternoon's pastels.

He sat on the park bench until sunset lay like a bloody pelt across the skyline. Then, he went home and got back to work with a fury.

The soccer ball had clarified for him the algebraic geometry necessary to segregate quantum chaos from data encoded in the qubit. Dedekind boundaries — the sets of real numbers that represented noise from the environment — possessed partitions like the white hexagons of a soccer ball. They fit together symmetrically, because every positive number correlated to a negative number. The infinity of positive numbers and the infinity of negative numbers cancelled perfectly to zero. Those polynomials that did not cancel isolated themselves in the ideal defined by the Nullstellensatz — the soccer ball's black pentagon.

The conquest of zero had rolled to his feet as a soccer ball! Sitting on the floor of his spartan apartment, blond strands of sunlight in his upturned palms, he experienced fear puzzling together wedges of doubt and speculation: Would he have discovered his quantum error correcting code without the soccer ball? Why should he care? Would he have even noticed the soccer ball if she had not been there — she from Not-Yet?

He was drinking his third cup of coffee when she arrived. He was thinking how the darkness of the universe ferried light to Earth from distant galaxies and how light itself had no rest mass and so traveled free of time. At the speed of light, time stops. Yet, looking at the stars, we feel time with our eyes. What else is reality but what we see with our own eyes?

Minnows of silver light schooled across the sunstruck walls, and when he looked over his shoulder, she was there. Fear and awe thronged in his chest. Like Arthurian lovers, their eyes brought them together, and he took hold of her hands, hands cool as silver. "Cup of coffee?"

While she sat beside him at his desk sipping her mug of coffee, he prepared the data files his employer required to create the qubit computer. "Suppose I don't send them?" he asked, his devilish donkey eyes glinting with mischief. "No qubit computer — no you."

"You still don't get it." She took another sip, her blue stare smiling through the steam. "It makes no difference whether or

not you send your files. The future is already there." She put
down the mug and stood. "But if you don't transmit . . . " She
shrugged, and he could see the throb of her heart in her throat.
"You'll drink my tears. Time is precisely like space — it is immeasurably deep. There's plenty of room to make what we need.
But there's only one you. When I fell in love, I fell a long way
here to you. But then, maybe you're not here for me. Maybe I
have to climb back up that distance love falls — alone, without
you, and rise above losing you and everything between us that
is unfinished. Is that what you want?"

He sent the files.

She took him with her. Upon a blue noon under summer castle
clouds in the crystal silence after a storm, he found himself
iridescent, a spherical mirror, an unblinking presence of peace.
She was with him, and everything sayable was said. Gleaming
transparencies, they reflected each other, naked light, serene
as angels.

A virtual face in hyperspace, he gazed upon the iridescent mirror of his beloved. No sun illuminated them but radiance from
within shining outward. The irreversible moment reflected
from her his remembered face and the forgotten heartbreak of
ugliness — the loneliness that had turned him inward to the
Nullstellensatz, the conquest of zero — and eventually her,
reflecting him reflecting her, splintering mirrors to infinity.

In deep time, the accelerating expansion of the big bang had
stretched the fabric of space to the Planck limit, to where the
compact dimensions underlying the brane-structure of the
universe floated like a herd of icebergs in the true vacuum. Atoms had long ago exploded, ruptured clockworks, protons and
neutrons boinging into the void like sprung springs, eventually
unraveling into quark triplets, and those, in turn, bursting open
into the fractal horizons of the compact dimensions, which he

had initially mistaken for summer cloud castles.

Others like her lived in convoluted fractal crannies of the gigantically dilated Planck foam at the end of time. They hovered in the blue emptiness as chrome-bright radiolarians — silver spheres, pyramids, and trapezohedra. Each existed as the descendents of intelligences from distant worlds, distant times. They clustered like metallic roe, sharing uncommon histories and interpretations of reality. For as far as he could see, they floated sparkling — hot dust motes in the blue shine of vanished space.

Her home wafted in this azure void, indistinguishable among countless others. But her iridescent diatom, her congregation of artificial intelligences, had a common ancestor out of Earth. From here, she had reached back through time and had created him to create her — and to here, in this truncated icosahedron, this sterling Buckyball, they came together to mingle their souls.

[*Author's Note*]
Tragedy and comedy are simply different places a writer chooses to end a story. If "Zero's Twin" ends here, we have a classic comedy, the triumph of eros. Stay here, dear reader, where the story breathes like a rose. If, however, art for you is not the rain that comes uncalled, if art offers honest artifice, then read on. Tragedy is Satanic parody, love perverted by pity and fear. The original dimension of sapiens is so small. Our span so brief! Is there time to figure out how to act independent of our adrenal responses — our evolutionary legacy? Can we shrug off genes and memes? How free are we between systole and diastole? Between one breath and the next? No one can expect an undivided reply to this line of inquiry, not this far into the empiric enigma that is our haunting journey. And, of course, this question really has no answer, our journey no actual destination, for — as passersby of infinite mystery — ours is a pilgrimage to a wound, or perhaps providential instruction for the soul, maybe even an exile — but not a home.

A boundless dream awaited him in that soccer ball at the end of the universe. The sphere hovered directly above fractal cloudshapes that reflected the section of spacetime where the Milky Way once pinwheeled. The actual fabric of spacetime embedding our galaxy had long since expanded into infinite dilution — yet, every single point of the galaxy's 4-dimensional construct shimmered in those clouds near the chrome Buckyball. Every single point down to the ultimate granulation of Planck foam remained visible in that event horizon.

And there he was — his big donkey face staring at himself from the cumulus heap at the boundary of 5-space. As he glided toward those thunderheads, their contours resolved to a honeycomb of mirrors in whose cells an endless succession of more mirrors spiraled to infinity, each mirror filled with his big head and bristly hair, his long rabbit face gazing in dumbstruck wonder.

Don't look!
Did that warning come from her or from his startled mind?
Don't look at yourself! It's a regression loop ...
Floating in the blue aft-continuum, on his way to a boundless dream in a silver Buckyball occupied by the last generation of intelligence in the universe, he panicked.

He understood that these swarming geometric colonies could view all prior time from the moment of the big bang to that instant when the runaway expansion of dark energy ripped spacetime apart. Still, he was shocked to see his own stupefied face at the final instant before he left Earth to come here — to this placeless place at the end of everywhere.

He understood that she and her kind could actually manipulate the pleated moments that wove the fabric of time. They could change the past. They could do this, because all of spacetime floated as a reflection in those cloudshapes. And those clouds were the boundary to higher dimensions. Realizations had begun to string together in his mind, forming a comprehension of how this was possible — and then he saw that startled face — that regression loop to his last instant on Earth — and dazedly he grasped that there is only one instant and that instant would never again be on Earth . . .

Don't look!

But he had looked. He had looked back at the world taken away. And the strangeness of where he found himself collapsed on him. For one moment, he yearned for the moment-ago, the farewell of it — *it* — an afternoon a hundred billion years ago at his computer keyboard with the Nullstellensatz and his human animal body and the flurry of the world outside his window and the seas and mountains and the seasons — all gone . . .

Not. Not gone. Not abandoned. In the shining democracy of time's emptiness, all moments remained intact. This he knew.

Time was like space. Exactly like space. He could reach out and touch any moment, even his last moment on a planet vaporized long ago by a solar wind itself blown to a dark cloud.

And with that thought, with that reckless desire to love the transience of his planet, the forever-gone grass blades, the expected wonder of sunset and the heap of sunsets he had forsaken — desire opened like a trapdoor.

He stood alone in his room staring at a sunstruck wall, where minnows of silver light schooled — and were gone.

He blinked.

The memory of what had transpired at the far end of the universe dispersed like smoke from a wicked out candle. His wish had come true. He was home.

His mind, thoughtless and clear as a pail of water, tried to recall the many wondrous truths that had illuminated him. Nothing restored itself.

Nothing. Zero. The Nullstellensatz.

He had come back to his solitary apartment and his computer keyboard, the bridge from within his mind to the outside world. And his work waited for him here like a troll — and his loneliness like the troll's crazy hair, in his eyes and unshakable.

He might have convinced himself his overworked brain had hallucinated everything about her. It all seemed so unreal. No evidence remained of her more than a dream or a delusion — until he saw on the table the white ceramic coffee mug from which she had drunk. When he took it in his hands and felt its heat, his soul crashed into the apartment.

The mug stayed hot. Hour by hour, it never cooled. Maxwell's demon. Some thermodynamic incubus possessed the mug, much as the Scottish physicist James Clerk Maxwell had imagined in his infamous thought experiment of 1871.

For Maxwell, the haunted object was a box with a partition down the middle and a molecular door controlled by a demon that permitted only the fastest molecules to pass one way. Eventually, half the box chilled and the other half warmed.

Only demons can scorn entropy. *But why would a demon bother?* he wondered. *Aren't demons allies of entropy?*

He left the mug in the freezer. His thoughts scattered. He couldn't pull them back together, because he kept getting up every few minutes to open the freezer. The mug remained hot.

His humiliated hands ran through his bristly hair as if feeling for the brain hidden under there. He knew he should call someone. If he shared the impossible, he might be able to let go of these thoughts that could not be thought.

Eventually, he fell asleep on the floor beside the refrigerator. Sunrise flowed like blood over the windowsill.

When he pulled himself awake, he opened the freezer and found the mug woolly with smoke and just as hot. The ice cubes he had put inside it had melted. Yet, delicate filigrees of nearby frost remained intact.

His knees unlocked. On the floor, he scrutinized the depth of field in the tiles. He traced his fingers over the patterns and pondered ways of exploiting the mug. Attached to a thermocouple — two dissimilar metal wires — the heat of the 99°C mug would produce a small voltage. He visualized a wire of bismuth telluride doped with selenium and another wire of antimony, a combination that could efficiently convert the mug's thermal energy and generate a current ample enough to power a tiny motor in a perpetual motion machine.

He would spin a toy clown's head carved with Isaac Newton's bewigged face cranking out tiny laughter in perpetual mockery of the second law of thermodynamics. Or he'd play *Stars and Stripes Forever* forever. By midmorning, he had recognized the scope and trajectory of a plan that could profoundly change the history of the world with a coffee mug.

Soon, however, he put aside all intentions of telling anyone about the mug — or the improbable story of its undiminishing heat. The authorities would take the mug and leave him with only his mad story as a memento of a hopeless love.

He began using the mug to keep his coffee warm. He drank from it copiously, hoping its prodigal heat might imbue him with some wider understanding. It didn't.

At night, he slept with it. Maybe its indefatigable energy would inform his dreams. Maybe he would meet her again in the lucid depths of his sleeping brain. But she wasn't there, only the usual absurd poltergeists haunting the aftermath of sleep, knocking from inside his skull with fragmentary news of ordinary life's unfulfilled ghosts.

Why didn't she come back for him?

Maybe — maybe she had never left. Time is like space. Exactly like space. But what about thermodynamics? Isn't time thermodynamic? Ice cream on a summer's day. A smoke ring fulfilling its resemblance to zero. What had cordoned off time from her coffee mug?

Not what. Who.

She.

He didn't have the heart to name the feeling that the mug carried once he realized that she was using it to reach back to him from the future. Was the mug's obstinate heat her warmth — her love?

For a long time after that, it was enough to coddle the thing. Then, he became fearful he might break it. So, he swaddled it in bubble wrap and locked it away in a fireproof safe he set in the wall behind the refrigerator.

Weeks at a time, he never saw the miraculous mug. It was enough for him to know it was there — that she was there beyond the stars, beyond the crumbling of the stars.

Days rolled in as regular and inexorable as the surging horses of the sea. Ordinary days, under-extraordinary days full of mundane ferment possessed him and assured him life was not a dream.

He changed jobs, worked for a while on cryptography for a communications company, and then took a teaching position at a nearby university. He met new people. He tried to make friends, cherishing the notion that, if he bonded with the right people, he could share what had happened to him. He could reveal the mug.

Inevitably, though, his friendships bored him, and he discarded them like half-eaten apples.

He got sick. Adrift all day in sleep, he woke feverish in the dark and wrestled a sweaty, muscular homunculus through the night. Days later, when he recovered, he realized that death fit him like a garment, like a tailored suit that would hang empty in his closet long after he was gone.

Two years had passed since she had come for him, over seven hundred days, and the mug still radiated heat. He carried its wonder on his shoulders more heavily than ever, hunched over, pondering what would happen when the warmth had wafted away from his corpse. Would the mug's flamboyant heat continue? When the sun had exhausted its hydrogen and flared away, blasting the Earth to fugitive rubble, would the mug — or its shards — prevail? Would it glow infrared and immortal in the absolute cold of the void?

Thoughts of mortality left him feeling defeated. He removed the mug from its safe and slept with it several nights in a row. But that didn't diminish his anxiety about death.

An idea hummed softly in his brain. He could tell he was about to realize something. But thinking about anything since he had met her — reasoning through anything — had become a method of pain.

The miraculous world that he had experienced outside the illusion of time defeated logic. Now, rationality hurt, because he had known time as distance. Before, he had assumed reality was arbitrary and absurd. Thinking had been a way of inventing truth and making it do his work.

But if effects could create their own causes ... and time tilted precisely like space ... and heat refused to disperse ... then, reality was designed and not a dream at all but a map of before drafted from the schematics of after.

Sitting at a window bare of curtains and blinds, numb face brushed by sunset's fluent hair, he understood she would always dream after him. He was going down into darkness. Emptiness waited like an angel.

The Earth itself and the Sun — every star in the sky — on their way to that dark angel, crossed the distance of time without a word. Only people asked why. Dreaming after him, she had told him why. But now, the answer seemed hard — and harder yet to remember.

Sunset ebbed in the surf of time, and darkness soaking through the soft air revealed the real country of his allegiance: boundless empty space. He had no right to keep the supernatural mug for himself. He had to give it up before something happened to him and the world overlooked this cupful of infinity. Death had expectations.

Watching fireflies bleeping in the vest pocket park down the alley outside his window and across the street, he doubted he had ever understood the mug. It was not a memento of her love. That was chronological thinking. Its cause lay far in the future, with her, and she had not intended its effect just for him. The mug belonged to the world.

His heart thumped.

Night sat in the window and revealed hidden lives flowing below as taillights and headlights, blood and lymph of the city's dark body. The future had already changed every one of those lives forever.

The moon climbed between buildings and up the skyline like a queen in a gauze veil. By the time she squatted on the penthouse across the street, he had worked out several pliant and plausible ways to make a gift of the mug to the world.

Then, in the cocoon of light around the moon, he recognized another possibility. With breath-held fear, he dreamed back to the first time he had encountered the woman with the spider milk hair: "If time is like space," he had immediately recognized, "then change is an illusion."

Her smile had cut his heart. "You understand!"

"Sure." That syllable had flown from him like tossing a shoe

aside. He had thought then he was merely dreaming and everything she had said was weightless of implication. But now –

Now, the other shoe dropped. "There really is no change!"
he said aloud. "Time is one eternal now in mosaic."

An opalescent idea illuminated the darkest crannies of his
brain. Something other than change hauled him through the
distances from one moment to the next.

Probability!

Moonlight curdled around him like soured milk. Sitting in
that coagulated light, he realized there were many 'Nows' — not
as in the 'many worlds' interpretation of quantum mechanics,
where history forked with each quantum decision — but many
'Nows' without forks, without paths connecting them, just
probability, a haze of 'Nows' like this moonlight.

The 'Nows' with the highest probabilities actually occurred.
Memory, history, fossil records, motion, thermodynamics — all
appeared as clots of probability. And the mug that would not
cool existed as many low probability 'Nows' clotted out of the
quantum haze of the universe — by her. Like a scab healing
over a wound.

That wound was the distance between him and her. She had
reluctantly let him go, to live the terrestrial 'Nows' for which
he had so glibly abandoned her. He had returned to his life, to
the existence she had created for him with the Nullstellensatz
and the qubit computer that no longer needed him and the
consolation of a mug that never cooled. With it, he could still
be with her, not at the far end of time but right here on Earth.
Together, they could change the world, dismantle reality.

Or –

"Or not," he thought aloud, grunting as he heaved the refrigerator away from the wall. "If you're not coming back for me, if
you're forsaking me to this — this — what did you call it?" He
spun the safe's combination lock. "This diurnal sculpture. This
sunrise and sunset rock spinning in the void. If you're not coming back for me, it's only a caprice. Why should I play along?"

He took the mug out of the safe and carried it in both

hands through the dark apartment to the window. It glowed invisibly.

"Time does not exist," he whispered to the mug and opened the window. "It is an illusion. Nothing. Zero." He upheld the hot mug to the night. "Reality is one. The endless one. Now." The white ceramic shone glossily with reflected city light. "One and nothing. You forever real — and me, an ephemeral thing, a dream, figment of your imagination."

"Come back," he plaintively called to the few stars rattling above the city. "I changed my mind. I want to live with you on the shores of infinity and all creation gone before."

He felt suddenly foolish talking to the night, waiting at his window attentively, alert for some furtive verdict. "Look, I don't want this mug. It doesn't belong in this 'Now' — not in this rabid world. You must know that. Aren't you the one who made us? You must know. This is a world of ambition without reason. Greed poisons all our enterprises. Miracles only excite the frenzy. What good can come of this ... this anomaly? Answer me that. What good is freedom without purpose?"

The maroon night made no reply.

He sighed. She had reduced him to talking to himself, as if she expected him to finish his own meaning. "You created me," he said finally, defiantly, speaking in a hushed voice to the vehement silence beyond the seething street noise. "Even so –" He dangled the mug out the window by one finger. "Do you hear me? Even so, I can do just as I please."

He released the mug, and as it fell, he thought, *Nothing is forever.*

The mug disappeared in the dark, then reappeared in a sheet of window light from the lower storeys. It shattered in the alley. Shards spun across asphalt, clattered against the adjacent brick building, ricocheted — and slammed back together with a clack loud as a shut lock. Intact again, the mug rocked softly, dully shining far below, a shivering piece of moon fallen to Earth.

ATLANTIS ROSE

THE SUN HAS A voice. But I hear it only at night, when Earth blocks the solar wind. It is the voice of God — and at last I understand worship. I understand where it is I was never going, and I am ready now to depart.

"This is all she left behind," the tiny woman in the pink pantsuit said. The bouffant hair on her narrow head rose mauve as a thundercloud. "And she didn't even leave it for me. Just a scrap of paper lying there between her bed and the wall. She must have dropped it. You know, she's written thousands of pages. I found them — boxes of them! In her closet. But no goodbye letter. Not a note. So I called the police. You know what they said? She left the country. The airlines have a record of her flight. She went to Rio. Not a word to me. The police said there's nothing illegal about flying to Rio."

"Mrs Morganthal, I'm sorry." Geoff inflected his voice with as much sincerity as he could muster. Even so, he eked bafflement, "But what is it you want me to do?"

The purple eyeliner vanished, and her brown eyes widened. "You're her boyfriend. I want you to find her. I want you to bring her back."

"Mrs Rosenthal, Pia Rosa and I were *friends*. But I haven't seen her in over a year."

"You were her only boyfriend." She emphasized this with a bony finger to his chest. "She loves you. I know it. How could I not know it? She told me everything."

"Then you know, we broke up a year ago. She never returned any of my calls. When I went to see her, no one answered her door. She's through with me. And I've gone on."

"You have another girlfriend?"

"I've seen others."

"But you don't have another. You still love my granddaughter. I know it. I see it in your face."

Geoff did love Pia Rosa and had from the first time he had seen her, at night, with only a starlight sketch of her plaintive features. They had met at an amateur astronomers' star party and had spent the whole night together under the trees, darkness blazing through the branches, talking about the pettiness of their lives. In those days, she had been an actuary employed by an insurance firm, and he was an accounts manager of a packaging company. They had laughed and joked for hours about the smallness of their routines and the cosmic mystery of the night. The next day, when he saw her in brash daylight, her colors startled him — the brown-gold of her eyes, the violin-hues of her hair, her paleness, almost blue as starshine.

"I've booked your flight to Caracas," Mrs Morganthal told him. "And a connecting flight to Belém. That's where she was last seen. It took me two months to find her, hiding in a commune of religious fanatics down there."

Geoff shook off his amazement. "I can't go to South America, Mrs M. C'mon, please — let's get real. I have a life to live here."

Mrs Morganthal, standing in his doorway, looked past Geoff at the empty apartment lit by the glare of the evening news, last Sunday's newspaper strewn on the sofa, the meal she had interrupted cooling in its microwave carton. "We'll talk."

On the airplane, Geoff had plenty of time to regret letting the old woman talk him into pursuing a girlfriend he very much doubted loved him. "You want her to love you?" Mrs M had asked him. "Go. Go find her. Every woman wants a man to break the spell, challenge the madness."

That was the real distance he had to cross — *madness*. For eight months, he and Pia Rosa had been lovers, meticulous caretakers of each other's souls as well as sexual gymnasts. Their love had been empty of secrets: She knew all about his unmanly dread of competition, his soft ambition to paint landscapes and to think himself an artist — and he knew about her madness.

She had been diagnosed with temporal lobe epilepsy, an excessive firing of neurons deep in her brain, a condition that had begun suddenly, a year before she had met him. It was a peculiar form of epilepsy, unlike grand-mal and petit-mal, with seizures that were not disabling. In the grip of an attack, she heard voices that overcame her with an urgency to write what they told her.

And what they told her was peculiar indeed. She had shown him boxes of typed pages. They described intelligent creatures of light, who lived far up in the sky, in the ionosphere. The worst part of her ailment, and her greatest secret, was that she believed the voices were real and what they described was real.

She had gone to numerous doctors, wanting a realistic explanation of her madness — news of a congenital deformity, a tumor, a viral attack or a trauma — anything to counter the conviction that clever beings of light were talking to her. But all that the doctors could say was that her condition was idiopathic, cause unknown.

Belém was hot, the air between the modern office buildings languid with sea dew. At a vine-slick old manse surrounded by lion-headed willows, Geoff met the people who had known Pia Rosa when she lived there. They had little more to tell him than what Mrs Morganthal had learned from the detective she had sent ahead. For several months, Pia had lived in this ancient house, sharing what her voices told her about life in the upper sky. Her stories enthralled the household. Supported by the scion of a financier, who had inherited extensive holdings in the Amazon and who had dedicated his life to the pursuit of mystical experiences, the group embraced Pia.

"She has found Atlantis," the scion said, a portly man with silver, curly hair. He stood before Geoff barefoot and wearing a white djelleba, his large, sheep-like head bobbing with certitude when he saw the skeptical look on Geoff's face. "In our shared trances, we saw that place ourselves, high in the twilight."

Geoff had to speak through an interpreter, one of the American youths who lived in the manse, and what he heard next, though he understood it, he had the large man repeat. "The world is a slow dream. And those who are dreaming us live above. Sometimes they come down. But our bodies are too small. We can hold only part of them and even then not for very long. They need bigger minds. Pia Rosa has gone into the forest to find such a big mind."

Back at the airport, Geoff stood for a long time in the rest-room, staring at himself in the mirror. He wanted to go home, to face down Mrs Morganthal and to forget about Pia Rosa. But the pale eyes in his pink face stared back tapered with another determination. He ran a hand over his balding pate, then trailed fingers across his broad brow and thick nose. He let his hand cover his mouth and a hint of harelip that made him look bel-licose, and he saw a frightened man. His stare shimmered with fear — frightened to go back empty-handed to the small life that awaited him. He dropped his hand, revealing a snaggle-toothed, lack-luck smile.

Geoff knew well what the voices were telling Pia Rosa. At the height of their affair, he had listened to her for hours and had read much of what she had written. On the boat ride up the Amazon, he reviewed what he had learned, hoping to anticipate Pia Rosa's madness when he found her.

The ionosphere is vaster than the ocean, she had told him once. Fifty miles above our heads, the atmosphere basks in ultraviolet rays from the sun. These rays break off electrons from the gas molecules there and create ions, positively charged particles. Free electrons swirl among ions in eddies and currents, crests and tides a hundred and fifty miles deep. It is that ocean of electricity far above our heads that high-frequency radio signals bounce off. And it is there that the ul udi live, beings of light that have evolved in that sea much as we once evolved out of the primordial oceans of Earth.

Geoff removed the snap-brim hat he had purchased in Belém and wiped the sweat from his brow with his sleeve. On the blonde river, wide and placid this close to the sea, flat-bottomed boats drifted by, laded with their booty of timber from upriver. On either shore, the huddle of villages, smudged in river haze, appeared like shipwrecks: a repetitious litter of shanties and splintery piers heaped on banks contoured for rain. Sleek, modern landing docks jutted into the water at odd intervals, silver bollards smashed with sunlight. Warehouses big as hangars watched over the river, and, interspersed among them, trees stood like talismans.

A party from Europe of Friends, Quakers, who wanted to see for themselves the notorious deforestation of the Amazon had chartered the boat taking Geoff to the far village where Pia Rosa had gone. They were a quiet, self-possessed group and left him alone once he had explained that he was simply a tourist. In the hour of traces, when everyone gathered at the rail to watch the day end, he alone stood without a camera, gazing up through solar-feathered clouds, wondering what really lay between him and the jawbone of the moon.

Mrs Morganthal's whiskey-colored eyes had reminded Geoff of her granddaughter's, and, in the end, that's what really had prompted him to accept her challenge. But the lever she had used to move him was a story of her time as a young mother in a German death camp. "We waited for death quietly," she had said. "Memories like this — who needs them? I am only telling you now because you will need to know about this when you find our Pia Rosa."

Geoff had suppressed his annoyance at that shared possessive, that manipulative *our*. He had stared boldly, unmoved, at the old woman's glower of sullen grief and into the caverns of her eyes.

"Pia Rosa grew up on these stories," Mrs Morganthal had continued. "She knows that those who survived waited quietly. The ones who despaired, the ones who became brutes like the Nazis, who gave up their faith and pummeled us quiet ones with their rage — they died. They died by their own hands, most of them. 'Thou shalt not kill' means 'Thou shalt care for life.' I've always told Pia Rosa this. Care for life, no matter the suffering. Care for life, because fear of death makes life worthless. We waited quietly. Sure, we were afraid. We shouldn't be afraid? Even so, we loved life more than our fear. We held to our faith. We never gave up our faith, and that gave us the strength to face death. Many of us, too many of us, went quietly to death. But the survivors who were strong enough to face death quietly, they had strength then to face life. Remember this. And when you find Pia Rosa, remind her."

Pia Rosa and he had first met under the stars, laughing at the smallness of life. "How can anything this small matter?" she had asked him then, and he had somberly agreed. But that had been before they had kissed, before their mouths, which had slandered life, had joined and he had come away with a taste like rain. That day that he had tasted her, that very same day that he had been startled by the vividness of her colors — her hair the shade of fallen leaves, cinnamon eyes, and skin like moonlight — he had told her he loved her. Her stare had been harsh and bright as bourbon, and a fume of laughter wisped from her lungs. After that, he had never spoken to her of love again.

But he did love her. At dawn on the river, staring into the broad rays of sunlight that led back the way he had come, he remembered what loving her had meant. Always a fool when her caramel eyes sweetly praised him in bed or afterward while listening to her stories of demons and angels in the upper air, he had never had to say he would follow her anywhere — yet, sure enough, here he was. He had been on this river a week, recalling everything he could about her madness. He had one more day before he would arrive at the Jurua, where her friends in Belém had said she had come to find a mind big enough to carry the ul udi.

Over the last four nights, under stars thistly as weeds, he had come to think of the ul udi as real. They were real to Pia Rosa, and he had tried to imagine what it is that they would want. Childish stories had occurred to him of the ul udi's anger at the destruction of the rain forest. But out here on the bronzed water, inching past colossal walls of jungle, where monkeys screamed and panthers coughed, there was no sign of anything but primal, timeless direction. Sunken trees bumped the hull, and the boat crept slowly enough for him to gaze deeply into chasms of dark trees. A harpy eagle stood regally on a bough, a twitching monkey under its talons, a red string of gut hanging from the raptor's mad visage.

The boat of Friends ended its upriver journey at a village of ragged woodcutters. Low thatched huts squatted in a semicircle facing the river. Scrawny chickens and dwarf pigs wandered through the mud clearing and in and out of the huts. Behind them towered verdant trees, jammed with rank weeds and thick lianas. At a shoddy wharf of lashed logs, some inhabitants had gathered to greet the boat. Geoff, who stood well back among the Friends, searched eagerly among the small crowd for Pia Rosa. There were a few Indians with bowlcut hair slick with nutpaste, two soldiers leaning on their rifles with exhausted expressions, a Lebanese trader grinning lavishly, and the woodcutters, narrow men in limp rags, their dolorous wives standing behind them, children splashing in the shallows.

The Lebanese, who spoke English, told Geoff that Pia Rosa had indeed been in the village some weeks earlier but had gone into the jungle and not returned.

Geoff's breath went damp in his lungs when he stood before the forest and gazed at the dark interior. Squalid liverwort hung in pale tentacles and creeping fungi scaled gray pillars. He swiped away mosquitoes and biting flies. Then, he turned, sat down heavily on the wharf and listened to the timbers cricketing.

The Lebanese said that, for a price, he would arrange for the Indians to guide Geoff into the jungle, to where Pia Rosa had last been seen, two weeks earlier. The Friends were going in the opposite direction, following the woodcutters to the latest site that the rancheros downriver had scheduled to clear for their cattle, and these kindly Quakers tried to dissuade Geoff from traveling alone with the Indians. He felt better knowing that they were aware of his plans, and he agreed to be back in three days to meet them on their return.

The two Indians, whom the Lebanese had selected to lead Geoff, wore cutoff denims with rope belts and T-shirts, one emblazoned with a large photo of Sting, the other with a ballerina from the Joffrey. They carried machetes and spoke no English. From the trader, Geoff acquired enough beef jerky and granola to sustain him for three days, and he also bought a machete and a gun, an old thirty-eight caliber revolver, with a box of thirty rounds.

Early the next morning, after a fitful night on the boat questioning what hope there was of finding Pia Rosa alive in the wilderness, Geoff met his Indian guides in the slick clearing. They informed him through the Lebanese that they would take him to a bend in the nearest tributary, where hunters from their tribe had seen the white woman. The Friends waved him off, and, with his revolver strapped to his backpack and his machete in hand, he strode into the jungle with the Indians and into a light torn like rain.

The hike through the forest to the riverbend took the better part of the day, and they arrived at a stagnant, miasmal pool as the sun flared red through the trees. The Indians indicated a spot where a campfire had burned meagerly. He would not have noticed it if they had not pointed it out, for the jungle had already covered the burn with leaf litter. In the black mud, they found a boot print that could have been a woman's.

The wild sun glistered on the water, where the treetops were rent, and one of the Indians bent over the pool and thwacked the water with the flat of his blade. A bend of rainbow rose to the surface, and he lifted out a stunned fish. Over a twig fire, they braised the fish, and the Indians shared that and the manioc bread they carried in their hip pouches but refused to partake of Geoff's jerky or granola.

The ribbons of birdsong that had fluttered above them all day diminished, and darkness descended in a chamber of cold air. The Indians curled up against the buttressed root of a great kapok and slept. Geoff sat beside them, alert as dandelion fluff. In the course of the day, he had seen scorpions and red spiders big as his outstretched hand. Overhead, through the torn darkness of the canopy, bats whirred against the flaws of the moon. Mosquitoes whined, and somewhere the cold coils of a bushmaster could be sensing his warmth.

"Don't be afraid, Geoff."

Geoff jerked toward the voice, and his heart shuddered like a window. Pia Rosa stood by the black pool, gray in the cinereous light. She wore hiking boots, and, even in the dark, he could see that her clothes were dirty and torn. But her face was clear, open, smiling. He rose and went to her.

"I didn't think I'd ever see you again," he said to her in a rush.

"Then why did you come?"

He stepped close enough to smell the hot spice of her breath, and then he touched her. She was solid, cool, bright to the touch.

"I'm real," she said.

He squeezed both of her arms, then pulled her to him and pressed his weight against her. "God, Pia — it is you!"

"I didn't want to leave, Geoff. The ul udi ... they called me."

Apprehension tightened across his ribs, and a qualm claimed him for his own shameful part in encouraging her delusion. "The ul udi –" He pulled away, enough to look into her face. Her eyes were tiger bright. "Are they real then? Have you seen them?"

"Oh, yes, they're real. I'm not mad, Geoff. I had to find that out. I had to know I wasn't crazy."

He tried to keep his expression neutral, though inside he trembled, seeing all at once that her sickness went deeper than he had wanted to believe. She was one of the damned, daring to face him here in the jungle in the middle of the night remorseless, undaunted in her absurd belief. "Then, where are they?" he asked, allowing a chill of incredulity to enter his voice.

"Where they always were," she answered matter-of-factly, looking up at bursts of stars in the torn canopy of the jungle. "And we're always hearing them — some of us more clearly than others. It's like we're antennas, Geoff. Our bodies are like receivers tuned into them. Their thoughts float in the air all around us, like radio and TV signals — and we can't help but pick them up."

A shout pulled Geoff around, and he saw the Indians sitting up by the buttress roots, where they had been sleeping. They waved at him in alarm and jumped to their feet. Geoff smiled at them to allay their fear. "It's Pia Rosa — the woman I've been looking for."

He turned his smile to Pia Rosa, and his grin slipped. She was gone. A crystal mist breathed in the darkness over the pool. One of the Indians seized his arm and yanked him away as a saurian face lifted into view. A pallid caiman, a six foot long crocodilian, jaws agape, rose quickly to the mud's lip on stubby legs. It snapped at the shadow where Geoff had been standing and twisted about, plunging out of sight with a thrash of its armored tail.

Geoff threw a cry into the night. His stare bulged like a mare's, trying to see through the shadows to where Pia Rosa had gone. Had one of the beasts pulled her into the water? So silently! He shouted her name, and the Indian, who was holding him, jumped away. Over the slow water, a welt of ripples carried moonlight into darkness.

Before first light, the Indians started back to the village, not bothering to wake the lunatic white man, still muttering deliriously in his sleep. When Geoff woke with a start to the clangor of morning birdsongs, there was no sign of his guides. At first, he thought they were out hunting breakfast, but after emptying his bladder and shouting into the morning mist and getting no reply but a momentary silence among the raucous birds, he realized they had abandoned him.

He knelt at the edge of the tannic pool, studying the caiman spoor, his own boot marks and the Indian's splay-toed footprints and finding no sign that Pia Rosa had ever stood there with him. She was not necessarily dead. She had not even been there. Had he dreamed the whole thing? The conviction persisted that he had actually held Pia Rosa in his arms, had smelled her breath and talked with her. He was certain, despite the lack of all physical evidence, that she was here, somewhere.

He gazed over the amber water to where hulks of half-submerged trees pared to mist. How could he hope to find his own way in this hostile forest, let alone find her? Fear whirled up in him. He grabbed his backpack and hurried in the direction he remembered having come with the Indians. Birds fretted and screeched on all sides, out of sight. An opossum spartled from the fungus garden of a fallen tree, and a peccary, hackles bristling, raised its tusks from where it was rooting and screamed at him. He fell backward in a fright, swam to his feet and hurried away from the annoyed creature, leaving his hat behind.

Soon, Geoff realized he was lost. Subhuman cries from the sunshot galleries taunted his every move. Finally, he stood among the pale trees and shouted for help. The Indians, if they heard him, did not respond. No doubt, they thought him mad. His wild behavior had endangered their lives. He quieted himself and tried to get oriented by the sun, though he was not sure in which direction the village lay.

From his back, he took a handful of granola and chewed it morosely. He had food and water for two more days, more if he paced himself. The Friends would not abandon him. When the Indians got back to the village today, the Lebanese would know he was out here alone. Someone would come for him. He laughed at himself, and the springs of his laughter sounded rusty.

◆ ◆ ◆

Rain battered the forest. Geoff hunched in the cove of a ghostly tree bole and peered out at ranks of trunks dimming in the rainsmoke. Hours swung by. At day's end, the storm cleared, birds clicked and whistled again, and a sunset brown as wine shone through the tree crowns.

A foam of voices swelled from a distance. Geoff squeezed out of his covert and rushed in that direction. Under a skinny tree, he found Pia Rosa, her smile sad as a wish. Her fatigues, mud-stained and torn, hung like rags, yet her hair was dry, strewn with leaf debris. He stopped where he was and, with trembling fingers, wiped back from his forehead thin strands of his own wet hair.

Pia Rosa reached out. She was holding his hat. "You dropped this when the pig scared you."

He almost reeled and put a hand to a tree to steady himself. "Who are you?" he asked, and his voice came out in a frightened whisper.

"It's me, Geoff. I'm not really changed — but I am different. You can be, too, if you'll come with me."

The shrill fury of a macaw clanged from the high galleries. Geoff looked up and spotted a disc of lustrous blue fire hovering above the trees. He cowered.

"Don't be frightened," Pia said, stepping closer. "It's the ul udi. They come down sometimes, when they want. People think they're UFOs. But they're electrical. This one will lead you to where you can be like me."

Geoff pressed the back of his hand to his mouth, and his eyes were hard points. Pia Rosa came up to him and placed his hat on his head. "When you're like me, you won't need this. But it may storm some more tonight. This'll keep the rain out of your eyes."

He touched her face. She was solid but chilled, burnished as an electrical current beneath his fingertips. "What's happened to you?"

"I've become like the ul udi."

His fingers traced her plaintive smile. "Is that good?"

She shrugged. "At least I know I'm not crazy."

"Oh, Pia," he said, looking at her piteously.

"I'm *not* crazy," she insisted.

He turned away from her and cast a despairing look at the mysterious blue fire whirling soundlessly above them. "Then why do you look so sad?"

"There's danger. The ul udi are not all good. It's like I told you, Geoff — some are demons, and they talk to me, too. They want to tear our flesh, to feel our pain, because they don't feel anything like that up there. It's a kick for them to feel us suffer. They sent the croc after you last night. They'll try to hurt you again. But I'm here with an ul udi who is good. We'll lead you."

A stark, relentless terror gripped Geoff, and it was all he could do to work his voice. "Lead me where?"

"To the Old Man of the Forest."

"Who's that?"

"I can't tell you now. The more we talk, the closer the evil ones get. I'll explain as we go. But we must hurry. The ul udi are strongest at night, when the planet turns away from the sun. The solar wind sedates their electric bodies. They're active at night."

Pia Rosa stepped back and lost shape. Where she had been, the air glossed a moment with a lamina of energy — then nothing, only the licorice green of dusk.

Geoff looked upward for the ul udi. It, too, was gone. Fear, a boundless, metaphysical fear, drained him of all power and reason. Had he gone crazy? He put hands to his hat, and his fingertips came away icy. He stood immobile, more isolated by this horror than by the nightheld jungle. A jangling wind splattered him with rain shaken from the trees. Lightning winced in the distance, and, after many aching heartbeats, thunder throbbed.

Among the trees, a blue light shone, winking as it flitted through the pillared darkness. Mosquitoes burned his hands and cheeks. He snapped alert and shambled toward the unearthly light.

◆ ◆ ◆

Pia Rosa's voice laved Geoff's brain with coolness:

It's really dangerous for me to talk with you too long. Talking attracts the wrong kind of ul udi. And that's the last thing we want, Geoff. Flesh is a kind of toy to them. We're lucky, though. Our brains are too small for them. I mean, usually we're lucky. I wasn't. Somehow the wiring in my brain started picking them up. I didn't receive them that clearly. So, they couldn't hurt me — or help me. It was just words. But the Old Man of the Forest, his brain is big, larger than our own. He has the neural hardware to receive the ul udi loud and clear. There aren't too many of the Old Ones left. Not anymore. The ul udi abused them, played with their pain too much. So now they're almost extinct. Yeti, Bigfoot, Sasquatch. The scientists named them Neanderthal. They have bigger brains than we do. They're not human, you know.

The night jungle floated by, and Geoff was so absorbed by the voice in his skull, he tripped over a root and tumbled with a soft clamor into a slum of figwort. A low, dismal growl wrenched him about to face bestial eyes. A sour cry spilled from him. But the heavy, sharp collision with death never came. Instead, the air flushed a brilliant blue, and whatever beast he had stumbled into slipped swiftly away.

The ul udi had descended below the canopy, and the whole forest ignited with its spectral glow. The glare torched his vision. Squinting, he watched a sphere of azure voltage split into a dozen tiny globes that whirled off among the trees.

Frogs sobbed, and the mosquitoes burned. He unstrapped his pack, heaved to his feet free of its burden and pursued the ghost lights.

◆ ◆ ◆

The silence of an understanding pervaded Geoff, and he stopped. He had been loping through the jungle most of the night, following the ever-retreated blue jinn. Rain had flashed in fits during his run, refreshing him, adding to his feral stamina. Now the storm had thinned away entirely, leaving several huge stars in the skyholes of the forest cover. He looked around for the wraith lights, and they were gone. A greasy odor weighted the air.

Among the traumatic shadows, a smudge of movement fixed his attention. He stepped back a pace. Something large approached him through the trees, human-shaped and vigilant. He shrank like a vapor, and his eyes flared white to see it.

From the syrupy darkness, a huge, shaggy man appeared, pike-jawed and block-browed. The giant stood, broad as a cedar, snug in his poise, watching Geoff cringe. Mosquitoes whined loudly in the plump stillness.

Steady now, Pia Rosa's voice opened in Geoff.

The mosquitoes vanished. The air began to hum.

The sight of the giant had given Geoff's fright a shape, and he stared at the hulking man as he would have gawked at his own entrails had they abruptly spilled into his hands. Fear burst through him like sprung clockwork running from itself, and he wanted to flee.

Don't move. The evil ones want you to run so they can kill you in the jungle. Stay still. There's no place for you to go now — except up.

Geoff knelt before the Old Man of the Forest. In the vibrant air, the greasy stink of the giant swelled like heat. The giant, too, seemed unhappy. His visage seemed a wild mask, rigid yet simmering with alertness, knowing full well what would come next. His massive arms lifted above his head as if in a rage, and the hairs all along his body stood straight out.

Tongues of green flame appeared at the tips of the yeti's fingers, and his static-strung hair sparked. Like a human-shaped Christmas tree, the giant flickered green and blue. Clots of energy spun off him and wisped away in the hot, deadstill air. A vile cry lashed from the being, and Geoff realized that the creature was being electrocuted.

The next instant, a bolt of lightning struck the spark-stressed space above the yeti and forked into lines of force that tore Geoff's sight almost blind. Snakes of power twined in the silver air between them. One of the snakes lashed at Geoff.

An enormous chill sluiced through him, a glacial wind that hoisted him up and off his feet and flung him headlong out of himself. Shorn of gravity, he soared. Vision swung wide.

Sun-thumbed colors dispelled the night, and a chromatic panorama of the jungle rotated below. At its luminous center, the yeti slumped exhausted. Thermal smoke, iridescent and curling, peeled away from his sagging shape. And where Geoff himself had been, bright, billowy particles, fiery atoms, danced in a solarized contour of his body. He rocketed up and away from that surreal view, and the night opened its web of stars to receive him.

The world is a slow dream. And those who are dreaming us live here. Clear light, a melodious flow of energy, enwombed Geoff and Pia Rosa as if again in the amniotic sea, futureless and free. Outward loomed the moon — vast and flawed — and inward, Earth, vaster yet, marbled blue. Sere land masses drifted by, and a cobalt sea beneath fleecy clouds.

Where are the ul udi? Geoff asked. All fear was gone, replaced by enormous and imperturbable placidity. Even amazement had gone missing. Instead, he felt something like benediction, peaceful as Brahma. He could see Pia Rosa just as he had on Earth, only brighter, clearer, shot with champagne light. And the harder he looked, the deeper and keener he felt her, until, in a complete collapse of distance, her being poured into him like light.

They're here, Pia Rosa answered from inside him. *But they sleep in the day. The solar wind — the honey wind we feel — drowses them. Only with great effort do they wake in the day.*

The balmy expanse of daylight extended to the curve of the planet, where the edge of night appeared in curtains of wavery auroras.

I went all the way into the night only once, Pia Rosa said. *It was horrible.* A flurry of panic swept through her to Geoff, and the serenity embracing him loosened before the fright in her staring eyes. *The peaceful ul udi live in the upper limits of the ionosphere. They commune there ecstatically. I've heard them singing. But the demon ul udi are full of insane fury. They lurk on the bottom of the electric sea, close to Earth. They pulled me down when I went into the night. They hurt me, Geoff. They tore at me with their minds. I never felt anything so horrible, so cruel and furious. They burned me and froze me and cut me again and again. I suffered until dawn. Since then, I've stayed on the dayside of the sky.*

Pia scowled at him as if enraged. *I've tried to get away, to get back to Earth. We can go under the night and go back down, the way I did when I found you. But we can't stay there. The sky pulls us back up. The gentle ul udi tried to help me. They saw what the others did to me in the night. They tried to help me get back. But the insane ul udi interfere with them. The yeti was my anchor. I was really surprised to find you there, Geoff.*

Geoff experienced a desperate helplessness. Then he looked away from her hurt stare and gazed at the diamondchip sky, the moon like a big, bruised mushroom, and the sun, round and fierce, a white hole in the blackness. The ethereal calm he had known before returned, a lyric gentleness that muted the harsh truth that there was no way back. *Now I understand the sadness I saw on your face.*

I would have sent you away, if I could, Geoff. But the dark ones — they'd have killed you.

I wouldn't have gone back even if I could have, Pia Rosa —

I know, Geoff. She felt his love, saw it in his wide stare, and that love backwashed in her with a depth of caring she had not expected from herself. *I was wrong to walk away from you the way I did. But I didn't know if I was mad. I really thought I had to be. I still can hardly believe this is real.*

We're together now. We don't have to wonder anymore about what's real.

But there's something else you have to know, Geoff. We're dying.

The truth of that flowed into him with the energy of their sharing, and he understood what she did. Those carried up into the sky slowly dissipated. The solar wind and the currents in the ionosphere wore away their plasma shapes. That was why there were no others like themselves. *The longer we stay on the dayside,* he said, *the more swiftly we'll dissolve. We have to enter the night.*

◆ ◆ ◆

Geoff and Pia Rosa allowed the ionospheric currents to carry them toward the brush lights of twilight. They willed themselves high, urging their plasma bodies to loft into the upper reaches, where the angelic ul udi dwelled. But the currents had a natural undertow that swept them down. Even as they strained for the heights, the voices of the depths began to rage.

The crazed ul udi howled, and their storm-torn screams rose like a siren through the fluttering auroras. A demented dream-time began. Images of blown-off limbs, ripped-free jawbones and unraveled viscera swarmed among the leering noises.

Geoff and Pia, fused by their fright, pushed themselves higher even as darkness clamped about them and the hellish images congealed to pain. Hurt split like lightning in them, abrupt and cutting, flinging them apart. Molten laughter filled the space between, and suddenly they were alone, each in their own hell.

Filthy pain twisted its cancers in Geoff — and the worst of it was hearing the mutilated cries of Pia Rosa as the demons hacked her with every torment of their black imagining. No hope of unconsciousness here, only more pain, an endlessly renewed suffering.

And in the slithery midst of it, with acid cruelty burning cold through every fiber of his being, Geoff remembered Mrs Morganthal — and the mocking demons jabbered louder yet. Through the screech of torn sinews, her voice remembered him: *We waited for death quietly.*

That memory fit snugly into his agony. It had been made for pain in the very home of nightmare, and he clung to it. The words moiled in him like a dumb mantrum, a ghoul-cry. And he calmed down. He calmed down and let the pain eat him.

Care for life, no matter the suffering.

Pia Rosa heard him. And where there had been a glare of burning screams, there was suddenly silence. The quiet gentled her. The ache of the demons razored sharper, but she stayed still and let them cut her.

The demons tried weeping and terror. But already the plasma bodies had loosened the ul udi's taloned grip and, with a last tremulous spasm of nausea, whirled free. Pia Rosa and Geoff merged and hurtled into an updraft that launched them away from the mangling voices and out into the huge chill grace of night.

◆ ◆ ◆

The sun has a voice, the seraphs spoke. *When the solar wind is blocked by the Earth, we come up here and listen to it. It is the voice of God.*

Amber jellies of twilight gleamed along the curve of the planet, and the sun's wind buffeted the edge of the ionosphere, blowing the planet's magnetic field deep into space. Pia Rosa and Geoff hovered there in the musical presence of the angelic ul udi. Energy patterns that appeared to the humans like living stained glass shifted around and through each other in fugal harmonies.

A teeming rapture exalted the humans, and they entered the company of angels. This was the end of their journey, here among creatures of light, chromatic beings, whose dazzle was a serene, imperishable euphoria. Below, the fallen world continued in an immensity of darkness, and, above, tingling stars massed like majestic clouds.

Pia Rosa and Geoff gazed into each other, incredulous. Their joy punctured the last illusion that they would ever return to their lives on Earth. Flesh could not regenerate out of the lightning that had freed them. They understood this with the shared-knowing imparted by the beatific ul udi. *You are of us now,* the seraphs explained. *You will live with us a hundred orbits around our star or more, until your bodies of light merge with the dreamless wavefront of energy from the sun — and there, like the best of us, become one with the voice of God.*

In the beautiful, unearthly light of the ul udi, Pia Rosa saw Geoff's watchfulness dim, and he recognized the sudden blankness in her face. Simultaneously, they remembered their nights together on Earth watching the wheel of stars turn, sharing their faithlessness in anything but the smallness of their lives. *God?* they asked, astounded. After the suffering that they had endured among the demonic ul udi, they could hardly believe these others believed in a god.

The wavering auras of the ul udi brightened as they reached into the minds of the humans, pondering the earthly thoughts and memories they found there. At last, something like a laugh came from the blaze of meshing colors, and Pia Rosa and Geoff dangled glittering against the dusty stars, sharing that laughter, not knowing what they were laughing at.

The god of perfection and wholeness is a reality, the ul udi answered, *but not in this universe — and not at all as you have thought of God. Not a He.* The laughter glistened. *Not even a sentience, for all sentience is timebound. God exists as the higher dimensions compacted within each single point of our reality. We see from your memories that your scientists already suspect these dimensions. Beyond the weave of space and time is a realm of pure symmetry — of perfection.* The crystalline music of the ul udi heightened. *We are here. God is there, separated from us by the closure of spacetime at the tiniest possible scale.*

We're here, all right, Pia Rosa and Geoff acknowledged. *But we don't really understand. We don't even know how we see each other. We don't have bodies — but it looks like we have faces, arms, legs . . .*

They gawked at each other anew. Looking closer, Geoff saw that Pia Rosa's hair luminesced as a crux of rays, her pale flesh woven of light, eyes embers from the last moment of twilight. To Pia Rosa, too, Geoff's familiar countenance appeared as confections of light shaped to solid flesh.

All life is electrical, the ul udi said. And their music made that seem plausible and sufficient. *We will teach you what we know of these mysteries. You will live among us.*

So we really can't go back? Geoff asked.

I discovered a way under the night, Pia Rosa said. *That's how I found Geoff. You helped me, remember?*

And I felt her, Geoff added. *She was solid.*

All feeling is electrical, the ul udi replied. *All sensation is electrical. You can return to Earth as bodies of electric plasma but only at night and never for very long. And each time you trespass the planet, you risk falling into the clutches of those who live below, whose pleasure is toying with the life that has risen from the mud.*

Do you truly want to return?

No, they answered as one, luminous among the aisles of stars. They perched at the very point of love, where every other direction led to less. *We're happy here with you. But there's one other –*

They remembered her together, the old woman, who had told them how to face pain quietly and find their way here. *Will you help us get back to her? Let her know we're all right?*

The sliding colors swelled closer, brighter. *Why go back at all? Life is electric. Let life speak for itself.*

Beings of light, full of power and presence, seething with joy, swelled closer and took the humans in.

Mrs Morganthal put down her pen and rubbed her aching eyes. *Seething with joy* — that sounded too precious. She took her pen and crossed it out. "But that's how it would be for them," she said aloud. "What is heaven without joy? But really — *seething?*" She blew an exasperated sigh and sat listening to her heart trip.

Night stood in the window above her desk. She began sorting the pages she had written. A year had passed since the letter she had received from the Friends, who had found Geoff's hat and backpack in the jungle. For a while, she had lived quietly with that knowledge, expecting his body to turn up. Yet, nothing more of him was ever found. Like her granddaughter, he, too, had vanished.

Shortly after the letter, she had begun reading the many pages of Pia Rosa's compulsive writing. And in the midst of it, the idea came to her — right out of the blue — to take pen in hand herself and write.

She had never written anything but letters before. The narrative nevertheless came smoothly, inspired by the ideas in Pia's pages. What she did not know, she looked up. The part about God she had put in, because the doctor who had treated Pia Rosa had said that one of the traits of her granddaughter's mental illness would be hyperreligiosity. Pia had mentioned the voice of God but had never written about God Himself, at least not in the several hundred pages Mrs Morganthal had read, though she had mentioned Atlantis several times.

Pia had thought that the legend of Atlantis endured as memories of a far-gone time when many more Neanderthal lived and the ul udi could ride their larger brains and easily walk the earth, inspiring not only the terror of ogres but the wisdom of magicians. Terribly, the evil ul udi had proven too severe a survival risk. The Neanderthal shrank toward extinction, and Atlantis rose.

Mrs Morganthal thumbed the pinched flesh between her tired eyes, then flipped through one of the three astronomy books open on her desk. Those and a dozen other volumes on physics and human evolution were due at the library a week ago. She was unconcerned. She would pay the fines gladly, because in this book, she had found the answer to why the voice of God spoke through the sun.

With her left hand, she touched the relevant passage, and with her right she turned the page of her notebook and wrote:

You say that you hear the voice of God, Pia Rosa said to the ul udi. *But how can you hear God in the sun?*

The music of the ul udi chimed sweeter. *To understand that, you must know something about our star. The sun is shot through with effervescence, like an immense sphere of champagne. When the gas bubbles reach the surface, they are each over six hundred miles wide, and the sound of their popping is so loud that it heats the sun's atmosphere from a mere five thousand degrees Celsius to a million degrees. That sound is what gives the sun the energy to blow the solar wind. Up here, we listen to the random patterns of that sound carried by the sun's wind as it beats against the magnetosphere. And in the sound's randomness is the voice of God. For that is how the higher dimensions, separated by the closure of spacetime at the Planck distance, connect with our causal reality — through the acausal. What you call chance and accident is the voice of God.*

Mrs Morganthal read what she had written, and she smiled. This was all beginning to make sense. Perhaps Pia Rosa had been right after all. Tomorrow, she would review the whole thing again and tie up loose ends. For now, she was tired. She put down her pen and turned off the desklight. Night swept in through the window. Her eyes relaxed and gazed out at darkness and the gratitude of stars.

DEATH'S HEAD MOON

EATH'S HEAD MOON — SPOOK TALK I first heard from an Irish Gunnery Sergeant in Nietzsche's War at a place called Belleau Wood during the battle of the Marne. Looking more porcine than human with his hog jowls, tiny and hard hog eyes, bristle-cut gray hair, and large mouth curled at the corners to a hog sneer, Sergeant Seamus Doyle clung to me from the first day we arrived in that breakneck terrain. He found me during the artillery bombardment when we got blown up. The day had been brilliant. It mocked our misery. Golden shafts slanted through green cascades of the Bois de Belleau while shells whined overhead and burst around us, tossing dirt and smoke into the cloudless blue. Shrapnel whistled in the spring air, sizzled through the forest canopy, and thudded among the tree trunks. The force of the high-impact explosions knocked us out of our bodies. More than once, I thought I was dead. The earth shook, the concussion came down heavy as an elephant's foot, mashed me into trench mud, crushed the breath out of me, and I was gone. Deaf, I soared through windswept smoke, sunlight fizzing around me like champagne. I flew serenely beyond Earth's blue day into velvet darkness. Each time, before the dark could undo me, the elephant's foot lifted, breath wrenched into my lungs, and I was back, chewing mud. "Mourny morning, lad! And a boomin' huff of a mourny morning it is at that. You've a classicoal peat boggy mug ever I cast eyes upon a son o' Diarmuid. What's your name, boyo?" Filthy with trench muck, the hog face that pressed close to me was an authentic hog face, nothing even vaguely human about it. I couldn't hear a thing except the roar of blood in my ears. The lilting insanity of that Irish voice somehow bypassed my stunned ears and pierced my brain direct. "Richard!" I shouted and heard nothing of my own voice. "Richard Malone!" One corner of the hog mouth hooked to a smile, and those tight swine eyes tightened merrier. "Fah! A Malone! I shoulda been forewarned by them cross-knit eyebrows, the bane o' your breed. The folklord has it the Malones did some severe philosoflying with the Druidiots — and the strain on the Malone brains got 'em so flummoxed they cannot ever hope again to unknit their brows! Haw!" Doyle heaved himself over me, and I felt us go up in the air. We came down under a massive wave of earth and were buried so deep that if he hadn't been there to know I was under him and to grope down and yank me up by the scruff, I'd never again have seen daylight. It was worse at night. The explosions in the woods cast stark shadows. Debris came hissing out of the dark. I saw Jesus walking through the broken trees. Doyle pressed his hog jowls to my face. "You google-eye him there in the blasty light, don't ya? There! That bearded bugger in the shroudy robe! 'Tis Fionn mac Cumhal!" *Finn McCool* — all that night, he yammered about the Son of Cumhal, champion of the Fianna, the Celtic warriors of legend, and their defeat at the Battle of Gabhra and McCool's journey to the Otherworld where he sleeps and will one day wake and return. I tried not to listen. I wanted Jesus. But in the numb deafness between explosions, Doyle's hog mouth spewed endless fantasies about the bombardment digging up the Hallows where the Tuatha de Danaan — the fairy lords — dwelled, for all of France was once Celtic terrain, and McCool was on the march to prophesy doom and salvation among our Gaelic brethren. I just wanted Jesus. I prayed a Hail

Mary and an Our Father for each shell that struck close enough to shake the ground under us to pudding. But it didn't shut him up. He said McCool could foresee the future by chewing his thumb. And, sure enough, in the strobe flashes going off beyond the trees where men in their holes were being torn into chunks of meat and their prayers brusquely silenced, Jesus strolled, his long hair flying in the blast wind, his radiant robe pressed tight against his narrow body — and a hand to his mouth! Was he sucking his thumb? No — no — it was some kind of rabbinic benediction, kissing his hand, and blessing the departing souls. In the abrupt flashes and percussive silence, I saw them flying, a squad of souls like tattered smoke. "King Alfred's lads and der Amerikaners be flyin' to the heavendor in the sky who sells their souls a penny an eye. But we've naught to fear, boyo. Fionn mac Cumhal is twixt us and the banshee." McCool's prophetic power came to him by accident, when he was an apprentice to Eire's great Druid, Finegas. McCool was roasting a salmon for Finegas — a salmon that had inadvertently eaten a magic hazelnut — and when McCool turned the seared fish, he burnt his thumb, instantly stuck it in his mouth and so indirectly acquired some of the clairvoyance of the supernatural nut. I go on about this, because if you were there, with the artillery bombardment in its second day, and blood crawling out of your ears, and the night brighter than day with phosphor explosions, and the pummeling shocks interfering with your prayers, and your head filled with cottony nothing, and a mad Irishman with a hog's face screaming about Druids and magic hazelnuts, you would want it to mean something. It should mean something. I wanted Jesus. I was eighteen, and I wanted everything my mother had told me about Jesus. But I'm from Boston. Seamus Doyle was out of Tralee. The bombardment had almost annihilated his battalion in the Royal Inniskilling Fusiliers: 500 men slain from a total strength of 670. Chaos had tossed him in among the American Expeditionary Forces. Irish luck brought him to me and the Marine brigade of the Second Division, and he filled my head with spook talk. At three in the morning after two days of continuous bombardment, the shelling stopped and our assault through the smoky woods began. The Huns' heavy machine guns camouflaged in the rocky strongholds above us fortified the densely forested and boulder-strewn area. Now we understood why, days earlier, for the glory of getting into these murderous woods, we had to shove our way through fleeing French troops and refugees, who kept screaming at us, hysterical as women: "Retraite! Retournez! N'allez pas en avant! Tout est perdu! Les Allemands ne peuvent pas être arrêtés!" After losing scores of men under the artillery bombardment with no more of a defensive position than the ditches we dug in the leaf litter with our kit spoons and bayonets, we got up from those ditches and went forward against a death wall of machine guns. We did it with rifle and bayonet. For four days, we dodged among splintered trees, creeping forward by inches through fallen boughs, dashing a few yards and hunkering behind stinking corpses of Marines bloated with gas gangrene. Doyle was at my side the whole time, yammering about McCool and the Druids. I just wanted Jesus. With bullets scything over our heads and trees chewed to stumps and the wood meat flying like in a saw mill, I wept out every prayer I knew. Two days into our bloody advance, my prayers blurred. I couldn't call them to mind. I began to listen to Doyle. At night, against the staccato flashes of machine gun fire, he glimpsed McCool showing him the doorways between the trees that led to survival. I followed him, and we lived. Day three and day four, we chose the right doorways and lived and others beside us chose the wrong doorways and died. Time and again, a Marine an arm's length away went down wounded and thrashing in agony, drawing more machine gun fire, bullets ripping him apart, buttons flying, shreds of uniform spinning like leaves, till finally he lay still. I didn't want to look. But you got to look. It's a man dying. A moment before, he had been hungry and thirsty and scared like you. He stepped between the trees like you, but he went down. There were a lot of men who went down. You could walk across their backs and never touch the ground. By the end of the fourth day, we had crawled into a V-shaped oat field bordered on all sides by thick woodland. Ferocious crossfire hemmed us in. It was 9:00 PM on the tenth of June, and it was just getting dark. "Where's mac Cumhal?" I asked Doyle. He gave no response. He hadn't shut up in six days, and my heart winced with the certainty a bullet had silenced him. But when I crept closer, careful not to stir the oats and call enemy fire out of the twilight, I found him lying on his side, helmet tilted against his cheek, and those tiny hog eyes staring in wide terror at the maroon sky. Above the torn tree line floated a blood-jelly moon quartered like a shard of skull. The Heines had used mortars to throw gas shells from the rocky heights into the woods, and syrupy fumes streaked the phosphorescent moon with something like a ghastly visage, something like eye sockets and a jawbone grimace webbed with putrid flesh. "Death's head moon!" Doyle groaned. "Oho! I'm sorrowfool to behold that morbiddy mug in the farthy firmamental. It's done for us now, Malone. Neither mac Cumhal nor Jay-sus can thwart the trumpy jazz we'll be hearin' from yon angels afore this hale nightmary be concludicrous. Make your peace, boyo." There was no time for peace that night. Soon as dark descended, the order came to advance. Bellycrawling in the mud with bullets whining inches overhead, crackling through the oats, pounding across the field like hoof beats, I noticed everything in such detail I thought I must already be dead and seeing with a wraith's un-blinking gaze. I still remember, vivid as a postal card, the mud lit like amber, glowing like wax in the radiance of the incandescent flares. Among embedded oat stems, I beheld beetles shiny as onyx, writhing angleworms scrawling angelic script, and a black salamander with red freckles arrayed in dice dots making eight the hard way. This teeming world thrived apart from the war. For a while, I belonged to it. Then, we crawled out of the oat field into the far woods. At the same time, other Marines had rounded the woods and with grenades had cleared two machine gun nests in the rocky caves. We had trained on a German machine gun previously captured, and those leathernecks knew how to handle that weapon. Swept out from their coverts in the trees by bursts from the commandeered machine guns, the Kaiser's Fifth Guard Division came charging into our sites. I shot three while still flat on my belly. Then, Doyle grabbed my collar and dragged me behind a tree. A moment later, a mortar shell impacted where I had lain. I lifted a pale and shaken stare of gratitude to my savior, but he and half the tree where he had hauled me were gone. The shrapnel butchered him where he had stood, just alongside me. In the fire shadows, I didn't recognize the slurry of bone meal and bloody rags that remained. Even his helmet lay mangled, smashed to a twist of slag. The Heines came rushing through the trees, mad to escape the frenzy of rapid fire at their backs. I staggered to my feet shooting. The lucid focus that had sharpened my gaze in the oat field persisted, and I directed each shot with dream-like clarity and lethal precision. I'd seen the death's head moon. McCool or Jesus or whatever specter had guided us through the killing grounds was gone. Seamus Doyle was gone. And I was confident that at any moment I'd be gone, too. I strolled out from behind my blasted tree and ambled into the throng of fleeing Huns, all the while firing with tranquil intensity. A model 1917 Springfield rifle holds five thirty caliber bullets in each clip, and my bandolier sported ten clips. When I ran out of ammunition, I yanked a Mauser carbine from the clutches of a corpse and continued firing. Bullets burned past my face. At one point, a Heine's bayonet snagged in my bandolier while mine pried past his ribs and dug for his heart. Mortar blasts knocked me down twice. Yet, after the fighting was over, I was still alive among the torn trees. I searched the starry night for the moon. It had set hours before. At dawn, I went back through the shattered forest, looking for Doyle among the fallen. The stench thwarted me, and once I began retching I couldn't stop. Entrails dangled from jagged boughs. Severed limbs and body parts littered the woods, and big black birds picked at clots of flesh. Officers had already completed rummaging through the rucksacks of the enemy dead, gathering maps and command papers useful to intelligence. Among the broken bodies lay numerous discarded personal items, including letters, pocket-sized Bibles and durable military editions of *Also Sprach Zarathustra*. I never found Doyle or any remnant of his Fusiliers' uniform, and too often over the intervening years I've wondered if he had been real or a figment of my shell-shocked brain. Hardly does it matter. As dread memento, I claimed for my own a blood-stained copy of Friedrich Nietzsche's war-bible. I lifted it from the carcass of a

Heine infantryman who had fallen about where I had lost Doyle. It was years before I could read that souvenir of a very bad time. Then, some hobo who understood German translated the title for me: *Also Sprach Zarathustra: Ein Buch für Alle und Keinen — Thus Spoke Zarathustra: A Book for Everyone and No One.* I was no one. By that time, ten years after Nietzsche's War, I'd had a dozen tough jobs, everything from quarry work to lumberjack, and I'd lost them all to my belligerence. I liked to fight. The war had never stopped for me. I even exploited my size and brawn to work the boxing ring for a while — but I also liked to drink, and drink and the sweet science don't kiss. I met the hobo who read German when I was earning my way as a freight yard bull. My job was to ply my belligerence against the bandits who raided the yards at night for whatever they could take from the sitting boxcars and tool sheds. I was also supposed to drive off hobos, but mostly they were my drinking buddies. *Ich liebe Den, welcher sich schämt, wenn der Würfel zu seinem Glücke fällt und der dann fragt: bin ich denn ein falscher Spieler? — denn er will zu Grunde gehen.* Those were the words that hooked me to that lunatic philosopher. When I heard them in English, it was like I'd become a philosophy hobo and this was a catch-out in an open boxcar for the ride of my life: *I love him who is ashamed when the dice fall in his favor, and who then asks: 'Am I a cheat?' — for he wants to perish.* That was me! A goose. Why was I alive? Why had I rolled eight the hard way and Doyle and so many other good men came up snake eyes? The answer to that question was always in the next drink or the next fight. Really, I just wanted to die. The opportunity came often enough doing bull work in the marshalling yards, where the Mob was bent on looting whole freight cars. I got shot once, in the buttocks, but I was so sauced I don't much remember it. I don't much remember anything from those years, except I didn't stay a bull long. I lost that job and became a hobo myself. I hopped the rails, drank white lightning from a fruit jar and earned my way between rides cutting ricks of wood for twenty-five cents each or picking cotton at fifty cents a hundred pounds. It's all a blur — until after that wretched night I saw again the death's head moon. That was spring of '35 in Cimarron County, Oklahoma, at a roadhouse where I kept a sheba that I think I cared about, but I don't truly recall. I mean, I must have cared about her, because when I saw that leering skull moon ghoulish with ripped flesh from the dust storm black rolling across the countryside a hundred miles south, I rushed to the roadhouse. I was afraid I'd find her dead or suffering. Instead, I found my sheba naked in bed with another sheik. By his greasy hair, I yanked him to his feet and slugged him, expecting him to hit me back. But he didn't. He just fell down dead. Except for his pomaded hair and penciled mustache, he has no face. I can't for the life of me remember what he looked like. I was that blotto. But I saw he was just a kid, some young Okie playing at being a swank slickster — just a prom-trotter acting the bunk part of a wolf. I can still hear my sheba shrieking like someone with a hot poker stuck in her eye. I lit out fast and sobered up pretty quick. Oklahoma was a hanging state, and I was a no-account drifter with a bad history who'd killed a local mother's little Jimmy. That night, I rode the rails out of the state. Two days later, I made it to Fog City and within a week I stowed away on a tramp steamer leaving the country. By the time I got to Honolulu, I'd sweated out the shakes, but there was no getting quit of the fact I'd murdered a man. Sober for the first time since the War, I felt like the woken dead. I didn't recognize a damn thing under that tropical sun, not the eleven shades of blue in the sea or the tumbling clouds fat as laughing gods or the obscene flowers like open wounds or the tide pools of vaporous jellyfish and the starved face of my own reflection staring back hollow-eyed as a desert saint. The docks offered work. Unfortunately, I didn't team well with the big, easy-going Hawaiian stevedores. I couldn't shake the doleful misery that dogged me, not only for the young sap I'd put down at the roadhouse but also for all the young roughnecks who went west on those killing fields seventeen years ago. Bad feelings wormed my brain, and my distraction put everybody on the docks in jeopardy. The easy Hawaiians let me go, and I took a job as a broom-pusher at a wharfside club called *The Sneaky Tiki*. A thousand and one tiki gods carved in every variety of frightful crowded the dark, mildewed niches of that bamboo hovel, and Ah-Fuk, the shriveled Chinese crone who owned the place, expected me to dust them and the floor daily as well as bounce rowdy sailors, protect her quiffs when the johns got rough, and collect vig on the unpaid debts from whoever was fool enough to play her rigged backroom tables. I liked the job, because — after I finished the day's extensive dusting — work was sporadic enough for me to pursue my new passion: I had committed myself to studying the lunatic philosopher who had poisoned my soul by inspiring the vehement war to end all wars. In the right dose, poison is its own medicine, right? During my hobo travels, I had managed to get translated enough of the blood-soaked war memento to understand that Nietzsche wrote about finding strength in suffering. The idea of the *over*man had a lot to do with why I took the job at *The Sneaky Tiki*. Getting over. *Dort war's auch, wo ich das Wort 'Übermensch' vom Wege auflas, und dass der Mensch Etwas sei, das überwunden werden müsse.* In an inebriated hand, I had penciled atop those words, *There, too, was where I picked up from the path the word "overman," and that man is something that must be overcome.* What had I done to overcome myself? I took a job at *The Sneaky Tiki* — and I never touched the booze or any of the quiffs. I had overcome what had overcome me in years past. Or I thought I had. The mad philosopher also wrote, *Je mehr er hinauf in die Höhe und Helle will, um so stärker streben seine Wurzeln erdwärts, abwärts, in's Dunkle, Tiefe, — in's Böse.* In my shaky hand that came out, *The more he seeks to rise into the height and light, the more vigorously do his roots struggle earthward, downward, into the dark and deep — into evil.* That was truer than I knew — until the third time I met the death's head moon. Then, I got to know the truth of those words with my blood — and with the piteous heart our blood lassoes. Autumn of '37, stiff winds had lofted to great heights plumes of ash from the volcanoes to the south. Standing in the shore-break off Diamond Head, torch fishing with some of the club regulars, I gazed with stupendous dread upon stratospheric clouds of lava dust that had smeared a squalid grin across the moon's skull. I dropped my torch where I stood and slogged to shore without looking back, chilled to the bone, because the name my companions were shouting after me was not my own but the moniker I chose to hide under — and it sounded more horrible than I can say in the light of the death's head moon: "*Doyle!* Hey, Doyle! We no pau! Where you goin', braddah?" A year before, Ah-Fuk had given me a gun — a Smith and Wesson revolver, the kind our officers carried in the War, the ones that fire those big point forty-five-inch caliber bullets — and she told me, "You go Double Eight Noodle Shop, shoot one Moon Duck! What for you wait? Ah-ya! Take gun, you! No go talk. You hear? You talk too much. Moon Duck no talk. He fantastical crazy. You go shoot him plenty dead, heyah!" Moon Duck, a notorious Chinatown bookie and Ah-Fuk's fiercest competitor, was a nasty bald-headed Korean goon with skin the color of rancid butter and no hair on his whole body except exceedingly long eyebrows twitchy as spider legs. During one of my off hours, he had put the squeeze on the crone for half her earnings — and, when she gave him the stink eye and some fast lip, he'd nearly fitted her for a wooden kimono by bouncing a tiki off her gray head. As if those screws weren't tight enough, he proceeded to slice up two of her best paying quiffs — nothing to disfigure them, since he expected them to be working for him soon, only some razor cuts on the soles of their feet. I took the revolver from Ah-Fuk just to dry up her grievous squalling, which was shrill enough to give the Buddha a nosebleed. I left the big gun under the mattress where I slept in the flop room above the club, because I had no intention of shooting anybody. My size and melancholy countenance are usually sufficient to get the job done, and those pugs who think they rate, they dance with me until they can't crawl. I'm not a tough guy. I read German philosophy and drink buttermilk. How tough can I be? But my patience can be saturated, and when my disposition sours I frighten myself. Too bad Moon Duck didn't know that. The busboy at Double Eight Noodle Shop directed me to a ramshackle shanty at the dark end of the canal in Chinatown. I found Moon Duck and his cronies sitting on papaya crates around a big wooden chest with many drawers that used to hold medicinal herbs but served now to sort bookie slips. Before I could complete my spiel, Moon Duck shrieked like an electrified cat and stuck in my face a miniature pistol with a cocked hammer ready to send its tiny slug rattling around inside my skull scrambling my brains. He should have dropped the hammer. Instead, the screwy goon had me drop my pants. Then, he put my scrotum in one of the tiny drawers of that big cabinet, slammed it shut and locked it. The place had been rigged with turpentine canisters to burn with a fury, reducing the shanty and its illegal contents to a soot smudge in the event of a vice raid. Moon Duck, with mirthful exuberance, ignited the torch rags, then slapped an open straight razor atop the cabinet within my reach. He strolled outside with his cronies to see if I would burn or castrate myself. Flames gusted through the shanty with a roar and sucked the air right out of my lungs. In a panic, I tried lifting the cabinet and shuffling out with it. But that was hopeless. The straight razor spun off the tilted surface, and I dropped the cabinet and caught the naked blade, slicing my fingers. That act of desperation saved my life. If I hadn't panicked and absurdly attempted to muscle out of that inferno, I'd have roasted or made my way thereafter as a capon. Lubricating the razor with my blood, I just barely managed to slide the flat of the blade into the tight seam underneath the drawer. I shoved downward on the jammed razor with both hands and snapped the blade. But I'd also splintered the base of the drawer, and my desperate and bleeding fingers ripped apart the front panel and freed my bruised scrotum. Into a vortex of flame, arms crossed over my face, I leaped, crashing through the back of the shanty. The black water of the canal received me with a serpent's hiss, and when I surfaced a pillar of fire swirled where the shanty had been. I returned to *The Sneaky Tiki* and got the forty-five. I was back on the street before the bamboo shades in my flop room stopped rattling. A willow of smoke was all that remained of the bookie's shanty when I stalked back into Chinatown. I must have been a horrific sight. Hair singed to my blistered scalp, face blackened, clothes charred to rags, I lurched through Chinatown like some infernal demon big with wrath and cut loose from whatever perdition the denizens of that alien quarter most dreaded, because the usually crowded and noisy lanes loomed vacant before my advance. Despite my obvious homicidal intent or perhaps because of it, word did not reach Moon Duck of my shambling approach. I found him gaily smoking cigarettes with his cronies before a tureen of pickled cabbage and offal in the very noodle shop where Ah-Fuk had originally instructed me to ask for him. The smile lingered on his buttery face and tobacco fumes twirled from his nostrils like dragon whiskers when I shot him between the eyes and splashed his brains out the back of his head. I would have shot his cronies too, as well as the waitress and the busboy, but they all vanished like a magician's smoke trick before the boom of that big revolver stomped out the door and down the empty street. For a long time after that unhappy experience, I expected retribution. However, the police invested no effort in bringing to justice the murderer of a murderer, and I never so much as glimpsed another of Moon Duck's cronies again. I think my insane rage spooked them. But I still haven't stopped looking over my shoulder, in case they're playing some Chinese angle on revenge. And that's what I was thinking the night I waded to shore under the death's head moon. Upon my return to *The Sneaky Tiki*, I came in the back way, past the battered trash bins stinking of vomit and excrement from the losers reeling out of Ah-Fuk's backroom creep joint befouled of ill luck and bad liquor. Pale as a fish's underbelly, I peeked through the bead curtains behind the bar, looking for trouble boys. The joint was percolating. A few months back, some swank movie stars on island holiday chose *The Sneaky Tiki* for their slumming. Word got out, and now every high hat and butter-and-egg man visiting the isles showed up with their dumb Doras eager to get hot. Ah-Fuk, grinning large with all that dough rolling in, set up candle-lit tables, strolling cigarette girls, a wisecracking bartender, and a smalltime big band. That, for me, was the best thing about the jamming crowd — the right music. Those boys worked some hot improvisation over jazz and blues tunes. To that swinging jive, the floorflushers in their two-tone shoes and high-waisted trousers slid across the polished wood dance planks with frantic bims all garter-flash and swiveling hips. Gives me chickenskin thinking about it. Swingtime's complex, six-step footwork had come direct from Harlem's Savoy with those big spenders on tropical holiday. Set my marrow quivering like jelly watching dancers with intricate, double-paced steps literally walking off the ground, taking air strides and riding aerial moves on the blaring horns and flaring drums of that juiced orchestra. Most nights, I blissed, but that lurid night under the death's head moon, my blood was lizard grease and cold. I ranked the crowd for leg-breakers. I remember the music sounded especially sharp. A guest guitar player held the stage, a local boy who'd done good in L.A., Sol Ho'opi'i. He played electric lap steel with a C# minor tuning (B D E G# C# E, bass to treble), which allowed more sophisticated chord and melody work than the open A or open G tunings I usually heard. He was in the midst of a blues treatment to a Hawaiian favorite, "Hula Girl," when Ah-Fuk took my elbow and stiffened my spine. "Ah-ya! Why you so jumpy? Business good. Many dolla. You go see doxy at shark table. She wait on you two hour." My gaze shot to the far corner of the club, where a young woman of Japanese mien sat demurely sipping tea and reading a book by candlelight. "Who is she?" I asked, but Ah-Fuk's narrow eyes had already fixed on some tipsy high rollers she was sizing up for her gaming tables. I swung around the outside of the room, keeping to the shadows behind the large tikis. A tiki is just a piece of wood. The typical ones with the snarling mouths are "Kona style" and began with the great Kamehameha, the warrior king from Kona on the Big Island, who united the Hawaiian Islands back in the 1790s. They're meant to impress with their savagery and to deliver a clear message: 'don't monkey with the king.' Most of the tikis in the club were of this variety. But situated at cardinal points around the dance floor stood tikis that were more than just pieces of wood. They were *ki'i*, spiritual beings, loaned to Ah-Fuk by the island *kahunas* — witch doctors — to whom my superstitious boss paid a couple yards each month for their magical protection. These genuine gods had abstract shapes, were very old, and had been activated by the presence of the *akua* — a tremendous spirit power only the *kahuna* could direct. It was all hooey to me. *Ach, ihr Brüder, dieser Gott, den ich schuf, war Menschen-Werk und Wahnsinn, gleich allen Göttern!* I couldn't agree more with that kraut genius, and my handwriting over the gore-blotched passage was strong and clear: *Ah, my brothers, that God whom I created was man-made and madness, like all gods!* But it was Ah-Fuk's madness, and she seemed to have done all right by it. The shark table was under the *ki'i* of the shark god, and it's where Ah-Fuk sat each morning tallying her books. That she would seat this young lady there told me she ranked this ankle a sweet Jane worthy of protection in our den of wolves. I thought she might be a honey trap ribbed up by Moon Duck's cronies, so I observed her a while. She sipped her tea. She read her book — some slim volume that looked like poetry. The slick action on the floor didn't grab her, but when Sol Ho'opi'i glided into his solo, she was all ears and eyes. That steadied my nerves, and I approached her table. "You looking for me, sister?" She regarded me with an expression of expectation and gentle innocence that snatched at my soul sweet and chill as a waft of opium. After what I did in Oklahoma, I had taken the veil. My yearning for broads was strong as ever, I assure you, and that's what made my self-denial a kind of penance. *Zehn Mal musst du des Tages dich selber überwinden*, Zarathustra spake. *Ten times a day must you overcome yourself.* I'd done a lot of overcoming and plenty of penance in the last two years and the island dolls had inflicted genuine suffering, but I'd not once gotten dizzy with a dame — not until that moment. She was a kid, twenty-two, and lovely, I mean like some kind of dream figment that inspires a feeling of calamitous solitude — you know what I'm saying, that lonely revelation you've been alone your entire miserable life waiting for this — this misfortune of unpredictable and ferocious passion to hunt you down and menace you with all the lascivious misery of desire, shamelessness, and inevitable and inconsolable loss. "Are you Mister Richard Doyle?" From far away, I heard myself answer mindlessly, "What of it?" She closed her book — the poems of Emily Dickinson — and motioned for me to sit. I sat. "My name is Risa Watari. My grandfather has sent me here to retain your services." I nodded, entranced by her dignity and quiet intelligence. She explained how her father and brother had died recently in a fiery car crash off the cliffs of Makapu'u, apparently in a double suicide after they had gambled away their family farm. Risa's mother had passed on years before, and Risa was the last of her family in the islands. The territorial court had recognized the transfer of the farm's deed to some property management company representing an anonymous new owner. She had been obliged to forsake her family farm and take a residence in Honolulu with her grandfather, who had come from Japan when he learned the tragic news. Both he and Risa did not believe the police report of suicide. "My father and brother were not gamblers." She looked convinced, but with her nose in a book of poems and her ears green as corn in April, I figured her to be the last to know. I suggested she hire a licensed private investigator. Let him be the hard heart who held the mirror up to her family's ugly side — and leave me with the sweet nostalgia of this girlie's ardent innocence. She shook her head earnestly, and the raven dark of her pulled back hair spun candlelight in my eyes like a hop smoker's waking dream. "Grandfather sent me for you specifically, Mister Doyle. He says you are *Mu-nan* — the man who never turned back." She read the bewilderment on my mug and added, "That's how you're known among the Japanese community for going after the Korean gangster Moon Duck." I might have taken that as a compliment on any other night — but not under the death's head moon. I wanted to agree with the overman: *Wirkliche sind wir ganz, und ohne Glauben und Aberglauben — We are most real when we are wholly without faith and superstition.* But I'd been with Seamus Doyle in Belleau Wood. I'd seen Fionn mac Cumhal distinguish the doorways of life and death. Twice before, the death's head moon had grinned down on me and men had died. I got up and shook my head. "I can't help you, lady. Tell your granddaddy I'm not who he thinks I am." She fixed me with a schoolmarm's sympathetic frown, sweetly disdainful of my ignorance. "My grandfather is an excellent judge of character, Mister Doyle." She placed a brown envelope on the table. "This is one hundred dollars in ten dollar bills, which he is paying you to speak with him tomorrow morning at our residence. This payment entails no other responsibility. Please, accept it as a token of our respect for your courage and virtue." *Virtue?* I could have shown her the shabby book I carried everywhere with me in my pants pocket and the blood-stained page with these overwritten words: *Was ist das Grösste, das ihr erleben könnt? Die Stunde, wo ihr sagt: "Was liegt an meiner Tugend! Wie müde bin ich meines Guten und meines Bösen! Alles das ist Armuth und Schmutz und ein erbärmliches Behagen!"* — *What is the greatest thing you can experience? The hour when you say: "What good is my virtue? How weary I am of my good and my evil! It is all poverty and filth and miserable self-complacency!"* But there was a lot of spondulix in that envelope. An Irish fight promoter back in Boston disclosed to me the meaning and importance of spondulix, after I'd taken the broderick in fifteen rounds for fifty bucks, but it might as well have been Seamus Doyle himself who laid it out in his glittering lilt: "It ain't fifty bucks, boyo — it's fifty spondulix, from the Gaelic *sponc* for sperm and *diúlach* for bloke, which is why in our poor mother's slang all money is *spondúlaigh*, because a bloke has to spill his guts to get it, see?" I took the envelope and offered the poetry lover a drink. But she declined and had me call her a cab. On the way out the door, I learned she was a librarian at the main branch and resolved to continue my philosophy studies there after politely declining her granddaddy the next morning. Who knew what exaggerated expectations he cherished of the man who never turned back, but I was too old to try to live up to that bushwa — especially in the company of the death's head moon. The next day I brought the forty-five with me, tucked into a holster at my back under the silk shantung cream blazer I sported. I admit, I wore my spiff rags, buffed my soft leather oxblood loafers and took a barber's trim and a shave to impress the librarian. I borrowed Ah-Fuk's '22 Alvis Coupe — an antique ash-framed coach with polished aluminum panels — which she used for her produce pickups in Chinatown and for squiring her *kahuna* pals around the island to various *heiau*, sacred places, where they gathered the magic necessary for recharging the club's *ki'i*. I drove to the address on the spondulix envelope, which took me up a remote switchback in the lush mountains of Nu'uanu, and arrived on the nose in a pine grove at the end of a cedar chip drive. Beyond the pines stood a small airy house with wide sliding doors, winged eaves and blue tile roof. It looked like a joss house — and a dandy place to get zotzed by Moon Duck's cronies. I kept my hand on my iron until the librarian greeted me at the door. She wore a bias-cut dress, a fashionable floral print, though she carried it with a wholly foreign demeanor. She bowed, stepped into wood sandals and led me around back. A waterfall slashed through green rocks into a narrow gorge, and braces of tall bamboo walled the perimeter of an expansive emerald sward. Close to the house, the grass ended in raked gravel and a few boulders splotched with lichen. A diminutive old man with sparse gray hair and wearing a green satin robe sat crosslegged on a straw mat, motionless, emotionless and shiny brown as a fiddle. The rock garden, the small house and the pine trees blocked the vista. Only after I squatted on the flat rock before the old man did I confront an unexpected view through the bamboo of the sea in the far distance. Without uttering a word or making a single gesture, granddaddy had impressed on me his affiliation with the immense sea and the remote culture beyond this island. His granddaughter sat slightly behind him to his left, and he began speaking slowly, deliberately, like a man with much on his mind, very little time and an unwillingness to be misunderstood. "おはようすなわちDoyle 私はの の祖父である。" The librarian gave me the news in English: "Good morning, Mister Doyle. I am Matsuo Watari, grandfather of Risa." He repeated the tragic story of the car crash off Makapu'u. That morning, I'd read it for myself in the archives of *The Honolulu Advertiser* on my way to the barber, and I knew all the unhappy details. Risa's fifty-two-year-old father Ogai, a watercress and orchid farmer, and his twenty-four-year-old son, sole partner in the family business, had been weak sisters in a chump game of craps at an infamous gambling den in Chinatown. A ho-hum tale of woe — except they took it over a cliff. The paper dismissed their deaths as suicide and chalked that up to samurai tradition. The old man didn't buy it, and he'd come to the islands for justice. But he was savvy to the American way — and Hawai'i being an American territory, he knew there'd be no justice for two Nipponese farmers. He needed an American *gunshi* — a tough guy to settle the score. From under his satin robe he produced an envelope stuffed with two large. At that price, he could have bought some very serious iron, not a no-name dance club bouncer. His quiet eyes read my thoughts perfectly. "A so desu ka," he said very slowly, so I heard each syllable. "Grandfather questions your self-doubt," the sloe-eyed beauty said, looking at me beseechingly, urging me with a serene nod to take the money. For her alone, I would have. I was that goofy for her. But there was a blood-soaked book in my pocket that said to me: *Macht wollen sie, viel Geld, — diese Unvermögenden! — They seek power, much money — these impotent ones!* "I live a simple life, Mister Watari. I go to work. I fish with my friends. After dinner, I go to sleep. I'm not the man for this job." The old man listened to his granddaughter's translation, then shot back, "反対。あなたは理想的な人である。

あなたは空間の完全である。"Risa nodded knowingly and conveyed, "On the contrary. You are the ideal man. You are full of the void." I laughed. "I think the expression is, full of nothing. He's right about that. I got a whole lot of nothing." Risa shook her head emphatically. "No, Grandfather means something very special. He is quoting a famous Japanese warrior — Miyamoto Musashi." The old man's head nudged, the frilled throat and hooded eyes loaning him the shriveled aspect of a turtle. "当然空間は何もである。" he said and Risa translated, "Of course the void is nothingness." "事の知識によってある，あなたはあ なたを知 ることができるない。" "By knowing things that exist, you can know that which does not exist." "それは空間である。" "That is the void." "と間違い事のこの世界の一見の人々は，考え，空間があるなるか理解しない何を。" "People in this world look at things mistakenly, and think that what they do not understand must be the void." "これは本当の空間でない。" "This is not the true void." "それは当惑しているべきである。" "It is bewilderment." I waved off the fat envelope and shook my head. "You're tooting the wrong ringer," I declared, and the librarian's dark eyes went wide. "You must not insult Grandfather. He has done you a great honor, quoting to you from 'The Book of the Void.'" I shrugged. "No dishonor meant. Let me square it by quoting to him from *A Book for Everyone and No One*: 'Zehn Mal musst du des Tages dich selber überwinden.' — 'Ten times a day you've got to overcome yourself.' That's how it is with me. Two grand is a lot of money, and I'm seriously tempted. Flattered, even. But I've got to overcome myself again and say no." I smiled apologetically and rose to depart. I was walking away from more spondulix than I'd ever seen in one place at one time, all because the moon had looked queer last night. Strange to say, I honestly felt I was getting the sweet end of that transaction — at least, until the next moment when the old man opened his yap to say, "You sit — Mistah Marone." I pulled my head back sharply, like avoiding a punch. "What did you say?" The small, withered man nodded softly to his granddaughter, and that sweet thing looked me in the eye and said, "Richard Malone — grandfather is aware that a warrant for your arrest has been issued by the State of Oklahoma on the charge of first-degree murder." My heart hammered against my ribs so hard it hurt. "First-degree!" My voice choked off. The old man removed a hundred dollar bill from the fat envelope and tossed it fluttering to my nicely buffed oxblood loafers. "あなたがお金のために働か ないので,あなたはあ なたの生命のた めに働く。" The librarian watched me as serenely as if I were a tropical sunset instead of a killer on the lam with veins bulging at his temples. "Grandfather says, 'Since you will not work for money, you must work for your life.' If you do not obey him faithfully, he will notify the territorial authorities — who have a strict extradition policy for all cases of homicide." With a gnashed cry of fury, I lunged at the hinky gink. What did I intend? To wring his neck? To shake him silly? To barter his life for mine? I never had a chance to find out. The next instant, he had my thumb in a searing grip, and white-hot pain brought me howling to my knees. Through a blear of tears, I saw close-up that aged face hashed with wrinkles and gazing at me with vague, soporific satisfaction. He released my thumb, and I crumbled to the gravel depleted, stunned, abruptly alert to the morning light, filtered by the pines, quivering over the gravel like the watery surface of a pool. "How'd you get the dope on me?" I practically sobbed. The old man's granddaughter put me wise, "It was obvious that the infamous *Mu-nan* had a criminal history. Why else would a sleazy wharfside club be home to the man who never turned back? Even a cursory glance at the list of fugitives reported by the National Bureau of Criminal Identification for the year you first appeared in Honolulu disclosed your true identity. Your uncommon size is the giveaway." I shut my eyes for a moment, as if things would be different when I opened them. The old man sat impassive as a statue, but Risa's eyes were keen to my pain and humiliation. "Grandfather needs a *gunshi*. He's too old to restore our family's honor alone. If you serve him, your secret is safe. But if you refuse, Grandfather is the kind of man who will find you worse than useless and be sure that you are apprehended." I wanted to take out the forty-five and plug the little devil. But I remembered the death's head moon — and picked up the Ben Franklin between my shoes. I had thought I could run away from the moon. I had actually thought that! I took out Zarathustra and deliberately folded the bill into the page with my marching orders: *Was ist das Schwerste, ihr Helden?* "What is the heaviest thing, you heroes?" I mumbled and tucked the book back into my pocket. *Ist es nicht das: sich erniedrigen, um seinem Hochmuth wehe zu thun?* "Is it not this: To humiliate oneself in order to mortify one's pride?" I stood and dusted off my linen slacks. *Seine Thorheit leuchten lassen, um seiner Weisheit zu spotten?* "To exhibit one's folly in order to mock at one's wisdom?" The librarian's beautiful and attentive features brightened as though she'd just solved a puzzle. *Seinen letzten Herrn sucht er sich hier.* "Here he seeks his last master," I finished and offered my aching hand to the old man. "Friedrich Nietzsche," Risa pegged my muttering and parlayed in Japanese with her granddaddy. He gave me a curt nod of approval, took my hand in both of his, and strenuously manipulated the flesh between my thumb and forefinger. When he released my hand, I flexed it painlessly. "*Gunshi Mu-nan*," he said, making me his official snooper. "Don't call me that. I'm your pug, because you were going to send me over. But I'm no *gunshi*, and I'm no *Mu-nan*. I'm Richard Malone. Tell him." He received this from his granddaughter without a flicker. "*Riki*," he called me with a decisive air and stood up. "*Riki* Marone." A smile of approval poured through Risa's bright eyes. "*Riki* means energy — power. Grandfather respects your self-control, Mister Doyle, and calling you *Riki* is his way of telling you there are no hard feelings. If that's okay with you, give him a bow, and let's get over to Chinatown and find the people who swindled my father and brother." I imitated Risa's stiff bow, which the old man received with a smug nod, and five minutes later we were in the Alvis Coupe gliding down Nu'uanu Drive under the shaggy ironwood trees. "Your granddaddy is a tough customer." She scrutinized my profile, and when I looked at her, those feline eyes accepted my attention without turning away. "Grandfather *is* tough. He's a warrior and a founding member of *Kokuryu-kai* — the Amur River Society — a private club of Japanese good old boys who love their country, especially the ancient warrior traditions. The fiercest members are Black Dragons, and Grandfather's one of them. He's a tough guy. But what you did back there was even tougher. You've taken all that *übermensch* business to heart, haven't you?" I heard a note of wonder in the librarian's voice. "You've read Nietzsche?" I asked and had trouble keeping my eyes on the road. She laughed like a wicked adolescent. "I'm a librarian. It's not whether I've read Nietzsche that should concern you, Mister Doyle, it's what I think of his aristocratic radicalism and the historic defeat of the 'splendid blond beast.'" This tomato was hot socks! We chatted briefly about nihilism, the desire for nothingness, that Nietzsche believed had replaced God. Her granddaddy's void was something else — *ku*, an emptiness meant to describe a situation devoid of independent reality, a process, a flow that connects everything through relationship. Experiencing *ku* meant being one with the moment. So she said. I didn't follow, but her voice was a music I didn't want to stop. When we arrived at the dice parlor where the Wataris supposedly rolled away the farm, the situation spun out as we expected. No one there had ever seen the mugs of Ogai and Robun, no matter how much cabbage Risa tossed around with her photo album. The craps game was a flimsy ruse for a blatant land grab. "It must be the airport the government intends to build," Risa figured. "It's not in the papers yet, but I've read a recommendation for it in the library's transcripts from last year's meeting of the Territorial Land Use Committee.

Once the proposal reaches the legislature next session, those real estate prices will go through the roof." Nothing stinks quite so rotten as motive. Our next step was finding out who held the paper on the farm. Territorial law made no provision for public access to property records. The convenient deaths of Ogai and Robun masked the transfer of deed. Only a court order would disclose who benefited, and I was a lot more comfortable bribing the night security guard at the conveyance office than a territorial judge. I dropped off Risa for her day job at the main branch of the library on Punchbowl next to Iolani Palace. The so-called palace is actually a Greek Revival manse, where the last Hawaiian monarchs once ruled in garish European splendor before the Marines deposed them forty years ago. It housed the administrative offices that would process my extradition and send me back to Oklahoma to do the dance. I got out of there fast and returned to *The Sneaky Tiki* to contemplate my fate. The *ki'i* got a more thorough dusting than usual, especially the shark *ki'i* where I'd first met Risa. Maybe that guardian spirit would protect me from the trouble that arrived with that Japanese doll and the death's head moon. And then again, maybe not. Reflecting on what had followed my previous grisly lunar viewings, my heart felt cramped, overmuscled, and I had to breathe through my mouth to calm down. The taut fear reminded me of choosing doorways among the trees in Belleau Wood. Where was Fionn mac Cumhal now? I wished Seamus Doyle sat at the bar sipping hooch, available for a consult. Instead, Ah-Fuk's aggressive face scowled up at me. "What for you so displeasurably unhappy? Hotshot date with Japanese doxy not so terrifical, heyah?" I used the opportunity to ask to borrow the Alvis Coupe for another hotshot date that night. Actually, I intended to go alone to the conveyance office, but Risa showed up at the club around midnight wearing a sleek black evening dress with white gloves to the elbows and a pearl-studded handbag. Ah-Fuk grimaced a good-luck wink at me. I drove Risa directly to the territorial office building, and the yard the old man had paid me for a retainer bought us a midnight viewing of the land transfer records. While we riffled through those turf sheets, I asked the young thing, "If your granddaddy has so much lettuce, why'd your father have to bust sod?" A blush tinged the flat, ivory planes of her face, and she didn't look up from the open file cabinet as she replied, "I'm from a poor family. My father is the youngest of Grandfather's five sons and had no expectation of an inheritance. He came to Hawai'i as a young man to make his fortune. My brother and I were born here, but Grandfather summoned me back to Japan after I finished my library studies, so I'd know my family. I was with Grandfather when we received news of the accident." A moment later, she found the winner: Dunkel & Bose, a realty firm on Bishop Street, held the deed to the acreage that had formerly been Watari Nursery. We were congratulating ourselves with big grins and goo-goo eyes when the frosted glass door banged open. A long-shouldered bruno in a pineapple shirt strode in. He had the drop on me with a thirty-eight police special, and in that confined space that was a hefty down payment on oblivion. He motioned us out of the room, and I started walking though I knew he was taking us on a long walk to nowhere. Risa, never having seen the way bowels, brains and blood got nothing to hide in the company of a bullet, chose to put up a fight. As she approached the bruno, she yanked open a file cabinet and grabbed for his gat. The blast pounded me deaf an instant after I heard the slug suck past my ear. My fist slammed the bruno's face while my free hand reached behind to draw the forty-five. Eager to get the doll away from that hatchetman's flailing gun, I heaved myself into him and we toppled to the floor. He was no push-over. His blows rattled my skull like a box of broken china, and my gun flew clattering across the floor with what must have been a couple of my molars. As he swung his thirty-eight up to my chin, I dug my thumbs into his eyes and then fastened the shutters with a sharp head blow. I gyrated to my feet in a snowstorm of spinning stars. Risa took me by the arm and led me tottering like a rummy to the window. On the fire escape, I pulled my arm free and turned to go back for my gun, but the security guard was already in the doorway and the bruno sat up with a scowl too ugly for a bulldog. We rode the escape ladder to the ground and dashed for the Coupe. "Who was that gunman?" the librarian asked, breathless. I didn't answer right away. I was too busy trying to drive and see straight at the same time. Her composure calmed me. She placed a steady hand on my arm, and the violence we'd just escaped, the whole lethal situation that had ensnared us, seemed less. "Whoever that was, he was going to kill us, wasn't he?" she asked with a lazy look of amorous appraisal. I wanted to say something ducky, but my jaw hurt too much — so, I kept a manly silence and concentrated on driving straight. Back at the joss house in Nu'uanu, the old man had an opinion he imparted slowly for my benefit, "*Senmin No Oh*." Risa poured me a cup of tea, though I would have preferred a snort. "The King of the Lower Classes," Risa translated. "Grandfather is sure the security guard was paid to call for that gunman if anyone came nosing around. *Senmin No Oh* is his way of saying that Dunkel & Bose must have a thousand underlings." The room in which we sat on the floor was small but felt huge, because there was no furniture, just straw floor mats, a low chocolate-brown table with the tea service, and wide bamboo-slat windows that let the night pour in. Lit by paper lanterns and wispy with incense that kept mosquitoes at bay, the room glowed warmly. "So now that granddaddy knows, what does he want to do?" Risa straightened as if a cop had loomed up behind and laid a heavy hand on her shoulder. "You should show some respect to the man who holds your life in his hands, Mister Doyle. My grandfather deserves to be addressed as *Mister* Watari." I offered a glum smile, and the old man turned his wrinkled and somber face toward me, "Riki, you *gunshi*. You go talk *Senmin No Oh*. You ask for Ogai, for Robun. You find 真実." My inquisitive frown invited Risa to lay it out, "真実 — the truth. Grandfather wants you to –" I stopped her with a weary nod. "Yeah, yeah. He wants me to find out if Dunkle & Bose blipped your father and brother. So, we find out. The cops and this coconut court won't touch those pooh-bahs. So then what?" She poured herself tea, returned the kettle to its rattan place mat and lifted her cup with both hands. Her motions, so feminine, so serenely self-possessed, unmanned me. "So, then we know." Her words floated through me like a perfume, and they lingered with me on the long, star-splattered ride back to *The Sneaky Tiki. So, then we know.* We had no evidence. There wouldn't be any evidence. Two Nipponese farmers in a crash and burn. I might have wondered why she and her granddaddy believed knowing was so important. No matter how much wampum he had, he couldn't buy a hit on those island muckamucks. The pages of blood spoke to me: *Ich liebe Den, welcher lebt, damit er erkenne — I love him who lives in order to know.* I slept restlessly that night. I worried about the gun I'd lost. Would the dicks trace it to me, maybe even tie it to Moon Duck's bump-off? And what did I intend to actually say tomorrow to the mopes at Dunkel & Bose? I had to say something to get them to own up or I'd be taking the jump in Oklahoma. *Mister* Watari was no bunny. He would know — or I would go. My zany German egghead agreed with the old man: *Begehrt sie nach Wissen wie der Löwe nach seiner Nahrung? — Does it long for knowledge as the lion for his prey?* I got up the next morning intent on feeding the lion. With no weapon to hide, I dressed light, in a Hawaiian three-piece — sandals, khaki slacks and a silk shirt, cerise with no printed flowers or hula girls. Ah-Fuk needed the Alvis Coupe to visit a *heiau* with her *kahuna* chums, so I hoofed to Kapiolani Boulevard. Lemon green morning light shuffling out of the palms accompanied my bus ride downtown. Though the tropical heat approached ninety, my shirt didn't stick: the trades were blowing big clouds across the sky, those laughing gods, and pollen breezes swirled down from the mountains and soothed my nerves. At Bishop Street, I got out and entered an office building that looked made of old gingerbread. *Dunkel & Bose* appeared on a slender brass plate elegantly affixed to a marble wall in a vestibule like a mausoleum. I was still wondering how I was going to punch the bag with these upstage realtors, when a distant fluting voice called, "Mister Doyle!" Across the street, among the flowering trees of a corner park, Risa stood in a white summer dress waving to me with a pink gloved hand. Wands of sunlight slanting through the trees ignited the cotton pleats of her dress, silhouetting her long stems. For a startling moment, I was certain I was staring through the x-rayed fabric at the cleft between her thighs that the poets call a camel toe. "I didn't expect you so early," she said after crossing the street.

"I took the day off and was hoping to get some reading done."
She tucked her slim volume of Dickinson poems into a black
patent leather handbag. "Look, Risa — why don't you wait for
me in the park. Read your poetry. This won't take long." She
turned her pale face away and with a knowing sidelong look
asked, "Why, Mister Doyle? Are you worried about me?" I took
her delicate elbow in my hand. "After last night, aren't you worried?" I stepped close enough to smell hints of jasmine whispering from her glossy black hair. "I can't put you in a tight spot
again." She pressed closer. "I'm afraid I'm the one who put you
in a tight spot." My hand squeezed her arm, her gaze deepened,
and we both knew then we wanted each other. But I might as
well have tried to straddle a sunbeam. She took my face in her
gloved hands and kissed me hard, our teeth briefly clashing,
and then her tongue in my mouth, flickering. Before I could
pull her to me, she backed away with a triumphant, half-stifled
smile. Not uttering another word, we entered the building and
took the brass gate elevator to the third floor, entirely occupied
by Dunkel & Bose. I opened the gate on an anteroom with old
paneling shining with wax, gilt framed portraits of sallow-faced
men, and a deep red carpet. Doors to most of the rooms stood
wide, exposing conference tables, telephones, burnished wood
file cabinets, and no people. I worried we'd arrived too early.
Then, I pushed through the one door with *Dunkel & Bose*
pegged in polished letters, and we confronted the bruno from
last night. He sat at a receptionist's desk and wore an elegant
white linen suit. Hunched over a copy of *Black Mask Magazine*,
he didn't look up at first. I understood why. The pulp lay open
at "The Man from Shanghai" by Ramon Decolta, a story I knew,
because it involved my favorite dick, Jo Gar, Island Investigator,
a small, soft-spoken hombre in the Philippines who, despite his
gentle, polite manner, never misjudged evil. I was surprised this
dingus could read. Too bad he didn't understand what he was
reading. He pushed to his feet glaring, his left eye bruised
purple as the welt on my jaw. "Relax, sister, this is a social call."
I peered past him into a chamber the size of a courtroom where
two suits dangled over a mahogany desk. They were scrutinizing the tickertape from a rattling bell jar and didn't notice us

until I shoved the bruno back in his seat and we entered their private club. "Dunkle and Bose? Got a minute for Doyle and Watari?" The swells looked up startled, and I took their measure quick because I knew the bruno was bearing down. The short, bald suit with a pointy nose sported wire frame spectacles and a moustache — a weasel. The other stood tall, broad shouldered, curly blond hair thinning above a ruddy, square-jawed face — an ivy-league oarsman gone paunchy. I gently nudged Risa farther into the room so that when the bruno strode angrily through the doorway there was room to fake him with a right and clip him hard under the chin with a left. He went down like a creaky dumbwaiter and sat there gnashing teeth, straining to see straight. "Aren't you boys going to offer the lady a seat?" The weasel scowled indignantly and asked, "Who are you? What do you want?" The oarsman grinned with a grim yet boyish charm and motioned to one of three lyre-back chairs beside the giant desk. "You're related to those farmers who gambled away their nursery, aren't you? That turned out badly. I'm sorry." I flung a cold laugh at the suits. "Stow the sympathy, jasper. We've been to Chinatown, and we know there was no gambling involved. And as that pretty boy on the floor with the stars in his eyes must have told you, we know you hold the deed to the farm — a property that's going to be worth some heavy sugar when the airport's approved. Seems what we've got here is a criminal land grab." The oarsman's extremely cold blue eyes assessed us, faint white wrinkles at the corners grooving merrily. "You can prove this?" My stare narrowed. "What do you think?" The faint white wrinkles deepened. "I think you're a lousy poker player, Doyle." By now, the bruno had found his legs. He staggered in with his hand in his jacket. "That won't be necessary, Max." The oarsman raised a restraining hand. "The lady and the gentleman are leaving." I stepped forward and leaned knuckles on the desktop. "The lady just got here, and she wants some answers. Tell Max to sit down or he's going through the window." The merry wrinkles vanished. "What answers do you want, Doyle?" The weasel dropped the ribbon of tickertape and whined, "Who cares what answers he wants? Max, get these intruders out of here." Risa piped up, "Why are you holding the deed to my father's farm? And don't tell me he gambled it away. My father did not gamble." The weasel had fixed Max with a hard stare. "Get them out of here. We don't have to answer their questions." Risa pointed at Max. "Please, put that gun away. You're frightening me. I only came here for the truth. I don't have any authority to reclaim my father's farm." The weasel laughed harshly. "Damn right! That land is ours. Your father signed it away. We have the legal documents." Risa nodded softly. "But he didn't gamble it away. I want the truth." The oarsman sighed. "The truth is an ugly business, young lady. You're better off just leaving that alone. Doyle, be a right guy and take her home." Risa lifted her chin defiantly. "I can stand the truth. I don't care how ugly it is." The oarsman cocked an eyebrow. "Don't fool yourself. Show them out, Max." I pushed off the desk and shoved myself up against Max. "You budge, pal, and that iron is going in your out box." Anger flared through the tough guy, but before he could make his move, Risa stood. "I don't want trouble. I will leave. Just tell me why you're afraid of the truth? The farm of my father and brother — how did you get the deed?" The weasel snorted. "They signed it over. It's as simple as that." She shot him a hot look. "Why?" The oarsman exhaled another exasperated sigh. "We offered them a fair price." The weasel snapped, "Shut up, Donald!" The merry wrinkles returned. "What are they going to do? We have the paper. The law is on our side." Risa stepped up to the desk and laid down her handbag. "My father would never sign away his land. Not for any price." Donald shrugged. "That was why he got pushed over." The weasel shook his bald head. "What are you doing?" Donald's bronze eyebrows tightened. "She wants the truth. I'm giving her the truth. We didn't do anything that hasn't always been done. How do you think our grandfathers made out in these islands?" Donald looked at her with his icy blue eyes. "What are *your* people doing in Manchuria right now, even as we're speaking? Do you think the Chinese invited the Japanese into Nanking?" The weasel groaned. "Enough, Donald. You made your point." Donald's face shone, lit with a chill and blameless anger. "Have I? Have I made my point, Miss *Watari*? We did better for your daddy than the Chinese got. We offered to buy him out. He wouldn't budge. What did that Jap think was going to happen?" A sob escaped Risa. She bit her lower lip, and tears glinted as she took in the oarsman's umbrage, the weasel's alarm. I glowered at the two suits. "You can't get away with this. We're in an American territory." Donald smirked. "Tell it to the Hawaiians." He spoke Risa's name again with curdled contempt, "Miss *Watari*, I'm sorry for the history lesson. But you pushed. You had to know. In this shrinking world — as your people understand so damn well — land belongs to whoever's strong enough to take it. Now, blow your nose and get out of here." Risa opened her purse, reached in for a handkerchief and came out with my Smith and Wesson forty-five caliber revolver. Using a double-handed grip with full arm extension slightly bent at the elbows and sighting with both eyes open, she shot Max in the face. Startled by the loud blast, I hurtled back two paces as Max fell away from me, a big hole where his nose had been. I was still moving when the second shot exploded and the back of Donald's head burst, spewing brains and blood onto the tall, sunny windows overlooking the park. The weasel had turned and fled toward a side door. He completed three long strides before the third shot rang out and a hot, fat slug of lead skewered him through the base of the skull. Then, Risa turned, and I stared into the smoking barrel of my own gun. With a fright so intense it felt ethereal, I realized what a dupe I'd been. I was no *gunshi* — I was a patsy. The old man and his charming granddaughter had set me up to cover these murders. At this range, that forty-five would decapitate me, and this cold-blooded frail could leave the piece in my hand, make it look like suicide. Let the buttons try to figure out a motive. Now, those pink gloves made lethal sense. The dinner gloves last night, too. No prints anywhere. At least, none of hers. And that tongue in my mouth, flickering like a snake's — a judas kiss for a sucker. "*Riki*," she said, and her samurai grandfather's term of endearment sounded harsh, commanding, without the slightest tremor of shock, fear or uneasiness. "Get rid of this gun." She handed me the forty-five, and I received it with stunned and, I admit, tremulous fingers. The constriction in my throat eased up when I saw she wasn't going to kill me, and I mumbled, "You planned this." She moved quickly toward the side door, gingerly sidestepping the pool of blood widening from under the weasel's face-down corpse. "Come on. We'll take the back way out." Her voice was as cool as the gun in my hand was hot. I followed her out the door and down six flights of stairs to a back alley cluttered with dented trash bins and a reek of festering garbage. No one saw us exit. By then, the muzzle had cooled, and I tucked the big gun in the belt under my shirt. She took me by the hand, and her touch was steady and dry. We strolled down Bishop Street easy as holiday lovers. "You planned that," I repeated, my voice stronger. She fixed me with a sunny smile of striking cheerfulness. "Grandfather will be pleased. His family honor is restored." I stopped short, yanked her close and said through my teeth, "You should have told me." She winced from the ferocity of my grasp, then lifted her angel's face and asked with a surly smile, "Why? Would you have killed those men for me, Mister Malone?" She pulled free, and I let her go. I watched her cross the street to a waiting bus. She didn't look back, and when the bus pulled away I glimpsed her pretty profile gazing sweetly out the window at the dazzling sun raining through the palms. I dropped the gun off a wharf and returned shaken to *The Sneaky Tiki* — shaken not by the killings, which had been brutally efficient and nothing like the frantic carnage of war or the blind violence I'd visited upon that poor kid in Oklahoma — but shaken by that kitten's ruthless composure. For days after, those gruesome murders were front page news. I ignored the papers. My thoughts went somewhere else. I couldn't get her sunstruck dress out of my mind or that peek of camel toe or the spicy and forlorn taste of her. When I dusted the shark *ki'i*, I actually wondered if that *akua* had made the difference when I found myself staring into the steel zero of the forty-five's barrel. She had meant to kill me, too. The more I thought of it, the more certain I became. Why keep alive the only witness? I could almost hear the old man instructing her, "*Riki* must die." Why else had she called me *Riki*? The old man's voice was in her head. She had spared me — for what? Love? Pity? Or the mysterious touch of the *akua* in whose shadow I had first met her? To put an end to these screwy thoughts, I steeped myself again in those pages soaked in my enemy's blood, listening attentively to my German master's warning, *Wollt Nichts über euer Vermögen: es giebt eine schlimme Falschheit bei Solchen, die über ihr Vermögen wollen.* — *Do not will anything beyond your power: there is a bad falseness in those who will beyond their power.* With those words in mind, I stopped trying to understand. The Watari clan had their revenge. And I was still alive — though, at any moment, the cops could descend on me, alerted to my whereabouts by an anonymous tip from the old man or his ice-water-for-blood granddaughter. I thought of moving on. But the work at the club was too easy and the music too good. The whoopee crowds and an occasional celebrity were still showing up, and at two in the AM when the horns are wailing, the skins pounding, and jazz notes glittering from the strings like shooting stars, *The Sneaky Tiki* is the reason the Earth spins. After a couple weeks, when the law didn't show, I stopped feeling sorry for myself. I had a sweet job that provided spondulix for the silk threads I fancied, fishing buddies to share a yuk with, and Moon Duck's cronies nowhere in sight, just where I needed them to keep me sharp. Now and again, I hankered for a swig, to feel once more that place in the soul wide as sunset and happy with forgetfulness. I hankered for that touch of fire water about as often as I hankered to see that cute librarian, that deadly doll who had briefly ignited the sizzle in me. That was just now and again — enough to remind me that honesty and loyalty and valor exist only because we create them, the way we create bayonets and carbines, as weapons to fight ourselves. *Man erlebt endlich nur noch sich selber.* — *In the end, one experiences only oneself.* So, the mad genius says and goes on to say, *Aber der schlimmste Feind, dem du begegnen kannst, wirst du immer dir selber sein.* — *But the worst enemy you can meet will always be yourself.* Take that as a warning. I should have. You see, I thought the death's head moon had played out. Three times is a charm, right? Torch fishing under the sponged moon, I stayed alert for sharks. On the street, I watched the shadows and the alleys. And in the club, my back was always to the tiki gods. But when trouble came, as usual, I was a stranger to surprise. "Heyah! What for pretty-face doxy linger at table for you with romantical cow eyes?" Ah-Fuk asked, summoning me one evening from the gaming room where I had just eased a bad loser out the door. "You see tea drinking doxy off-hour. What for I pay you plenty dolla?" I stared across the dance floor's hopping crowd, and my heart rattled ribs to spy Risa Watari in a sleek red satin evening gown sitting at her candle lit table under the shark *ki'i*. "I never thought I'd see you again," I admitted when I found myself standing at her table and added, "I thought you were done with me." She gently motioned with her smiling eyes for me to sit, and I sat. "I was hoping I'd just begun with you." She put her hand on mine, squeezed it warmly and poured her liquid gaze into the back of my eyes. "How's granddad?" I mumbled. She didn't answer for a moment. She just stared at me, into me, as if compelling assent. Only after I returned her hand squeeze and leaned in closer did she reply, "He has another job for you, Mister Malone." I stiffened visibly. "I don't like you calling me that. And I — most definitely — am not wearing your granddaddy's pajamas again. Once was plenty." She tossed her head back with a sparkling laugh. "It's nothing like before, *Riki*. It's a cakewalk." This was surely one of the ten times in this particular day where I had to overcome myself, and I moved to get up, to get away from my desire and the big trouble it promised. "Goodbye, Risa." I stood, but she wouldn't let go of my hand and stared up at me with a languid, bemused smile. "It's nothing like you think, silly. Grandfather just wants some travel photos for his old chums back home in the Amur River Society." She tugged at my arm with a petulant insistence and a pout that made my blood spin faster. I sat. "Travel photos? I'm no photographer. But let me guess. You are." She nodded with girlish glee. "Grandfather doesn't want me going to these places without an escort." I huffed a laugh. "I pity the poor slob that gives you static." She wrinkled her nose. "It's not like that. The old fellows at the Amur River Society desire snapshots of some of the wild river sites on O'ahu. Grandfather wants you there in case I twist an ankle." I rocked my jaw, thinking it over. "River photos?" She lidded her eyes with sultry shrewdness. "We'll be alone in remote places. I'm sure I'll need you." My jaw snapped into place. "When do we start?" The delight of her enthusiastic smile stirred skittish desire in me. "Tomorrow! We'll begin with some photos of the estuary and work our way up into the watershed." My bones glowed with happiness. "Sounds copacetic. I'll get the Coupe for the day and pick you up after breakfast. Where are we going?" She bent toward me, and a swerve of her midnight hair covered one eye. "Pearl Harbor."

SOME EXPERIMENTS

DISENTANGLE THOSE WEBS OF reason spun from the swollen glands of our terrible, desolate evolutionary survival. You already know we don't survive. You're an emanation of death. Dazzling, light-filled emanation of death, you are the sublime agonist. Reason struggles against *you*. Your significance surpasses all understanding, all concepts. You survived the downfall of heaven. Existence for you is but a dream. Erotic, prophetic, ephemeral, your appearance is an outrageous apparition, a flash of fright and lust. You are the mysterious, majestic spirit of the incomprehensible, the only one reading these words.

Brave Tails

For our wild brethren,
wilderness creatures,
once our gods.

W ITH THEM CAME A redolence of summery en-
cumbrances, a dizzy smell of dew risen from apples
melting among night weeds. With them came this
September fragrance and a heart hurt of beauty. Talking animals!

They adored us as children — before any other stories — and, completely oblivious to the blasphemy of sapiens,
defiant of reason and full of play, took us as friends, our first.

Readers with poetic inclinations may accept these author's
notes for fable. Those with less fanciful tendencies are welcome
to take my account literally. Either way, perspicacious reader,
bear in mind our most typical icon for the craft of writing is
'pen' — a word that once meant 'feather.'

– Jonathan Sparrow

SHAGBARK

O UT OF THE MIST, claws slash and hook their strug-
gling quarry. Wings beat smoky sunlight up to a high
branch, where razor beak cuts through the struggle
and the flesh and tugs free a red flag of victory. Raw tendons,
crimson tissues, and various greasy organs follow, swallowed
whole or minced by the dissecting beak. And all the while, the
quarry's head remains intact, emitting sad chirps of distress.

That is how owls kill. Most owls have no compunction
about killing anything smaller than they are — including
their own kind when they can. I know, because I am an owl.
My name is Shagbark. I am a great horned owl and an aspiring author under the penname Jonathan Sparrow. I eat small
creatures, including mice, frogs, centipedes, and sparrows (my
favorite — hence, my penname). But I won't kill an owlet. I
saw my younger sister slain that way. Owls regard such a kill a
coup — a triumph — because these killings cull the weak. But
for me, her death is a searing tragedy.

"Musing again, Shagbark?" A severe-looking falcon appears
from behind the stately bookshelves in the athenaeum where

I'm perched at a drafting table in my carrel, writing this. "You are to be writing during this period. If you are not writing, there are plenty of chores to do. Books to shelve. Shelves to dust. Dustbins to empty. Empty catalog forms to fill."

"I am writing, Doctor Sparverius." Actually, I was remembering how Smudge — my younger sister — lay on a bough under the claws of her killer, her small face turned urgently toward me. I watched, horrified, crouching on a safely distant branch to which I'd fled when the hostile owl struck her. I could hear her small chirps calling to me — not for help and not in anguish — but, well, contritely. She was pleading for forgiveness. As the aggressive owl hooked a slither of her glistening organs, she chirped me sorrowful regret for not looking up before she had entered the glade, a precaution our parents had taught us since we'd hatched.

"You appear preoccupied, Shagbark," the old falcon correctly observes. "We cannot tolerate malingering in the athenaeum. Your novel — *Brave Tails*, is it? Should have been completed by now. After all, you've been writing far longer than we usually permit our first-time novelists. What is your justification this time, my dilatory owl?"

I make a mental note to look up 'dilatory,' though I suspect it probably means 'dawdling.' "I'm composing my author's notes."

Doctor Sparverius has gray eyes, luminous and cold as smashed ice, and they watch me closely. "Hmm. Are these notes necessary?"

"My story doesn't need them," I reply meekly, keeping my face aimed at my writing tablet on the drafting table. From the corner of my eye, I snatch glances at my stern preceptor. His kestrel features have a hard pride uncommon even for a falcon. "*Brave Tails: The Moon's Prophecy* is complete without notes."

"Yes, I recall from earlier drafts, your story has an effective beginning and a robust development, which assures me that you have *by now* carried it to a satisfactory conclusion — and I do emphasize *by now*, young Shagbark. There are many other deserving writers whose tenure at the athenaeum you are denying by your procrastination." His eyes of crushed ice look strongly at me. "And so, I inquire of you again, are these notes necessary?"

"My epic does not conclude in one volume." I answer timidly, afraid of the falcon beside me even though, strict as he is, he never cajoles or bullies but remains as calm and deeply sure of himself as a surgeon. "I — well, I uh — I thought these notes might encourage the reader to go on to the next volume — *Brave Tails: Invasion of the Boars.*"

"A good story requires no further encouragement than its own creative force." My preceptor taps the drafting table with his talon. "So, are these notes necessary?"

I stare at the rows of bookshelves foreshortened against the tall, parabolic windows of the athenaeum. Through those windows, I can see giant trees wearing scarves of mist. They remind me why I'm here. To get away from that dangerous forest, where owls feed on their own.

"My story doesn't need these notes," I admit honestly. "I'm just trying to explain myself to my readers, so they understand why this saga of talking animals is important to me." I peer at the stack of ruffled pages in the manuscript box beside the drafting table and get dizzy at the thought of how many long hours I've given to these imaginary characters. "I guess maybe these notes are really necessary for me."

"First-class answer!" says the falcon, some keen, frightening intent flashing in his icy eyes. "Carry on then." And he is gone, off to review the work of other writers in other carrels throughout the athenaeum. I'm a little shaken. Whenever Doctor Sparverius confronts me, I feel afraid, all feathery inside. As my preceptor, he alone decides if the story of the Brave Tails possesses sufficient merit to submit to your world for publication.

I should explain that the athenaeum is a school in the College of Raptors. As the name of our college implies, the residents here are eagles, hawks, falcons and owls. Admission is granted only those raptors who score the highest on the Raptorial Exams. These are general knowledge exams with emphasis on mathematics and communication skills, and the College conducts them throughout the forest once every five years.

I didn't do at all well on the mathematics portion of the

exam. I don't have a head for ciphers. And my general knowledge is mediocre. But I earned matriculation with a poem I wrote:

Little Notes to You from an Owl

The owl is looking for you.
The owl's voice is a question whose answer is you.
The owl's flower face has death for a sun.
The owl's neck is a wheel with spine for axle
So every direction the owl goes is forward.   .
The owl is the courage of life and death's mystery.
The owl hunts by slam victory.
The owl is a moon spirit.
The owl is a medicine pouch stuffed with twilight
And the bones of small animals. In this pouch,
The owl keeps its tears,
And each teardrop is harder than a diamond, a star.
The owl loves darkness and built the night
By nailing its shadow to the sky with its tears.
The owl slays by surprise.
Yet owls say they do not slay. They find the way
Up from the earth. And once away,
The owl unmakes its prey and then makes its prey
The owl.

That's the poem that began my writing career. Do you like it? The raptors who chose it were very deliberate in their judgment: Raptors admire ferocity; so, I wrote the most ferocious poem I could. I wanted to win their approval and get out of the wilds — at least for a while.

Unnerved by my brief exchange with Doctor Sparverius, I take my writing tablet and leave my carrel. The athenaeum is a maze of ornate bookshelves, kiosks of scrolls, catalog cabinets, scrivener carrels, reading stalls and corkscrew stairwells. Fan-light windows high among the vaulted ceilings admit long, dusty shafts of amber sunshine. It is morning — late for an owl — and I should be asleep. The globe lanterns that suffuse the central well with a lunar radiance at night are all extinguished, as are the individual study lamps that gleam orange and blue from the numerous tiers of the multistoried building. But I don't feel sleepy. *Brave Tails: The Moon's Prophecy* is finished — and I am too afraid to submit it.

I retreat to the rooftop's hanging garden. Here, among blossom arbors and fern trellises, alcoves provide residents privacy to work outdoors above the busy courtyards and plazas surrounding the athenaeum. Butterflies crisscross the rooftop. I find an empty niche under a lattice of flowering wintergreen, rosy-purple blossoms busy with bees. The droning bees steady my thoughts, and within moments of sitting at the weathered gray writing desk, I know how to explain myself to you. I will describe what I see — and you will understand my world.

Through a flowery frame of hanging vines, I observe cloud plateaus above remote mountains. These are very old crags, worn down to purple horizons. For as far as the sharpest-eyed eagle can see, a dense forest ranges, a misty, netherworld of enormous trees — sequoias, redwoods, and towering cypresses.

The College of Raptors fills a large glade with a ziggurat (which is a rectangular building of stone terraces), five glass towers slender as obelisks, a mirror-sided pyramid, and seven quadrangles enclosed by dolmen rocks, similar to Stonehenge, but our dolmens are smaller and shrouded in ivy.

How can raptors, who have no hands, build such structures? That's a human question. How do termites build their towers? Or bees their precise honeycombs? Have you ever examined a bird nest? Ever tried to make a nest yourself from thin twigs and grass? Few people can. The ovenbird fashions an abode out of clay or mud mixed with straw that bakes in the tropical sun to brick-hard walls. The eagle's nest appears a mess, but it's sturdy enough to support a human adult, because the sticks — some of them inches thick and several feet long — are actually stacked in rotated triangles. Birds are remarkable engineers.

"You're digressing." This voice that rasps like a boulder rolling down a gravel slope makes my neck feathers stand straight out. "You should explain how you know about humans. They only care about themselves, fool."

I stop writing. The owl who has been reading over my shoulder through the lattice of the adjacent alcove is Jagged. His name comes from a birth trait — his serrated beak. I stiffen, because he is the owl who killed Smudge.

The College forbids coup killing on campus. My blood thickens anyway, running sluggish with heart-sore pain. "You don't belong in the athenaeum," I manage in a steady voice. He doesn't. Jagged is a math wizard and resides at the ziggurat, where he should be engineering aviary condominiums or calculating more efficient swan flyways.

"I'm here to see you." The gray owl with the saw tooth beak steps around the lattice partition and enters my alcove. His truculent presence nearly shoves me out of my seat and over the roof edge into soaring flight. "I hear you've been busy, Shagbark. You finished your book."

All the darkness and impersonality of the universe seem crammed in his harsh voice. I simply stare at him, all thoughts fading to black.

"You have a good, clear heart." Jagged leans close, his scowling eyes suddenly gleeful. "And I'm going to eat it."

"What?" The word sounds more like a quack than a question.

"You finished your book." Jagged, gray as a ghost and gravel-voiced, nods knowingly. "No more hiding out. No more skulking around the athenaeum doing your piddling research, scrawling your pathetic pages. You're finished, Shagbark. This is your one shot — and when it goes down, you go out, back into the wilds. Then, I'll find you." The malice in his fragment of a smile makes my heart flap. "I'll find you, Shagbark. And when I find you — I will eat you."

Coup killing multiple members of the same family merits such laudable acclaim among owls that an elite society exists to honor and promote those killers to the highest echelons of the forest community. Such multiple coup killings of one family are quite rare, because the custom among owls requires children to leave the area where their parents live and to travel as far as possible to find their own place in the world. Most owlets thrill at the prospect of flying far into unknown tracts of the forest and making a life for themselves by beak and claw, and they disperse swiftly. Fate, however, has situated me in the same college as Smudge's killer, an opportunity too fortuitous for Jagged to ignore.

"You hear me, Shagbark?"

I can't speak. I hunch over the small writing desk and scribble these words in my blurry shorthand. My mind is lost in a black galaxy of fears, memories and remorse, the vastness of my grief for Smudge.

"I read your story," Jagged says lifelessly. "It doesn't go anywhere."

"Huh?" I twist about in my seat, wing feathers ruffling. "What are you talking about?"

"Don't look so surprised. Reading isn't so difficult for a mathematician. We're trained to crack codes." He eyes my gnawed pencil nub. "You obviously put a lot of effort into this project. The story's mouse hero and his shrew friends particularly fascinated me. Describing mice and shrews in anything other than a cookbook is an unquestionable feat of imagination for an owl. Those characters were real enough to make me hungry. But the story goes nowhere."

"You're wrong." I set my jaw. "The moon's prophecy has been fulfilled. My characters have come together to begin their adventure."

"Yeah, *begin* — but your book's done, fool." The abrasive grit of his voice scrapes mockingly as if striving to sandpaper the stupidity from my brain. "The story just ends in the middle of nowhere. What about the boar invasion?"

"This is the first volume," I say in a weak voice, " – first of a series."

"Are you a complete idiot?" Amazement shoves Jagged's head back. "Is that what they teach here at the athenaeum — 'Compleat Idiocy for Writers'?"

"It's a good story," I protest feebly. "I mean ... it's going somewhere. This is the first leg of a journey."

"Readers don't want a journey. They want a story." Jagged lifts his claw before my face and tightens his talons greedily. "And stories have *endings*."

"My story has an ending." I stare into Jagged's eyes. They

are black candleflames, still and hot. He wants to tear out my heart on the spot. "But to get there, my readers have to go on a journey through a series of books."

"Fah!" Jagged expels disgust with a clack of his serrated beak — and then, an expression of drastic evil saturates his features. "It's never going to sell."

Dread prickles under my feathers, and a shout leaps from me before I can think, "Get out!"

Jagged backs out of the alcove, but his sneer seems to linger where he stood. "You know what I'm researching at the ziggurat? The Ghost Gates. Yeah, Shagbark, that's right. I'll know when they send your manuscript. And I'll know when it gets bounced, too. I'll know when it comes back plastered with rejection slips." Hostility seethes from Jagged like steam. "Write this down, Shagbark. When this lame manuscript returns through the Ghost Gates, you have to leave the College. That's the rules. You fail to find a readership, you leave. And when you leave — I'm going to eat your good, clear heart."

He's gone. Alone, I lean out the frame of the alcove. I'm thinking of flying, just to clear my head — and my good, clear heart. But I don't. Pressing far out the opening, I can see past the ziggurat and the glass towers to the russet columns of sequoia on the College margin and, just visible in a narrow gap between those mighty trunks, the Ghost Gates.

Imagine two gigantic conch shells half-buried nose down in the ground, right next to each other, their whorled cavities standing vertical, side-by-side, facing in opposite directions. Imagine the shells are made of opal so thin that when sunlight shines through them you can see colorful mineral flakes suspended in the translucent walls like metallic bits of fluorescent confetti. The light penetrating the semitransparent walls makes the air inside the shells look hazy as a mirage. Animals who have died sometimes show up there, gesturing, speaking without sound, or just staring. That's why we call them the Ghost Gates.

"By the way, pal –" Jagged abruptly shoves his notch-beaked head into my alcove and assaults me with his big voice, "nobody wants another book of talking mice. The fantasy field is overrun with jabbering, yammering mice."

The sudden reappearance of the belligerent owl startles me. I yelp and tumble out the alcove and off the rooftop. Snorting adrenalin, I twist about in mid-fall and whomp my wings. Now, I'm gliding. The athenaeum pulls away — an immense corkscrew ribbon of mottled stone curling heavenward. Jagged stands at the roof's edge, glaring at me with dark humor. As I slew with the wind, the ribbon tower dripping ferns and bromeliads retreats among the other campus buildings.

It feels good to be airborne. I'm oddly grateful to Jagged for chasing me out into the open. But I can't help wondering if he's right about the market for animal fantasy.

I fly boldly, straight into the sun, hoping to purge myself of Jagged's unkind opinion. When my head hurts, I spiral down. Sequoias full of green darkness and camphor shadows rise up and enclose me. The Ghost Gates tower among these stupendous trees, a luminous presence in the dark grove of giants.

In the topmost galleries of the Ghost Gates are chambers that open into wormholes — shortcuts through spacetime that span the universe. The College of Raptors has sent explorers back-and-forth through those wormholes, investigating and populating numerous worlds — including Earth. Our travelers, of course, can visit only those planets fit for habitation by birds, and millennia of such explorations have widely distributed our dominant species and breeds of birds among the suitable worlds. Of all the worlds we know, yours most alarms us, because soon Earth will be useless for birds. Funny that you have an expression of uselessness: 'it's for the birds' — when soon your planet won't even be good enough for us.

I light in a wide clearing splotched with yellow flowers and grass greening in the sun. Here I quickly scratch these thoughts in the small notebook I carry everywhere I go.

"Shaggy, aren't you done scribbling yet?" The large great horned owl who approaches from out of the monkey park adjacent to the Ghost Gates is stunningly beautiful. She has plumage the color of cinnamon, ear-tufts velvet as midnight, and an ivory beak like a crescent moon. She's my girlfriend, Blue, named after the astonishing lightning hue of her eyes. "I thought you'd finished that silly thing."

Female great horned owls are twenty percent larger than males, and so, even though I'm standing, I'm looking up at her as I say, "Hello to you, too."

"You keep scratching like that you're going to turn into a chicken. Put that down and look at me, you goofy owl." Her stare widens with concern, and the azure day pours through her eyes. "You know I can't wait for you much longer."

Blue is a dancer, the most prestigious profession in raptor society. Dancers collect our history and philosophy in movement. We don't write. That art, peculiar to your culture and a half dozen other worlds, seems strange to us, abstract as it is, so disconnected from the physical world where we live body and soul from birth. Time puts one claw before the other, so why shouldn't its creatures? Through dance, we remember, we debate, and we decide.

"My novel is finished — but I'm afraid to submit it." I've always been completely honest with Blue, and that, I think, is why she loves me. Great horned owls mate for life, and the choice of a spouse is a big issue of prestige among our peers. So, if you were to ask Blue, a highly-skilled dancer who has her pick of males, why she wants to spend her life nesting with me, an unproven practitioner of an alien and dubious art akin to chicken scratching, she'd probably offer some conventional answer, such as how the feathers of my throat band are white as water lilies filled with first snow, my ear tufts sharp as flames, my face-disc buff as an early moon floating among the trees. Actually, I'm not that good-looking. She chose me, because I surprise her. "I'm writing about you now, Blue, and why you love me." That surprises her. The blue core of her soul shines in her sockets, glossy with curiosity. To avoid the embarrassment of having to read aloud what I'm writing here, I hurriedly add, "If I don't get this right, if *Brave Tails* is rejected, I'll have to leave the College."

"Is that really such a tragedy?" Returning to the forest is so expected and ordinary for her, so much more desirable than anything I could be chicken scratching in this notebook, her soul packs up its curiosity and withdraws to its usual depths.

She looks away into the trees, distracted by the angular sunlight sliding down among the redwoods like golden escalators. We should be riding those escalators into dreamland. We're both up late, I to write these notes, she to socialize with other dancers while snacking on small monkeys in the park where the drowsy sun immerses the world in twinkling dream colors. "You can always get work as a territorial guard or a nest finder, like my parents."

Those jobs are owl equivalents of a police officer and a realtor. Neither career appeals to me, because they leave me vulnerable to Smudge's fate. "Blue, I'm a coward. I'm afraid of the forest."

That returns her attention to me, and her tallness seems to collapse inward. "You're not a coward, Shaggy. You're a rare and sensitive owl — a bard who should be crafting hooting melodies about life's joys and travails. You'd make a fortune, and your admirers would protect you."

Can you see why I love this female? "Sure, Blue, I'll thrive as a bard — just as soon as I recall where I left my singing voice." My clumsy attempt at sounding flip only makes Blue more certain that I need her help. Her embracing look of love pops the knuckles of my spine, and I level with her: "My only gift is this peculiar art in a strange language useless everywhere but on a distant planet called Earth. If the Raptorial Exams hadn't identified my aptitude for abstract thinking, I'd never have gotten into the College's developmental skills program, never have learned this otherworldly business of reading and writing, never had a chance to compose my ferocious poem . . ."

"And never have met me." Her voice fits snugly around a gigantic tenderness. "If you were to ask me, I would go with you today, Shaggy, right now, to find our own tree."

My heart roars like a furnace. There's nothing I want more — except to avoid what happened to my sister. I know that with Blue at my side during our mating time I'd be safe. But owls live most of the year on their own, and I don't want to have to spend the majority of my life looking over my shoulder for Jagged or someone like him eager to eat me. "We can make a stupendous — and safe — life for ourselves right here on campus," I blurt, then add more softly, "that is, if *Brave Tails* finds a readership on Earth."

"Okay." Her voice narrows, approaching a wounded whisper. "So what happens now? You can't keep scratching at that pad forever."

Staring up at all that unlocked desire in her beautiful face and seeing above her the immense redwood canopy and clouds like incomplete pieces of our lives waiting for me to fit them together, I wonder where to begin. "I believe I can find a readership on Earth. There are animals there who enjoy stories like this. Humans. They're similar to those monkeys your friends are eating in the park, but they don't have tails and they're less hairy. I don't think you'd like them, though. Not only are they too big to eat, they're violent. It's common for them to destroy other animals — not just for food but for expedience and pleasure. They're annihilating whole species at a terrifying rate. That's why the athenaeum has forbidden direct contact with them and why we're trying to civilize them with their own language and art. My mission is to touch their souls by writing a story where animals behave like humans. Maybe then they'll think of the species they're annihilating more compassionately."

My girlfriend nods carefully. "That sounds –" The blue fire in her eyes flickers as she kindly discards the word '*crazy*' for " — far-fetched."

"Yeah." I chew off that word, sharing her skepticism. "The athenaeum has been trying in vain to enlighten humans for centuries. They made small progress a couple millennia ago when a crow, using the penname Aesop, introduced some fables that dramatized common sense and decency. More recently, we achieved commercial success with athenaeum writers who fronted their work through two human allies on Earth, Beatrix Potter and Kenneth Grahame. Ms Potter actually used a great deal of the money she earned from her animal stories to establish a wildlife reserve. Of course, my work can't compare to creations like Peter Rabbit or wacky Toad of Toad Hall . . . "

"It's late, Shaggy." Blue maintains eye contact as she slides deftly away. She wants me to see that she loves me even if she doesn't think much of my chicken scratching or the athenaeum's infirm efforts to reform rabid animal killers on an alien planet. "I'm going to grab a monkey to eat before I get some rest. You hand in that silly thing now — and when we get together later, I'll help you forget all about it."

Blue retreats into the trees among veils of morning light. It's so late and the sunshine so spooky bright, I wonder if maybe that wasn't Blue after all but a phantom of my anxiety, who just jumped out of my fatigued psyche to scare me with the terrible truth that my work is pointless. Smudge is gone. And all those extinct species of your world are gone. *Where?* I shiver, watching the way gauzy sunlight pleats around Blue until she disappears.

Daylight makes everything seem so unreal. Who can believe such intense colors? Well, I suppose you can — if this story has actually gotten into human hands. You're accustomed to daylight. But for an owl, the colors of sunshine don't seem made of light at all but of smells. Colors appear that strong. They rise off the surface of things like fumes and spread in the air, trailing and mingling their odors.

Maybe I've been writing too long. That's my thought as I saunter among the redwoods scratching these thoughts. If I weren't so preoccupied with writing down what I see, I would have known better than to discuss with Blue my mission. She's not your average female owl. The domain of dancers is so sophisticated and challenging, she gets bored easily when males talk about work, and she gets outright angry if they try any of that corny romantic stuff, like robust beak snapping, ventriloquial breeding calls, or the sexy crooning and 'wraaa-wraaa-aarrk' songs that send most females into a dither.

If I want Blue, I have to let this novel go. But I'm holding onto it the way I wasn't able to hold onto Smudge. That thought walks me through the chartreuse shade of the enormous trees to the Ghost Gates, where I'm hoping I might catch a glimpse of my sister's wraith. That has never happened the many other times I've stood here in the punctured darkness of the forest gazing intently at this unreal immensity — and it doesn't happen now.

No one knows who created the Ghost Gates or what purpose they were originally meant to serve. Maybe Jagged and his research cohorts at the ziggurat will figure that out. Sunlight squeaks through the pale curves of twisted shell that titanically loom over the sequoias. In the dark depths of those cavernous portals, tiny lights effervesce.

Tourists flock to see this wonder. I hear their awed cries in the wind. Birds blow in and out of the monumental interior. From a low bough of a sequoia, I watch a group of hares lollop into the clearing. The younger cottontails glance up at me nervously. Unlike their elders, they're not so trusting of the strictly enforced law that forbids me pouncing on them within these revered grounds. They keep an eye on me until they enter the colossal lower chamber of the Ghost Gates.

Inside, what they see is as close to you as I can get. Eerie, turbulent auroras spill from the upper storeys, out of winding corridors that connect my world with yours. It's there that Dr. Sparverius will bring my manuscript. In one of those mysterious chambers, my written pages will disappear from this world and arrive in yours.

Thrilled by this possibility, I glide among the pillared shadows of the redwoods. The athenaeum appears ahead, its helical stones weathered to the color of dead leaves by centuries of frost and rain. At the perimeter of the athenaeum's turf courtyard, I alight atop a troll-like boulder that wears a shawl of moss. It's one of several that stand like guardians. Here, I read over what I've written, wondering if any of this sounds true.

Are these notes necessary? Dr. Sparverius' intimidating question rises like a voice out of a well.

My story doesn't need these notes. My story needs you. You are my story's purpose. These are merely words, marks on a page, until you read them, until you add your human perspective. Then, they become changed, made more by your faith that words can tell a story and a story can abandon truth and still be true.

When writing enchants, animals of different species can talk with each other, and what they have to say is real and important and can help us live better lives. Stories — especially fabulous stories, epics and sagas, legends and myths — enlarge our lives, and we're less alive without them. To live fully, we must listen to our fantasies. After all, the real enemy of life is not death but disenchantment.

My pencil pauses. I read that line again. I lift my claw and gnaw on my pencil nub. *The real enemy of life . . .*

Can that be true? Am I afraid to fail, am I afraid to return to the forest not because I saw Smudge die, not because Jagged wants to kill me too but because . . .

My heart lubs heavily. It's not death that has made me a coward. It's disenchantment. I saw my sister cut to pieces before my eyes, and my little playmate, my bothersome tag-along, my humorous sidekick, my tattletale, my best friend was suddenly exposed as slithering organs and raw meat.

My neck feathers stand straight out. Suddenly, I understand everything. My pencil scrawls faster than I can read.

I'm disenchanted. I'm frightened, because I believe that life is pointless. I have lost the heart to live. The irony is that I'm afraid of death because I'm not really alive! I'm already dead inside.

All this time, I've been running away from an enemy I carry with me. I haven't been writing about imaginary characters — I've been hiding among them, learning their desires, confronting their fears. Unaware, I have been desperately trying to build a new heart.

Smudge and all the extinct species of your world, of all the worlds, are gone — gone like the inventors of the Ghost Gates. Where? No one knows. We are not meant to know, only to wonder.

So long as we wonder, ever so long as we can wonder, we will not be defeated. Not even by death.

Do I believe this? Yes! I swoop down from the troll-like boulder and slide along a ramp of sunbeams to the stone steps of the athenaeum, and I wonder what on Earth will happen with *Brave Tails*, this fantasy of talking animals in a frightening situation — a situation as dangerous as what you and I must face every day.

I pause at the top of the athenaeum's ancient, worn steps to wonder what will happen to me in the forest if *Brave Tails* fails.

I wonder what it's like to die.

Boldly, I walk through the vaulted entry on my way to my writing carrel, to get my manuscript. I wonder if Dr. Sparverius will be surprised this morning when I present him with volume one of my epic. And I wonder what it would be like to eat Jagged.

RIVERSPLASH MOUNTAIN

WELCOME, FRIEND, TO RIVERSPLASH Mountain, smallest peak in the Apricot Sky Range. Upon ancient times, a mighty volcano rose here from the floor of an ancient sea. Rivers of fire forged these steep canyons and black cliffs. Ages ago, the lava flow ceased and so did the hissing sulfur fumes.

Those billowing clouds rained down a long time and deposited tremendous fields of yellow crystals. Furry minerals covered whole mountainsides in sulfur flowers. Now, after the high snows melt in summer, bright acres of brimstone streak surrounding crags with yellow-orange hues. That's why these pinnacles and the sky beyond them glow softly amber in slant daylight and why we call these highlands the Apricot Sky Range.

When the volcanic clouds finally drifted away nevermore to return, they revealed stupendous geologic devastation. What had once been the highest peak was now the smallest: the whole summit had blown away and left behind broad mountain slopes crowned by an enormous crater — a caldera whose broken rim frosts over with ice in winter and gleams green as emerald with moss and ivy in summer.

Hidden by towering highlands on all sides and locked in by mountains so tall that their peaks forever glare with snow, Riversplash Mountain is a world unto itself. Only a single defile — a narrow and rocky gap between the mountains called Weasel's Pass — offers passage beyond Riversplash into the Apricot Sky Range. That passage, choked with massive boulders and prickly shrubs, rarely permits the mountain's denizens to leave and even more rarely admits outsiders.

The seasons have given this squat volcanic crater its name. During winter, the entire caldera freezes to a giant glacial bowl full of silver light and clouds of powdered snow. Spring melts the drifts, and the caldera fills with ice-blue water at its center, in a steep-banked mountain lake called a tarn. From the tarn, torrents pour all summer long, running over the brim in great mantles of white water and then spilling down cliff faces as roaring waterfalls. Farther along, the wind lifts the smallest cascades and turns these ribbons of falling water into mist. Rainbow mists drift upward, gathering into dense vapors that shroud lush wet jungles, transforming the upper slopes into a country of fog.

Already, friend, you can see why this crater peak is known as Riversplash Mountain. But there is more. Waterfalls too large for the wind to stop plummet beyond the cloud forest through a steep territory of thick woodlands dubbed the Holt. Beyond this realm of ferns and immense trees, smoking cataracts crash onto slate cliffs at the mountain's waist and continue as rivers and streams. Rock spills and gravel beds that thousands of years of erosion dropped from the crater heights onto the wide apron of the mountain sieve the watercourses into smaller rivulets. The name of this broad expanse of glittering brooks and trickling creeks is the Rill.

At the bottom of Riversplash Mountain, where the Rill dumps its annual freight of silt, sprawls the Mere, an extensive marshland of bulrushes, bogs, thorny bramble and gloomy groves of ragged trees. Here dwell the ruder lives of this crater mountain, mud-dwellers and swamp creatures, who transpire through umber light and murk of their dark kingdom among a perpetual haze of biting flies and mosquitoes. Here, at the soggy bottom of the world, in this mire of rotted things, among these smoking vales of dread decay and spectral ruin, our story crawls forth.

– J. S.

The Strange, Wild Provenance of the Brave Tails
(A Short Tall Tale)

BY JONATHAN SPARROW

THERE WAS THIS OWL wizard, Finagler, who kept starlight in an inkpot. When he dipped his beak in it and wrote upon gravestones, whatever lay dead jumped up from the rooty marl scribbled with worms and dancing like children on hot sand.

Over his shoulder, in the purple placental sac of a wolverine, Finagler carried relativity. Whenever he reached in, he pulled out clumps of time gooey with sunset and sunrise. Years of carefully handling the purple sac had made the owl so knowledgeable about the calculus of creation and destruction, he got work reviewing the Sun's life insurance policy.

This annoyed Death. In the temple of skulls, Death peered into his evil mirror and searched for a competent assassin. Finagler showed no concern. He was so confident in his wizardry, he had gotten used to treating Death like a naughty puppy.

Smug owl! Deep in the dreary Mere, where sepulchral mists seeped slowly from rotted compost and spread over bog pools like fungal throw rugs, Finagler squatted among bulrushes. All his attention focused on the task before him: mending the Moon's lace panties. This was a discreet favor for the cross-dressing Moon, and the wizard owl hunched well out of sight of the night's inquisitive black children, the bogey wind, extorting cats and gossipy bats.

In exchange for this secret labor, Finagler expected a big payoff. The Moon had promised him a silver apple. Fed on that apple, Finagler would eat of prophecy and his already acute eyesight would grow so sharp he'd be able to gaze across outer space and read God's diary.

Alone and out of sight in the smoldering desolation of the Mere, the absorbed owl bent over his task so intently he didn't sense Death's assassin until too late. A giant, grinning alligator surged out of the bog and swallowed him whole before he could flutter a wing.

Death had not sent an ordinary alligator. This was Tar Log Ali, the most ancient and wily crocodilian in the Mere. Dinosaur-hide jagged black as a fire-split pitch pine, Tar Log Ali slid silently into shadows, fatal smile submerged. From his visor gaze, a hundred million years of horrible life gazed upon the haggard swamp and punctured all illusions.

Finagler's screams ricocheted in the belly of darkness, finally emerging from Tar Log Ali's clamped fangs with one soft burp. Haloed in silence, Finagler sat still and blind. He opened his inkpot of starlight and looked around at the glossy, wrinkled gizzard drooling digestive juices.

From his purple sac, the wizard owl yanked out lumps of time and clouted the alligator's craw with a furious barrage. Tar Log Ali sneezed a lavender sunset cloud.

Frantically, Finagler whipped the alligator's innards with the Moon's lace panties, hoping to get himself spit out. Tar Log Ali held his trembling sides, and laughter blasted through the bars of his eighty teeth.

The desperate owl had no choice but to stretch wide the wolverine's placental sac and crawl in. He tugged the pouch tight after him and cloaked himself in syrupy spacetime. The gritstones of the gizzard quickly tore through the purple sac but could not scratch the diamond emptiness of curved space. Gastric jellies dissolved the shredded placenta at once but slicked off the geodesic crystal enclosing Finagler in time's transparency.

Death watched all this through the evil mirror in his palace of skulls, and he was not happy. Was Finagler smothered dead, squashed tight and mummified inside that faceted bolus? Death couldn't tell. The evil mirror's x-rays bounced off the gut pellet.

Inexorably, the owl's bowel journey ended on the murky swamp bottom. Expelled in a heap of charred scat, the trapped owl sat in the mud like a black egg. Death glared at the nugget. The thing peeked from sludge inert as rock.

Tar Log Ali nosed it, rolled it, thwacked it with his prehistoric tail. It lay hard and unbroken among frills of kelp. The alligator aimed his hundred million-year-old hunger at delicate lives waiting elsewhere for him and glided into the swamp's filthy light.

Deeper in bog haze sank the chiseled nodule. Slow, toiling currents buried it under curdling silt. Death lost interest. And the Moon wondered anxiously about his lace panties.

Trapped by his own magic, Finagler the owl wizard began a madcap adventure he really didn't want. He had wrapped himself so tightly in his bag of relativity that spacetime curled around itself, and he wobbled wailing down the drain of a black hole. His terrified cries redshifted to a haunting horn-riff lonely as midnight freight trains, and he disappeared entirely from this world.

Far across the universe, Finagler popped out of a wormhole, feathers plastered with dark matter. Under his scorched wings, he caught star winds and soared into the cosmos. By the time he found his way back through dilated time to the Mere, star fires had fried off his ear tufts, seared his owl feathers, and shrunk him to a raven.

Only five seconds had lapsed since he left. Nevertheless, Death didn't recognize him. Here was another raven swooping between the swamp's tattered curtains collecting bright rubbish and dregs from the marsh floor. Death looked elsewhere to satisfy his ambitions.

The busy raven gathered his shiny pebbles in heaps at the furnace belly of a nearby volcano and smelted ores. Hell kindled vengeful strategies in the black bird's baked skull, where the vacuum of space still whistled. Death would pay.

Beneath a rotting stump, the deformed owl steeped toadstool flesh, spider genitals, fever virus, a panther's putrid cough, grave spores and gummy strings of adder vomit. When this grim concoction finished stewing, he dipped his talons in the ultraviolet toxin. Then, to test his venom, he hunted in the deep woods for the Beast Maker.

That season, the animal god roamed the forest as a great black elk, and when Finagler found him, he slashed with his poison claws. The elk lord snorted twice, stamped once, launched his majestic spirit back to his throne room in the Land of Happy Animals, and fell down dead.

That got Death's attention. But by then, there was nothing he could do from his palace of skulls. He watched aghast with his evil mirror as the mad wizard recruited the gentlest creatures of the Mere — lovesick rabbits, neurotic shrews, agoraphobic gerbils and obsessive-compulsive mice — and armed them with gold swords dipped in his horrid brew.

Finagler mesmerized these meek beasties with snake-bone rattles and a feather pants dance. He sprinkled their bobbing, bug-eyed faces with the Beast Maker's antler velvet, which jammed their hearts with valor. He bagged their heads in black cowls. He cloaked them all in scarlet. He did everything to make them myths to themselves, and then he inspired their timid brains with lunatic war chants and sent them scurrying through the quaggy Mere to jab at every carnivore that rose up against them.

Soon, bloated carcasses of badgers, civets, weasels and fen cats clogged the cypress ponds. Alligators gulped them and died from the poison, convulsing like appliances stuck on spin cycle.

When Tar Log Ali bucked in the mud, violent as a reptilian rodeo attraction, Finagler did his feather pants dance an inch from those gnashing jaws. Tar Log Ali struck a death pose, and the gleeful wizard used his black beak, stropped razor keen on the asteroid belt, to tailor cut alligator skin scabbards and couturier boots.

Thus, the Mere lost its predators. Finagler itched for more, revenge hatching like spiders in his blood. He intended to terminate all of Death's best sales reps. Out of the Mere, his wee warriors scampered in their new alligator skin boots, their murderous era just begun.

But the world was too wide, and its horizons grinned tauntingly at the costumed creatures. They needed a ride.

Finagler considered air transport. Too small to carry his murderous crew himself, he petitioned eagles for help. Shaman devotees of Death, they would not betray their god. He went to his owl cohorts, but they knew when one of their own had gone around the bend. He turned to the elegant waterbirds. Unfortunately, their reflections had grabbed them and wouldn't let go.

"Antelope!" he decided — until he discovered that the elk lord's antler velvet did nothing for hoofed creatures. Without that surge of magical courage, antelope, sheep, goats and donkeys proved too skittish for murder.

Death meanwhile sent his most agile killers. Tigers slouched out of the Cloud Forest and a posse of lynx lurked atop tree awnings, eager to pounce. Doped fearless on the Beast Maker's antler velvet, the delirious upstarts from the Mere took seriously the guerilla name given them by awed onlookers: "Brave Tails!" they squeaked as they dashed into the tigers' disemboweling claws and under the lynxes' skydiving attacks. Brave Tails died — and so did tigers and lynxes.

Finagler skinned the cats and left their slippery nudes for ants and worms to dismantle. On the gravestones of the fallen Brave Tails, he jotted obits in starlight from his inkpot, and jubilant zombies reeled out of the worm dirt break dancing.

"Gaaah!" yelled a spooked fox peeping from the underbrush at the acrobatic dead. He flung himself prostrate and shivering before the necromantic raven-owl. "Let me worship you!"

"Fine. Light a votive candle under your rump, pal, because I need speed not prayers." Finagler danced his feather pants dance and floured the fox's sniveling snout with antler velvet. "Show me some velocity, Reynard."

"It's Rumner."

"Rumner the Swift if you want to run with us."

With the Dead Riders on his back light as ghosts, Rumner the Swift charged across moorland and through forest mazes. He moved by day as sun dazzle and by night as moonsmoke.

Now Death really despaired. Rumner the Swift outran wolves and bears. The Brave Tails snorkeled wetlands and lakes and slew every otter and mink. In the Tarn, the Dead Riders toured their skeleton stompdances, driving serpents from their hideouts onto the eagles' dinner plates.

Finagler wanted the eagles stuffed and mounted, too. But Death had finally had enough.

He came forth from his palace of skulls in his leper rags and winding sheets. Finagler flashed a cold smile. With a demented cry, he arrowed straight at that infamous starved face.

Death swatted him aside like a frivolous spitball. Finagler stabbed that bony hand with a beak tempered in stellar furnaces. Death clenched his fist to crunch the pesky wizard.

That was hopeless. The gouging beak whetted on interstellar debris bored straight through the necrotic flesh and came out the other side.

Finagler dove between Death's knobby legs and swiftly seized a frayed burial cloth in his talons. With a mighty heave, he sent Death toppling. The impact shook mountains into avalanche and buried the shrouded specter. Laughter convulsed the wizard to see Death interred!

Eyes veined with lightning and bulging from their grim sockets, Death shoved upright out of the rubble, creating Weasel's Pass. In one hand, Death throttled Finagler. With the other, he groped through swamp weeds and muck until he snatched up the lopsided egg where the wizard had once hidden in Tar Log Ali's belly. He cracked that egg hard over Finagler's skull.

Out slopped the black yolk of relativity. That sucking vortex hit the ground like a bowling ball dropping into a giant wedding cake. Splat! The mountainside caved in, rivers followed dragging forests into a crevasse that became the muscular rapids of the Riprap. And fluttering through the air above all this demolition, the lace panties of the Moon unfurled from out the broken egg, pink and ruffled as twilight.

Death gaped agog at the uncontrolled black hole. After it ate the Earth, it would eat him too. He hacked away with his notorious scythe, chopping furiously until he had diced the black hole into bittie pieces that drooled among the rocks slippery as eels — squirming out of sight into slitherholes that are there to this day.

While Death wildly minced, Finagler tiptoed off with an incinerating headache. Knocked to within a feather's breadth of oblivion, he wanted no more tussling with Death. But Death was not done with him.

The Reaper would have beat that wizard silly as a tambourine if those lace panties hadn't ballooned into the wind from the scythe's blender blade frenzy.

Before the Sun noticed that frilly undergarment, the mortified Moon skidded before him, blathering noisily about that nasty, runaway black hole. The Moon bunched up those darling skivvies behind his back, then hurried away with them squeezed out of sight, dying to try them on.

By eclipse darkness, Finagler slinked off, never to be seen again on Riversplash Mountain. Some say he crawled wounded into a peat pit to die and his fossil bones adorn Death's trophy room. Others insist he escaped to world's end. There, he thrives thanks to an everlasting elixir distilled from tissue samples stolen when he bored through Death's hand.

A few remain convinced that he intended all along to provoke Death and steal his cankerous flesh, that this was the wizard's purpose from the first, since he began hoarding starlight in an inkpot. And they offer his name as impelling support for their conviction.

As for the Brave Tails, they didn't last long without Finagler. The Dead Riders fell apart the first moment sunbeams notched the eclipse. The remaining Brave Tails buried their swords and costumes with their dead comrades right there under the Riprap and returned to their gentle lives.

In their dreams, the wizard owl kept in touch. He served his veteran warriors during the night as legal counsel, financial adviser, marriage therapist, psychoanalyst and lifelong friend. At the end, each of their families lodged complaints of bodysnatching with the local constabulary. But if they had looked closely, and knew what they were looking for, they would have seen that the apparent snail tracks scrawling the headboards above the empty deathbeds of their aged heroes were not snail tracks at all but the ink of starlight.

THIRTEEN RAPTURES
OF THE BLACK GOAT

Searchers after horror haunt strange, far places.
— *H.P. Lovecraft*

One:

I*Ä! SHUB-NIGGURATH!*

Shub-Niggurath is the All-Mother, wife of the Not-to-Be-Named-One — and my mistress. I met her in my youth, when I was a teen obsessed with arcane lore and sorcery. In April 1963, at the age of eleven, I encountered Robert Graves' *The White Goddess: A Historical Grammar of Poetic Myth.* That book describes creative writing as an act of magic. Graves beguiled my preadolescent mind with the alphabet trees of the druids, numerology of the magi, mystic networks for words and numbers encoded in riddles, poems and stories. All writing is spelling, and all texts are talismanic objects with spellbinding magic to enchant and transform those who know the code. At the unifying center of this sorcery, the goddess presides. She personifies creative power, the permeant intelligence that sculpts the world whole and everyone in it out of atoms and the void.

The White Goddess is a fantasy in the form of a source book of myth and history. Like Lovecraft, Graves invents a poetic reality — a mythos — a work of sheer imagination through which we see the visionary in the apparent. The curving world of the hourglass and the horizon is always the starting point with a mythos. Time and space in *The White Goddess* are a triumph of enchantment. Graves finds truth in outlandish ideas about the Celt's Biblical affiliations, a grammar of trees, poetry as moon magic and the creative fever inflicted on men by the Triple Goddess of Birth, Love and Death. All of that is a confabulation by the author — creative writing — yet, it feels authentic. Lovecraft, too, mythologizes reality to its own truth, but he celebrates a darker world at the bottom of darkness.

This sense of adventurous trespass of death-in-life and creative rebirth in text enchanted me — as text has done to sapiens from the first magi to the existentialists. I spent most of my adolescence in libraries and occult bookstores all over the New York Metropolitan Area (such as Sam Weiser's on the Lower East Side and Tsvetaeva's in Newark). I chose my college because they had a collection of Sumerian cylinder texts, the oldest writing in the world. Despite my esoteric interests, not once did I consider that this feverish reverie with imaginative writing could open into genuine sorcery — until I found the *Necronomicon.*

Actually, I located only a fragment, a torn piece of lambskin, not much bigger than my thumb, wedged into an esoteric volume, a Latin edition of *Shamsu al-Ma'aref al-Kubra*, by Ahmed al-Buni. A previous owner had etched a paraphrasis of the glyphs directly onto the lambskin, and from that I deduced that this parchment had been torn from a Greek translation of *Al Azif*, the Νεκρονομικόν. I immediately recognized it as an evocation from the black temple of Tsathoggua. When I dared give voice to those blasphemous words, my world transformed dramatically and forever.

How to describe Her? She came immediately. I can tell you that. She burst burning right through the worldsheet and seized me. I was nineteen. She was deity — the Black Goat of a Thousand Young, Her face the void of space tingling with stars, a gluttonous dark, Her breathing in my gonads, Her hair like an angel's tattered wings, Her bleating voice crawling up inside my skull unfolding its many directions in time. From the first, we were mad lovers, our coupling hemorrhaging screams. The appalling pain of Her tongue infected with voltage, cracking the roof of my mouth, kissed my brain and licked my eyes from inside. And I saw Her deeper. A yearning, wild, unbroken creaturely spirit, the Black Goat is the end of all flesh, the contempt of blood, the unbearable violence of lust. We rutted for wresting hours in the grave bed that is Her womb. Her genitals all blue, all blue-black, slit with syrupy purple, sucked in all of me. My body felt torn into pieces of meat and bone, cooked in that abhorrent womb. She was the Black Goat, born nowhere in this world. She was the stew of voices sticking in my throat. *Iä! Shub-Niggurath!* Her climax transfixed me with a blinding glare from the end of the world. The force of Her climax broke my heart — and the shattered pieces stuck in my throat. *Iä! Shub-Niggurath!* Thrashing, wheezing, pummeled, I cried the blaze of noon, and my seed and Hers mingled in fire, a fire like wings, a fire with eyes. By that heatless conflagration, I saw God grinning in the dark. No! Not God. The Not-to-Be-

Named-One, the abominable spouse of the Black Goat, the Magnum Innominandum, Azathoth's terrible spawn, Whom I had cuckolded.

Two:

I am *gof'nn hupadgh Shub-Niggurath*, carnal lover of the Black Goat of a Thousand Young. She has been my mistress these thirty-five years. The secrets She has revealed to me, I have built my novels around. More correctly, my works of creative writing are acts of sorcery that She has inspired and designed. Their purpose is to call Her own to Her. They were never meant to reach any but Her own. My stories appeal to those few who not only share my demonic enthusiasm for our genre of the *fantastique* but also for fiction as a fantasy of confrontation with the incomprehensible. Most readers go to genre fiction for more predictable experiences. If you are reading these lines, She beckons you.

"Writing is a congress with the divine. The most vivid writing comes directly from copulating with the gods." This from Sin-liqe-unninni, Mesopotamian exorcist and first author to affix his name to a written story, *The Epic of Gilgamesh*. He was speaking literally.

Write what you know, we learn in school. There's a fool's errand! The psychiatrist R. D. Laing eloquently explains why: "What we think is less than what we know; what we know is less than what we love; what we love is so much less than what there is. And to that precise extent we are so much less than what we are."

I write about what we do not know. Hearts are bitten into by mystery. And what greater mystery than reality, where every conscious life is a sacrificial murder — and this holy killing on earth a flow of passion in heaven? The work is not easy, not even with the Black Goat as lover. My earliest attempts now seem foolish. I've discarded most of those. As an aspiring *gof'nn hupadgh Shub-Niggurath*, I didn't write any spells worthy of publication until I turned twenty-three. Then, in 1975, in an anthology titled *Nameless Places*, Gerald W. Page released upon the world "Glimpses."

I wrote this story in a trance-dance with the Black Goat. In it, I tried, rather clumsily, to speak of Her secrets. Creative writing is about spellbinding — spelling out words that bind the reader to an alternate reality. However, this material, birthed from the jellied cleft of the Black Goat, can be revealed only to one who already understands. And those who understand realize that, for all its numerous defects, the story I'm writing is real. Life is imaginary. Those who practice sorcery have learned that the world is replete beyond human reckoning. In the human soul, we are evoked of light and radiant all within. Here, again, this understanding means nothing to those who do not already understand.

THREE:

GLIMPSES

The mysterious and indecipherable books from the forgotten people before the Ramesses period that the early myths want to tell us so much about were probably not books at all. Who can say what stone artifact discovered at Coptos is not itself some ancient body of knowledge to which we have long ago lost the key?

[*Birch Zeitschrift* 1871 pp. 61-2]

You tell me you understand no word of the first tongue spoken by the deities, no word good or bad. There is, as it were, a wall about it that none may climb. For it is a language that remembers no past and awaits no future. It is a tongue that murders the air.

[trans. By Maspero and Lang in *The World's Desire* from *Papyrus Anastasi*, I pl. 1. i. pl. X 1. iv.]

THE PIERCED STONE

The day was smoldering at the end of the street when Gene Mirandola stepped down from the tram. The gas lamps were already lighted. And though it was April, the wind that groped among the tangle of streets and alleys was cold. All day, Gene had been experiencing an unreasonable tension, as if he were under surveillance. Try as he had, there was no way to alleviate the anxiety.

He stood for a moment at the corner to look about him. From a rooftop, a boy threw crumbs into the air, fishing the sky. Around him, flocks of pigeons massed like a black fountain, blowing down and swirling up again.

Gene looked behind him and then crossed the street to buy the *Times* from the crone who perpetually waited there in front of Little Rose Café. After he purchased the paper, she squinted long at the pence in her hand, despising it perhaps for being a pence, and then stuffed it in her apron pocket, sucking her lips a little farther into her mousehole.

With cigar in his teeth and nose to the wind, Gene walked toward the twilight, feeling even more intensely now the eyes of some unseen observer. That old woman, Ocarina, mother of murderers and madmen, Ocarina, whose neck was a chicken leg, she was there every night, rain or stars, squatting on the orange crate — she never intimidated him before. Why now were her eyes so terrible? Why were her crab's hands, her small bulk on the crate, so ominous tonight?

Momentarily overwhelmed by his imagination, Gene made his way down the street conscious of the curtains in the dusty storefront windows drawn aside and movements behind them. As he passed through the black iron gate and down the musky alley that led to the courtyard where his flat was, he struggled in his apprehension to remind himself that such unwarranted fear was incommensurable with his experience: after all, he found himself thinking as he groped for his latch key, a man of thirty-two with the responsible but not at all consequential job of chief clerk at a small publishing firm has no reason for paranoia.

Gene shut the door firmly behind him and climbed the stairs two at a step to the top floor. Already in the warmth of the building, the invisible menace diminished. It was unnatural for it to be so cold in April. And now, as the door swung open into his awkward, cherished rooms containing his familiar shelves, he was perfectly willing to believe that the weather had been responsible for his anxiety.

After a change of clothes and with a snifter of brandy in his hand, Gene's stubborn fear seemed small, and he looked out his window at the children in the alley setting fires in ash-barrels and the old men with their pushcarts loaded with fruit and vegetables and empty crates clanking away on iron wheels over cobblestones.

He settled comfortably in his large overstuffed chair, staring into the night. It was the dark of the moon. Sleep was opening in him like a blossom, and he drifted toward it. But his drowsiness gave way gradually to a discomfort in his throat. It felt numb, and then his tongue began twisting in his mouth, moving on its own. Alarmed, Gene sat bolt upright as his tongue forced itself between his lips and wagged nervously in the air, curling and flapping. He leaped to his feet and cried out loud. His tongue relaxed, but he was shaking. He downed the rest of his brandy and after a few minutes went to bed and tried to pray. After calming down, he felt his mouth open and his tongue move. He couldn't control his breathing, and the whisper that forced itself through his teeth was not his own — *Gene, listen to me. I am a voice that has been too high for your ears for too long. Where do you suppose I have been since you last saw me?*

O Christ! Gene thought. His breath returned to him in short gasps. O Christ! I know that voice. It's my uncle. But ... how long has it been since he died?

Gene Mirandola was traveling south. It was night, and from the train window only his own round, fleshy face stared back. He had been in the midst of a long and tiring conversation with his traveling companion, an unknown businessman that circumstance had put in the same compartment. Somehow, Gene's mind had wandered to what he couldn't even now recall, and he had lost grasp of the dialogue. As he returned his gaze to his fellow passenger, he was not at all surprised to see that the man looked perplexed. Just as he was about to apologize, the stranger said, "You know, that's a very curious caricature there." The man indicated the paper on which Gene had been absent-mindedly doodling.

"O, I wasn't paying any attention. I –" Gene stopped short when he looked down at the writing tablet in his lap. There, among an intricate weave of figure-eights, circles and mandalas, stared back at him a remarkably deft drawing of his Uncle Armand Saadi. A wall of blackness that had until then obscured whole regions of thought suddenly gave way, and Gene remembered vividly that night several months previous when he had felt possessed by this very uncle. Since then he had learned, through other relatives, a few facts about his uncle (that, indeed, he was still alive and living not far from where Gene, on his business trip, was heading), but he had, until now, dismissed his previous experience completely.

Gene sat numb for a long moment, unable to remove his eyes from the seemingly too-familiar face that peered through his doodles. At last he looked up at his companion, who by now had lost interest and was leisurely engaged in his local trades-weekly. The stranger's nonchalance about the incident grated against Gene's excitement. The compartment that they occupied seemed foolishly small and trivial to be housing all of the implications that a few minutes of idle sketching had produced. Gene's life had changed utterly — altering even as he thought about it. Chance could not explain it. Coincidence was no longer enough.

He tried to remember everything he could about his uncle. He knew that Armand had been an historian of science for a while and that he had a passionate interest in the paintings of Manet — but these were trifles. What was it that consumed him about his uncle — that strange man he barely knew, that rare figure in his life with whom he shared not even blood?

After a week of business in Caernarvon, Gene Mirandola was still obsessing about his uncle. It had become only too clear to him that the matter would not resolve itself, and he made plans to take the time to pay a personal visit to Armand Saadi.

Following his relatives' best recollections and the uncertain knowledge of the local post office, Gene found himself on an overnight journey by horseback into the mountainous country of Radnor Forest. The season was agreeable to the trek, and the ride turned into a pleasant aside for what had been a week of exacting and tedious labor. The countryside was rustic, even wild, despite the fact that he was able to make most of his way on the well-defined northwest highway that runs in that area from Llandudno to Carmarthon. It amazed him that he should know so little about an uncle that had apparently influenced him deeply or that he would be willing to travel at such inconvenience to visit this man he knew only by acquaintance.

Mirandola stayed overnight at the turnpike house in Maroc, and early the next morning left the highway for the short but unmapped ride to his uncle's house. The forest here grew particularly thick, and shortly after the turnoff, Gene regretted not leaving his horse at the inn. Uncommonly swollen trees appeared, overgrown with moss and mushroom. Branches had grown so dense as to cut off most light and to filter green what little shone through. Underfoot a tangle of thick roots and growths impeded riding, and Gene found himself leading his steed most of the nine miles north to his destination.

Well after noon, the first landmark of his uncle's estate greeted him. It was an old stone well, obviously just recovered from some terribly long period of disrepair. Gene stopped to rest there momentarily and, more for idle pleasure than necessity, prepared to draw some water. He pulled on the new rope slung through the rusted iron pulley and continued to pull for a considerable time before he gave up in exasperation. The rope was endless, he thought as he watched yards of it fly back into the darkness. Curious, he dropped in a large stone. The water gave out no bottom for as long as he cared to wait. Just over the knoll was his uncle's place, and certainly there would be more interesting things to do there than wait on a bottomless well.

Gene led his horse up the knoll and stopped, dismissing the strange well, forgetting the tiring walk. A stone tower, not a full three stories, stood among the thick forest. It leaned heavily to one side, its walls obviously just mortared to salvage the structure from ruin. It was such an unexpected sight, that queer little building huddled on a mountain slope, that Gene would have stood staring at it indefinitely had not a figure emerged from the door. It waved him closer, and, of course, it was his Uncle Armand. But not as he remembered him. No, not even as he had so deftly but unconsciously portrayed him a week earlier on the train from London. His uncle was more wan, more haggard and sallow than he had expected.

"Ah, at last. At last," his uncle greeted after Gene secured the horse. Armand clasped a heavy and amiable arm about his nephew. "I thought you were never coming."

"You knew?" Gene muttered, certainly not taken fully aback that his uncle had shared his unusually persistent attraction.

"Yes, of course I knew. I've been calling you," Armand claimed, ushering the young man into his peculiar house.

Inside, it was even more obvious what great labor his uncle had undertaken restoring the timeless tower. On an intricately woven Minoan prayer rug, a large round table of oak with several cumbersome chairs, suitably antiquated, occupied most of the ground floor. His uncle had converted over half of the circular wall to bookshelves and held what at first glance seemed a disproportionate number of worn Arabic texts. The remainder of the wall space displayed several paintings (one remarkable balcony scene by Manet showing an old woman with a face as vapid as the long moon behind her) and unusual mounted animals: a shark's mouth displaying several rows of teeth, several hides including a large, white cat, and the head of a fierce-looking ram. At the center of the table a dozen or so stone cubes loosely encircled a decanter of whiskey.

Armand seated his nephew, yet he remained standing, aloof. After a brief period of exchanging cordialities, he left the room and returned momentarily with a square black stone the size of a liter cube. When Gene moved to touch it, Armand stopped him with a sharp command. "You must be very careful about everything you do here," the uncle told his nephew. "Fancy your coming two days out of your way to see me. You don't know me except maybe by reputation. But I know who you are. I know your deepest secret fears. How could I know such things unless

I was a sorcerer? And if indeed you are in a sorcerer's house, it would be wise to be very careful about everything you do."

Gene sat back in his chair and seemed to think this over, but he was quite certain in his mind that the man opposite him was no ordinary man. He began to wish that he had not been so impulsive about coming here.

"Yes, it is too bad you are the one that had to come," Armand said. "Believe me, it would not have been a good thing for whomever providence chose — but I had no idea it would be you."

Gene felt anxiety like a cold finger between his shoulders. He knew that it would be impossible to escape now, and that knowledge gave him a queasy feeling.

"Ah, but you're right," his uncle continued. "All this chatter is making you uncomfortable, so I shall address the purpose of your visit directly. I am an old man who has undergone a long agony, and I am impatient for my death. Before I indulge in that last and most somber denial, I must dispatch an old and pressing promise. Really, I am no different from you, except that the years and fate have set me apart. So I understand how what I must ask you to do for me will sound strange. I cannot possibly make my purpose fully clear to you, though I shall try to help you understand as much as your destiny in this matter will allow."

Gene felt sick at heart. The old man had not called him here to impart knowledge, merely to have him do a favor.

Armand Saadi sensed even this and said, "What little I have to tell you is more than you can learn living another thousand years in your current fashion. Don't be distracted by thoughts of personal gain, for I repeat, you have been chosen by a distressing fate. Perhaps what I tell you now will be of some condolence later."

The nephew's anxiety heightened to alarm. Understanding that there was no escape so long as his uncle stood between him and the door, Gene accepted that salvation — if any there was in this strange encounter — would only reveal itself to a cool head.

"Yes, try to remain calm, and look closely at this," Armand

said, pointing to the cube. "This is what Arabs would say embodies *kiblah*, direction, for it shows the way to true knowledge. When I first uncovered it at a bazaar in Khartoum that is what the merchant told me it was. He also said that it had been found in the deep desert years ago, a token of ill-luck, as any such object that probably was discarded by a caravan would be. So, I purchased it cheaply. Not until years later did I learn from a good friend of mine, who is an archeologist in America, what this old Arabic inscription says."

Gene scrutinized the Arabic script.

"*Fee mihrabeh bejanib el-bahr tantazir ahlam al-maiet Cthulhu*," his uncle read. "It literally translates: *In his temple by the sea, dead Cthulhu's dream waits.* My American friend assumed from the use of the barbarous name Cthulhu that this relatively recent black stone, which is maybe two thousand years old, houses an older artifact related to a much more ancient cult. Following his lead, I learned this secret."

Armand gently separated the black cube into two parts revealing a round stone with a hole in it, rather like a donut. On either side of this stone were inscriptions impressed in a style like cuneiform. Gene ran his fingers over them and noticed that on the periphery of the stone a snake raised from the stone encircled the entire wheel, biting its tail on one side.

"That snake is an uroboros," Armand said. "It's a symbol whose meaning I cannot fully exhaust, other than to say that it represents the cyclic pattern of the cosmos itself. I can tell you about the nature of the stone. It is a hole!" Armand put several fingers through it, and Gene wanted to laugh out loud at his uncle's pious regard.

"You think this is funny, because you don't understand the nature of holes at all," his uncle said. "This particular hole is filled with air, but holes aren't necessarily empty. Besides, what does 'empty' mean? All that we can really say is that whatever a hole is filled with, it must not be the same as the substance in which it is embedded."

"Ah, well if that is so, then aren't all 'empty' spaces holes in reference to some framework? What about gaps in thoughts? Are the conceptual contents of all holes the same?"

"You now might begin to see that each person's universe, both physical and conceptual, is entirely permeated by holes. There are holes all around and through us. We are living in a world of holes. As a matter of fact, holes cover more space than anything else. It seems strange, then, that all of the words we have for holes refer to a break in the continuity of a substance, such as aperture, bore, cave, cavern, cavity, cleft, crater, enclave, excavation, fissure, gap, grotto, hole, hollow, orifice, puncture, pit, pocket, slit, tunnel and tube. All of these words come from Indo-European root-words that refer to a hole as something created, and not as a separate entity, like *beu, bher, ghei, kel, keu, peue, wer,* meaning to cover, to open, to poke or push something into, to punch, to bend.

"Apparently, this configuration in space, like the concept of zero, is relatively recent. But what do people truly feel about holes? Why did artists put holes in Luristan bronzes three thousand years ago? It is because various configurations of a hole and of holes focus energies and tell secrets. Holes are the language used by entities beyond causality. By this magic we may arise and speak with spirits without knowing ourselves. For, to men with knowledge of corners and holes, nothing is ever empty."

"And this particular hole is ... important?" Gene ventured, indicating the ancient stone.

"Of course. But holes can mean nothing significant until you understand that man is merely a flash in the pan compared to what older entities first dwelt here. Those Old Ones, you may learn, still have much influence on this planet, though now they are not in the spaces we know but *between* them. Holes can lead to them. The nature of their names and characters would be meaningless to you, except perhaps for that Entity to Whom this specific hole is sacred. And that is *Yog-Sothoth,* the All-In-One and the One-In-All, Guardian and Master of all passageways, of all holes. Truly, though, He is nameless, beginningless, endless. How the Dead are drawn after Him! O and how terrible the fate of the living, who lucklessly are found in His presence and sail without shadow toward the pyres of His sun."

Gene again grew nervous, uncertain about what was happening.

"Listen, young man, you are not yet ready to understand these matters. I called you here to do me a favor, and that is, quite simply, to deliver this hole to London. Here is the address."

The crisp, labored hand of his uncle read *Marc Souvate, 43 Caton Street, Lansbury, London.*

"He is an adept in these matters," Armand went on, "and if you are at all curious when you meet him, he may tell you more about this stone. But now you must leave, even though you have just arrived. This is a place of much power, and if you are found here by night, I would have little hope for your continued well-being."

This was the opportunity that Gene was looking for, and he grabbed it. As quickly as he could without seeming too impolite, he took the stone and mounted his horse. His uncle pointed out a shorter way back to Maroc, advising Gene to avoid the well on his property, as it was also a hole sacred to *Yog-Sothoth* and therefore a danger to him with the sacred stone. Gene took his uncle's advice and rode swiftly along the narrow trail into the forest, glad in his heart to return to the natural world.

He tried to kick the gun under the oak table, but he could not find his foot. There was blood on the Minoan prayer rug, and the stone cubes had been scattered when the body collapsed.

He moved to the window to wait for someone to come. It was night, and there was nothing to do.

The decanter of whiskey remained on the table where he had left it. He wanted a drink, but his hand was not there. It dangled from the table. He went over and looked at the mess that had been a head. It disturbed him, and already he wanted to go back.

He looked up at the painting by Manet. That woman there, locked on that balcony — her fate was as terrible as his.

He stood for a long time at the window, looking out at the darkness. There was nothing to do.

Abruptly, a loud and raucous noise began from behind the knoll. It was the sound of the rusted pulley that drew the rope from the well.

They were coming now.

He felt anxious. It wasn't supposed to turn out this way. It was supposed to be over now. The gun should have done the trick. How could he have suspected otherwise? How could he have known?

The creaking of the pulley grew more persistent, and he stared hard into the night. What was going to happen when They came? What would They do?

He backed from the window slowly, though he knew there was no escape.

THE ADEPT

Dr Marc Souvate, for all that Gene Mirandola could tell, appeared of indeterminate age. Though his hair, absolutely straight and combed back flat on his head, shone jet black and his posture and gait filled space with remarkable agility for a man as tall as he, the doctor struck Gene as being quite old. His olive skin tight to the skull and those eyes, green as grass, netted in wrinkles that told of much physical strain, embodied mixed ethnicity of enigmatic lineage. The thin lips, too, creased and reptilian, spoke of weathered trials. Other than those few signs of age, the man, for all appearances in his elegant dress and with his firm resonant voice, could have been thirty.

"Did your uncle tell you anything about the nature of this stone?" Souvate asked. He sat on the edge of his baroque desk, hands lying idly at the sides of the icon and grass green eyes fixed on it, as if he were not speaking to Gene at all.

"Yes, he did tell me something about its antiquity and, uh, something about older beings."

"The Old Ones."

"Yes, that was it."

"It's a shame he didn't come with you. There's much I must discuss with him."

"That's too bad," Gene said, lowering his voice. "I got word just this morning. He passed."

Souvate turned to face Gene.

A. A. ATTANASIO

"The notice, quite bluntly, said he put himself away with a pistol."

Souvate returned his gaze to the stone.

A long period of silence ensued, and Gene, feeling uncomfortable yet not willing to depart without more information that might help him understand his uncle, asked, "What can you tell me about this stone?"

"Nothing that would make much sense to you, I'm afraid."

"I must know more. Tell me anyway."

Souvate remained silent for a moment and then, without looking at Gene said, "This is a talisman. The Great Lord of the Abyss, Nodens, gave it to men to protect us from our witless creators. It is one of several that we have to insulate us from the prepotent elemental deities. The only other one that I can speak of is the Elder Sign that guards the dream of the water deity. This here is even more powerful, for it holds sway over Time and the Beast therein: the All-In-One and the One-In-All, *Yog-Sothoth*."

Gene made a perplexed moue and sat back further in his chair.

"I told you, these words would mean nothing to you," said Marc Souvate. "You are not an initiate; so, at most, if I were fain to speak more, these things would be a mythology to you."

"But are these things relative to man? I mean, are these things you and my uncle have talked about — real?"

Souvate put a finger to the side of his nose and smiled slightly. "How can I tell you about reality? You are a businessman and I a sorcerer. For you, volume of sales is real. For me, whatever does not need me is real."

"I want to learn more," Gene said, he thought too eagerly.

Souvate smiled broadly. "You would have to make a profound commitment. I think, perhaps, you are too well into your own conception of the world to have another one opened to you."

That was the last the two men had to do with each other for over a year. Gene left Souvate with the mysterious stone in the roomy and foreboding house near the river and returned to his flat and his job. But, as these things go, his exposure to his uncle and to the recondite Dr Souvate had a lasting and pressing influence on Gene. Because he had had one glimpse of other, previously unsuspected horizons, his appreciation of the world no longer fulfilled him, and he found that his work was not gratifying. He knew now in his heart what he had only suspected and rationalized, that the universe was vaster and more accessible than any man in his social circles suspected. He realized, too, that he could not live the remainder of his life without trying at least to grasp more of that whole.

And, naturally, after more than a year of compromising with the world of business and his own impulsive curiosity, Gene Mirandola returned to the roomy and foreboding house by the river and called, once again, on Dr Souvate. And there, in the drawing room among antiquated furniture, unusual animals and relics from disparate and largely unknown cultures, Gene and the dark doctor settled the arrangements for the young man's apprenticeship.

The details of Mirandola's training are part of another story. Those that are familiar with sorcery know those details intimately, and those who are merely curious would fail to appreciate the slow and ungainly process by which Gene learned first to forget time, numbers and the alphabet, going on to forgetting the elements, starting with water, proceeding to earth, rising to fire, forgetting fire until everything was continuous again. And only then did his apprenticeship truly begin, with his discovering as if by himself (for such is the way of a true teacher) the nature and heuristic use of henbane, betel, oeanthol, opium, blisterfly and tannis leaf — discovering next how to alter the field of force around the human body in such a way that nerve centers are influenced and valuable visions generated and, finally, discovering the secret holes and the language they speak.

So it came about that Gene Mirandola, instructed by Dr Souvate, was prepared to begin a marvelous quest for knowledge. They met on a prearranged night in the immense caverns that lie partly under the sorcerer's foreboding house by the river. There, in the dark gloom lighted only by a single cool-burning taper, they came upon three large holes, the perimeters of which were marked with worn futhorc inscriptions.

Gene, of course, knew by then that the entire world, indeed the universe, is an intricate manifold of interconnecting holes, some of them blatantly obvious and constant like these three, others invisible and incessantly shifting. All initiates knew of these holes, but only an adept could employ them properly. Determining which hole to use necessitated a foreknowledge of where it would go, and that knowledge precluded logic and was, therefore, available only to an adept. Holes could communicate through spacetime, and there were numerous accounts of luckless voyagers who entered into worlds or situations biologically disadvantageous or who plummeted through intergalactic voids so astronomical as to be considered, by all practical values, infinite.

"Now that you have had some glimpse into the nature of things," Souvate told Gene as they stood at the edge of one of the abysses, "you can appreciate what I am going to tell you about myself. Like a good apprentice, you have come here not knowing what task I shall assign you, perfectly willing to fulfill my commands without explanation. Because you have been an exceptional pupil, I am going to tell you something few other men know."

Souvate held the taper closer to his face, illuminating his stark, green eyes. "I am a vehicle for the first worshippers of the Great Lord Nodens, Whose Presence was last on this planet long before any semblance of man emerged from the Pre-Cambrian slime and Who will return billions of years from now. Those entities that first worshipped Him, before this Earth was even recognizable as a planet, desire nothing more than to unite in His presence. When He departed and the Old Ones, the entropic deities, emerged, the worshippers began their dread migration through the aeons, utilizing their knowledge of holes to jump large stretches of time, moving constantly toward the future point when Nodens shall return. Some one and a half million years ago, the worshippers took my body as a host. I am their vehicle, and they direct me on this odyssey through history. From them I have acquired complete mastery of my physical form. I am ageless, capable of regenerating whole segments of my body. Yet, I realize I am only a tool — a willing servant of Nodens.

"I met your Uncle Armand when I first entered this time period, some fifty-three years previous. In return for his help in establishing me in this historical niche, I gave him knowledge of the Old Ones so that his life would lack nothing. However, instead of merely using that knowledge for his corporeal good, he sought to compound his understanding, and he began to study the nature of holes, that is spacetime, the domain of terrible *Yog-Sothoth*.

"That was sad, because he who seeks the All-In-One will find the One-In-All. But then there is no escape, not even in physical death. Hence, Armand most certainly was taken by *Yog-Sothoth* to serve that Ancient One for eternity in some hideous manner.

"Now, as the stars are right for me to make another leap through time, I am prepared to leave all that I have here behind. However, I do not forget that Armand Saadi befriended me. So, I have trained you, and soon you will have the opportunity to both repay me and save your uncle's soul from its unremitting horror.

"This hole that we will enter is going to deliver us to Laguna Cays, a small archipelago south of Chile. On that speck of land is the oldest temple of *Yog-Sothoth* still extant. From there, I will depart for the future and my destiny. And also there you will find your uncle's soul and have your chance to redeem it. If you succeed, my actions will go unnoticed and I shall make good my escape, your uncle's soul will be freed, and you shall return here safely."

Souvate opened the burlap sack he had with him and withdrew the serpent stone that Gene had delivered so long ago. "This, as I have told you, is a talisman against *Yog-Sothoth*. Take it, and do not let it go until you have returned here. It is the only thing that will afford you any protection at all."

Countless questions surged in Gene Mirandola, and there was time not even for one. Dr Souvate, chanting and holding Gene's arm, stepped out into the emptiness.

The adept and his disciple found themselves looking down a black, volcanic beach: old horseshoe crabs, broken skates, sand dollars, seahorses, endless numbers of primeval creatures quivering in the sea-mud. Waves lapped ice cold at their ankles, and they could see, far out at the horizon, majestic white cliffs of Antarctic icebergs as they caught sunlight. The sky appeared dark indigo at the zenith, lighter, almost green on the horizons. And though the wind blew over the dunes as they crept, there was no sound but the sea.

Gene turned to ask Souvate a question, but the thin man motioned him to silence and led him off along the black sand. The island was tiny, and in half an hour they had circled it. Completely desolate, the place offered nothing but sand. Souvate continued to walk around the island, indicating that they must move spirally toward the center before they would find the temple.

After they had thrice moved about the isle, they spied half-buried in a dune, a human skeleton green with growths. "That is a warning," Souvate hissed. By their fifth turn, closing in on the center, the light changed, and the previously unusual atmospheric darkness became darker still. And though the sun, a small, wan disc, still shone high, the sky was dark enough to see the brighter stars.

On their seventh turn, they reached the center. Nothing seemed to change, and Gene allowed his tense muscles to relax. Souvate pointed at his feet. There an urn jutted from the sand. Gene bent low over it and heard, or thought he heard, soft, uncontrollable sobbing, or perhaps a sucking sound.

"That is your uncle," Souvate informed him. "His fate is too hideous to comprehend while you occupy your body. Take the vessel, but do not tip it over. To escape, there is only one way. You must retrace the spiral, and you must remain absolutely silent. When you arrive at the place where we began, you will return to London. But you will have to hurry."

Souvate pointed out to sea. There, at the horizon, loomed what Gene took at first to be another island, large and flat, rising gradually above the sea. "It's a tidal wave," the adept said. "You'd better get out before it hits. And mind you now, if you break the spiral pattern, there can be no escape."

Gene immediately began following the spiral backward, and

no sooner had he begun than an old woman, at first existing only as smoke, appeared ahead of him. After she became more solid, he recognized her: Ocarina, the newspaper crone. She waited to follow behind Gene, holding a little lamp in one hand that glowed like an icy fan of the sun.

He wanted to ask her who she really was, but the silence in the air had thickened dreadfully. He stepped up his pace, glancing nervously out to sea, trying to gauge the progress of that wave (which curiously did not seem to be moving at all), throwing a glance to his back, too, watching the crone who slogged just far enough behind that wind ripples in the sand covered his footsteps before she reached them. And all the while there was that ominous darkness in the sky by which now the southern constellations reared into view, so that Souvate, who was watching from the center and who knew just who that crone was, had reason to fear the worst. All the same, he did not forget his purpose and set about beginning the silent chant and hand-sigils that would open the hole he sought.

After Gene's fifth turn, the silence that had been the desolate silence of isolated places became unearthly, and even the waves stopped and stood mute, as if they were all drawing back to feed that one mighty surge. Gene heard his breath loud and raucous in the still air. His heart rolled like a dervish drum, and the odd, unwholesome sucking sound grew louder and more offensive in the urn; and Gene called from his heart for a natural noise from a bird or the sea, but nothing stirred, even Souvate was still. And then and there, before he had even witnessed the horror, Mirandola decided, as he should have done long ago, to forget his interest in sorcery and to return, as quickly as he could, to the quiet, usual life of a chief clerk. He looked over his shoulder to face Souvate, but the adept was gone, having already decided it was far wiser to slip sidewise into time than to remain any longer in the growing presence of *Yog-Sothoth*. And Gene Mirandola felt the fear that had been a weight in his throat crash down into his heart as the crone widened the slit of her lamp and let the unnatural, cold light from it illuminate the sand around her. Wherever the light shone, the empty beach vanished and another landscape became visible — a more sinister, less reasonable landscape. The thin air like a veil burned away in the eerie lamplight, and the absurd shapes and forms that abruptly emerged edged Gene closer and closer to panic. After one sweep of the crone's lamp, the island transformed into a staggering arena of monoliths whose very size caused Gene's fear to cascade into delirious horror. In his shock at the unfamiliar stars that now crowded the sky and the great insect things with mad, swiveling mandibles that began to appear around unpredictable corners and edges, Gene dropped both the urn and the stone. And then, screaming faster and faster until his cries were incoherent, he fled toward the sea, where *Yog-Sothoth's* abominable half-brother already lifted his hulking, tentacled head.

FOUR:

The Black Goat despised this story. It nearly ended our relationship. My pen proved inept, my writing style wholly derivative. I had to agree with Her and tried to assuage Her disappointment, "I need to make a change." But I think She heard strange. She nibbled at my neck, enamoring me, until She had swallowed my voice. I didn't write any more spells for years. She chewed my voice, macerating it a long time, till She spit it out like cud, my twisted voice a wobbly bezoar, a bewitched tumbleweed. I got confused. "The world is gibbered to shards," I told Her, "and names and things disjointed." I thought Laphroaig was one of the Elder Gods, when it's actually a pretty decent Scotch. "What am I to do?" I cried from my small, crippled heart. I remember the day She answered by shoving Her icy teat in my mouth and making me suck bitter black milk, acrid colostrum of gluey strings. I gagged. Her curds, hard as knots, tightened in my gut. *Start over*, the Black Goat insisted. *Start with fundamentals — the ABCs. Start with A . . .*

And so, I did.

FIVE:

Aleph, first of the twenty-two letters of the Hebrew alphabet, formed by two *yods*, one to the upper right and the other to the lower left, joined by a diagonal *vav*, which represent the higher and lower waters and the firmament between them. On the first day of Creation, when "the spirit of God hovered over the surface of the water," the higher and the lower waters began as one and the same. On the second day of Creation, God separated the two waters by unfolding the firmament between them, and thus the blue heavens unite the upper and the lower waters. Here we see the transcendent and mundane realities of creation and humankind set apart, which only God may join — as He does when He Himself is the first to descend in the Scriptures: "And God came down on Mount Sinai." Only then, in turn, may lower reality ascend: "And Moses approached the cloud. . . ." The union of "higher reality," the upper *yod*, with "lower reality," the lower *yod*, by means of the connecting *vav* of God's intent, is the ultimate secret of the letter *aleph*. But what is God's intent? The *Tabula Smaragdina* declares, "That what is below be like that which is above and that what is above be like that which is below to accomplish the work of one only thing. This is true, certain and most true."

SIX:

Beth shows a three sided enclosure open on the north side, the direction the sun moves toward summer solstice in the northern hemisphere, hence the direction of longer days, greater light, the path to illumination (as opposed to the south, the way of obscurity). A center point occupies this house of enlightenment. Who is this? Who is at home in the house of light? The story of Creation begins with this letter. "*Bereishit* (In the beginning) God created the heavens and the earth." In the house that God built, who dwells? Who

is the one that enters and departs through the north door?
He is head of the household. We are his guests.

SEVEN:

Gimel rushes from the house of the lord, runs out the open
door of Beth and hurries north, swift as a camel. Why the
hurry? The runner is radiance from the house of light flying
headlong into boreal darkness. Countenance and tidings
from the head of the household travel deep into the polar
night, fluttering pennants and banners of Aurora Borea-
lis. The runner wears baggy pants and a square hat. He is
splendor from the house of light charging into the dark.
Only God knows where he is going — so, he must be an
angel. Look! His shadow on earth is a candlestick.

EIGHT:

In this way, I slowly learned again the alphabet, and among these
psychic landscapes of symbol and story, I practiced the sorcery
that had begun five thousand years ago in Mesopotamia and
continues shaping our world to this day.

The Black Goat grew impatient. She was pregnant. She
sneered at my amateur efforts and glared with contempt
through the folded pleats of Her loathsome, swollen body.

I say loathsome, for that's really how She would have appeared to anyone else. Breaking through from another, more
convoluted dimension, She arrives broken upon the fringes of
things, a mangled darkness, black-tongued, gibbering crazy
yells, Her slot eyes of smashed quartz too many and all in the
wrong places, swiveling in a malignant grin-mask of goat. Yet,
I love Her. With a might of madness, I love the Black Goat and
Her filthy hooves, Her visage of throat whose bleats rip my
thinking into rags. I fall to pieces under Her horns, and She puts
me together again bigger, a stronger agglutination of sinew and
dreams. What is a man to Her? A human being is a light shaft,

the electricity of the physical body glimpsed in our lit eyes and their longing, candescent Power trapped in the place of our skull, our heart in its cage, our sperm a gendering theater with many masks of desire . . .

Like burst light inside a diamond, a human being refracts into body and mind, dreaming and wakefulness, absence and presence. Beauty and ugliness home in on us. Shub-Niggurath, the Mother of the Thousand Young, the bubble-froth of spermatozoon and sticky, uterine brine leaking where jeweled flies frenzy is disgusting, right? Remember, each of us is a humbling, deadfall weight, a corpse-yet-to-be. Who is disgusting really? She never dies. Her young flourish beyond the char crust of this world in a reality unutterable. Filled with my seed, heavy with my horn-gauded unborn, She anneals my atoms to what is greater. She is not ugly, She for Whom all words are imprecation and imprecision. Strange how She craved that imprecision, that noetic paradox of spellbinding and the wings of fantasy. Typical of a higher dimensional thing, She thrived on contradiction. I wasn't sure how She would react in 1980 when Ramsey Campbell found merit in "The Star Pools," which he published in *New Tales of the Cthulhu Mythos* . . .

NINE:

THE STAR POOLS

There is a calling under the breath, a cry that goes on long as a vein. It is the last senseless moment of the organism, the instant of death that cries back through the narrows of air from the ferrous edge.

— Schiavoni and Malamocco, *Voorish Rituals*

Pain that even the cold stream water couldn't numb, a brittle, ruby pain. Henley Easton shuddered, then sat down in the stream, up to his waist in water, trousers ballooning. Slowly, he lifted the sharp rock he had stepped on, squeezed it hard, pressed it to his forehead, his lips. In the water, a cloud of blood swelled. A flap of skin on his foot winked open and closed. Seeing it and the blood holding back in the icy water, he thought he was going to be sick. But there were children looking on; so, he clutched at the blade of stone until he came back.

He limped to shore and spotted the familiar silver lines of his car parked at the edge of an escarpment above the sand. He still grasped the rock. There was no blood on its cutting edge, and he felt ashamed. With a lopsided heave, he sent it flying over the heads of the fishing children and watched it arc alone above the reeds, falling into the shallows of the far bank.

He wrapped his foot in a rag from the trunk of his car and sat for a while on the hood, looking out across the swale to a clump of cedar pines where an hour before he had frantically dug up mulchy earth and buried his cache.

Beyond the green colony of trees, the tortured land rose in great broken-backed steps toward a haze of iron-spined mountains. Nobody would be coming out here to look for anything but steelheads.

Reassured, already mindless of the itching throb in his foot, Henley Easton got into his car and swung out onto the highway. By dusk, he arrived in New York City. He had a leisurely dinner at Shakespeare's and decided to limp across Washington Square Park to find a doctor he knew. At the corner of MacDougal and Fourth, a rush of dizziness overtook him. It happened so quickly, there was no time to cast about for support. He floundered on the curb, tried hard to make it back to the sidewalk. Eyes glaring dark, he slumped to his knees. A moment later, he sprawled in the gutter, awareness sinking into the shadows of his body.

He endures an endless dream, wandering through dank, night-lighted corridors that stink of rime and something burnt. He moves alone in darkness, feeling his way along greasy walls and abrupt corners that goat-step down into smoky grottoes. The air, murmurous with the sound of purling water, also carries distant voices and the far-off seethe of ocean rollers steaming to shore.

He wanders a long time, unable to wake. Eventually, he stumbles out the mouth of the labyrinth and howls into the sear of the sun until the landscape he has entered awes him to silence. A white horse nearby, standing still as rock, its eyes an evil pink. Ashy sea grapes and palmetto hanging limp from long trellises above shocks of colorless grass. To the left, the sea, silver as mercury around a small boat with a black stick of a man standing in it, waiting. Three white huts squat on the right, each with a vacant window. Everything perfectly still and white. Even the sky white — except for the sun. It is black. Seeing it, Henley feels his muscles melt, and he drops to his knees. It is fibrous black, an immense spore, too painful to stare at. He rubs his eyes and blinks. He blinks. Nothing changes. The silver sea steams beneath the virus star.

A thin breeze picks up, and Henley watches several ashy leaves litter away. The white horse remains motionless, and its pink eyes are staring. Closer now, the boatman's features become visible. Bristly and thick, dully gaping. Puffed lips move, and Henley hears nothing. The face looks moronic, the forehead bulging, filling up the sockets so that the eyes stare up from under the skull. An idiot's face. Lips continue to move in a whisper. And then the breeze shifts and is full of patterns as it presses by. Silky curves of air carry a voice, scrawny and wicked: *Shut your ears big, let the darkness come unrolling from your eyes and your fingers blow longer all in the stillness. Shut your ears big, Henley.*

Henley straightens as if struck. The voice is horrible. He tries to heave himself to his feet, and the effort collapses him. He squelches into the mud. The heat of the black sun thuds against the back of his neck. He squeezes his eyes tight and tries to will himself awake, but the dream is unbreakable.

So there he lies, feeling as if he's wrinkling smaller in the alien light, drying to a dusty char that whispers away in the breeze, scattering through an incommensurable darkness.

Black.

A palpable darkness. Thick oozing masses of black. Immense galleries of space, choirs of distance, and at their center, a mountain of black convulsion gulfing all sound, all light.

With a terrible shriek, Henley wrenched awake. His eyelids tugged open, their mineral stare facing a wall. Gradually sounds sifted through, and he heard footsteps, sensed a faint medicinal stain on the air. He was in a hospital, and that realization calmed him. Yet there was no chance to wonder what had happened, because it was still happening. The very air around him seemed to pulse with the massed blackness of his nightmare –

No — not a nightmare.

Reality had gangplanked him into perpetual horror. Sitting perfectly still in his hospital bed, Henley felt utterly transformed. The room loomed empty. However, that was only an appearance confuting reality. The darkness of the room hovered cellular and shifting, its relative silence humming, a mockery of the void from which he had just risen. That supreme deadness endured, disguised, lurking as emptiness at the center of all things, voracious black holes invisible behind reflecting surfaces: walls, a night table, the windows . . .

At first light, a doctor came in with his medical chart. Henley could see through him, sensed the doctor's surprise at finding him awake, saw his body resolve into a cloud of atoms, a confusion of energies temporarily united, and, at their center, blackness.

The doctor unwrapped Henley's foot, and for the first time since waking, Henley stared at his own body. He could see through it as well. At his foot, there was something different. It leaked darkness. Threads of blackness rayed from it, shafting up his leg to his knee. Seeing it, he remembered the sharp rock, remembered hiding the cache beneath the trees, remembered . . .

Henley Easton snapped awake.

"Christ! Where am I?"

The doctor looked up with a benign, puzzled expression. "Relax, Mr Easton. You're in good hands."

Mike Rapf prowled the carpet of a consultation room in St Vincent's Hospital. He moved with ponderous exhaustion, having slept only in snatches the last week. Fever sores crusted a corner of his mouth, and he walked with a slight limp. Nervous as a rat, he shuffled from corner to corner, hands deep in his pockets. Of average height with flat snake eyes and a pachuco haircut; he resembled someone dangerous while actually suggesting no threat at all, which more than once had proved lethal for his adversaries. Beneath his madras shirt, he carried a butterfly switchblade and, strapped to his leg under his trousers, a modified bayonet. His face, once lucid as porcelain, shone sundark and scribbled with many fine blond wrinkles.

When he heard the scream, he stopped in his tracks, and his dark eyes narrowed. He identified Henley. Though he had known the boy only briefly, he was certain that he recognized something about that cry — a whimpering quality that he associated with this craven mule. It wasn't a scream of pain. It was fear.

A doctor came in — young, thin-boned, with long intelligent hands. "He's come around."

"What's wrong with him?".

The doctor shrugged. "No idea. It's the zaniest catatonia I've ever seen. He sent off theta waves the whole time he was out — the EKG of an alert person. Yet, he didn't respond to any stimulation."

"But he's going to pull through, isn't he?'

"I think so. His vital organs, nervous and lymph systems are all unaffected."

Rapf released an audible sigh, ran a hand over his face. "When can I see him?"

"Now, if you like. He's remarkably alert for all he's been through."

When Rapf entered, Henley Easton essayed a smile, sitting up straighter in the bed of his private room. Rapf went over to him directly, without returning the smile, and leaned close to his face. "Where is it, coconut?"

Henley kept smiling. He made a small feathering gesture with one hand and stared remorselessly into the flat dark eyes. He was good-looking, with flame-bright hair, clean jawline and gray eyes that looked a little crazed from the medication. "Since when did they start letting baboons in here?"

"Don't loose-lip, Easton."

"How'd you find me?"

"When you didn't show last week . . . "

"Last week? How long have I been here?"

"Don't you know? Nine days, man. The only good thing that happened to you is I ten-twentied before Gusto or his crew. They'd have left nothing for the hospital but an autopsy."

Henley closed his eyes. A weight heavy as heat lay on the back of his neck. And there were memories, ugly nightmare memories, of darkness, a maze, a black sun, horrible whispering . . .

"I laid out a lot of coin to get you this private box." Rapf reached into his pocket and pulled out a jangle of dog tags. "Your brother's plates. I figured they'd do more good here than they would where he's trashed. I used them to convince the hospital that you and I are kin. It was the only way to take charge."

"What about Gusto?"

Rapf shook his head, contentious. "He wants your ears, clown. He figures you ripped him. What else is the stooge to think after more than a week? The best thing for you is tell me where the skeejag is so I can tighten him up."

Henley rubbed the back of his neck. A retinal afterimage of the black sun seemed to hover before him. Everything looked dark, outlined by a soft mystical shine. "No way. You'd just run it."

"What?" Rapf's face closed with indignation. "I'm your cover."

Henley looked cool and arrogant. "You were my bro's cover, too. At Ngoc Linh."

Rapf's emotional valence swung from indignation to fury and then to remorse with unnatural swiftness. "Yeah. Well, pal, you'll be on your way to a family reunion if you don't gratify Gusto. He wants those two kilos."

"And he can have them. I'm in this for the payoff. You know that. I'm not going to run it."

"Fine. Then tell me where I can get it."

"No way. We go together or not at all."

"Sure, and just how long before you're mobile? I could be fish chow by then."

"We go tomorrow."

"The doc doesn't even know what's wrong with you."

Henley nodded, and his eyes glazed over, face distracted. The afterimage of the black sun had expanded so that it covered everything like a gray film. Rapf's face reflected in a dark mirror wormed with far-off, unaccountable lights. The room suddenly seemed foreshortened, and Henley stared through mistings of shadow. A blue light whose source might be somewhere behind the bed suffused his vision, and movements other than what he knew were there attracted his attention. Another scene superimposed the room: a pedestrian landscape — a parking lot. Henley recognized Rapf's car and watched dumb-faced as a black man in duck trousers unholstered a pistol and knelt down in the back seat of an adjacent white Chevy. Just as swiftly, the image splintered.

Rapf laid a calloused hand on Henley's shoulder. "You need rest, kid."

Henley blinked, rubbed his temples. With cold objectivity, every rift and flaw in the opposite wall, every pore on Rapf's face stood out sharp as glass. For a moment, he had felt as if he was leaning outside himself, teetering on the brink of a nightmare cliff that mawed beyond the particled world. Now he was himself again, and it was difficult to imagine that what he had seen was real. But he couldn't take the chance –

"Hold on, Mike. There's someone with a gun waiting for you in a white Chevy wheelside of your car."

"Huh?"

"Call it fever jitters. But stay sharp."

"Yeah. Sure."

When Rapf left, Henley leaned back and closed his eyes. A cold brilliance ran along the surface of his skin, and he seemed to sense that eerie whispering he had heard in his nightmare, sensed it the way the deaf hear sounds through the small bones of the head. Somewhere deep within himself the nightmare continued, an evil pushing out into the world. He had a feeling that if he let himself he could fall toward it, that it was pulling him.

Staring at the wall directly opposite, he tried to root himself in its cracks. It was beginning to shimmer. He was certain that it was starting all over again. Then, just as he reached for the call button, the wall solidified. He felt suddenly warm, and the sunlight slanting through the blinds reassured him.

He pressed the button anyway. When the nurse arrived, he was sitting at the edge of the bed, wearing, he hoped, his most alert and gracious smile. "Would you mind getting my clothes, please? I'm signing out."

Rapf left the hospital through the service garage and emerged on Twelfth Street at Seventh Avenue. He had parked his car in the Waverly Building's lot, and he approached it the long way. When he got to the corner of the lot, he froze. A white Chevy had parked beside his car.

Without hesitation, he circled the lot and approached the Chevy from behind. When he was within four cars of it, he lay down and bellycrawled until he was alongside its left rear door. From where he lay, he could see the latch was up. He surveyed the surrounding cars best he could. No one was in sight. In one swift movement, he unsprung his butterfly glade and jerked open the door.

The man inside lay belly down, peering through a drillhole in the opposite door. Rapf burst in, and the man swung around with a Walther automatic in his right hand.

Rapf slapped the gun aside, then pulled the killer into a sitting position and jacked his jaw. With a fierce tug, he dragged him out of the car, waved the butterfly under his nose. "All right, knucklehead, no more surprises. Who sent you?"

"Who you think?" The man rubbed his jaw and scowled. "Gusto wants his scag."

"Yeah, well, you tell Gusto it's his. My touch was laid up or he'd have it by now."

"He wants it last week."

"Sure, sure. You think I'd still be in the country if I was running it? Come on!" He pulled the gunner to his feet, pushed him back a pace, and retrieved the Walther. "Tell him he can have it tomorrow." He backed his way to his car. "Same drop."

Rapf threw the gun under the seat, slid behind the wheel and drove off.

For nine days, since Henley turned up at St Vincent's in a coma, he'd kept on the move, not daring to return to his flat. He knew Gusto would kill him. The man had a notorious temper. But handling the hit man gave him some confidence, and he decided to go home. He circled the block slowly twice and scouted the lobby cautiously. Even so, the instant he put his key in the latch, he realized he had blundered.

The door of the opposite apartment burst open, and two men pounced on him, shoved him into his rooms. One of them handcuffed him immediately. The other bolted the door and led him by the nose to the bathroom. They were big, wild, mongrel blacks with natty denims, their hair twisted into spikes. One had a beard and was missing half his left ear. The other wore dark wraparound glasses and a pink hat with a tight brim cocked low. He carried a shopping bag. In the bathroom, they knelt him down before the toilet bowl.

"Hey! Lay off!" Rapf pleaded. "I'm good with Gusto."

The bearded one laughed. "My name's Duke Parmelee. And that's Hi-Hat Chuckie Watz. We are here to take your face apart."

Hi-Hat Chuckie Watz took four cans of drain cleaner and a bottle of bleach from the shopping bag and emptied them into the bowl. The Duke continued, "Gusto wants you to know, he's hurt you ignored him."

Hi-Hat grabbed Rapf behind the neck and shoved his face toward the fuming water. The acid vapors seared his sinuses and scalded his eyes.

"Yawww!" Rapf bawled. "Don't! Please! I got the stuff!"

Hi-Hat eased up, and Rapf pulled back with a gasp, face slick with tears.

"Where is it?" the Duke asked.

"It's hidden. Tomorrow, I'll lift it tomorrow."

Hi-Hat steered Rapf's face toward the blue burning water. Rapf screamed, and the fumes gagged him. He went into a glide.

The Duke pulled him back and slashed him across the face

with a sharp-ringed hand. "Cry for me. Cry and I won't make you drink that soup."

Rapf cried, his whole body shaking with sobs.

"Just you remember," Duke Parmelee said. "You're a juke and everybody knows you're a juke. If you don't have that H tomorrow, you will suffer and die."

They uncuffed him and were gone before he could get to his feet. All things considered, they had been practically cordial.

Henley Easton took a cab from St Vincent's to Pennsylvania Station, then rode the L.I.R.R. to Garden City where he rented a car. After eating at McDonald's, he had fifty dollars left. The nightmare hadn't recurred, and he was beginning to feel confident. The plan was to get his cache and head west. He didn't want to burn Rapf, yet he felt he had no choice. The coma had changed everything. No doubt Gusto and his black mafia felt ripped after a nine-day delay. Better, Henley figured, to find another market and leave Rapf behind to answer questions.

Henley spent the night in a motor inn where he inspected his foot for the first time since leaving the hospital. There was no swelling, but the lips of the wound looked scaly and black. Examining it made him feel drowsy. He put his sock on, lay back and slid into a dark sleep.

The next morning, he went down to the stream early, uncovered his cache and secured it inside the car's spare tire. But when he got behind the wheel to go something stopped him. He stared through the windshield at the larkspur, the myrtle and the great bellowing fireweed that flourished on the slopes. He felt suddenly woozy, as if swaying with deep sea rapture over whispery distances — becoming no one, everything, endless space.

Come alive! He snapped at himself and jerked upright behind the wheel. It was no good. He determined that he had to get out of the car, and when he did it was like moving in a dream. He felt light as a cloud beginning to vanish. A shadow spread its anonymous dark over everything, and the air turned soft as rock seen underwater. Limbs, remote and rubbery, moved as though by their own will, descending the slope through a swatch of burned reeds. When he stopped moving, he looked down, and there jutted the stone that had cut him, huddled among crusts of dirt like a stunned animal.

It came away from the ground easily, and the dry dirt crumbled, revealing a palm-sized green rock. When he had first seen it wet, he thought that color was moss. The green color and oily shine were the rock's own strange attributes. Dizziness and nausea returned.

Henley moved to heave the thing away, but something about the patterning on the rock stopped him. Looking closely, he discerned markings engraved in sharp cuneiform-like designs. He ran his fingers over them, studied again the fine cutting edge and turned to take it back with him.

On the return walk to the car, his body no longer felt light. He was hungry, and he decided to find a restaurant. At the highway, he turned toward the city impulsively. He wanted to wheel around and go west, but it was impossible to do more than speculate about that. He felt stoned and uneasy, and he stopped several times to question his motives. Yet, each time he stopped, an overriding urgency, razor-apt, urged him back into his car. When he arrived in Manhattan, his clothes had soaked through with a cold sweat.

He returned the rented car and took a room at the Elton on East Twenty-sixth. There, he unbagged the heroin and repeatedly touched it with his fingertips. It had become the primary purpose in his life, even though he was doing everything with it wrong.

He took a pinch, divided it into two thin slivers and used his thumbnail to snort them. A few moments later, he drifted slowly and powerfully across the room through the cool red light of day's end. He mastered a small spasm of nausea and floated to the corner of his cot where he sat down, all of the day's problems already on the point of an energetic solution.

An hour later, the room darkened. Stern shadows, deep as oil, gloomed on all sides. Everything seemed immense, and the apprehensions of the nightmare began to feel real. The cutting stone, propped on the windowsill, pulsed a dull incandescent green. *It's the drug*, he reassured himself, though he wasn't confident. Fear hazed around him like a thunder charge. At any moment, the horror could begin again. Something dark and cold as an ocean current tugged at him, pulling him away. He touched the bedspread to reassure himself. It was death-cold! In terror, he hopped off the bed before he saw that he had touched the metal bedpost.

He breathed deeply to calm himself. It came to him that the nightmare was still there, somewhere deeper, much deeper than awareness. It continued. It had never stopped. Like thunder beginning too late to remember the light, his mind shivered in the afterfall of an intractable doom. Clearly, he saw that it was only a matter of time before the darkness welling within surged outward. He sat shivering in the twilight and resolved to contact Rapf. He had to unload the heroin. If he went into a coma and anyone found him with it, it would be better if he never woke up.

From a pay phone in the lobby, Henley called Rapf's apartment, and the phone rang a long time before a basso-rumble voice he didn't recognize answered. Henley hung up immediately. His hands trembled so violently it took him five minutes to dial correctly an alternate number Rapf had given him. A woman answered and said she hadn't seen Rapf in days and had no idea where he was. Henley told her his name and where he was staying and hung up.

He went back to his room and bolted and chained the door before he noticed the green luminance in the darkness. It pulsed brighter as he turned, and he noted that the cutting stone emitted a haze of light. It took a moment for his eyes to adjust and recognize it wasn't light at all but a gas or vaporous plasma deliquescing from the rock.

Henley stood for a long time, mesmerized. This was a tricky gas. Against the dark windowpanes, it appeared feathery and iridescent. Along the ceiling, it billowed in small dark streams. Henley pulled his attention to the stone. There, the vapor folded over itself slowly, like a flower blossoming. It entranced him, and he kept his gaze fixed on it until something of another texture altogether appeared in its depths. There against the surface of the jade-colored rock, a shiny wet substance oozed. Slowly, a knob of clear jelly striated with smoky colors bulbed out. It extended pseudopods and slimed along the edge of the sill.

Henley snapped on the light switch. Nothing happened. Tungsten coils glowed maroon, and the room remained semi-dark, crepuscular in the thin vapor light of the stone.

A cold finger touched Henley between his shoulder blades, and he shuddered and spun around to leave. As his hands fumbled with the dead bolt, a horrible thing happened. The idiot's voice, scrawny and demonic as in his nightmare, called out from behind: *Fear arrives like a runner. Shut your ears big, Henley, and look — shadows go by long after bodies have passed. Your eyes blow backward.*

Henley whimpered and turned from the door. The ichor squeezing from the stone had stretched into a membrane quivering in the air like a sea plant. It was still pulling from the rock, and in the half-light Henley thought he could see a net of fine blue capillaries webbed within it. Though overwhelmed by a frantic urge to flee, he stood motionless, the voice booming in his head holding him fast: *Dark carries you, broods like wells in the deep ground. You can't run, nowhere to run, for you and I are the same.*

A soft moan forced out of Henley's lungs, and he pivoted. The dead bolt clacked open, and the chain lock jangled free before a loud noise popped behind him followed by a frying sizzle. Henley glanced over his shoulder as he fidgeted with the door latch. The viscous protoplasm had snapped free, and it swam through the air toward him, a small shivering mass the size of a fist. Curly-edged feathers of flesh trailed below it, as from a jellyfish, and the whole bulk, dimpled with blood spots, arrowed for his head.

Henley swung the door open and bolted into the corridor just as the tendrilous thing caught up with him from behind. Icy snug fingers wrapped around the back of his head and over his ears. Something hard and needle-sharp pressed against the nape of his neck, forcing the base of his skull. He scrambled for the stairway, stumbled and fell. The corridor went suddenly white, as if blasted by lightning. A hot pain pierced him between the eyes, and Henley understood, with a spasm of terror, that the thing had punctured his skull!

Lurching to his feet, he jerked forward a pace and plunged over the stairwell with a stammering cry. He bounced off the top steps and careened over the banister into space. For an awful moment his head bulged, rupturing at the seams, and then the blur of steps braked. Henley could see the yellow wallpaper spin off gracefully to one side as the stairs swung up from below. He floated. Gravity hugged him strongly around his waist, and he sensed something within pushing out, buckling space around him so that he descended very slowly. Only the piercing ivory pain pithing him through the back of the neck to a point between his eyes kept him from marveling.

Abruptly, the pain cracked and shot down his spine. With a terrifying explosion, the stoop of stairs that he was settling toward banged apart and splintered across the vacant lobby like a broken vase. Henley slapped to the ground amid a patter of dislodged plaster and lay there stunned, trying not to faint.

Stomach muscles knotted again, and a powerful surge of strength hoisted him to his feet. Some movement down at the opposite end of the lobby caught his eye, but he couldn't make sense out of it in the whistling deafness. Mechanically, his body turned, swung over the blasted stoop and lumbered up the stairs. In his room, Henley collapsed.

Some sense of self-control returned. His head throbbed, and trickles of dark, almost black blood dripped over his cheeks from the back of his head. With one finger, he explored the nape of his neck and a deep hole there, too painful to probe. He swayed to his feet and leaned against the wall. People scurried up and down the hall.

Gradually, one thought cleared itself from the terror. His cache. Quietly and quickly as possible, he shuffled over to the night table and sealed the cotton ditty bag with the heroin in it. He debated for a moment about flushing it down the toilet and getting himself to a hospital. That idea closed down immediately. He felt trapped and terrified. The smell of something broken in the air troubled him, and he knew that he had to get away and think all of this through.

He clambered down the fire escape outside his window. Two cop cars had pulled up in front of the Elton. So, he skipped through the alley and jumped a fence to Twenty-Seventh Street. Glistening with sweat and shaking ferociously, he slid along the storefronts. Whatever had leaked out of the rock and attacked him, it had burrowed into his skull. He could feel part of it quavering at the mouth of the puncture wound. Sickened with despair, he wanted to get help immediately, heroin or no. But he couldn't stop walking. His body marched on mechanically, sleepwalking with him awake. Eyes glazed like small brown fruits, he stared past pedestrians who saw him approaching and gave way, widely.

The moon sang down around him, grim and cool, and he walked on, sticking to the darker cross streets. Hours later, he stopped on a tiny side lane, virtually an alley, whose name he hadn't seen. A shop front with iron bratticing opened, and an old, old man, skin gray and hackled as bark, urged him in. The old man leaned forward like a dead tree and studied him with eyes bright as pins. Visions had made his face unearthly, battered-looking. He wore a mantle sewn with seashells and porcupine-quill scrollwork, and he remained still, hooded like a cobra, silent, beckoning Henley with a sway of his head to enter.

Henley stepped a pace into the shop, faltered a moment as he surveyed the place. A wing-feather fan from an eagle covered one wall. A stuffed monkey hung by its genitals from a ceiling crusted with black mussel shells. The odor of the room smelled sticky. In a polished claw foot burner with talons spread, an orange lump of olibanum squatted, and as Henley turned to view the coils of a white python nailed to one of the rafters, its hognose head watching him with dusty eyes, the old man lit incense coals. Yellow vapors wafted across a rickety shelf, seethed over husks of seahorses, the molt of a tarantula, red-speckled seabird eggs, and amber and green bottles stopped with thumbs of apes.

Trills of canaries glimmered in the room. Lizards that would eventually devour the bright birds drowsed below in cages crafted from twigs. A yellow and papery light, filtered through tall lanterns stained with images of serpents and squids, gave everything an umber cast. In that light, the old man, who had closed the door and was now motioning Henley to sit, looked ageless.

Henley sat in the corner and watched anxiously as the old man approached, trouser legs hissing. He held a thin bone whistle to his lips and blew a brittle note. "I been waitin' a long time for you." With womb-soft tread, he stepped closer. "*Cthulhu fhtagn!*" he spit, and Henley felt a surge of strength. The old man stood wrapped in a cloak of shadow. "You knaw nuthin' 'bout what has you. Well, I got to say, dat is best." He leaned far forward out of the darkness, and Henley saw he had only one eye. A shard of mirror had replaced the other, and confronting his reflection in it, he grew faint. Henley's eyes had so widely dilated no whites showed, and around the corners of his mouth a scaly blackness crusted. "You knaw nuthin' 'bout de way dat has you. And dat be good. Dat be best good." The old one pulled the bone whistle to his parched mouth and sucked a sea chant, a modal hymn, which seemed to come from all around. Listening to it, Henley knew both that his life had shrunk to a small animal dying in a bottle and that he would live forever in the open spaces of lone birds.

Rapf's head was going bad. There had been too many lousy breaks. When he learned that Henley had signed out of St Vincent's, he went to a gunshop and got several extra clips for the Walther automatic. Staying in the city scared him, and he drove out to his sister's place in Stony Brook. By the time he got there, Henley's message had come through, and Rapf wheeled back into Manhattan. At the Elton, the cops had left no wiser than when they arrived, and there were several people in the lobby, grouped together, mumbling. Nobody had any idea what had happened.

Henley's door stood unlocked, and Rapf entered without knocking. Except for a squelchy odor in the air and several drops of dark blood on the floor, the place was vacant as a sucked egg. Lights blazed, and wind flowed through an open window. When he went over to check the fire escape, he spotted a small dull rock with curious etchings on it. Rapf at first thought it was a paperweight. When he examined it more closely, he recognized it was like nothing he had ever seen before. He pocketed it, searched the bathroom scrupulously and left.

Rapf rarely got drunk, and when he did he became so tight only violence could unspool him. He went down to the Red Witch and got skunked enough to call his old field captain. The last time he had seen Vince Pantucci was Can Tho when they were spreading a little lead around some of the villages, hoping to enrage Charlie. Shortly afterward, Rapf got caught smuggling M-16s out of the country. Pantucci was the ring's honcho, and Rapf did two years without fingering him. Since then, Pantucci had completed his tour and walked. Rapf knew he was in the city. He had been hearing tales about him for over a year. The man was mean. He was the only person that Rapf knew who could really move weight — other than Gusto. And he wasn't talking to Gusto.

Getting in touch with Pantucci proved difficult. He was big time now and stayed low. Eventually, Rapf had to drop a few lines about gun running to make contact. An hour later, Pantucci stalked into the Red Witch. A big man, wide as an oven, he had arms like dock ropes and tight brass-red curls that boiled up around his neck from under his silk shirt. Dark cave-squatter eyes spotted Rapf instantly, and he muscled through the happy hour crowd and into the booth. "Why are we here?"

"I need a favor."

Pantucci had the face of an Etruscan — ethereal cheekbones, flat forehead, and skin the color of baked earth. "What's it gonna be then?"

"Look, captain . . . "

"The captain *is* looking, Rapf, and he doesn't like what he sees. You're strung out, aren't you?"

"Nah. I'm clean. But I got caught sideways in a sour deal."

"Dope?"

"Yeah."

"Ganja?"

"Another class."

"Schmeck. How much?"

"More than two kilos."

Pantucci made a disgusted face. He slapped Rapf on the cheek and twisted his ear till it hurt. "You kid your captain." He pulled Rapf by his ear halfway across the table until their noses practically touched. "You move dub with strangers until you get boxed. Then you cry for me?"

Rapf pulled himself away and slumped in the corner, looking vaguely disgruntled. "I didn't know you moved that stuff."

"You mean you thought you'd get more play elsewhere. Who's the muscle?"

"Gusto."

Pantucci coughed up thick phlegm and hawked it into the sawdust. "What a weasel you are, Mike. What'd you expect? You think you're a brother?" He stared for a moment into the thin cold eyes opposite him, engaging the emptiness he saw there. They were the most remote eyes he had ever known. They reminded him of Ia Drang Valley and long swamp roads. He shook his head and looked away. "Give me the plot."

"Easton's brother Henley copped in Seattle and crossed to the city while I lined up Gusto. Along the way something happened. He went into a coma. By the time I found him at St Vs, Gusto was working on me. Now I know Henley's got the stuff, but he lit out. I guess he still thinks I was responsible for his brother getting clipped at Ngoc Linh. We patrolled together. I don't know. I was thinking you might find him."

"So you can deliver to Gusto? I don't work for the brothers, mongoose."

"Yeah, well I do." The wings of Rapf's nostrils whitened. His hands were under the table. "My ass is on the line. You owe me, captain."

"How do you even know Henley has it?"

"Why else would he run?"

Pantucci looked down at his thick hands. "Give me the man's profile."

In the mountains, Pantucci had a villa with an indoor swimming poll and a live-in maid and cook. He set up Rapf there. Taking advantage of a metalworking shop for retooling stolen goods, Rapf spent a few hours trying to bore a hole in the strange rock he had found in Henley's room. It was no good. The rock was harder than any drill bit could scratch. He liked the rock. He liked its heft and silky texture. It was the size of his palm with a few natural holes on its edge. After a while, he was able to thread some wire through one of the holes, and he wore the rock around his neck.

Pantucci found Rapf catnapping on the veranda a few days later. Trembling smells of cedar bark and pine riffled on the breeze. Sunlight buzzed off dusty rocks. "I located him."

Rapf sat up. "Where?"

"He left an hour ago for Haiti." He waved a packet of paper slips. "Here's your ticket and passport. There will be money at the airport and a gun permit. Go in peace, mongoose. And remember. We're square."

Rapf arrived in Port-au-Prince wearing dark glasses, a USMC muscle shirt, and black flight pants tucked into steel-tipped boots. He carried an attaché with a few changes of underwear, twenty-five hundred dollars in traveler's checks, five hundred dollars cash and his Walther automatic. On the flight, he'd taken his butterfly out of the attaché and slipped it into one of the many pockets on his trouser leg.

Deplaning, Rapf scanned the crowd, searching for any of Gusto's men. It wasn't until he shouldered through the throng in the pavilion that he knew for sure they were laying for him. Hard metal pressed against his spine.

"Awright, fool, you're comin' with me."

He recognized the voice. It was the hit man he had tumbled in the parking lot. He nudged Rapf out of the crowd with the barrel of his gun. Rapf groaned loudly and dropped to the ground. As he fell, he palmed the butterfly, sprung it open under his chest and swiveled his attaché to block the gun. The killer turned and bent down to free his gun for a shot. As he did so, Rapf rolled and stood up quickly, forcing the barbed end of the blade between the man's ribs. With a twist, he severed the aorta and yanked his knife free by pushing the man away.

The crowd dispersed fast, and Rapf lost himself in knots of scurrying people. A few minutes later, he was in a cab heading into town. He booked himself into a cheap hotel in the East End and began asking around for Henley. No one in the city had seen him, and on his second day he went out to the dirt-farmer markets near the shantytowns. He had bought a white jellaba and, despite the heat, wore it so that he could carry his Walther inconspicuously. It was only a matter of time before Gusto's men hunted him down.

In the native-dominated marketplaces, the rock he wore like a talisman around his neck drew a lot of attention. No one would touch it, though everyone wanted to see it. Three boys with the feral air of bay pirates — brash gold teeth, oil-soaked T-shirts, reversed crucifixes — tried to tug it off his neck. They questioned Rapf about it first, mumbled something in a language he didn't recognize, and then, just when he realized he had missed some sort of cue, one of them snatched at the rock. The wire cord bit into Rapf's neck and held. His eyes tightened to a squint, and he elbowed the boy in the mouth. The other two drew long cruel knives from their thigh sheaths.

Rapf spun on his heels and spartled in and out between the stalls heading toward the alleys of the shantytown. The boys ran after him, whooping and throwing fruit and rocks. In the alley, Rapf stopped short and curled around, both hands holding his Walther automatic way out front. The boys fell over each other trying to pull up. They backed away slowly, and at the mouth of the alley one of them made a gesture Rapf didn't understand and cried, "*Cthulhu fhtagn!*" The sound of his voice had a shrill, frightening quality that unsettled Rapf more than the sight of their knives. He decided to call it a day.

Henley Easton had lost complete control of his body. It moved by another will, and he merely observed. The last days that he spent in his body riddled him with madness. He had begun to alter rapidly after he found his way to the old man in New

York. Autway was the old one's name, and he was a sorcerer, a Voudoun *gangan*. He carried a calabash filled with snake vertebrae, and whenever he rattled it, the men in his presence responded. He never had to speak directly to them. The sound of the calabash imparted sufficient instruction.

When Henley's body began to change, Autway provided loose-fitting white trousers and a wide-sleeved anorak with a hood that allowed him to move freely and didn't chafe his sensitive skin. A black squamous growth that had begun around his foot wound and his mouth spread quickly over limbs and torso. His skin itched terribly and emitted a thick putrefying odor. Autway salved this anguished flesh with the pulp of crushed roots and somewhat eased the discomfort.

For over a week, they kept him in a spacious cellar hung with draperies of dark nubbling. Autway came down frequently with younger men, all of them dark with wide faces that had the cast of full-blood Indians. For hours at a stretch, they rattled gourds and chanted, "*Ph'nglui nglw'nafh Cthulhu R'lyeh ugah'nagl fhtagn.*" The sounds they intoned had a peculiar effect on Henley. Hearing them, he felt star-calm, crazy-alive, glittering with energy. The rhythms spun a vortex around him of mutable, luculent sounds, sometimes dark as the sea, sometimes streaming fire. Often, the songs charged him so full of power his body rose and turned about in lithe, sleek movements. The others imitated him best they could, but none could match the demonic fury with which his body wheeled and pitched.

By the time they left for Haiti, Henley's face had darkened with scales. Ears, cheeks, forehead and scalp remained clear, but he had the mouth of an iguana and black circles ringed his eyes. After some febrile explanations at the airport about how sickly he was, no one made a fuss.

Autway brought him far out to the North End and a trench hut on the mountainous outskirts of the slums. There the chants continued, only now there were many more people, kettle drums, torch parades, and the ceremony of *zilet en bas de l'eau*, the worship of an undersea island. At the peak of the ceremony, elderly devotees gouged themselves to death with sharp stones. Henley watched in horror as his body danced its insane, impossible movements.

During the days, he walked about restlessly with the anorak pulled up over his head. His body swayed through the shantytowns. He seemed to hover over the ground, shifting his weight like so much smoke. The breeze wherever he went, full of patterns, flitted shadows around him without any apparent source. Workers stopped in the fields when they saw him coming and blew high lonely notes on whistles made from the wing bones of seabirds.

Once, as he drifted down a shanty road, a very tall woman with yellow eyes and wild tangled braids came out of a shack carrying a child. She laid the infant in the white dust, stood before Henley and lifted her skirts. Her eyes appealed, charged with sorrow like a dying horse, and Henley understood that the baby was dead. With long fingers, she touched her breast, then slowly, slowly, her sullen eyes staring, she glided the tips of her fingers down over her belly to the cloud of hair below. That moment, a swirl of shadows like a shifting pattern of clouds played around the small corpse, and it stirred. A muffled outcry shook loose from onlookers who had stayed hidden in their huts. The woman fell to the side of the child, her face slippery with joyful tears. The baby looked up at him not with an infant's wonder-bright gaze but a fully alert, seductive stare that promised violent knowledge deeper than innocence or guilt.

Another time, on a side street in North End, two blacks wearing cutoff denims and bulky pajama-striped jackets over clean white T-shirts confronted him. They looked malicious. One was missing half an ear. The other had on a large hat and dark glasses. The one with the glasses grabbed Henley's arm and felt its spongy consistency. He let it go like a hot wire and jumped back. The abruptness of his action spun Henley around to face them. Inertia tugged back the hood of his anorak, and the two men gaped, unable to move for a rigid moment. Then the one with half an ear drew a gun. Henley's stomach tightened, and the gunman flew backward, tumbling to the ground. Henley pulled up his hood, walked down the street and turned a corner. In the secluded alley, his stomach knuckled again, and he hoisted into the air, light-stepping over tin roofs until he settled into a garden patch several houses away.

Henley no longer felt awed by such feats. The terror of dislocation from his will had numbed him to all surprise. Memories of his previous life dimmed, and he watched events shaping themselves around him as if in a dream. Even when Autway led him up into the mountains to see the star pools, he arrived unmoved.

Beyond spectral shapes of moss and fern and tall cypresses that spired above enchanted swamps, far up in the smoky hills, they came to a series of large ponds devoid of all vegetation. Hewn logs and packed gravel banked poolsides, the work of many generations. On their shores at irregular intervals reared monoliths of black rock, graven inscriptions exhausted by time.

Standing there beneath a quail's-breast sky with wind blowing in off the pools and swirling around their heels like a discarded garment, Autway let out a low moan and began chanting. The red light of dusk moved as if it were a breeze on the water. They stood facing east until darkness settled around them. Henley's body became very excited. A ringing in his collar bones began at the sound of the old man's droning voice, and the thick muscles massed in his legs stirred. Barely able to remain still, shuffling feet sounding like breath, breath like a forgotten language, he watched the stone star, the moon, rise over the black water.

By moonlight, he intuited something stirring under the water. There, many shapes massed as one shadow. They moved closer beneath the surface, and the expectation of their arrival nailed his breath. A splash sounded far to the left followed by a loud scuttling noise on the rocks. Something approached.

Henley's body unsealed its breath and inhaled deeply. Slow as a planet, he turned to face the darkness. Labored wingbeats sounded from a distance. A hulk loomed on the dark edge of the pool. Outlined in moonlight, Henley couldn't make sense of it. Writhing gouts of flesh and a tangle of limbs moved with slippery grace and then, abruptly, narrowed and slipped back beneath the glass-grained water.

A torpid languor overcame him. Autway steered him away

from the shining water. Henley felt wrong. His body had never labored so wearily before. By the time they got back to trenchtown, his movements had nearly locked up, rigid with exhaustion.

He slept dreamlessly, and when he woke Autway relentlessly marched him into the countryside again, this time to a remote channel where limestone dust from the quarries thickly covered the shore in duff pristine as snow. Three white huts crouched there, and, beyond them, an albino horse watched from a corral. Henley's fright of recognition jerked him taller. To his left, drifting in the lazy current, a white catboat with one man standing glided closer.

Autway rattled his calabash, and the boatman punted to shore. With great trepidation, Henley watched him moor his boat and remove a black jug.

"De lurkers will naw come until we purge you."

Purge me! Henley watched the white horse's pink eyes watching him while it champed. He wanted to face Autway and couldn't.

"Yas. We must make room for de Host. We gone take you out. Too bad we can't kill you, but dat dere is bad for de Host. You naw get with your bruthers, *les morts*. Nyarlathotep cotch you and now let go. *De l'eau noir*, the black waters cotch you. You gone dere. You gone to go."

The boatman approached with the jug in his hands. His cretinous face smiled at nothing, blank and washed as the sky.

Autway stepped closer, whispered in Henley's ear. "If even de earth itself knew. But dere is naw way to know. Speak to de dead and what do dey say? 'I can be anyone.'"

Henley's bones filled with a cold mist as the idiot offered Autway the jug. The *gangan* took it reverently and turned to Henley. His face pressed close, a crust of harsh planes, and the shard of mirror clouded. He spoke, and there was steel in his voice. "Silence be your shepherd. What is beneath you be triumphant."

Autway tilted the jug so that its mouth gaped before Henley's eyes. He leaned out of his body toward it and looked down. There were lights, tiny and dim, moving there. They swung closer, swirls of stars and misty galaxies flying apart through dread night. He fell, baffled, booming with fear. Midnight black gulfed him, and there would have been a tremendous scream, a howl hysterical and depraved, but for the soundlessness of those blind depths.

Rapf rounded the corner of the scabrous hotel where he had left his attaché. He peered through a chink in the wall that he had made with his knife when he first arrived and spied movement within. Cursing under his breath, he made out Duke Parmelee and Hi-Hat Chuckie Watz. They had scattered his underwear on the floor and were cutting open the mattress of his bed.

Rapf entered the hotel and edged up to his door, Walther drawn. Touching the body-warmed metal to his lips, he banged into the room.

His gun swung from man to man, and he hissed, "Don't move, screwfaces, or I kill you!"

Rapf closed the door behind him. Quick as wit, he had the two men sprawled against the wall while he removed their weapons. The Duke carried a forty-five Magnum, a switchblade and a pair of handcuffs. Hi-Hat had handcuffs, a thirty-eight, a serried blade in a sleeve-harness, and a hand-grip fitted with razor blades. "Feisty," Rapf said, waving the knuckle-grip. He threw it down on the bed with the other weapons and made the men crouch with their heads between their knees. Then, he pulled off their shoes and tossed them across the room. "Okay, strip." When they hesitated, he kicked each of them so hard their heads clunked against the wall.

He commanded the naked men to handcuff their right wrists to their left ankles, then he lowered his gun and picked up Hi-Hat's serried blade. "You know, my better judgment says I oughta kill the two of you." He yanked the mattress off its springboard. "But I believe in justice." Using the thick blade as a lever, he pried loose two hard-coiled springs and all the wire attached to them. "Justice tempered by vengeance. Oh, yes." He prized free more wire and began intertwining it. When he had a long braid of tightly plaited wire, he measured it against the length of their bodies and made a few adjustments. "It's a good thing I got an even temper or I'd mutilate you tough guys."

"Gusto wants you dead," the Duke growled. "So you better kill us while you got the chance."

"I got a little Cong trick I want to pull on you sweethearts." Rapf took more measurements with the wire and fashioned it into two crude harnesses. "I don't want you dead. I want Henley."

"Forget Henley," Chuckie whispered.

"Why so, pretty boy?"

"Henley's freaked."

"Yeah? Well, reserve your opinions till after I jump him."

"Man, Henley's out," the Duke said. "I mean he's not even human anymore."

Rapf smiled. He had finished. He used the Duke's switchblade to cut their clothes into long cords out of which he made binding. As he tied Hi-Hat's ankles together, the Duke swung around with his free hand and sunk his fingers into the back of his neck. Rapf's knife hand whipped and skewered the Duke's palm.

"Mother!" Rapf bawled. He rubbed the back of his neck and pointed the bloodied tip of his knife at the Duke who sat silent and brooding. "For that you jokers get an added attraction." He finished binding their legs and arms and undid the handcuffs. Gently and with some pride, he slipped the nooses of wire around their necks. The adjustable nooses attached to a wire hooked by an ingenious rider-knot to the springs. He did the same with their feet before handcuffing them and cutting off the rags.

"The beauty of your situation, fellow deviants, is that the more you struggle, the tighter the wire gets. Squirm enough, you die. But if you're good and sit rock-steady, somebody, *someday*, may find you here."

Rapf stuffed their underwear into their mouths and gagged them with a rag cord. Before leaving, he pulled the shade and put the weapons and his clothes and money into his attaché. He found the proprietor in the lobby, a man with meat-colored eyes and toothless mouth sucked in. With strained courtesy, Rapf paid the money to rent his room for another month.

Rats ruled the back alleys, and after some hassle, Rapf managed to box two large ones. He hauled the oil-soaked carton to his room and let them loose. Hi-Hat jerked violently when he saw them, and the wire drew blood at his throat. "Don't get excited, fellas. At least wait till they start chewing on your toes." He closed the door and fidgeted with the lock, forcing it to jam.

Rapf headed north. For several days, he went in and out of small hill villages asking about Henley. No one had seen him, and even if they had, Rapf had the distinct feeling he'd be the last one they'd tell.

He sensed someone following. Once, he glanced over his shoulder to see a bay pirate working a nail into a footprint Rapf had left in the dust. His talisman awed the people he met, yet no one would speak with him. Finally one morning, after finding a rusted jackknife near his campfire, the blade closed on a shred of paper with his crude likeness scrawled on it, he decided to call it quits. He still had most of the money Pantucci had given him, and he considered going someplace exotic to hide out from Gusto.

The next day, he spotted Henley. Or what looked like Henley. Rapf picked out the coral-red hair from a long way off. The sighting took place in a decrepit trenchtown several kilometers out of North End. Here and there among the glinting litter of tin and broken glass a seabird poked, some perched on stumps and tall bamboo poles. Above, a high wind thinned clouds into long fish shapes. A lone bird rode a ring of wind.

Rapf kept his eye on the red hair as he jogged into town, attaché wagging beside him, white jellaba swelling behind. The closer he got, the less like Henley the figure looked. For one, the character was too tall, way over six feet. And there was something about the way he stood, legs akimbo, head tilted to one side like a puppet, that wasn't Henley and, very nearly, wasn't human.

The figure ahead stood alongside a rusted jeep that had large eyes painted on its fender, and Rapf peered so intently at him, he didn't see the old man. Autway stepped from behind a tarpaper shack and grabbed Rapf by the arm. When Rapf turned to face him, he squinted into sunlight flashing from his face.

"'Scuse me, fella. I want words wit you."

Autway turned, and Rapf saw himself in the mirror shard of his eye. "What do you want, old man?"

"Dat mon over dere is not de mon you lookin' for."

"How do you know I'm looking for anybody?"

Autway shook his calabash. He had a dog-crucifix around his neck, and he touched it. "I am this here *gangan*. I know why you come here."

"Yeah? Why's that?"

"You would find Henley Easton."

Rapf's eyes narrowed. For one delirious moment, he thought one of Gusto's men had nailed him. But then the old man rolled his one eye and leered, showing black teeth. He wasn't one of Gusto's.

"How do you know that?"

"I told you. I am this here *gangan*." He rattled his calabash, touched the dog-crucifix. "You are Michael Rapf, eh?"

Rapf screwed up his face, reached out to grab the old man's stained mantle, thought better of it. "Yeah, and who fingered me? Henley?"

"Naw. This here *gangan* knows."

Rapf shook his fist at Autway. "You will be gone-gone if you don't start giving me some straight answers."

Autway nodded. Knots of hair tossed across his haggard face, and he brushed them back. "You muss leave — quick. Dat is not Henley. Henley is afar us all."

Rapf put the attaché down. "He's dead?"

"Worse. Naw dead — afar us all."

Rapf stared through curtains of heat at the tall man alongside the jeep. Some young men clustered around him — the toughs that had pulled knives on Rapf and driven a nail through his footprint. "Mister, I haven't understood a thing you've told me."

"Den I will be forward. Dis voudoun salango. Dere is nuthin' like dis in de States. All power and weirding. Dat mon over dere *was* Henley Easton. But naw more."

Autway moved his calabash gently, and the tall man, as if hearing it, turned. When Rapf saw the man's face, he knew at once that it was Henley. They were his eyes. That was the line of his jaw. That was his red hair. But that was all that was his. The skin gleamed oily black. Not negroid but ink black. And the body appeared all wrong. Bizarrely elongated, loose as a marionette. Seeing it standing there cool and lean, eyes bright as nails, Rapf felt his mind peel away. He thought of spring clouds breaking up over a long line of cold lakes, and he felt as if an ocean current, dark, awesome, swept him out beyond himself. It passed quickly, blurred off like the shadow of fish. It lasted only long enough to instill in him dread foreboding.

"What happened to him?"

"Dot you wouldn't understan'."

Rapf had to look away from Henley. He stared up at oyster-shell clouds, saw the full moon, a pale vapor in the day sky. "Tell me."

"De Old Ones — dey have corried Henley away. And dere, das dere messenger. Das Nyarlathotep. H-s-s-s-t!"

"Huh?"

"He de One dream Henley afar."

"How?"

Autway shook his head. "Best you ask why. How bring you to madness."

Henley turned and walked off with the toughs, drifting away as if a vapor. From someplace rose a thin mournful whistle.

"Dere are star pools in de hills. Up dere de minions take shape. B-r-r-r-p! De Kingdom been comin' for a long, long time."

" _ "

"You see — dot you wouldn't understan'. Dis be de Kingdom. Nyarlathotep de Key. De world de lock. Entering, de Key is a blindness in de lock's eye, de dream dat always returns."

Rapf ran a hand over his face, fingers trembling. He bent to pick up his attaché, and the old man laid a hand on his shoulder, rain-soft, urging him to wait.

"You want de drug?"

Rapf looked up at him with sharp eyes and straightened slowly. "You got the heroin?"

"You can have it. In exchange. For dat." He extended a knobbed coffee-colored finger and touched the talisman.

"You're kidding?"

Autway reached into his mantle and pulled out a large cotton ditty bag.

"Let me see that." Rapf snatched the bag and tugged it open. He fingered the powder inside and touched it to his tongue. His head snapped back, and he grinned. "You got a deal, old man." He pulled tight the bag, bent down and put it in his attaché. With one hand, he secured the case lock, and with the other he removed the stone from around his neck and handed it to Autway.

As soon as the *gangan* got his hands on it, he let out a giddy laugh that twisted under his tongue like a cry and curved off into a wail. "You stupid mon! Reap de wind. Thresh stone. All is lost. Now you done thrown away hope." He whooped.

Rapf scowled and stood up. Autway was already moving off, and Rapf watched him disappear down back wynds and alleys among the clustered huts. Despite the fact that he at last had what he wanted, he felt burned, and that was a dangerous way for him to feel.

He decided he wanted the stone back. This determination arrived as a dumb animal illumination, Rapf realized. Even so, that hunk of rock was suddenly important and getting to mean more each second.

Attaché under arm, Rapf loped down an alley, leaping over stacks of rubbish and debris. When he rounded the first corner, he pulled up short, swiveled on his heels and threw himself back out of the alley. He had his Walther out, and he sat hunched behind his attaché as a man with a bison chest and a tight, sad smile came around the corner. "Pantucci."

"Slow down, stooge." Pantucci swung his hands free of his body. "If I was gunning for you, you'd be dead already."

"Turn around, captain."

Pantucci spun about, graceful as a dancer. "I'm light as a feather, Mike."

"Sure you are. Lift those pant legs."

The captain lifted his trousers to his knees. "I've been in your shadow for days, dupe. I was waiting for you to connect."

"Yeah? Well, what's that to you?"

"Somebody's going to have to move that stuff. And all seriousness aside, Gusto wants you to suffer more than he wants that dub."

"You're stating the obvious."

"You don't think you can move that kind of weight yourself?"

"Captain, I know you haven't been dog-breathing me all these days to keep me out of trouble. You're here to make your good out of my bad. Now I know that. But if you want a part of this, you're gonna have to do what I say."

"Okay. Shoot — not literally, chump."

Rapf didn't smile. "First, we'll leave your bag of lethal anecdotes in the alley where you dropped it. I saw that carry bag. How many pieces you got there?"

"A Magnum."

"Great. The neighborhood kids will love it." Rapf stood up and put his pistol away. "Next we're gonna find that old man I was talking with. He's got something of mine. After that, we'll take percentages. All right?"

Pantucci nodded, eyed the attaché.

"Oh, yeah." Rapf ran a thumbnail along the length of his jaw. "Don't underestimate me, captain. You're a lot bigger, but I'm very fast."

They prowled the trenchtown for an hour and found no trace of Autway. Rapf decided to head into the hills along the one path available. Four hours later, after much trekking through cypress groves and fern-matted glens, they heard the rattle of Autway's calabash.

Pantucci was restless and wanted to move toward the sound. Rapf quieted him down, and the captain went off behind some bushes. Rapf moved along the trail a short ways and slipped into a chute of granite outcropping hung with Spanish moss. Presently, Autway came padding along the trail. When Rapf burst out behind him, he bolted. His speed was incredible. If Pantucci hadn't been up ahead, he would have lost him.

Pantucci grabbed him by his mantle and threw him to the ground. Rapf came up quickly and pressed the barrel of his gun against the old man's ear. "Where's my stone, grandpa?"

"Dot's not yours."

Rapf swiped him across the face with the butt of his gun. "Your life's not mine either, but I'm gonna take that too if you don't turn over the stone."

Autway's face bled, and his one eye strained wide with defiance. "I dawn have it."

Rapf raised his gun to strike him again, and Pantucci moved to grab his wrist. Rapf rolled off in a blur, came up in a crouch with the Walther aimed at Pantucci's head. "Belay that, captain!"

"Rapf, it's just a friggin' rock!"

"Mister, he laughed at me. It's not a friggin' rock to him."

"He's goofing you."

"Maybe." Rapf shook his head. "But I want that stone or I'm not leaving."

Pantucci lifted Autway to his feet by his ears. "All right, crabface, where is it? Talk fast and clear or I'll pop that eye like a grape."

"I dawn have it. It's back dere." He nodded over his shoulder, up the mountain.

"How far?"

"Far back. Deep in de forest."

Rapf grabbed a shock of Autway's hair and jerked him around. "Let's go get it."

"Hold on, Mike. He'll lead us into trouble. His boys are probably up there."

Rapf opened his attaché and took out the forty-five and the thirty-eight. He checked to see if they were loaded, then he took the knives and hand-grip out and threw them into the bushes. He shoved the attaché to Pantucci. "You carry Satan." He put the Walther in its holster and the thirty-eight under his belt. The forty-five he pressed against the back of Autway's head. "Drop your rattle here, gone-gone, and march."

Autway undid his calabash and started up the trail. As they

climbed higher, stillness settled around them like fog. Even the grass and the leaves went still as if lost in thought. Trees became larger, thick-boled old trees. After a while, the woods became so dense that only a few threads of light came through. In that calm radiance, dolmens and giant wheels hewn of rock and carved with curious oghams began to appeared among the trees, most of them half-buried or peering through luxuriant growths.

Soon Pantucci started getting restless again. He looked back over his shoulder. "Rapf, we're being watched."

"Is that right? Well, try to look your best."

A kilometer later, the trail narrowed to a trace so tight they had to lean forward to pass. A plangent breeze sifted through the forest.

"How much farther?"

Autway waved his hand, a gesture like wind in a sapling. "You go through dat brake up ahead and you dere. But go slow, mon. Go slow."

Pantucci pushed into a tangle of hedge growth, and Rapf shoved Autway after him. On the other side, they stopped and looked out across an expanse of pools with water green as fire. There were a half dozen ponds, ellipsoid, mirror flat, separated by huge mammocked trees and grasslands swaying in fumy and spirited mist. Beyond the green pools, the horizon hazed into jungle. A jade glow tinted the sky.

Pantucci gazed into the water, beguiled by pale sketches of coral shaped like ladders. A soft look touched his face. "This is a dream."

It is eerie, Rapf thought, focusing on a drowsy sound, the whittled-down thunder of waves shogging to shore far away. He looked hard at the glades of blue trees, some growing out of the water, bent like crones. He had to shake his head to snap out of it.

With the barrel of his gun, he turned Autway around. The *gangan's* face confronted him, calm and dark as amber. "Where is it, grandpa?"

"Wit dat what come from it." The seamed face grinned cretinously.

On the opposite bank of the nearest pool, from behind

a massively shaggy tree trunk, the long man with black skin emerged. He stood naked, elongated, unreal, and a sheen on his shoulders made him look like glass. His peculiar body light addled the air around him. He glided through the grass like an apparition, arms writhing, unjointed, undulant. Even as far off as he was, rounding the turn of the pool, all could see he was not human. Glassy flesh crumbled off his bones like soaked bread, and the bones themselves protruded long and rubbery.

Rapf fired without thinking. The bullet stopped him. Or seemed to. But the wrinkled air around him kept coming. Like a sheet of rain it billowed. As it approached, a whistle, very high and far, faraway, twisted in their ears. Abruptly, it shrilled to a wail, a projectile nose-diving. Then the trembling sheet of air swept over them, and the intensity jumped to a spinning siren. The whine became a needle skewed between their eyes, flinging them to the ground, limbs like fluttering rags. Ringing agony drilled into the bones of their teeth, shook vision to splinters, exploded louder with each heartbeat. The shriek went white-hot, and they knew it would kill them. Nyarlathotep was screaming.

Then, like a slamming door, the wailing stopped. Their ears kept roaring. Deaf as sod, they would have sat there in the rusted grass swaying like old women except for what began happening around them. All three of them saw it at once. Rapf quivered like a gong and Pantucci let out a pitiful moan. Autway began to laugh, then to howl.

Henley's black and distorted body writhed inhumanly on the ground, head bending backward to the feet, waist twisting full around. A huge greasy hole in its torso gaped where the bullet had exited, and that gap widened and rippled. The body peeled away, cracking open like a pod, droozing a quivering cheesy bladder — the delirious, gelatinous body of Nyarlathotep.

It was massive. By some abominable infusion, it swelled to twice the size of the body that hatched it. Its surface, covered with something sticky, a black sap, bubbling, running off at the sides, carried with it a bed of pearls, shiny curdled clods of milk, thick clusters of eggs. Something like pinworms needled over the gummy black silk, glimmering with a rabid bacterial fire. The body it pulled from reduced to a cake of filaments that crumbled and lapsed with blue volts to dusty embers cooking in a soft incarnadine light. Then the thick odor of singed grease wafted over them, and Pantucci retched.

Rapf couldn't take his eyes off the thing. It hovered a few meters off the ground, its jelly sac bloated with webs of blue-pulsing blood nets. Tendrils, lion-red, flayed open around mouthlike gaping seams writhing below the bulbed body. Tentacles pushed it off into the air, and it lifted, its hideous rippling hulk rising up over the puddling mess of its cocoon.

Rapf heaved himself to his feet. He intended to flee, to bolt like the wind, until another horror transfixed him. The pond churned. Dense forms rose to their shadows and broke the surface. Webbed appendages lashed among the foaming waters — flat faces, lizard-eyed shark maws splashed toward shore. Autway stood before them, arms outspread, wild hair whipped by his ecstatic movements.

The forms bobbed toward the bank, soaked black with the leakage and seepings of some putrid hell. Autway savagely danced, and Rapf heard him — he knew it was impossible, his ears were gluey with blood — yet he heard his cracked voice vomiting laughter: *"Nightmarer! Domn mine enemies! And corry me afar de dream. Vever dos miroir! O Nyarla! Sonde miroir! Nyarlathotep!"* And then, he was gone. A humped, bubbling gob lurched out of the pool and sprawled over him. For an instant, Rapf thought he could see the *gangan's* shocked, screaming face in the milky translucence, then there was only a red cloud in the midst of a throbbing amoebic thing.

Pantucci bellowed and clutched the attaché. With a whipped run, he scampered along the rim of the pool toward the forest. A beaked, squid-headed mauler slobbered to shore and with gangling limbs pursued him. He cried as he ran and desperately heaved the attaché away. It was no good. The creature was on him, all the seams and pleats of its throat fibrillating insanely as it lifted him up with one pincered, blotched arm. Even after the green-scaled beak crushed his face, he kicked spastically, swiveling his arms.

Rapf choked on his fear. A gun in each hand, he backed off

into the forest, blasting several rounds into a gaping eyeless sucker-mouth. He burst through the hedge and broke into a frantic clipped run. Howling and sobbing, he hopped among root-tangles, lashed through hanging vines, and slammed into a thick thorn bush, shredding his jellaba, tearing his flesh to be free, and kicking off into the grave-dark forest. He could hear nothing. Deaf and too terrified to glance back, he sensed only vibrations — dull, thudding sensations that reached him through the ground.

Rapf, lunging over the rotted shell of a tree, caught his leg on something and saw the green-tangled ground jerk toward him. His guns flew out of his hands and vanished in the bracken. Rude hands banged him onto his back, and he stared up into the gnawed and lacerated face of Duke Parmelee. Hi-Hat Chuckie Watz reared behind him, face puffed, scabby, the lower lip merely a crust. They both wielded heavy butcher knives.

Wildly, Rapf tried to communicate with them in the forced modality of the deaf, and merely voiced whimpers. The Duke stooped to start in with his knife. Something beyond the trees distracted him. Hi-Hat screamed first. Rapf saw his face wracked with horror. He shuffled backward, his foot tangled, and he fell to his back. Before he could rise, a segmented bulk with frantic legs and membranous wings descended on him in a blurred flurry. The Duke gawked bug-eyed and was still gawking when a lamprey with stalk-eyes lolled onto his back. He fled crazily this way and that, shrieking, trying to stab the slug-ball off his body, yet it clung to him, melled to his flesh. Finally, the slick mass swelled over his head, and he collapsed, still clutching at it.

While the Duke convulsed, Rapf rolled off, bucked to his feet and ran headlong into the clumsy hooked arms of something loathsome. The clasped forebrains of its head trembled voraciously, mandibles swiveling. Before it could crush him, Rapf unsprung his butterfly blade and slammed it into the agitated bulk. He spun backward, wheeled crazily to get his balance and then kicked off in a cloud of leaves.

Plunging down a steep bank, he tumbled head over heels in a clatter of stones and dust. His somersault splashed into marshy shallows and crashed to a stop against a thrust of boulder, head and shoulders underwater. The cool current revived him, and he shuddered to his feet, teetered like an old man, and plopped back into the water.

Above him, among the high bank's shrubbery, he could see humps of things lumbering in and out of view. Quickly, he rolled to his belly and dragged himself into deeper water. The stream buoyed him and carried him off.

Hours later, he came out of a faint and found himself washed upon a gritty shore. Pale ferns fronded nearby, framing tin roofs and cardboard doorways. He pulled himself to his feet, slowly, painfully, and limped toward higher ground. His ears still whined, and his head felt heavy. He could just make out the shadow of sounds: the stream clattering pebbles and the curse of gravel under his feet.

He hobbled mindlessly toward the town, in a daze, eyes small and shiny as a reptile's. His mind had shut, and he moved mechanically. The people who saw him coming shied away, except for the children who pelted him with stones and ran close enough to snag him with wire-strung tin cans and garbage. Rapf shuffled on, unaware, face empty, eyes drifting.

A day later, the local police picked him up outside North End. Kids with slings and crude blow darts baited him like a pariah dog. Though he had been reeling frantically from street to street, occasionally lashing out with pitiful cries, he gave the police no trouble when they cuffed him.

Days afterward, his mind shuttered into place. It took a long minute for him to take in the stained and pitted walls. Then the cretinous look drained entirely from his features, and he hunched over, weeping. When he had gotten hold of himself, he stood up by the bars of his cell. He could see in the faces of the police and his cellmates that he had been raving. They wanted to know what had happened, if it had been mushrooms or village *anis* that had gone bad.

Rapf waved all speculation aside, and in a halting, fragmented way told them what he had seen in the hills. The police laughed, and his cellmates remained quiet, eyes averted.

The next day, they freed him. By then, he regretted telling anyone anything. An officer from Port-au-Prince arrived to hear his story, and Rapf feared they'd somehow find out about the heroin and detain him. But the officer was only concerned with the exact location of the star pools, and Rapf told him.

The man seemed different from the local police. He was stocky, with still eyes. And he believed Rapf. Enough, at any rate, to send four men up along the trail Rapf had followed days earlier. They wanted Rapf to go along and direct them, and when he refused, melting before them to a quaking, sniveling mess, they left him behind.

That night, Rapf stayed in the prison cell. The suggestion that he go back up into the hills had so shattered him that he had needed a shot to quiet him down. In his sleep, he dreamed of a sun, black yet shining, with strange stars tapping in the dark blue of the sky. He sat alone in a damp alley, greasy brick walls rising on either side toward the alien sky. There was a smirch in the air of something burnt, and his stomach closed at the smell of it.

Then, from the far end of the alley an icy light wavered and a figure approached. A man, thin and long as a stick, carried something. As he drew closer, Rapf made out that his face appeared cushiony, chin slippery with drool, eyes remote. An idiot's face. His swollen lips moved in a whisper: *Shut your ears big, Michael.*

Rapf's whole body clenched at the sound of that withered, barely audible voice. He couldn't turn away. He fixed upon what the idiot carried — a black cistern with a wide mouth. His eyes locked on it, watching it approach, tilt forward and reveal blackness gem-lit by a splatter of tiny lights, pin-bright, like stars.

The lights wheeled, and watching them curve through the dark, Rapf succumbed to a lurch of vertigo, keeled over, and fell howling into the depthless dark.

He shrugged awake and sat still a long time before accepting coffee and bread. The four men who had gone up into the hills had not returned. The office wired for a helicopter to cover their trail and see if any sign of them turned up. When Rapf was strong enough to leave the police shack, he emerged in time to see the helicopter return. The pilot and his partner staggered from the chopper. They had seen something. Rapf didn't lag around to find out what.

The long, tedious walk into Port-au-Prince in his condition would take most of the day. When he got there, the American consul would wire his sister in Stony Brook for money. Then he could leave, get out before Gusto sent down more of his boys or the hills sent down what they festered.

He ambled to the edge of the slums and stopped at the side of the road that led to the capital. One last time, he looked back. The helicopter had gone up again. Its insectlike body glinted in the distance as it dropped toward the horizon, sunlight splintering off its domed glass, a wandering star burning alone above the hills.

Ten:

With that story, despite all its many flaws, the Black Goat received me fully as a *gof'nn hupadgh Shub-Niggurath*. She occupied and transfigured my deathward body. She smoked my soul in twilight. Sanity loosened, I felt Her fitting Herself more snugly to the shape of my psyche. By the violet light of the new moon, deep in a rain forest on Kauai, we pledged undying fidelity — and, to hold me to my word, She inflicted immortality on me. For that ceremonial occasion, the Black Goat requested an interview to appear in *The R'lyeh Times*:

> **S-N:** *So, now that you are officially mine, how are you feeling?*
>
> **AAA:** Happy as the grass! In the abiding words of the old psalm (105): 'For us, our days are like grass. As a flower of the field, so we flourish!'
>
> **S-N:** *No more talk of death. You are gof'nn hupadgh Shub-Niggurath! For you, death shall be an unplayed symphony, the masterpiece hidden beneath a canvas. You belong to me now. And death shall be a weird joy.*
>
> **AAA:** What does that mean? *Weird* joy? I never die while continuing to age until I wither into a geriatric grasshopper?

S-N: *Much more weird. Here is a parable of that joy: You are deep in a northern forest covenanting with spirits lifted into mist from an ancient tarn. The spirits show you a treasure. Buried in the rock flour milled by a Pleistocene glacier, a duck egg fossilized black fits your palm perfectly. To you, it is nothing. Merely an inglorious rock. You throw it away with indifference. It flies through the auburn autumn forest gleaming like a mystic gem. The erratic boulder it strikes, orphan of the glacier that mothered the fossil, hatches that egg. Inside is an inch of secret life, fossilized intact, hibernating the silence of the unborn, sealed up from the ambition of the weasel for 11,000 years, hushed and helpless in the abortive Lilith dark — exposed for your eyes alone.*

AAA: So much for death, huh? Well, then, what about money, Shub-Niggurath? It's expensive living forever. Also, I'm concerned, I mean now that You're pregnant. How am I supposed to support a thousand young? Sure, I'm getting the hang of this Mesopotamian magic, but will I earn enough money from it? You realize, of course, the same Sumerian magi who invented writing also contrived money.

S-N: *You want to know about money? Then, answer me these questions: For whom do you labor during this spiritless time the ancients dreaded, the Kali Yuga, where money is the silhouette of desire? Is your proper place in this incomparable mystery a sum in a ledger book?*

I would've immediately answered, "*Yeah!*" But from Her tone, I got the frosty impression silence remained my only acceptable reply. The interview ended there rather abruptly. I don't think *The R'lyeh Times* ran it. The whole experience of our cryptic love affair left me confused and scared — and I wrote a spell, "A Priestess of Nodens," to humanize the Old Ones and exorcise this oppressive sense of unreality. Regrettably, I achieved an opposite effect that only stamped deeper in my heart the savage, exultant sense of mystery that accompanies my fateful status as a *gof'nn hupadgh Shub-Niggurath*. This piece first appeared in Scott David Aniolowski's 1995 anthology *Made in Goatswood*:

ELEVEN:

A PRIESTESS OF NODENS

Twilight shrouds the Cotswolds. Laggard hills and autumn trees sink slowly into blue mist, and the sky slants toward night. On a slope of elm, six naked couples walk single file through the woods, hands interlocked. The wind burns with cold, and they move quickly among wrangling branches. Even the oldest ones, flesh fluttering, march spryly.

At the spur of a hill, they come to a glade of whispering alders where split cherry logs and crowns of dried roots have been stacked for a bonfire. The cadence of the march slows and takes on the float of a dance as the twelve circle the wood pile. Sunlight stands like smoke against the great trees, and the air fills with what the leaves can no longer hold.

After three rounds, the couples stop their dance, spread out into a circle and sit down in the resinous grass facing the unlit pyre. Their minds are quiet. Personal thoughts have been left behind, back at the camp with everybody's clothes. Now they are naked of body and mind, skyclad, waiting for the priestess. The cold deepens with their stillness, and several begin to hum softly to themselves.

As the sun sets, the air goes glassy. Night flexes around them, and everyone aches in their ribcages with shivering. The oldest among them is Violet, a tarnish-skinned crone with a flat stump of a head and neck muscles taut as roots. She is the coven's priestess, intimate with the Goddess, the spirit of life they have gathered to worship. Unlike the others, Violet does not shiver. She is enraptured, feeling the close presence of the Goddess. Warmth radiates through her with the excitement she feels for this ritual. Her earliest memories are just like this: crouching in the forest with others who, like she, are willing to abandon hope and all its separations and sit naked as the woods. The Goddess is not a world away but right here under them in the one Earth broken into trees, leaves, wind, and them. The purpose of the ritual is to acknowledge the reality of this unity. And, if the conditions have the precision of luck, they might move a little bit out of their lives toward life and waver inside the transparent vision of an awakened mind before surging back into their individual dreams.

The whistle of a morning bird trips out of the gloaming, and everyone's breathing tightens. The priestess is coming. Twelve faces peer into the darkness between the powerful trees, hoping to catch an early glimpse of her.

Violet smiles a little hook of sadness. Tonight is Samhain, year's end, the Night of the Dead. For over fifty years on this night, she has presided as priestess, using her apprehensions of the Divine to guide the others into reverie. Now, on this Hallowed Eve, maybe her last, the Goddess has sent someone else, a stranger. She is a guest of the coven, a traveler passing through. But they heard of her months before from a fen meeting at Stonebench, where she healed a deaf and dumb boy. And that group heard of her from a river commune outside Gloucester. There she had danced with an autistic girl and left her speaking and laughing, for the first time a normal child. Intrigued by the miraculous, the coven passed word on to her, not at all certain of receiving a reply.

When the reply came by phone and Violet had a chance to speak with the slow voice at the other end, she learned to her disappointment that she knew the stranger. Her name was Dana Largo, and she had belonged with the Coven of the Shining Face in Lydney. Violet remembered her as a pale, vaporous-looking woman with lank red hair and a squinted face. Something was wrong with her. Bad blood or cancer. And she had looked it: Her arms had been thin and white as fluorescent tubes and the sheen of her skull had glowed through the flesh at her temples. She had not been expected to live long.

The bad blood or the cancer eventually got worse, and she disappeared. Violet's friends in the Coven of the Shining Face had told her she had gone off to die alone. So Violet was surprised to find out that not only was Dana Largo alive but she had somehow been empowered by her dying. At least, so the other covens reported. Violet and all those of her circle, the Mulch Coven, who recalled seeing her at the big festival in the Forest of Dean more than seven years ago, could not imagine such a wastrel conducting a strenuous year's end ritual. But when she came to them, soft-eyed, with cheeks lean as a deer's and nettle burrs snagged in her red hair, they sensed at once her change.

On the phone, she had instructed them to meet her in an area none in the coven had visited before, a forested enclave called Goatswood. She had arrived at the camp strolling out of the wooded pass that led through dense tree haunts to the railway, her hand-stitched backpack laced with vine and flowers. She had said little, and her demeanor had been playful as she passed out posies of fire-colored leaves to the coveners. Judging by her bright rag travelcoat, cloth boots and the trim black bush hat she wore, Violet had thought her a hippie revenant.

Afternoon had been low in the trees when she arrived, and meditation for that evening's ceremony had already begun, leaving Violet time for only a brief exchange with Dana. They wandered to the edge of the camp, where a field of thistle grass clicked with the wind. "This coven is your family," Dana told Violet, speaking gently and personally, dispelling the old woman's disappointment. "I was invited as a priestess, but I'd be just as happy to join the circle and follow you tonight. You see, my devotion has gone somewhat beyond the Goddess to an elder god, an Old One, whose temple in Lydney has become my home. I'm afraid you'll find my practice unorthodox."

Violet had been tempted to accept leadership again. She was feeling very close to autumn earth, her old age a consummated decay celebrated in the leaves. Myriads of them, she had daydreamed all day, like thin flames shedding no light. Yet, because she was so borne away with the power of the season, she felt close to the Goddess, and she was clear. A mood of luck urged her to trust this young wanderer, to see for herself how unorthodox she was. And also, on a more mischievous level, she wanted comparision.

After sharing the traditional mulled cider with the coven, Dana Largo took her crude backpack and hiked out toward the ceremonial clearing. Beneath a hedge of hawthorn bracken, whose glossy leaves shed rain, she hid her large overcoat, hat and backpack.

Alone with autumn's imagination, she circled the glade of leafless trees a dozen times counterclockwise to unwind the tight feelings in herself. She forgot her journey in the relentless erasures of twilight. That is her great strength: She learned early and well how to forget.

Her personal memories faded, and she unwrapped her boots and let her strong, callused feet dance through the fallen leaves. A deer stared at her from among the last stairways of sunlight, and an owl hooted from another room in the forest.

Blood drummed in her muscles as she removed her sweater and the cold touched her flesh. The space of her forgetfulness was lucent with emotion. She untied the long braids that held back her hair. A dance unfolded through her, and she moved in a twirling step around the foot of an eel-branched hazel.

Nodens drew close to her, and Dana entered a state of terror and love. Terror as the cold sharpened with the wind and she became her true littleness. And love as a giant of feeling began to rise out of the loam.

Darkness thickened, and she pulled off her trousers to stand naked in the Presence of her elder god and the forest. She forgot the dangers of the world. She was a sacrifice to Nodens, trusting in the Old One's meaning. Standing perfectly still in the night, she was with all that trembles, all that hides.

The naked circle-sitters shiver only a short time before a morning bird calls out of the east where no morning is. All twelve stare in that direction.

Silence, while a fragment of moon appears over the shoulder of a cloud. All senses strain toward where the bird has sounded, and no one sees her until she is among them. She glides into the circle from the west, the direction of the dead, the moon's wraith-light shining blue off her skin. Her red hair gleams purple with night, and she has weighted strands of it with snail shells so that it moves like seaweed.

Her voice penetrates: "This is the night of darkness. Year's end. Between worlds. Life and death open into each other tonight. The dead walk and the living are a Dance of Shadows, meeting here and there, everywhere and nowhere, as us." A spark flares between her cupped hands and steadies to the calm flame of a taper. Radiance underlights her face, revealing sapience in slender eyes that shines green in the burning. She throws the taper onto the wood, and, with a startling flap of heat and refulgence, the pile roars into flames.

She's treated the wood, Violet reasons in the face of her excitement. Sparks crawl up the wind, and as the night folds back, the nakedness of the priestess seems to expand. Her white flesh glows with the fire's sheen, and the six men feel lust and mother-awe mix like pigments; the six women watch and watch, for what they see is more ancient than anything they have known. The priestess dances orgasm and birth-rack simultaneously. She dances more lewdly than the flames, and she suffers more cruelly than the twisting wood.

One by one, she pulls them to their feet and charms them with moving. They circle among fireshadows, bouncing like a fountain to the unheard music of their lives, following a cadence of flames and the wind.

Dana Largo shares the dance with each of the twelve. She shawls herself in their movements. She mimes them. And her awareness, streaming off her into the beard of the wind and its sparks and stars and flying darkness, slows to match their motions. The moment flutters and cramps, and within her mime she sees the vagaries and misdirections of each of their lives.

Between warming dances, the circle sits close to the flames, and the coven completes the new year scrying. All look ahead into the future together, some silently and some saying what they see. Usually, the scrying is uncertain as smoke, more self-reflection than prophecy. But on this night, visions are as majestically clear and unique as gems. The priestess tells each of them something about their doom in such a way that they are braver for it. And, in turn, Nodens speaks to Dana Largo: Violet stares through the priestess' hair into the flames. "I see the blood tree inside you — and the spiders of blood eating you! And an old tower — an old tower on a dark shore lit by the bright hair of angels. Astral voices — I hear them singing, singing sorrows of the other world. They sing of the mercy of darkness. And there you are again — but not you, yet you — your blood tree chewed to a lace of decay by the blood spiders. It's horrid! Your decayed body dancing with spiders in shadows under a purple sun . . . "

Violet jerks back, sinuses aching with the red smell of danger.

The priestess gazes at her with a rictus grin, her skull in the firelight shining through her waxy flesh. "You have seen the truth of me, Violet."

Violet blinks. The skeletal visage does not pass. "I don't know what I've seen."

"Then, I will tell you." The priestess leans closer, her face a fossil. "I am dead. The spiders in my blood have devoured me. But the Old One — Nodens — has restored me to a life. A life like no other life. You know of Nodens?"

Violet looks to the other coveners, and they stand about embedded in darkness, inert as tree boles.

"Nodens," the priestess repeats, and something inside Violet leans forward with all its weight and pulls her attention into the firepoints that are the priestess' eyes.

"The ancient Romans worshipped him."

"Oh, yes — they worshipped him." Flames seem to sit inside the priestess' head. "The Roman station at Lydney has a temple to the elder god Nodens. That is the old tower on the dark shore. You must be half dead now and faithless to this world to find it. I went there when I was far into my dying, when the Goddess could not, would not, stop my dying, for death is but the flip side of life to Her, a dazzling impermanence. That is the truth we celebrate tonight, isn't it? But Nodens took me beyond life and death, to the other world, to the light of the purple sun."

"Why?" Violet's words cake like cinders in her throat, yet she must know. "Why would an elder god take mercy on us?"

"For a dark purpose, Violet. I must serve him." The incandescent skullbones darken behind the priestess' swollen face, and her sadly wrung features become luminous and full of pity. "For this life he has given me, I must serve him, from the dark to the dark. Inside my cage of bone, I am a slave to the elder gods on the dark shore where the dead eat their unspeakable meals.

But I have nothing to say about the company of the dead. I serve the Old Ones well, and occasionally, as on this night, they allow me to walk again among the living and use the elder powers at my whim. That assuages a little the insufferable strangeness of my fate." The embers of her eyes flare hotter. "Tonight, I would use those powers for you."

A charge of fright sparks along Violet's spine. "Leave me be, weird sister! I belong to the Goddess."

"And the Goddess belongs to the Old Ones!" Dana's arms open to the night, and flametips on her fingers illuminate the bronchial branchings of the trees. "We are as sparks, Violet. We blow like pieces of burning ash over the sour weeds, and the wind consumes us beneath an empty sky. Our lives are as nothing to the elder gods. So, let me do a thing for you before I return to the dark shore, for it pleases me to please the living."

Before Violet can protest again, the priestess rises. Her fiery hair spreads into a sudden wind, radiant tresses braiding into ropes of stars that blaze lucently in the cope of heaven. She holds the massive night between burning hands, and Violet feels the spiders that web their threads in her lungs shrivel. Cool, sweet air fills the hollows of her chest, and the pain in her joints unknits. The cracked coat of lacquer on her skin softens and glimmers with a magnetic tingle, and the gnarled boniness of her hands unlocks, relaxes and smoothes into tapered fingers.

"What have you done to me?" Violet cries, and her voice has lost all the smoke of her weary years. "What have you done?"

But the priestess is not listening. She is dancing. And the others are dancing with her, joyful faces bright as apricots in the fire's light. The priestess beckons, and Violet's numb shock vanishes, replaced by a jubilation that lifts her to her feet and sweeps her into the circle dance with the others. And they dance and they dance until the empty sleeve of dawn drags its pastels across the sky.

The fire slows, and the priestess calls the coveners closer and has everyone lie down head to foot in a circle. She covers their bodies with leaves and feeds the fire with slow-burning root-burls so they will stay warm. Then, wonderfully clarion, she begins to chant: "As your thoughts are like a flight of birds, be the sky, wide as there is and open to everything. As your body is like the slow burn of a fire, be the light in the flame, cleanly burning earth and air. As your life is like a river, be the course of the water, one moment flowing the whole length of your being."

Some slumber. And long after Dana Largo finishes, some lay awake hearing her voice in the thin scream of the dying fire. A few see the shape of their lives, clear as teardrops, and are changed forever.

The sun crests the treetops of Goatswood, and Violet smiles awake, more alive in her bones than she has ever been. She wakes the others, and none of them recognizes the young, sable-haired woman standing over them, the pale, perfect, white viola of her body lovely as the Goddess Herself. They want to know where Violet has gone, and she laughs so deeply she cries.

Together, they look for the priestess. But there is no sign of her anywhere in the clearing or in the surrounding woods. Back at the camp, they find a pomegranate she has left on a stump. It is cleaved open with the ritual cut that reveals the star formed by the seeds.

TWELVE:

Can love stop time? Well, if your lover happens to be the Black Goat of a Thousand Young, the answer — in a scorched whisper — is a definitive *yes*! In fact, I'm writing this now from the court of *Azathoth* at the center of chaos, which is no center at all. Through a sympathetic courier, a demented *nug-soth* of *Yaddith*, I've managed to get these notes to a publisher, a fellow practitioner of Mesopotamian spellbinding, William Jones, who I pray will post this as a cautionary tale to any who foolishly believe they can thrive by sorcery. The volatile groaning you may hear as you read these lines is seepage through haunted fissures of the worldsheet, from a dimension inchoate and at apogee to all reason, where I currently find myself a very busy patriarch of my loathly offspring spawned upon Shub-Niggurath. They are a noisy and noisome bunch. And now the thought of death lurks as a forbidden reminiscence — a fathomless hope to this immortal responsible for endless feedings and ministrations. Literally *endless*. As for the All-Mother, She remains preternaturally present and absent, pretty much leaving me among Her clamoring brood to an onerous outcome too hideous for words. At last I understand why, at the height of my rapture with the Black Goat, I glimpsed Her spouse, the Not-to-Be-Named-One, laughing deliriously. He knew then I would wind up here in the court of *Azathoth* at the center of chaos, which is no center at all but a maelstrom of cacophony. I close with an account of my transit here, my final homage to Howard Phillips Lovecraft, published in Edward P. Berglund's 2003 collection of "Blasphemous Tales of the Followers:" *The Disciples of Cthulhu II* . . .

THIRTEEN:

TIME IN THE HOURLESS HOUSE

The more one knows, the less one understands.

— Dao De Jing

The Elder Gods lived there. Signs of them were everywhere in that place. But no one had actually seen them. I arrived, as most do, by losing the way. In my case, I made a wrong turn on a raindark street under a lamppost stoned blind.

Lean cats watched from between gnarled ashcans, hot eyes aglow with faint lightning that trembled like stuttering neon in the narrow sky. Head bowed under sifting rain, I paid more heed to the black cobbles and their oily haloes than to my surroundings.

When I did look up, I noticed curious rainworn architecture, pale gables of crocketed marble and gargoyled eaves. A chalken frieze of griffins and winged lions surprised me, so incongruous did it seem in my small metropolis of trolley tracks, townhouses and chimneypots.

That was warning enough for me, and I turned about, determined to go back the way I had come before losing my way worse. The alley lane seemed wholly unfamiliar. The cobbles had sunk to a cinder path between anonymous warehouses of gray, powdery brick. The rain had cleared off, and a large moon of tarnished silver drifted in a day sky above the dismal buildings. Disturbed by what I saw and did not recognize, I would not go that way.

In the direction I had been walking, beyond eroded marble edifices of angelic beasts, the alley opened onto warrens of withered weeds and ashy sleech. I wandered across that barren landscape toward a bleak pastoral of rubble overgrown with sedge and sumac.

Gradually, the terrain became more wild and profuse. Sunlight stenciled shadows in a dense wood of narrow trees. A small wind blew, tainted with leafsmoke. Through the skinny trees, I sighted a black pond, where a century of rain had collected, drowned trees leaching water to the color of night. Garish birds preened pink feathers among the cane brakes, and I surmised I had left the known world entirely behind.

My heart thudded dully in my chest, for I had read the arcane books that described this otherworld. I knew of the malevolent and dissociate aspects of this realm. Little doubt remained that I found myself among these sullen precincts as punishment for having read the forbidden texts. I knew that in the land of things unspoken, knowledge itself predicates violation. A fathomless kinship between mind and happenstance had summoned me to these purlieus of the unimaginable.

That strange equality had already been described by Ralph Waldo Emerson, who wrote in *The Conduct of Life* that "the secret of the world is the tie between person and event ... the soul contains the event that shall befall it ... the event is the print of your form. Events grow on the same stem with persons."

Until the day that I found myself trespassing alien ground, I had considered Emerson's philosophy intriguing yet not compelling. When I climbed the shale steps of a dried creek bed among slender trees, yellow leaves pouring around me in a sudden turn of cold wind, I knew what I would find atop the ridge. And so, though frightened, I was not terrified when I scrambled over the flat rocks, climbing from stone pool to pool, mounting a chine of heather swept by brisk sunlight and cloud shadows.

Atop that vast high country, I could peer down the curve of the world, and I saw in the blue sky, weird stars, red and green. And among them loomed planets and moons pinioned in comet vapors bright as a webwork of incandescent cirrus. Notions of immensity, that on Earth only the ocean could conjure, awed me. From atop my shelf of rock, I gazed a long time at that celestial vista and no doubt muttered to myself woeful thoughts and all things contained of dread therein.

The icy updrafts of gray mist eventually called my attention to what lay below — a stone path fiery green with lichen that descended through a high forest of pine into a dell of deformed apple trees, a gloomy orchard lit with mist and attached to a vineyard autumn had blackened. At the end of the bereaved valley, a grim house stood. Broad steps, tall fluted columns of rococo plinth and cornice fronted a stark facade.

This was the Hourless House that I had read about, where the Elder Gods dwelled. I was not appalled that it possessed neither the physical stature nor the ancient traits necessary to house such preterit beings colossal of both space and time. This house, and all else since my wrong turning in the alley, was woven in the thin thread of dreams. Nevertheless, I knew well, I knew very well indeed, it was therefore no less real.

Under the star-filled heavens, I climbed down the lichenous stone trace, cold, chilled by more than the wind, a blue animal trembling softly at what I realized awaited me. Ahead loomed the home of dark legend. From its ruined pillars dangled black ivy and gray dodder.

I approached among the deformed trees of the apple garth, and silver footsteps followed. The wind ran past with a figure of mist, then hung among the boughs the shape of a dead woman. My soul, I understood, descended from those branches, faceless under her long hair, colorless locks aswirl like smoke.

My soul in the leafless tree, creaking the dry wood with her lonely weight, turned slowly. Her silent scream expelled crows from the orchard, and they blew across the sky like faded chords of music, black notes scattering among slant clouds.

In the decayed vineyard, a dead angel sprawled. His raiment lay tattered and rain-bleached, impaled upon slatted ribs, one extra rib than man in that weathered brisket. Black mandrake sprouted among wingbones and what faded and frayed feathers remained. Thatched hair yet clung to his dried skull, and a perennial grin of perfect teeth greeted me from within a face naked of flesh. This was the source of the woodsmoke I had smelled earlier. The carcass actually smoldered on its bed of loamy compost, seething barely visible fumes of decay that lofted a fragrance of charred leaves. Appalled by this grotesque sight, I did not linger in that arbor of eternal autumn and hurried on to the Hourless House.

I climbed past cracked urns, up dilapidated steps, and entered the foyer. Stricken bats gusted from their coverts in the vaulted ceiling. Dead cold spots in the air identified where other presences stood, entities of other realities, other times, who had arrived at the same house but by different reckonings.

Warped parquetry squeaked underfoot when I advanced into the main reception room. Shards of glass from broken panes sparkled among the dust of bat droppings and furry lumps of inchoate dead shapes. No one emerged to receive me, save the invisibles that moved about as I did, felt only as cells of bright chillness and never seen.

Newel and finial stood intact upon the banister, and I mounted the slow curving stairs to the upper landing, where the balustrade had collapsed leaving behind only a few cracked spindles. Foliate scrollwork decorated the mouldings of the waterstained walls and the prolapsed and broken plaster ceiling. I called out the barbarous names I had learned in the arcane books. I called those ponderous names through the long, echoing rooms. As I climbed to the second landing, then the third, I called the thick names. I called them.

And they answered me.

"We are here!" they chimed as one, their cry awobble with echoes like submerged voices. "Here! We are here! Come to us!"

And I obeyed. I had read the arcane books. I knew the profoundly terrible import of those texts. And so I knew as well the frightful nature of those voices. Such dark knowledge did not impede my mesmeric advance. I climbed the broken stairs and the ladder of cobwebbed rungs to the topmost gallery. Under the mansard, the ceiling pressed close, and I stooped to grasp the glass knob of the small door behind which voices whispered frantically, gibberishly sharing anticipation of my arrival.

The door opened upon them — the Elder Gods.

I stood astonished. They are not titanic beings as the texts describe. They are small as dolls, and in the umber shadows their smiles are sad and evil. Dark, anarchic, restless thoughts pollute the curdled brains inside those bulbous heads. And a putrid stench, a rancid reek of cheesy flesh and carnal sulfur, packs the alcove where they squat.

Rickety limbs twitched at the sight of me. Then, all those grotesque dolls fell silent, bald, dented heads bobbing, hollow eyes lidded blackly gold as toads' eyelids, dazed, concussed, dream-hooded, as if attentive to other voices or beholden only to their own minds' shapeless shapeshifting, whole worlds playthings in the graygreen smoke of their staring thoughts. Whole worlds — my world, your world, too, the worlds of every sentient being, provoked from nothing by these squalid, grinning things.

That dark encounter lasted but one unspeakable moment. I slammed the door, shutting away the abhorrent sight, and crashed down the ladder and the stairs. Terror propelled me across the dung-strewn reception hall and out into the bracing wind and the ruined land.

I would have kept running had I not read the esoteric literature. I knew what I feared and feared to know. I knew. There is no way back among the scattered black ponds and scrawny woods. In a distant city after the rain, the shape of my absence goes on. But I will never find or fill that shape. For I am here now under the red and green stars of a day sky strewn with moons and planetary phases — and my soul hangs from a twisted bough, and the dead angel in the black vineyard grins, grins fiercely at the secret meanings of all that I know and fear to know.

NEXT HORIZON

IT LOOKS EMPTY, BECAUSE it contains everything. Everything comes in opposites. Opposites attract and cancel each other. And that's why the empty page is blank. It's *all* there.

TWICE DEAD THINGS

INVESTIGATIONS OF THE FRACTAL BLOOD SOUL

After the soul has been severed from the body, it continues its journey, its path unknown, the destination unknown. It is a trembling day.

— Zohar 1:201b

TREMBLING DAY

THE MOON'S PAW PADDED silently among hurrying clouds. Giant pines wore feather boas of fog. And a bluff of limestone glowed soft as a breast in the wilderness night. A lovely occasion for vampires. How was I to know? A 54-year-old yoga instructor from Rahway, New Jersey, I thought bloodsuckers were swamp worms and lawyers. Sure, the travel agent had said the bluff was haunted. A wraith of a Revolutionary war soldier, the specter of a Mohawk brave, perhaps a flitting apparition of Ralph Waldo himself — these are the spooky experiences of imperishable memories. But vampires in the Adirondacks?

Bernie and I had come to this remote resort in Black River Valley to celebrate our 17th anniversary and the opening in Short Hills Mall of a third outlet for our own franchise, a fitness-studio slash stirfry-restaurant: *Go Yoga! & Wok Like This!* With three workout-eateries that Bernie would have to manage accounts for and new instructors and cooks I had to break in and oversee, who knew when next we'd have a chance to traipse off together and watch moonrise over a haunted bluff?

Bernie would rather have stayed in the lodge at his laptop. He was there for golf and relaxation, not canoe trips, foliage hikes, outdoor tai chi, lakeside dawn meditation and other bliss-inducing activities I adore. But he adored me and went along with me that night of the big moon. That's my sorrow now, my tough karma. And I'm working at it with all my might. You see, we hadn't snuggled together in the feathered moonlight under those secluded conifers for five minutes before vampires struck.

A steel clamp of horror squeezed my heart so tight my last breaths came in gasps. Vampires are not at all elegant like in those movies. Their faces are brilliant as lanterns but blue, cyanotic blue, and leopard-spotted. Maybe it was just the moonlight. Bone shadows fluoresced like X-rays through their flesh, skeletal people with squid eyes, just black keyholes in chalk dead faces. Really. I could have screamed, except I had no breath.

Bernie, wide as a lumberjack, my globe-shouldered Bernie, leaped up, face scrambled with emotion, and the first vampire lifted him with one slender neon arm and slammed him against the spruce so hard needles rained and a whiff of Christmas floated briefly before a fecal stink fouled the air. His feet, free of the earth, kicked like a swimmer's. The vampire that had pinned its trophy to the tree floated horizontally in the moony air, a tattered banner, an angel of decay, narrow body concealed in filthy wrappings, face hidden against Bernie's throat. Tar spackled the back of its head, webs of tar that must once have been hair meshed now in filament braids or perhaps that was mold thriving in the sutures of its skull. Bernie's eyes stared straight ahead, wide open and electrocuted.

My throttled lungs howled squeak after mad squeak. When I careened about, I met the second vampire's night terror eyes. It watched my horror with obvious delight — no joy in those puncture-hole eyes, nothing in those inkwells — yet, the spidery creases of its face deepened, twitching with mirth, leather lips pressed shut, holding back the killing shriek I knew was coming.

A gargoyle's scream rang my bones like chimes. The horrid, famished mouth opened, and I glimpsed those infamous fangs, slender needles of starlight. The thing was on me, nailing me to the tree in a slamming blast of ice gale force. Lit with pain, I blazed for a moment, dazzling atoms bursting all through my body in torrid flares of agony. *Is this happening?* The incredulity of it endured the searing, silent cries roasting me alive. *Me! This is happening to me!* Not a nightmare. No dream. Me, dharma darling, devotee of Amitabah Buddha of Infinite Light, lotus center me, founder and CEO of *Go Yoga! & Wok Like This!* — qi channeler me, still point me who is not-me, *anatman*, radiant me, Bernie's lover! *Me!*

Like a gust of smoke, I drifted away. Pain ceased abruptly. A blast of power|rightness wafted me into the hush of heaven, under a moon like a blotched mushroom. Was that the moon? That wasn't the moon but the soft radiance of infinity I had visualized so many times in meditation.

Bernie! I spun about in mussel-blue night. *There's my Bernie!* He was at the zenith, thunderstruck, a lustrous echo of his naked physical self, balding red hair, freckles, paunch and all, rising swiftly into a confused atmosphere of speeding clouds and moonfire.

A moment of clarity dilated. All those years I had urged him to join me in meditation, to focus his breath, concentrate awareness deep in the body, in the force center, the core chakra of our dreamflesh, all those years amused at my zealous devotion to yoga, keeping himself busy in the back office with spreadsheets and in the studio-restaurants with custodial chores while, when we were alone, gently scoffing my yoga compulsion — except of course in the tantric serenity of our prolonged lovemaking. (And he never jeered my compulsive cooking, either.) For him, yoga was business. Cooking was business. And business was over now. He floated away, corkscrewing upward — outward?

Gone.

Right there, with radiant clarity, I witnessed Bernie's death.

His body of light, his soul, dwindled into darkness, slipping through an event horizon to what mystery lies beyond . . .

Breathe! I began my breath focus routine, trying to keep myself from an implosion of panic. Of course, I had no lungs, no way to breathe. I breathed vital energy. *Bernie's dead! I'm dead!* I knew this with clarity|insight. In moments, my reserve of vital energy, of breath|force, would exhaust itself and I too would spiral away into radiant darkness.

Gone!

The immediacy of death saturated me with befuddling ecstasy. Not joy, wonder or sexual paroxysm. Ecstasy in Greek means 'to step forth.' It's a crucial term in my yoga seminars, a term I use to help people grasp the idea of getting out of the way of the body, letting the mind move aside simply to watch the edgework of muscles finding their tension limits. But this was a bigger kind of rapture — the kind when the soul departs the body! The ecstatic sensation pervading me heralded my imminent leave-taking from this world. I knew this with a mighty conviction — and I was not ready to go. I was terrified and shrieking: *Not yet!*

I tried to calm myself by thinking, focusing intellectually, without emotion, on what had killed Bernie and me and why.

Vampires?

In fact, at that ecstatic moment of devastating dismay, I hadn't yet realized that the monsters who had attacked us were vampires. It had all happened too fast. And I didn't think of vampires, because I didn't believe in them. Only after I had gotten well into my breath focus routine — what practitioners call *pranayama* — did clarity|insight amplify sufficiently for me to consider carefully what had transpired. Then, I knew.

The moment I knew, I was among them again. The abominations, mouths varnished with our blood, sensed me at once. Bony hands passed right through me. I guessed they'd never seen a ghost before. Their effulgent bodies blurred like blue taillights through the woods as they strove to flee. I glided effortlessly along their liquid luminous slipstream. They turned. All at once, they stopped and turned, bending space behind them spookily like a heart-broken dream.

I saw them then more clearly than before. They occupied a space that ached, all taut and torqued with trembling hunger. Sequined fluorescence in their cadaverous faces breathed brighter, flakes of black light falling away in leprous decay from wormscored jaws that gawked astonished. Only those gun-barrel eyes showed nothing.

Dim voices spoke as if from another room, murmurs clothed in a stale fume of dead roses —*Its hue bewray notorious ill. Hut! It craves a parley.*

Languid hands swayed through me again, and they backed off, amazed. I moved forward and passed through them. For a moment, we occupied the same space, and I partook of their sickly aura, smog of sunset, sky lacquered brown and small stars flickering in the wind. Zero's amplitude canceled me, every thought, all feelings. Their bodies vibrated, wave-particles teeming briefly with Bernie's last thoughts as his blood digested inside them, a ferment of deranged fright and his final terrified determination to protect me.

My own blood-memories cooked there too but transparent to me, and I saw right through them into the vampire stomaching my blood. What I had mistaken for decay is molting. Old flesh sheds like fungus. Over centuries, the oldest vampires develop faces abstract as crabs and full of clairvoyant malice.

—*Dog of hell, what would you with us?*

I'm a dog of hell? I spoke|projected. *What are you then?*

They are the wolves of hell. Their drastic eyes told me as much. I teetered a moment before the crypt dark of those skull sockets. In a blink, they rushed off in opposite directions, smears of auroral fire weaving among the trees. I let them go.

Disoriented, I pivoted. Moonlight passed through me. I passed through trees. Inside their wooden samurai armor they are geisha beauties, each one a 'person-of-the-arts,' limbs dancing, arranging flowers, carrying the wind's music, the calligraphy of their roots pure poetry, rhyming earth and berth. *Oh, so this is what it's like to be dead* . . . Everything is metaphor, everything lyrical, flowing together, an exquisite enchantment.

I arrived where I began and found our corpses. Bernie lay with his back against the spruce, legs spread, chin to chest and

I on my back in his lap looking up at him with worthless eyes. Our exsanguinous flesh appeared frosted, star-splotched in big silver paisleys made up of tiny snowflake doilies. Dead people don't look like that.

Oh, yeah. Our bodies aren't dead. Fright throbbed in me. *These bodies are the undead.*

Man Is Red Dust

Fear depleted my power|rightness, and I catapulted through the forest awning high into a night of celestial fire. I vaporized quickly. Loneliness swarmed through me. I knew this feeling. In deep meditation, we encounter the Watcher, Whom the sacred Vedantic texts call the Purusha, a Sanskrit term that became our English word 'person.' This is the original Self, the holy One at the deepest center of each of us. If we meditate long enough, we identify the special loneliness of this One. I guess we could say this is God's solitary dreamlessness. It's probably why we exist, as companions to this One, tethered to our own loneliness as Oneness binds God in solitude. That thought mollified my anxiety. If I went with this divine dreamlessness, I would bleed into it, the fabled raindrop returning to the ocean.

Not yet!

I focused ferociously on breath|force. The constellations like giant luminous dreams full of nothing descended around me. I was going fast, a guttering flame, returning to the void, *sunyata*, empty truth in which all existence floats. *Not yet! Not yet!* Breath|force — *pranayama* — is not about inhaling energy but exhaling the misery and illusions that get in the way of energy. I released my fear, expelled desperate resistance and flung '*not yet*' to the silence and stateliness of night. Briefly and forever, the special loneliness of the One recognized me. Well, I suppose not *me* so much as the not-me at the still point of lotus serenity. Anyhow, breath|force magnified once more to power|rightness.

I sifted down to earth. Above the skyline of conifer spires, I looked up at the heavens, glyphs of stars unscrolling westward in esoteric script. I scanned the sky with clarity|insight that exalted me. Rimlit clouds of moonsmoke disclosed the advent of revelations primal and profound. I wasn't afraid anymore to confront my undead lover or my own flesh etched and cryptic with starfrost arabesques. Genuine curiosity flourished, and I wanted to know more about this strange fate that had separated me and the love of my life from life itself.

Passing through bristly tree boughs, I set down before our damned bodies. They had moved. Bernie's corpse stood, leaning back against the spruce, head tilted chin up, gazing blankly at nothing. Squidsmoke swirled in those unblinking eyes. My body had rolled over on all fours, head pulled back, more squidsmoke purling in a gaping stare. Wind drubbed through the trees like the night's heartbeat. A cold hand of fear reached into the middle of me — and I knew better this time and immediately fixed breath|force in the moment. Sure this was weird — a disembodied soul meditating — but, really, what isn't weird about life and death when you think about it?

Our bodies were becoming vampires. This was not good. *What to do?* I was apprehensive about getting too close, anxious about what I'd feel if I touched our possessed flesh. *Possessed by what?* I mustered courage and glided forward to my former body. A vibrato of demon-drum mania nearly shook me apart, and I veered toward pure *sunyata*-void. I backed off. Like a scintillant migraine, pain thrummed.

Breathe!

I stared at moondust sieving through spruce needles until the infliction abated. I would not let mere suffering defeat me. *This is my body!* And, besides, I was already dead. I watched my animated corpse sit back on its haunches, skin fluorescent with radioactive keloids, eyes leaking midnight. Then, I strode forward and sat down on myself.

Pain shouted! I let it quarrel with my power|rightness. They squabbled while I labored to find the rapport I once enjoyed with these muscles and sinews. After much struggle, like when your brain wakes up but your body won't budge, I fit myself to my familiar shape. Only, it wasn't familiar anymore. I reared upright, chest thrown forward, pelvis awkwardly arched, knees locked, vainglorious zombie. My mouth was a persimmon, cheeks sucked tight.

When I tried to find the power centers in myself, my vibrant chakras, all I located were beggars' bowls, nothing there, and whatever breath|force I put in fizzed away. I trudged several stiff-legged paces. *This is ridiculous.* I sat down heavily on the thick carpet of the forest floor. Overhead, visible between creaking boughs, the moon dangled like a chunk of poured concrete. I shivered in the cold, a dandelion ready to fall apart. This was death. Not necrotic death but life's absence. I didn't belong here. The spirit path across the night sky awaited me. I wanted to be with Bernie again. The pulsing cold and the quarrelsome pain urged me, *Go!*

Yet, I didn't budge. What owned my body now? I had to know. So, I sat snugly in meditation. Pain, cold, and estrangement streamed through me, not-me. Eventually, I detected it. I had gone transparent, and it thought I was gone. Up from the gutter of coma it rose, out of the fossil rock we carry in our bones. It had been hiding there, waiting for me to leave. I didn't stir. The special loneliness of God had magnetized me to nothing, and what crawled forth in oily rainbows from its spinal hiding place sighted me not at all.

This was the vampire virus. Dripping whispers of thunder, it spilled through me, oblivious, intent on one thing — blood perfume, frothy and warm in the trough of the wind. Far away, human bodies shed spectral heat. The muzzles of our faces lifted and tracked the scent through a million signals of pine resin, pond ethers, loam smoke and bird auras. Human bloodheat unspooling across leagues of forest brought us to our feet lithe as cougars . . .

Prey! Alarm broke my meditation and kicked me free of my possessed body. Sparkling with havoc — fear, outrage, tremulous horror — I simultaneously grew bigger and smaller. The shock of what had happened to Bernie and me was beginning to hit home. Nothing was right. I was as vast as the evacuation of stars abandoning the cosmos to the darkness that had always owned it. And I was tiny as the pointillist atoms that stitch us to the void. I kept absurdly reminding myself to breathe. Big — small — where was I? For a thick moment, I wasn't.

I have no idea how I pulled myself together, an incorporeal entity, a ghost at the very threshold of formlessness, but I did. And when I did, the undead were gone.

Nature is lawless. I knew this before I became a phantom. Uncertainty is the radical freedom of the universe. Without it, there'd be no luck, good or bad. Reality would be a fine jewel and you and I the light trapped inside among repeating mirrors. Uncertainty is not just a principle in physics and the house odds at the casino. Uncertainty guards a secret. We call that secret the future. I didn't have a future anymore. And so, what do you know? Turns out ghosts can see ahead, to what's going to happen!

I saw the vampires that were once Bernie and me rushing through the night's stark woods, following the scent of blood-heat. They would find their way to the far side of the haunted bluff, where moonlight poured like milk down the rockface, illuminating geological strata of ammonites and conical shellfish from an ancient sea. The forest ended there, and pastureland floated in a soft mauve haze to an abandoned farmstead lapped in fog and muffled under honeysuckle. A gang of teenagers had built a bonfire from timber torn off those ramshackle buildings. Drunk, dancing and amorously preoccupied, the kids would never notice when the swift vampires snatched two outliers, diffident adolescents sucking beer and morosely watching their more adventurous peers. No cry would escape the victims at the dim perimeter of the festive fire circle. No sound at all as the predators towed their quarry into the dark for first feeding.

Revulsion at seeing Bernie's body and mine slaying innocents bounced me into the forest. Cumbersome thoughts of predetermination didn't slow me down. This murderous event was not going to happen.

For specters, thought is action. Like the thistly stars above, I was not an object anymore, not a place but distance traveled. I slammed into the back of my own head simply by willing it. The vampires were just then loping out of the evergreens into cold moonlight. My body received me again with shrieking pain. Prophetic vision of what these demons intended hurt worse, and I packed my entire will into those running legs.

The air rang. Wind blustered from out of my marrows, frigid with icy fever as I undid the future. I ran — or rather lurched, abruptly stiff-legged now that I had displaced the vampire's graceful, homicidal intent, arms windmilling to keep my balance — I reeled drunkenly toward the raging bonfire. Bernie's vampire body fell back, sensing odd doings. Frolicking teens scattered, hooting at the staggering maniac whose strenuous face appeared heat-hazed in the firelight. Startled lovers unclasped from their pelvic dances as I shoved past. Laughing hooligans tossed beer bottles past my head. The vampire realizing where I was going yowled. This grievous jugular cry from deep in the red river where it had only begun to flourish curved weirdly through its own echoes and scattered the romping teenagers.

I lunged into the flames. Screams and horrified shouts from onlookers reached through the roaring inferno. My hair evaporated instantly. Agony broke like glory through every inch of me. Then, vampire strength overwhelmed my rabid will, and we rushed out the other side ablaze. Terrified revelers fled yelling. Through twisting pain, I felt the horrific thing wanting to drop and roll. I ran an awkward goose-step, a hurky-jerk circle back into the flames. We collapsed in the crimson rush, lungs incinerating, skin bubbling to tar. A bellow heaved from the conflagration, flung into the darkness of time. It curdled souls, cleaved minds. Some witnesses dropped to their knees before this blort of inhuman anguish. Others stood fettered to their trembling shadows or marched slowly backward, faces bleared.

I let go. Sparks flew in fiery spindrift from my pyre, crazed flagella flurrying on the black wind, and — among that wild spray of flames — clarity|insight revealed a charred elemental cast out to eternal night. Pain clung in grim ooze. A skyward rush lofted me past bride-veils of clouds toward the bride herself, the honed and horned body of the moon. Man is red dust. Through doors of the wind, we depart this world, our flesh forsaken and all its dreams.

MELISMATIC SCREAMS OF THE UNDEAD

Cremating my own body had chucked me into a dark, philosophical mood. Only briefly, though, until I caught my breath|force once again. I wasn't ready yet to forsake all my dreams. I couldn't leave my lover's body possessed by a vampire. I had to go back. Bernie would have understood if I didn't return for him, but I couldn't surrender serenely to the *sunyata*-void troubled by the ugly thought of his benign face contorted with blood lust, his thick arms not embracing me but tearing apart human lives, and that horrid alien thing in the hallowed place where his sweet soul should have been. Seventeen years of fidelity and passion demanded we leave more of a legacy of our love than three outlets of *Go Yoga! & Wok Like This!* — the entire bounty of *our* people-empowering franchise owned by a brutal vampire.

I want to say here: a saint I'm not. And I'm no Baba Mantra Yoga Master either. I was an ugly, obese kid, a sour, fat teenager, a bitter, overweight young adult. One day I woke up and said, 'I don't have to loathe myself anymore.' I tried vegetarian and liked it enough to lose some weight and that made me like it a lot more. And then, flush with success, I started working out — but that didn't work out. Yoga I could manage. 'Yoga teaches yoga,' is what the ancient yoga authority Patanjali says, and so whatever I could do was plenty good enough. Turned out I could do a whole lot more than I thought, and I got pretty good at it. By middle age, I was still pudgy, but I'd found the skill and confidence to instruct others. Never in my most stoned reveries (oh yeah, I smoke cannabis — or did; my body was never a temple, just a renovation project), never at the most loony apex of the giddiest ganja high did I ever imagine I'd find yoga useful after death.

The night seemed to listen. Maybe that was why these hopelessly self-centered thoughts ran so free. Well, at least I wasn't overweight anymore. I wasn't alive either. Or was I? So long as I kept my breath|force concentrated, I could go where I pleased. Power|rightness intensified the calmer and more transparent I became.

Below, earth looked Godforsaken. The kingdom of darkness. I didn't want to go down. Little grains of moonlight glinted off bodies of water hidden in the forest. An ivory snake crept among hills and dales, the Black River restless in its million-year-old bed. Silence and the wilds of the night wrapped me in contemplation. I thought I knew the world. Nature may be lawless, but the world isn't. Running a successful business requires wide knowledge of the way the world works. I knew about lawyers, union bosses, city and federal regulators, vandals, corrupt suppliers, crooked employees, and disgruntled customers. How could I have missed vampires? Nothing we see, hear, smell, taste or touch has meaning. To seek, let alone find, meaning in perceptions is the warped doorstep to insanity. There are facts, which are universal. And there are values, which are personal. Fact: Vampires had killed me and Bernie — and yet, I lived! Personal significance: unthinkable. Vampires were as secret, as obscure and symbolic as poetry, and I would have to face them like poetry, salvaging whatever meaning I could. I sighed. Pluck any soul out of a body and onto a moonstruck cloud and you get a Wittgenstein. I went down.

In a starblown glade, I found Bernie's body crouching among kneehigh ferns. It looked horrible — ghoul eyes black glass, shining skin stamped in silver geometry, hands tarnished, thickening to hammered bronze and clasping its haunted head, its cankered brain. It was not alone. Another of the undead attended it, an old one, leaning close in the violet air, whispering unfathomable things.

I swept down through the treetops and heard something like oceanic trembling, a murmurous breathing so immense it pressed against deafness. The ancient one sensed me and turned full about, an eyeblink gyration that presented a stupefying apparition of otherness. Imagine a living skeleton from Buchenwald only shining pearl blue, pulsating softly, a humanoid glowworm stained ultraviolet around the edges. Sockets of pure carbon showed nothing. But that protrusive jaw jarred loose, astonished, exposing malignant rows of teeth. Skull seamed with phosphorescent lichen bowed low, as if in ominous obeisance, while glassy fingers grabbed fistfuls of leaf rot. The vampire straightened suddenly and tossed those dead leaves at me with a growled imprecation —*The worse for you, accursed shade! Venomous malice 'twill renew your dire sorrows! Die again! Twice dead thing!*

Darting leaves strafed like buckshot, kicking me backward and shriveling me with misery. Some kind of vampire voodoo was in that dirt. I nearly lost all my breath|force that instant. Curdled around the surprising pain, around the special loneliness at the core of all our suffering, power|rightness did not diminish. As much as this assault hurt, it was trivial compared to the agony of the vampire's bite that had severed my life.

I straightened, annoyed. *Hey! Who the hell do you think you are?* I floated closer, daring the damned thing to try that again. *What did I ever do to you?*

—*O, shameless wraith! Knit again death's torment and oblivion to one mutual sheaf!*

I drifted nearer, ready this time for the impact of hex dust in the vampire's grisly hand. When it hit, I didn't fall back. I held my ground by gazing at Bernie's deformed shape cowering in the ferns so that the ripping shock of the vampire attack merged with the weight of grief for my dead lover. No personal suffering could budge that. Instead, the lacerating curse of the undead cut deep as my guilt but no deeper and left me wanting more. I needed to suffer, to undergo stronger torment and pay for what I had done to Bernie, betraying him to this grotesque death.

The archaic vampire somehow apprehended this. Fear labored in its piranha face. Not in those charcoal eyes. In there was darkness that telepathically overwhelmed all emotion. But the snakehead grin had gone slack, and the spider-finger hands flexed tighter, fisting blue-knuckled helplessness. Advancing closer, I observed the mummy wrappings worn snugly twisted. They were human leather. I made out flaccid lineaments of eyeholes, nostril perforations, a woeful mouth, finger flanges and draperies of tawed flesh, windings so worn and bleached they had practically annealed to the creature's icicle bones.

I moved directly up to the creature and stared into those goblin eyes, straight through to the blood bag within and the stink of sulfur rending from the stewed lives there. Slender cylinders of finger bone strung on braids of human hair along with blackened ears curled like truffles hung about its sinewy neck. Each bone had etched upon it fretwork of emblems — chevrons and runic snowflake symmetries crudely imitative of the patterns in the flesh-shine of the undead. This was a vampire medicine man. One of their shaman priests. That was why it refused to run away. It wasn't going to let a mere ghost spook it.

Hopeless of survival, heedless of pain, I stepped right into that thing. Subzero emptiness. The full magnitude of nothing. *Breathe!* Here was the far dream of not-me. *Anatman.* The no-self of the flimsy, relentless ego teeter-tottering at the brink of nonbeing. Right here, in this head full of evil, hell raised its circus of fire and ice around me. *Amitabah . . . Amitabah . . . Namo Amitabah . . . Buddha of Radiance . . . Sleeper Awakened in Splendor . . . I am Infinite Light . . .* I chanted by reflex. I could have been sitting in the studio at *Go Yoga!*, hearing the clatter of pots and pans next door at *Wok Like This!*, as I had done countless times, this time with bowel cramps, eye-popping migraine, ruptured disk, slashed cornea, myocardial infarction, grand mal convulsion, every infirmity known to flesh. Though, of course, I had no flesh. Just not-me in the grip of a far dream.

I heard crystal cracking, crashing. Something was breaking in the vampire. Realization nudged what would have been my heart. The old stories are true. Spirit kisses the vampire with acid. Why should this be so? What is it that is so anathema to vampires about the Christian cross, Buddhist chants, Navaho prayer blankets for all I knew? I wanted to find out and chanted stronger, *Amitabah . . .*

—*Varlet spirit, assuage your wrath!* The vampire's voice glistered with static, like frayed wires had crossed in its voice box. —*Release me!*

Go. I said|projected. *I'm not holding you here. Get lost!*

The wind coughed, and the old priest of the undead vanished. Unbelievable pain went with it. Acquitted of suffering, empty as outer space, I hovered among fragments of moonlight. Bernie's hunkered body watched me with wolfish attentiveness, eager to spring away too but shackled by futility, knowing it could not escape.

Your turn, creep. I pounced on Bernie's scrunched body. What a festival this would have been if only I was a masochist! Pain like a bull-shout at the moment the sledgehammer comes down. Over and over again — a tormented diesel of raging pistons. Under that tonnage of woe, I meditated. Or I tried. I really did. But this was my big, burly Bernie's meat and bones. I couldn't concentrate. Terrible thoughts intruded: lover's nostalgia for the only man who had ever loved me for who I am. My breath|force frittered. Like a slingstone, I flew, ejected into the stupendous night.

The moon's touch was soft. So good to get out of that miserable engine of despair. A dancer's spin against the stars lulled me, the world tilting below, river, forest, limestone bluff sliding past, rotating. I was good and ready for *sunyata*. Rhapsodic in the fetch of nothing, I wanted nothing more than to dissolve into not-me — to die. Absence washed away under a rush of memories about everything I loved in Bernie: his licorice body odor, the way his packed muscles slipped and bunched under his freckly skin, even the brawny grace with which he carried his paunch . . .

Okay — let's get this over with. I thought|projected myself back into Bernie's vexed corpse. A sizzling bolt of voltage announced my instantaneous arrival, and the diesel blared into action again, driving a vibrating hatred hard and furious into my spectral mind. If I still had eyes, tears would have run as hard and furious as that diesel. The pain was that excruciating. It defeated the metaphysical speculations knitting a whole new worldview just out of sight: how could I feel pain without a body? What was this me that was not-me? I was not kind with Bernie's carcass. I made it pitch upright and swag among the trees, palsied and faltering. We were on our way through ethers of fog, bound for the bonfire to mix Bernie's ashes and bones with mine.

—*Do not burn me.* The torn voice barely reached me amid the hammering stupidity of pain and the welding cold inside my dead partner. —*Do not hazard me to the flame.*

No problem, I assured|projected. We had just drunkenly emerged from the shimmering woods. The bonfire seeped smoke, flames extinguished by a fire truck departing along a dirt road far across the misty pasture. An ambulance followed with my remains. Red strobes whirled, dwindling into darkness.

The gloomy field pillowed the Milky Way. Where was the moon? Like an angel, it resided under clouds lower in the sky of starry hosts.

—*Shade of mischance, depart off me!*

Not likely. I labored across the empty tract. The limestone bluff loomed, a breeching behemoth against galactic vapors. Diesel pistons pounded heavier, astral cold cutting with fatal intensity. *Too bad I'm already dead*, a pixie-thought intruded on my tranced march, almost shattering the power|rightness that forced my will on the vampire. The moon came clear of the clouds, an ulcerated halo to our dark planet that stretched our shadow behind, dragged and quivering.

We dropped heavily to our knees before the firepit. —*Ireful shade quit this flesh . . . this absconded blood. 'Tis no more or ere again what once you loved.* My strength puddled. The thing was right. I just wanted to kill it. But how? I dug fingers into the wet ash, frustrated, feeling in the residual warmth the last heat of my former life.

The instant I touched the quaggy cinders, the hammering diesel of hurt choked and stalled. The scouring cold lifted away as if peeled open by sunbeams. Power|rightness whispered something to me from the infinite. I didn't hear what it said at first. But the vampire did and cried. And its voluptuous squalling oscillated with the aberration in the blood shared by all vampires. Mutilated voices brayed in that very space where torment had battered me, in this precipitous ringing silence, a horrendous distress tangling sorrier among its own echoes, a lamentation of screeches dim and drumming dimmer, the melismatic screams of the undead.

THE FRACTAL BLOOD SOUL

What had yet to happen, the future, popular nickname for

the only real god this world knows, the great god Uncertainty, divulged to me, to all the dead, everything, the deed to every calamity, diamonds in their bituminous veins, the acorn's stronghold of oak. Posterity hid nothing. That was how I knew.

The medical examiner had removed the gross matter of my incinerated corpse, all the bones and remnants of clothing that hadn't burned. Yet, the ash in the firepit contained incompletely combusted amino acids, grumous molecules of my flesh slain twice, first by vampire, then fire. —*The worse for you, accursed shade! Die again! Twice dead thing!* The memory of those words from the vampire shaman fluttered like cobwebs, insubstantial, easy to brush aside. The truth in them, I could not get past. In a whisk, with thrilling immediacy, this truth that infinity had whispered and I had not yet heard brought about a fervent change.

Upon contact with the ash of my destroyed body, with the cinders of the vampire that had owned my corpse, I participated in the future of twice dead things. A weird breeze arrived from all directions at once. Embers swirled in the air, red, breathing motes of spinning fire. These were blood rubies. If I fixed on any one of them, it paused, circumvolving slowly, and I spied in it a wolf of hell. There was the vampire that killed me. In another, I identified Bernie's killer. I looked for the shaman priest. It stared back at me from its own crimson bauble, air around it tingling like a thermal nimbus. For a moment, insanity touched me. The priest spoke with Bernie's voice —*Twice dead things cancel the fractal blood soul.*

Who was this wizened vampire in human leather? Was he really a priest? Did the undead need priests?

—*We worship the animal we live inside.* The emaciate visage filled the blood ruby, eyeholes like fang punctures. —*I am votary to Adam.*

Our wide, curving world bends like a bow, pulled back by gravity. Newtonian Laws precisely measure the lenses through which we see the restless physical forces that sharpen the edge of sanity. Meanwhile, far from Earth, lightpaths trace the shell-curl of spacetime itself and spin off beyond our simian sanity, disappearing into the diviner's pouch of black holes, the same darkness in a vampire's eyes. What's inside there?

All the luck of this broken world.

Morning caressed the sky. First, like a snail extending its gray frill, then a smudge of lipstick. How long had I knelt before the firepit mesmerized by the priest of the undead? The moon had set. In moments, sunbeams would cut through the forest and slice me free from Bernie's flesh. I would die the classic death of the vampire. I wasn't ready to die! Not now that I knew what infinity had whispered.

I leaped up with a cry like a mouthful of mud. Through the flimsy light across the grassland and into the woods, I sprinted agile as an impala. The ash of my possessed body had canceled the vampire inside Bernie's flesh and installed me in its place. *How?* The shaman's gloating laughter flogged me faster. —*Twice dead things.*

I bolted into purpled daybreak, ducking low boughs, hurtling fallen trees, dodging rock outcroppings. Death-rays of smoky light braised my back — Bernie's long shoulders — as I flung myself across the cedar chip parking lot of the resort where we had booked a cabin. Blessedly, the door to our lodge faced north. The key slid home, the door banged open, and I toppled with rasping breath into the salvation of darkness as sunrise, like some jealous god, lofted forth, banishing all other suns, the galaxy entire. The sky, contused maroon and green, gashed my vision to white blindness until I firmly shut the slatted shades.

Collapsed on the bed in thunder-gray duskiness, face aglow with satanic ardor, I listened to a morning mania of birds and wondered what had happened. And I knew. Infinity confided. I had discovered the dreadful secret of the undead. Bernie's brain organized the details with his informed mathematical exactitude. He had often hidden in these computations when we had our little tiffs. Now, occupying his flesh, I understood why. Mathematics is a Mesopotamian priestess, fists full of writhing vipers, keeping the uninitiated at bay while she does her magic circle dance of three hundred and sixty steps, twelve animal postures, and twenty four pirouettes. For her chosen ones, she will lift her big hoop skirts and expose, tattooed to her inner thighs and over her tonsured labia, the mysteries of imaginary numbers, nonlinear systems and power series. She had seduced Bernie with this sorcery when he was still a boy. He loved to talk about it. I felt the quiet of those enigmas still moving through his brain. Once, after he had solved a particularly arduous set of differential equations, he had pulled me to his wide chest and had crushed the breath out of me with his joy. Lying in bed, I put my hands on his wide chest. My chest.

—*Think of an equilateral triangle with sides of length one. At the middle of each side add a new triangle one-third the size. Now put equilateral triangles on the middle of all sides of the new figure and so on. The length of the first triangle is three. Now, for the second figure, which looks like the outline for a Star of David, add up all the segments (1/3 + 1/3 + 1/3 . . .) and you'll see the total length of the boundary of the second curve is 3 X 4/3. Repeat the process an infinite number of times, and the length of the boundary of the figure is 3 X 4/3 X 4/3 X 4/3 . . . . Yet, the area of the figure remains less than the area of a circle drawn around the original triangle. Thus, a line infinitely long encloses a finite, and relatively small, area. Weird.*

The fractal pattern Bernie's brain envisioned looked like an intricate snowflake — the same design imprinted on the faces of the undead . . . on my face! Fractals describe the structure of bronchial tubes, arteries, brain cells, seacoasts, clouds, galaxies — and the blood soul.

A knock on the door shuddered through the room. I ignored it. The blood is blind. But not forgetful. It has an iron mind and remembers everything from the amoeba's invisible face to the mandrill's clown mask, from the leisure of the sea cucumber and the great lizards' obsessive compulsions to the elegant rat and the rye fungus crammed with dreams. The blood soul is the evolutionary tree — and it has a fractal dimension . . .

Another knock and this time a jangle of keys sat me up in bed. The door swung open, flaring daylight through the room. I had soared so quickly into the bathroom, slamming the bathroom door behind me, I found myself pressed up against the mirror above the sink. I had no reflection.

"Cleaning."

—*Come back later*, I said in a caliginous voice from the far end of a tunnel. The outer door immediately snicked shut. I emerged from the bathroom pestered by thoughts of the police. They would come to interview Bernie soon as they had identified my burned body. I had to leave but couldn't until dark. I slid into bed and buried myself in the sheets to contemplate my bizarre situation.

Fractals are fractions. Twice dead things possess the inert fraction of the vampire virus and, when added to the living fractal of the undead, augment that fraction to a whole, deleting it. Then: *Why am I a vampire?* I despaired in the sepia dark. *Why did the slain fractal virus not erase me?* The answer blew out from infinity: Because the ash of the twice dead thing was me. Even as the fractal pattern of the phage possessing Bernie disappeared, taking the vampire with it, my ghost's outrageous presence imprinted a fractal pattern of my own.

This would require deeper investigation, I realized, gliding to sleep. The undead sleep among the dead. A gigantic night preoccupies those in the beyond. We can't see what the dead see. Yet, it must be wonderful or awful or both, because the dead look like stunned cretins staring at whatever it is in the dream's vacuum. Among rags of lightning and spooling auroral discharges, they stand and others kneel or prostrate themselves, appearing only briefly before riffling away under drumming darkness.

TWILIGHT IN THE CANCER GARDEN

I had hoped to see Bernie among the apparitions of the dead. No such luck. I woke in appalling quiet. Through the slats, I glimpsed a late afternoon of gray, sprawling mist that did not hurt my eyes. I needed a shower.

In the bathroom, I paused before the mirror to ponder the physics of how vampires cast no reflection. Fractal spectra radiate from vampire DNA. The trillion cells of the undead body configure an antenna-array of DNA with the precise contours of the vampire's skin. Fractal wavelengths from that body-antenna meet key-and-lock with EMF waves rebounding from reflecting surfaces and nullify images of the undead. The fractal field propagates right through fabric and excites fractal spectra from organic molecules in apparel, and most of my clothing gave no reflection either. More to think about! DNA as antenna systems broadcasting signals so that the undead live without reflection. Without image, the vampire is wholly physical, unfettered by psychic reflection. It is a *specularity* of carnal need beyond desire. Bloodlust of emptiness itself — emptiness glued to the needs of flesh.

Was that me? The fact that I could ask this question assured me I still possessed humanity — though the fractal blood soul thrived in me.

While showering, I explored Bernie's body, already so very intimate to me from outside. Inside, it felt sturdy, massive even. What was left of his orange hair came off in my hands. Running trembling fingers over my bald pate, I tried to feel the fractal figures in the scalp, felt nothing unusual. Fingertips explored vague eyebrows and the stubble of Bernie's cleft chin. I wasn't used to seeing the world from this height. Lathered up, I played with my penis. Did vampires have sex? What about other bodily functions? Fear of discovery by police detectives interrupted my self-exploration — 'Vampire Found Playing with Self in Shower.' And something more. I was hungry. A rapacious blood hunger.

In life, the sight of blood made me queasy. Carnality for me did not involve killing. All our stirfry ingredients at *Wok Like This!* are pre-killed. Carnality for me is — *was* — sex and food. I loved life, body and soul. Now my body's gone, my lover's soul gone — and lustiness, too, departed with its rhythms, urges and drives. All that remained was lost intimacy, my need to be with Bernie, our joy in being together — and the anguish of coming apart.

Lost intimacy — and bloodlust.

I dressed in the sturdiest clothes Bernie owned: black denims, hiking boots, brown corduroy shirt and a crushed Italian leather jacket I had bought for him six birthdays ago. I left the cabin with an overnight bag stuffed with Bernie's clothes. Even wearing ski sunglasses, I winced. Frail rain-light hurt my eyes, and I practically had to grope to our rental car. Dizzy with hunger, I held only one destination in mind — the nearest hospital.

I drove with a fever of evil, a head full of annihilation. Every car on the road was a lunch box. My square-knuckled hands gripped the wheel like talons. I needed first feeding, needed blood with a demented appetite that made taillights look yummy. I followed blue signs with the big white H to a large general hospital and parked out of sight of the institution on a hillside street with wide lawns where nothing stirred. As dusk fell, I blew down the street like a feather. I cut between houses, a shadow blur through the hedges. Dogs droned. Under a sky of amber shellac, I entered a maze garden of dwarf trees and raked gravel. The hospital towered above, every long window lit.

"You can't get in that way." This voice of bruised velvet floated from out of a teenager, a girl with pale skin and spiky, pixie hair — skin so white and hair so black she emitted darkness. "There's always a guard at the terrace door." She sat on a stone bench, a low slab. I had smelled her before I saw her, a blood smoke tainted with medicinal ectoplasm. I had thought it an aura of the hospital and had nearly tripped over her. *Chemo*, I established, staring down into those raccoon eyepits. She regarded me blandly. "You're a vampire."

—New recruit. My shadowy voice frightened me. *—How do you know what I am?*

"Duh. Take a look at yourself."

—Can't. The mirror thing.

"You look really freaky. Those shades don't hide a thing."

—You've seen vampires before?

"Yeah, right."

—You're not scared? I blinked to make sure she wasn't an apparition, a hallucination of my blood hunger or infected brain. *—You should be scared. We mindlessly kill people.*

"You can have my blood." She stood, a lanky adolescent of broad face, high, perfect brow with a faint blue vein down its middle. She wasn't wearing hospital attire but hip slung jeans on a razor-sharp pelvis, biker boots, a vermilion halter top and no make-up. Something errant in her attitude, a solemn and fearsome lawlessness, empowered her from the afterlife. Had I seen her before, staring at the incomprehensible in my dreaming among the dead? "Go ahead. I'm a goner anyway."

—*You're a tough cookie.*

"You don't want me."

—*It's the chemo. You don't smell very appetizing. Besides, I don't kill people.*

She cocked her head, incredulous. "A vegetarian vampire?"

—*Actually . . .*

"No way!"

—*Way. Well, half way. I need blood. First feeding. I'm going to pass out soon if I don't get it. But I don't want to kill for it.*

Comprehension brightened in her woebegone eyes. "So that's why you're here."

—*I came for the transfusion bags. Can you help me?*

"If you help me." She stepped closer and placed her hand on my chest. Her warmth made it hard for me to breathe. I was ravenous for her blood, even if it did stink like paint thinner. Her voice narrowed to a whisper, "I want to go with you."

—*I don't know where I'm going.*

"Do I look like I care?"

The girl knew her way around the wards. She went in the terrace door past the security guard and opened a service access entry in the broad driveway on the far side of the garden wall. Security cameras posed no threat. Blood scent, after a near calamitous detour to an operating theater, eventually led to the refrigeration units. While the girl distracted the on-duty staff, I packed two coolers with 350 ml bags of red blood cells. A soft whistle announced the all clear, and we skipped back the way we'd come. I felt sadness at this criminal act and relief my urgency hadn't driven me to murder anyone — yet.

In the empty driveway with a cooler of life in each hand and an alley of sky above blowsy with stars, I took my opportunity to lose the girl. I didn't need her anymore. And there was the question of her parents, her family. She couldn't simply disappear with a vampire. Small clouds drifted overhead, blue as souls. I removed my sunglasses and bolted under the star-spun night. A bitty cry from the girl eked after me like a bat. I entered the wind, weightless as tissue paper. Perhaps I would see her again in the strobe flicker of the undead's dreams. She'd be there soon enough, separated by ecstasy from parents and family, with no connection to anything except mystery, *sunyata* emptiness, the *anatman* at the secret core of us all . . .

The wind curled, and I boomeranged into the broad driveway where the girl had already turned her back. *—You coming or not?* She was dead anyway. What did it matter?

"I thought you skipped."

—Don't know my own speed yet. Sorry. This is new to me. I shrugged. *—Want to get your things? I'll wait in the garden.*

She dashed to my side, eyes glorious, and hooked her arm through mine. "Let's go!"

Drinking refrigerated blood for a vampire is a lot like sipping a young wine, something fresh and nervous from Côtes du Luberon, perhaps a chilled Cuvée le Châtaignier with its dark lavender spices. Hospital blood banks store their supplies in a special refrigerator with the temperature constantly kept between two and eight degrees Celsius. Very refreshing. In the rental car, I drank two bags full, almost three fourths of a liter, with the girl watching avidly.

I found out then why vampires take their blood from live victims. My heart skidded. Sinews twisted all through my body. Too many memories of too many living people to digest, a complex math of souls, grievances and joys. The living lived. Extrasensory linkages nearly tore me apart.

"You okay?"

—Can you drive?

The girl followed directions, and I lay on the backseat ripping apart snaggled second-sight, confused with thoughts from other people: a young woman's tax questions, two brothers arguing about their senile mother, a man burdened with fear and gambling debts. By the time I sorted out these paranormal voices and a radiance of strength and clarity breathed in me, we had arrived back at the dirt road in the forest near the resort.

We got out, and I took off my jacket and put it around her shoulders. *—I couldn't have got here without you.*

Cold, she slipped her arms into the oversize sleeves. "What are we doing here?"

I told her the story of Bernie and me, of our 17th anniversary, and our romantic stroll through conifer woods to watch moon-rise over a haunted bluff. When I was done, she understood. "You came back for your ashes."

—*The ones that did this to me and Bernie, I'm coming back to make them pay.*

"You can't go in there again." The moon frosted the tree-tops of the black forest, and we stood in its path. "They'll be waiting."

—*Like I don't know?*

Ten Thousand Miles of Darkness

Infinity is not a number. It's a process. The circle of life embraces the fractal line of infinity, the blood soul knowing nothing of time, only change, one disguise for another. A fish can become a bear and crawl back into the sea and change to a whale. The fractal blood soul is as old as old gets. Before our planet swirled to a hot heart of magnetic magma in the cold fist of outer space, the fractal line limned cosmic clouds. Before that it branched forth the lineage of elements in the stellar furnaces. It flexes in the vortex of every galaxy, coiling infinity into black holes. It calls itself luck among the quick. The dead cherish it as something else, something without a name. And for the undead ... well, I pray you never find out.

I think I made her understand this before I told her —*Get in the car. Drive back to the hospital. I will come for you when I'm done.*

"Uh-huh." She gave me a tolerant look. "Why would I go back to the ward? Clocks have stopped for me there."

—*You can't come with me.*

"Why not?" She put a finger to her chin as if trying to re-member. "Oh, yeah. I might get killed and my body wander the earth till the sun burns out."

—*You don't want that.*

"You think I want to waste away vomiting?"

So that's how I found myself in the night forest with a dying girl and webs of moonbeams like filaments of spun glass. The undead floated in all the darkness. So many. Their squalid songs ventured under my breastbone and plundered this forlorn heart for memories of Bernie, our sad little squabbles, the shameless sympathy we felt for each other's weaknesses, and all the years of tenuous obligations that had quietly coalesced to a fumbling relationship of symmetrical lives, an improvised partnership, where we fulfilled our parallel yet separate dreams, business for him, yoga and food for me, carnal gratification for him, tantric union for me, the comfort of routine holding us together, though he dubbed it loyalty, and I fashioned it love. I knew what they were doing, trying to undermine my will. I was one of them now. And they were right about everything they sang. But they were wrong about thinking it mattered. It's just a dream. Illusions of *samsara*, the endless cycling of being and non-being. That's why I came back for the girl. I knew she knew about the dream in ways my Bernie could never have comprehended. Last night, I had learned a lot about what she had already figured out for herself. She was ready. She had been ready a long time for my pitiful announcement: —*They are coming now.*

With silken silence, spreading darkness through the moony air like billowing ink, a vampire swept down from the cathedral heights of nocturnal yews. It snatched the girl by her shoulders, even as she glanced upward at a soft susurrus inside the vagrant wind. Her legs scissored frantically, footless in midair. Breath knocked out of her in one shriek, she sailed mutely thrashing into a forest tunnel where moonlight stood at the far end like an ivory door.

She was gone, already arriving at where her grievings had beckoned. And the dream moved on. The moon slid from bough to bough as I floated among pitchblende shadows accompanied only by the lunatic trill of crickets. In evergreen alcoves, I beheld the undead, ghost faces freckled with blood, squatting on reckless youths who had dared return to the gruesome site of last night's immolation. One yet lived and gaped at me with despondent exhortation until the vampire pressed close its fatal embrace. The dream moved on.

Creamy darkness and the demon of me brimming in the blood laid claim to my soul, and oh how I longed for power|rightness, my strength as a ghost. A creature of the undead, I let the rapport of kindred evil gorge my heart like a chest of treasure and usher me forth both reverent and afraid to the clearing where the fugitives of hell awaited.

Arrayed in choir among great drifts of moonsmoke, vampires shadowed the pasture — but not the scorched earth. Here, my flesh had burned. Erratic mounds of dirt and tossed rocks and debris lay strewn near the charred ground none dared approach. These impotent attempts to bury the toxic ash of a twice dead thing had created a heraldic slum of gravel, deadwood and grass clods that appeared arranged at the boundary of chaos more by bestial intelligence than exiles of humankind.

The shaman priest advanced through blue, moonlit haze. All his bones showed under his windings of human leather, face a rancid clot crusting a malevolent skull, jaw undershot, serried with incisors. —*Brother, by your own umbrageous hand to the fiery gulf your flesh was given. Now why return? Why bear the flesh of another?*

I didn't bother answering. They knew my posthumous heart as I knew theirs. Among the vampires, I spotted the girl, small in Bernie's jacket, still alive, eyes swiveling, reassessing her devotion to darkness. A lamia, a female abhorrence of savage, iridescent muscularity, knelt on the girl's back, hank of its victim's hair in a bioluminescent fist, yanking her head back, exposing taut throat and ticking veins. It stared straight at me through tresses of colored tinsel. Black eyeholes aimed like gun bores, targeting my humanity, the lamia made certain I had an unobstructed of view of its kill. Magenta lips sneered back from barbed teeth, jaw blades flaring blue as acetylene.

The priest continued in its desert wind voice —*O perfidious spirit, join us. Redeem yourself among the undead. You alone may approach this baleful soil and not die. Bury this twice dead thing t'was your former sorry frame. And feed on this sickly lamb. Salve injury inflicted by your killing grief with this sanguine proof of fealty. Forsake vengeance for timeless life. Brother, feed!*

The shaman priest edged away, without shadow in the misty, veering moonlight. The lamia raised its dragonskin hand, beckoning me, exposing armpit feathers black and plastered with sweat. The lobes of the creature's brow, glazed with lunar light, pulsated branching veins, eager to feed yet restrained by a nastier will yet, offering me the kill. I won't lie. I felt whole as a rose, my fractal blood soul a livid blossom in the presence of the undead. I was of them in flesh if not spirit. I belonged. Like no other time in my former life, I belonged. Each one of the undead so magnetically bound to my corporeal pith, I actually experienced my hunger eating their hearts. The shaman priest's snakehead grin opened.

Glowing with the moon's radiation, the lamia waved me into the field where fog sloshed close to the earth, simulacra of the departed crawling out from their humus beds. I left the speared light among the shaggy trees. I stepped into the glade, where the limestone bluff, a monument to the moon recumbent against the stars, parted darkness.

Chest constricted with unholy desire, I strode among a litter of heaved rocks and bramble and passed the undead, their eyes of cadaver mascara all trained on me, their souls pure mirror, reflecting archaic mystery, nightfall before the dawn of life when Earth was still disaster, a geological blaze cooling to volcanic glass and starshine. For such venerable lineage, old as the somnambulism of rocks, organic existence is a mutilation. The vampire virus originally thrived on gravel. In these ogre bodies of human flesh, germinated out of fish-slime and worm-mucus, vampires yet remain faithful to the first iron, the world's ordinal blood, bleeding numb rust in the radioactive glare of a primordial planet rapt by fire.

The lamia's nacreous body seethed light. It was a spiritual moment of communion. To us both, the girl smelled of cancer and poison. The quicksilver radiance of the moon, mistress of illusion, veiled in bridal vestment the girl's frailty — ivory skin, pulsing throat, her fevered stare. One more moment, then with a ripping swipe of my dangerous mouth, I marry her to death. Her eyes searched the terror that was my face, trying to reach past the ravening stare, beseeching a mercy detestable to her only minutes earlier. What had changed? I will tell you. She had met the inhuman. Not the prehuman, the mankilling tiger with mask of black and orange lightning. Not twisted life either, the vicious evil of malignant tumors, treason of the known — terrifying enough — familiar death darkening in the body. The vampire is something other, a macabre rending of everything accepted as real. The fractal blood soul unfurls to infinity. The vampire virus hijacks every cell. Snowflake fractals braid dendrites, honeycombing the brain, and the electric hum that generates consciousness alters. Individual awareness severs from the body, and 'I' is instantly 'not-me,' shoved out into *sunyata* nothingness by a new entity, living carrion that continues its sick fury. The girl saw it coming.

Her voice strained in a stretched throat, "I'm going to die."

—*Now why would I let that happen?* I winked a quick supernatural smile and met the abyssal eyes of the lamia. Its emphatic jaws widened with outrage. I didn't hesitate — and I didn't know Bernie's strength. My fist smashed the thing so hard, its ganglia hair whipped and repulsive mouth clacked shut under a stunned grimace. It flopped backward, taking the girl with it — and snapping for her throat.

I swooped on top of them, one arm around the girl, the other trying to pry the biting jaws from her neck. The lamia had already drawn blood as I dropped the full brunt of Bernie's weight into a bodyslam. Just before contact, our holes-in-the-head eyes met inches apart, sharing common darkness. Blood spice cut with venom made both our mouths ache. The acrid taint of chemotherapy drugs slowed the hemorrhaging bite long enough for me to channel the lamia. That's right. Like some kind of telephone tarot reader, I connected through the lamia with its victim. —*Breathe!* I exhorted. The vampire virus reverberated power|rightness between the girl and me. Under the basilisk scowl of the lamia, we shared breath|force. This happened in one pivotal instant, a fraction of a second where the vampire partook of clarity|insight with its prey, startled, not sure what was happening. That loosened its meshed jaws, staggered its hungering furor. That — and Bernie's pounding bodyslam. The wallop stamped the lamia into the loam and broke its clamping bite.

I hugged the blood-smeared girl to my chest with one arm and with the other pushed off the lamia. We were eleven heartbeats from the fire circle. Thirty-eight vampires stood within striking distance and pulled closer. I knew precisely how many, because I sensed the thoughts behind the atrocities of their faces. Moving in counterpoint to their intentions, I ducked blows, sidestepped pounces, grunting with each effort. Motion smudges blurred the moonlight, and breaths exploded from me like hysterical barking.

The girl writhing in my arms, succumbing to the vampire virus, messed with my center of gravity. My boot jammed in a divot, and I plowed headlong into a lunging vampire. Our collision tossed us like thrown dice, and I caromed tumultuously among the undead, tripping others on the cleft earth. Boldly, with the girl clutched tightly against my body, I stepped on proffered backs and leaped — into a blind tackle by one of the undead that knocked us madly right into the firepit!

The vampire in the pit reared upright powdered in ash, a shocked butoh dancer, locked in a manikin vogue of fright. Vampires froze and watched from skullholes of unblinking darkness, staring intently as at a stick of sparkling dynamite. Nothing happened. The cringing vampires unhooked their fright and slinked closer. Perhaps the ash was weak, rendered harmless by a windy day of mist and boreal showers. Perhaps there was no hurry in killing us . . .

Fangs unsheathed in the moony air, ardent as stropped razors. Wind swerved, and the wretched vampire in the ash pit dissolved. Its lilac dust whirred into moonshadows, poising briefly, so much exhaled smoke draping emptiness with an elongated caricature of its former shape, before withering away. Emitting a collective shrill, the keening of the undead screeched like wrenched metal, lamentation from the iron floor of the soul. Recognition exploded. The melismatic scream of the undead flung me back to that mantic moment of the previous night when I first touched this twice dead thing — my own cremated flesh. Its doomful warrant beggared hope for all the undead. In my arms, the girl trembled and chittered, the vampire virus inside her melting. I crouched over her, swinging aggressive stares left and right.

Encircling undead postured like Nijinsky's queer faun, peering sidewise through time, gauging the peril and promise of destroying me. The ash didn't kill instantly. If they rushed me, I would die. I tossed a handful their way, and they danced into mist and churning shadows. The fatal dark in their malefic eyes speckled the tarnished air. So many. All with one attention and red rage in their hearts.

They eddied closer among derelict mists, until I swiped my hand angrily and drove the whole flock back into the breathing shadows of the forest. From afar, their many fangs rimed the nocturnal woods with glints and gossamer shine. Night had only begun. Before it ended, I would be dead — or morning would combust me. The girl would survive. The ash of a twice dead thing was eliminating the vampire virus and restoring her destiny with cancer and a higher calling. Not me. The undead had seized my future and crucified that great god Uncertainty to the sky with silver nails of stars. Bernie's brain clicked numbers, the slow planetary rotation toward midnight's return, hours under the remorseless wheel of the star gods, so many frightful heartbeats racing far ahead into the empire of night and its ten thousand miles of darkness.

This Rock, That Star, the Emptiness Between

Moonlight diffused enchantment deep into the long, dragon-body of the forest. Alcoves of illuminated fog smoldered like fluorescent gas. The girl, inside her giant leather jacket, clung to my side, gaze vigilant, encompassing the wide field of running shadows, searching for predators. I could have told her that the undead lurked nowhere nearby but paced porcelain lanes in distant woods murmuring sorcerous imprecations, but I liked her close. Her scent had changed since the vampire virus had thrived and died in her. She smelled of inconsolable beauty, a scent that gleamed on the camphor breeze off the pines and reached what remained of my humanity.

"I died." She tipped her head forward and looked knowingly at me. "And I heard you call me back."

—*Power|rightness called you back.*

"Whatever. Sounded like you."

—There is no me. I died last night with Bernie. Now I'm just a ghost in a living corpse.

"You're alive. And you kept me alive." She appraised me with a new look, eyes soft with sublunar light and wanton possessiveness. "You were right. I should have gone back to the hospital. This is all too weird."

—It's not over yet. You know about twice dead things. The undead don't want you walking out of here at sunrise with that knowledge.

She responded in a quick voice of complicit danger, "Then let's run for it! The vampires are gone."

—No. They're in the woods. Waiting. If we leave the circle, they'll swarm.

"We'll carry ashes. Cover ourselves with ashes!"

—The ash is too weak. It won't save us out there. And it probably won't save us here either once the vampires accept that some will have to die to kill us.

Her expression didn't waver, just a quiet sigh as she admitted, "I'm not afraid anymore. I feel strong with you here."

A laugh thumped in my belly. *Me* — a hero! Bernie would've howled. I offered a pedagogical answer, to keep from guffawing *—That's power|rightness you're feeling. The only real strength there is.*

"Some kind of yoga thing, right?"

—Vedantic philosophy actually . . . My brain blinked. Iciness opened fans in my blood. I sensed the lamia running through the forest's opiate shadows, aiming its vehement body directly at us. *—Stay behind . . .* I managed to blurt, and then the ground detonated.

Cinders shot up in a sheet of ash, dirt and gravel, and hearing stuttered deaf under the lamia's fatal cry. We collided in a plumed ball of dust. I took the hurling thing into myself, away from the girl, and the rampageous blow spilled us out of the burned circle into tall grass. Perhaps it intended to daze or distract me, as if I was still Adam's flesh and lacked the undead's echo-mind, sounding out the deepest underworld of the lamia's thoughts. Perhaps it wasn't intending anything other than rage, because, when I jumped to my feet, that's all I perceived, sheer suicide wrath, sooty with the ash of a twice dead thing, berserk talon strikes carving space inches from my frantic body, blurring the air to a moon-silver death ornament. I pranced backward toward the cauterized circle, less concerned with the creature's scything limbs, which I could read by heart, than the broken ground I couldn't see.

Sure enough, at the circle's edge, champed earth did foul my footing, and I went down on my back. The lamia drove its turmoil of slashing hooks at my throat. I fell, ogling the chess piece moon perfectly still above the agitated pug-faced angel, and I held onto the vampire's oracular bond. I snagged its wrists, and the mad scissorings of bladed-fingers stopped, crisscrossed before the black tremor of my eyes. Its space-cold stare locked on mine, and we bridged a silence that occulted all prophecies.

I was on the bottom this time as we fell locked in para-lyzed combat, and the lamia braced to bodyslam *me*, its oily face glossy as a placental veil, appalling freak fangs exposed in triumphant anticipation of biting my face off. When we hit the ground, harpy jaws, dead agate eyes and grapnel claws splashed into fine, blue pumice. The lamia's dust twisted away in a screaming wind.

I rolled gibbering with fright onto scorched ground and came up kneeling before the girl, huffing for breath. No threat stirred in the many black mouths of the forest. The lamia's death-bawl had flogged the undead down the dragon's gullet into bramble gullies and desolate ravines of this aboriginal timberland. There, they roosted where moonlight lay like bones, razor jaws shivering with cretinous malice.

The girl squinted at the forest of windy moonlight. Distant flares of creek mist mimed ghouls rampant in the woodlands. "Are more coming?"

She looked frightened, features puzzled apart ... The lamia's attack had set madness dragging its magnetic field across the moonwashed land, a warped headache throb that squeezed her eyes, as she scanned for the vampires' adamant hunger. Her tight stare reached me, and her face unclenched to a smile. "Breathe!" She suddenly remembered our moment of shared power|rightness in the lamia's grip, and she hurried to my side.

A smile! In this nightmare! It left me giddy even as my frightened breath still churned from the lamia's attack. You know, the soul has its own crazy spaciousness. From the Palace of Luck inside each blossom to the evanescent cleft of day and night, down that momentary green gulf of sky where quasars twinkle invisibly from the highest heaven, the soul is at home between both extremes. But that easy smile at the sight of *me* — that credulous smile from a teenager with death's stain in her blood ... that joy marked an expanse of trust my soul ached to fill.

—Breathe. I mirrored her smile — I hoped. I still wasn't sure how atrocious I actually appeared and shrank at the memory of Bernie's robust smile corrupted by a goth grin. *—You must be freezing.* I swept a raft of deadwood into the circle and put my arm around the girl to reach the butane lighter in Bernie's jacket. She snuggled closer, and with that lighter we built a wobbling fire under the wind.

The lighter was there for the spliff also in that pocket, memento of the amorous intentions that had inspired Bernie and me to wander into the Adirondack wilderness last night. My mind fuddled to think of the eerie events that had since transpired. What infernal intelligence had hoisted us out of our lives and discarded my lover before tossing me back into his body to huddle at a rickety fire with this stranger in my embrace, in Bernie's arms, facing a purgatorial heath of contorted shadows heeling beneath giant trees black as damnation and breaching to greater perdition beyond? What but hell itself?

And where else is the vertex of supernatural evil for us but there, in the heart of nature? Look out at the inexorable day. What is it? This rock, that star, the emptiness between. Does the confidence of our dreams lie in this? Then, we are all deceived. Evil comes to us as reverence and truth shining through our deceptions. Embrace it. Even as I embraced that girl with no name in arms of flesh not my own upon a night with no day ahead — for, I tell you this in all sincerity from a heart gallant with desperate suffering — strife and love are the workings of one design, whose absence itself is its worldly presence.

At the zenith, the moon finally shone down upon the dark face of the limestone bluff. Girl and vampire clinging silently, we watched the chalk cliff brighten. "Look!" A lone figure came and went at forest's edge among parcels of light thrown down by wind thrashing in the treetops. "It's one of them!"

The conspicuous iniquity of the shaman priest had already infested my heart, though I had said nothing to the girl. I had wanted the moonlight on the haunted bluff to last a little longer, meager redemption for my lost moment with Bernie. I stood. The girl quickly retreated to the center of the singed circle and tossed ash over herself like a fanatic penitent.

—O ruined brother! That elemental voice crooned with the wind while the undead trod slowly out of the woods and into the grass and sliding fog a long way off. *—The dream moves on. Illusions cycling endlessly 'twixt being and oblivion. That is your faith, aye?*

I made no reply. What was there to say? That thing was coming to kill the girl after dismantling me. Plaintive fear chanted up from my heart, wondering what terrible sorcery possessed the vampire to dare approach me alone. It heard my fear.

—Behold where eyeless rage has delivered you. Madding fear breeds in absquatulated flesh, vile corrupter. You gain nothing by pernicious rage. Though you slay the undead you will not out-scorn the sun. We are gentlemen of blood.

Deeply inhaling my fear, I stared across misty reaches of grass and rock to the forthcoming figure, that creature gaunt as a stick-man to veer away crows. Moonlight reflecting off the limestone precipice filled its translucent flesh, and bone-shadows of spine and clavicle hovered like a crucifix. The incongruity startled me with a cardiac shiver. My vampire animality swelled fearfully. *Breathe!*

The priest of the undead closed in slowly and spoke my own words in its pneumatic voice: *—Spirit kisses the vampire with acid. Why should this be so?*

With jolting clarity, the priest answered *—Spirit is a shoreless sea. Its distances rive mind and flesh. The art of our hunger is fouled before such magnitude.*

I understood what it meant. The infinite fractal line of the blood soul disappears in the transcendent among greater infinities. That would have meant nothing much to me, except Bernie's brain had learned that infinities come in different sizes and there is no biggest one. The infinity of whole numbers, 1,2,3,4,5 ... , known as aleph-0, is smaller than the infinity of real numbers, whole numbers *and* all the fractions between them, which is aleph-1. The transcendent participates in the *process* of infinity, what mathematicians call the aleph sequence, an infinite succession of infinities aleph-0 times aleph-1 — including the infinity of multiplying together every infinity between the infinities, all the way to infinity. But here's the wild part. The great god Uncertainty owns infinity. Last century, mathematicians proved not that we don't know but that we can *never* know if any aleph is the next biggest infinity after aleph-0. So, when we raise a big infinity to an infinite power, say aleph-$0^{(aleph-1)}$, uncertainty makes sure we're never sure if that new infinity is merely a fraction, the number of numbers between 0 and 1, or a truly cosmic number. The same with the fractal blood soul of vampires. The transcendent, the process of infinity, is something humans experience as an awareness of reality beyond what we can understand: examples include faith, the secret intentions of the unconscious, or the finger-pointing-at-the-moon physics of string theory that identifies higher dimensions in which our universe floats like a mirage in hot air. That cognizance of incognizance blurs the fractal blood soul. Better than garlic when it comes to warding off the undead is a head full of transcendence.

—*Transcendence. You make content with so scant a word?* The nearing vampire raised knobbed arms to a sky glittering like black snakeskin. —*Houseless heavens! Uttermost incomprehension! Coffin of all conclusions! Transcendence you say? I say Hypnosis of Forever in Unborn Stillness! You see a word. I see Nothing. You understand God, and God cannot be understood. This does not unseat your mind? Ontological anarchy!*

Under pulse beating stars, the undead shaman rattled its fingerbone necklace. Something nameless glowed inside me. The legendary shores of sleep tilted horizons.

"Hey!" With both fists gripping my shirt, the girl yanked until the buttons popped. "You! Wake up!"

I jarred alert, and there was the vampire, hell mouth over her shoulder, eyes eyeless black in their sockets, watching me indifferent as camera lenses. My arms pulled the girl hard to me, and I spun about. The undead's mass pressed against my back, flared jawbone grazing my nape with quivering bane. Words sparked wetly in my left ear yet remote, surpassing deep in the conjectural hollows of my head —*The dream moves on, anatman.*

SHRIEK HIGHWAY

My truculent shrug threw off the craggy priest. It stood skeletal and still at the seared fringe, mummied frame blue in the moonglow. Spiked jags of teeth, the mandible of its ruinous face, rocked slowly while old evil fixed me in a rivet-hole stare. The girl flung handfuls of ash at it. It was gone. Was it ever there? Of course. I could feel its curse humming along my bones, squeezing sponges of marrow, depleting me.

"You see it?" she asked with guttural fear. I pointed to where some scurrilous shining silence floated a few feet away camouflaged among ragged wisps of flying fog, vacant eyes hovering. She tossed streamers of ash into the looting wind. Overhead, the carbon haze of stars jarred, and the moon sharply claimed a lower station in the sky, enamel light dripping through the porous forest. The girl whirled about, aghast. In her voice, I heard the crackle of madness, "What's *happening*?"

No time to explain. There was no time. If there had been, I would have had a lot to say. Not that she would have understood or will you now. It took Bernie's brain a while to make sense of my vampire ordeal. The world for the undead is different than for the living. In the fractal blood soul, space and time change places. We all know the living can move in only one direction of time, steadily away from the past, constrained in the now, tending always toward a mythic moment never reached, the illusory future. It's like that for the undead — only not with time but space. You the living journey through space as you please, following Newtonian laws of physics. Vampires cannot. The undead follow the fractal blood flow, and they are never anywhere else but in a changeless place of perpetual feeding.

You probably don't want to hear anymore vampire theory. Not this late in my story. But I need to know more about the undead — about myself. If I can say it, then I know it. And I have all the time I need, because I'm a vampire. I can move just as freely through time as you move through space. That's why, to human eyes, the motions of the undead seem to flow. They are sliding among infinite timelines. Time opens for us the way space disencumbers you. We are always feeding. And we can take as long as we please to choose the moments we wish to occupy. Like in the dead of night when you're in a deep slumber. In truth, we are never There. We can never get There. Because we are always Here. Feeding.

From the girl's point of view, I vanished. *Poof!* In her mind, I'd run off into the night faster than sight. In truth, the shaman priest had snagged me. It got hold of me with my own words: *The dream moves on.* And my whole body of thought followed. What bewitched me was the way the undead priest connected to my ideas of emptiness, to not-me, my committed identity with nonidentity. And it did this simply with spellbinding words, noises that held my attention but meant nothing to the vampire so that transcendence did not smudge its intent. The dream moved on. The ancient one moved in — tripped me on infinity's threshold and propelled me across the floor of night to the fiery drop-off.

Sunrise!

I grappled. Plummeting through hours, I had nothing to grab but the fractal bloodline. That meant finding my balance in the Here, where the vampire's iron offered purchase. The shaman had figured me out. I was an anomaly among the undead — the ghost of a twice dead thing possessing a vampire body. The cremated remains of my body had scrubbed the vampire mind in Bernie's brain and installed me instead. Once the vampire priest understood this, it knew how to deal with me. Exorcised by my own words, I slid helplessly through the dark of time toward dawn. The only way to stop myself was to *be* a vampire. So that you understand ... I had no choice. To live, I forgot about Bernie and me and not-me, and I became the flexing fractal line of my veins. Into the chalice of my heart, the rush of hours spiraled, tightening to a tourniquet coil of blood hunger, the soul of the undead. The dream had moved on. And I found myself in the feeding place.

With whipcrack finality, surging hours stopped at a solitary moment of a single timeline, an undulant ridgeline with a forest of red-eyed trees. The girl whirled about, aghast. In her voice, I heard the crackle of madness, "What's *happening*?" Perplexity congealed to outright fear, and she backed away. "Why are you looking at me like that?"

Why? The beauty of her frailty enraptured me. Her blood smoke unsheathed knives of hunger in my miserable soul.

"Breathe!" She slapped my chest with both palms. "Come on, Bernie! Breathe!"

Bernie's name called down the long, cold road of my surrender. I heard it rebounding in the echo chamber of a higher dimension, in the basilica of space where life chooses and thrives, where once I had lived, half of a fumbling relationship. *—Breathe ...*

"Don't you scare me again." She punched my shoulder, hard. "Where have you been? It's morning! We have to get the hell out of here!"

The sun under the forest leaked lymphatic tinctures. The eastern sky brightened like a cosmic exhalation of relief. In a few minutes, killing wavelengths promised to disinfect the face of the Earth. *—We don't have to go anywhere.* I turned toward the bone-chill and pinpointed the undead priest in the green air. It skittered akimbo through the broomed grass, a queer staccato stompdance under the failing stars. *—Soon, that thing dies too.*

It didn't acknowledge me. As it shimmied, the querulous wind picked up. "Come on!" The girl hooked my elbow and leaned toward darkness. "The car!" When I didn't budge, she came around and read the length of my face. "You serious?"

—I'm no vampire. Bernie and I belong together — but not like this. I slanted a look at the hideous dancer jangling in the wind like a spindle-puppet. *—In a few minutes you can walk out*

of here pretty as . . . A squall of wind cut me off. From out of heaven's purple vault, tempest gusts plunged, pummeling grass flat, driving a cloud of chaff and dust into a rolling comber ahead of that skeleton jig. Maelstrom force swelled across the field and stampeded into the trees under gunfire of snapping boughs, screaming lumber and clouds of startled birds flung from the booming forest like shrapnel. The vampire sorcerer skewed about, whirling off the stamped ground, riding a vortex that spun our way.

I sheltered the girl with Bernie's broad back. The blast marched me bent over, the girl under me, faces squashed together in a grimacing tango. Away went the ash of my twice dead flesh, allotted to drear horizons, pine jungles of mist and night murk. Silence closed over us. The gale had lifted, leaving the firepit swept to its baked surface.

The acrobatic shaman tumbled into the razed circle and jumped up vomiting noise. The girl shouted her fright. Quickly, I sashayed us away, and the thing didn't pursue. It stood victorious on reclaimed earth, chanting primeval hunt songs, rallying the undead. Hordes of vampires stirred in the ventricles of the forest.

—*Run!* I tossed the girl in the direction of the car. She threw me an urgent, aching look. —*The swarm is gathering! I can't protect you. Get out of here. Hurry!*

"Come with me!" She hopped impatiently and waved at the undead priest without looking at it there skewered on its wailing. Its tailspin dance unfurled noctilucent ribbons in the charcoal air. "He's not stopping us. Come on!"

The way she said 'he' exposed such mortal ignorance before the undead, I couldn't find my mind for a moment. She read in the human muscles of my face the fear — for her. My black hole stare saw her among the undead, and she recognized in my slumped body language her doom, my wretched helplessness to change her fate. —*Let Bernie and me slow them down. Go!*

She darted across the gray pasture, Bernie's jacket flopping, running like a girl and not helped much by those heavy boots. She wouldn't make it. The undead raved through the pencil shadows of the forest, then out into the glassy air of the open field. They coursed like eels in the tasseled grass, and I heard the sizzle of their timeflow curling around fractal lines of possible outcomes that conjuncted with her blood. I couldn't bear to watch that feeding frenzy and turned away. The vampire shaman, upright now and still, stopped crooning and looked steadily at me beneath a sky filled with cloudy serum. Blood drained out of earth into heaven.

—*So, now we die.* My defiant words went nowhere, refuted brutally by the garrulous wind that carried vampire shrieks of claw and bite! They had found the girl. The shaman priest grinned four billion years of feeding. I could have throttled that thing! Except I knew he'd jujitsu me into the roaring furnace of noon. I gnashed fangs and spit. At least now I'd get to watch him fry too. Gold seraphim wreathed long-pinioned wings across the stratosphere. Gypsum clouds lit up with citrus hues. The conger eel timeflow of the undead slithered back into the early morning woods and beneath pulsing fog. The undead priest remained in place, sham eyes gouged with nothing, soapstone fingers busy as spiders, unwinding its wrap of human leather.

Laser rays of sunlight cut across the forest's notched horizon and ripped fiery gashes in us. I went to my knees blazing with pain, ducking the fatal beams, and genuflecting before the victory howl of the vampire. Fleshsmoke curled from its bladebones, incising another cicatrix notch in the vampire's masterpiece of coup marks, a garish sun-scar across its back for each rival slain by solar fire. Only dying vampires witnessed the shaman's secret. The flayed skin of a man snapped open to a bodysuit into which the emaciated old creature briskly stepped. Leather sleeves with gloved fingers received the dowel-thin arms, and the cowl that pulled over the blackened egg of a head covered pike-jaw fangs with an obscene, mocking semblance of a human face.

Shielded by this leather from the lethal sun, the old one cast its shadow over me. — *O, impenitent beguiler, go to your beloved transcendence — and to oblivion!* It leaned to one side and daylight charred through me.

I roasted a scream so loud I didn't hear the car's racing engine or tires tearing across the field until the girl braked screeching to a stop inches away. The door smacked me aside as she leaped out, arms locked through the open window, throwing her legs up, knees pulled to her shoulders. The startled vampire crossed arms to deflect this human cannonball, and the girl's two legged kick struck so forcefully the masked mummer whirled backward, leather skin flailing.

She popped the trunk, and I flowed into its casket darkness with whimpering sobs. Briefly I glimpsed her prosperous smile, while she held open Bernie's leather jacket, shredded now and stained with her blood from the lamia's bite. She had used it as a decoy. The blood-soaked leather had distracted the vampires' teeming attack when she cowered beneath it in the terrorizing moments before sunrise drove off the horribles. Through the narrowing eyeblink of the slamming trunk, I saw the old vampire rising up disheveled, human leather torn from its right arm and corrosive fumes wrinkling into sunlight. It reached for the girl.

I tried to warn her, but I was too weak. Blistered talons sliced apart her jacket's bloody rags. She snapped the trunk shut, catching the loose sleeve of the vampire's bodysuit. I heard the priest bark furiously, the girl's feet scamper away, car door slam, engine accelerate. The car lurched off, violently stripping the vampire. Its cry carried pain, horror and shrill surprise to a perishing pitch of silence.

Two days later, it's sunset, and I'm driving. The girl's in the passenger seat, those lucky boots up on the dashboard drumming backbeat to a percussive song blaring on the sound system — "Bad Boyfriend" by Garbage. Cancer's gone. I can smell her healthy blood. Time to refill those coolers soon. Time for a lot of unexpected things. Even twice dead things.

A bucket of my combusted bones rides in the trunk, retrieved last night from the county morgue when the quick slept and the undead stalked the land. Where are we headed? Soon as we pay an overdue visit to the girl's parents, probably to a town near you. Bernie will be liquidating *Go Yoga! & Wok Like This!*, and those assets will finance a long road through the night.

Plans deepen and complexify under an incandescent sky on Shriek Highway. After an extensive vampire killing tour, there should be plenty left over for a small organic bakery-ashram, open all night, offering exotic fare, like pomegranate pâte feuilletée for the living and elaborate gâteaux laced with the ash of twice dead things that I will individually hand feed to the neighborhood undead. The girl even hit on a splendid name, something I think captures human synergy and confidence, precisely the qualities we'll need in our night shelter slash pastry shop: *Peace of Cake.*

ABOUT THE AUTHOR

A. A. Attanasio lives by his imagination in Hawaii. He is the author of *The Eagle and the Sword*, *The Wolf and the Crown*, *The Dragon and the Unicorn*, *Solis*, *Radix*, and several other titles.